中国海洋大学"985工程"

海洋发展人文社会科学研究基地建设经费资助

李萌羽 著

跨文化沟通与中西文学对话

中国社会科学出版社

图书在版编目（CIP）数据

跨文化沟通与中西文学对话/李萌羽著. —北京：中国社会科学出版社，2017.4

ISBN 978 - 7 - 5161 - 9871 - 1

Ⅰ.①跨…　Ⅱ.①李…　Ⅲ.①比较文学—文学研究—中国、西方国家　Ⅳ.①I0 - 03

中国版本图书馆 CIP 数据核字（2017）第 031389 号

出 版 人	赵剑英
责任编辑	安　芳
特约编辑	席建海
责任校对	李　莉
责任印制	李寡寡

出　　版	中国社会科学出版社
社　　址	北京鼓楼西大街甲 158 号
邮　　编	100720
网　　址	http://www.csspw.cn
发 行 部	010 - 84083685
门 市 部	010 - 84029450
经　　销	新华书店及其他书店

印　　装	北京君升印刷有限公司
版　　次	2017 年 4 月第 1 版
印　　次	2017 年 4 月第 1 次印刷

开　　本	710×1000　1/16
印　　张	21.5
字　　数	335 千字
定　　价	78.00 元

目 录
CONTENTS

跨文化沟通与中西文学对话

第二编 中西文学关系研究

第三编 跨文化沟通与对话

附录 部分代表性英文论文原文

第一编
跨文化认同与中外文学综合研究

跨越差异

——论全球化语境中的文化认同

在众声喧哗的全球化问题讨论中，不同的理论学说各执一端，众说纷纭。其中，对全球化概念的不同解读，其定义被不断重新阐释、修正的过程，反映了这一概念的复杂性、不确定性与相对性。全球化曾被理解成一西方标准化的单值意义概念，但这一概念后来逐渐遭到解构，被放到了一个与本土化辩证联系的关系中进行阐释，从而还原了其内涵的相对性与多义性。

一

全球化是否仅仅指向一种适用世界各地、千篇一律的单一经济、文化体制？对全球化这一概念的不同理解，反映了人们在全球化与本土性关系上不同的倾向性。日裔美籍政治家福山在《历史的终结》中认为，西方式的自由民主意识形态已压倒一切，其体制可能导致人类进步思想的终结和人类统治的最后形态，也就是"历史的终结"；美国学者亨廷顿也竭力宣扬美国文明模式，反对多元文明，他甚至说："如果多元文化盛行，如果对开明的民主制度的共识发生分歧，那么，美国就可能同苏联一道落进历史的垃圾堆。"① 从表面看来，全球化是在西方化、现代化的运动过程中，

① ［美］亨廷顿：《美国国家利益受到忽视》，《外交》1997 年 10 月号。

不同国家与民族所呈现出的一体化的发展趋向。在现实世界中,我们看到西方的资本经济与消费文化的确在试图制造一个同质的社会,故美国现代化理论认为,始于西方的现代化过程具有转化全球的内在含义,它将把世界引入单一的西方现代文明体系。这种全球化理论在多种意义上反映了一种西方"主导叙事"的观念。

但全球化作为西方"主导叙事"这一单值意义概念在后现代主义的语境中被逐渐解构。一些学者尖锐指出,全球化这一概念实际上代表着西方的霸权,全球化不过是帝国主义的另一名称。霸权的背后隐藏着一种单向的思维范式,在其建构的话语之中,全球与本土存在着褒贬分明的二元对立关系。而在后现代解构大潮中,这种片面强调全球单一文明的观念逐渐被修正。欧阳桢认为,全球化"这一现象中全球和本土不是那么对立地作为两极并列在一起,相互排斥的因素互相融合或共存"①,故他用"glocalization"这一英文(由 globalization 和 localization 两个英文词——"全球化"与"本土化"各取其词根拼写而成)来阐释全球化这一复合体概念。因而,全球化这一概念具有不确定性、相对性和包容性。它不是一个绝对、纯粹的概念,而是本身就包含着其对立面——本土的存在,超越了二元对立的单向思维模式,全球、本土之间只能是一种"我中有你""你中有我"的水乳交融的关系。

全球化的辩证法给我们提供了一种开放性视野来理解全球文化与本土文化的辩证关系。它使我们以超越全球化、地方化,东方、西方的二元对立的思维模式开掘人类全球共同体的丰富而多样的精神资源。希腊哲学、西方文艺复兴和现代启蒙思想,不仅构成了西方文化最具生命力的内涵,而且在全球化的过程中深刻地影响了世界各地人民的生活。而东方哲学、文化思想的博大精深也对西方文化产生了深远影响。据学者考察,一元神教(基督教、犹太教和伊斯兰教)都源于东方。印度教徒、佛教徒和道教徒的生活方式均展现出一种基本的洞见、繁复的仪式,以及社会制度和日常生活实践紧密相连的精神境界。全球化打破了地域狭隘的边界,使不同

① 王宁、薛晓源主编:《全球化与后殖民批评》,中央编译出版社 1998 年版,第 56 页。

民族、不同国家的文化各自冲出封闭、绝缘的状态，而相互渗透、影响，共享人类全球共同体丰富的精神资源。

全球化使世界不同的国家和文明更紧密地联系在一起。在多种文明的融合中，人类可以需求到更多的共同点。美国哈佛大学学者杜维明认为，全球多种文明千差万别、各具特色，但人类仍可以遵循、共享一些最根本的价值观，它们即为人道、公正、文明、智慧和信任。这些共同的价值观为人类开展文明对话，培育更高水准的全球文明提供了基本前提。

但全球化并不是一均质的过程，人类文明将归于单一发展模式的简单化推论无法解释当今社会在全球化的过程中日趋复杂的文明、种族冲突。人类深深扎根于"原初纽带"（primordialties）之中，这种"原初纽带"不可能轻易被改变，"我们拥有强烈的情感，崇高的愿望和不尽的梦想经常与某一特殊的社体相连，通过母语来表达，与某一独特的地方有关。"① 因此，在描述当前人类生存条件时，我们不可能忽略种族、性别语言、本土、阶级、年龄和信仰的差别。任何试图放弃"原初纽带"成为世界公民的说法都是不切实际的。"原初纽带"给全球共同体以丰富的个性。全球化不但没有削弱人类的这种"原初纽带"，反而进一步强化了本土意识。正是全球化促进了殖民体系的瓦解，造就了全球化的后殖民社会。原殖民地国家在摆脱了殖民统治，获得独立后，首先觉醒的是民族意识，他们正是通过对民族文化的强调来重新确立其独立地位。弗兰西斯·福山曾指出，农耕时代，民族主义根本不存在于人的意识中，在转向工业社会或其后，民族主义迅速成长。因而，我们应该用全球和本土来界定我们的身份，我们既是各自国家、民族的成员，同时也因世界的相互依存，成为全球人类大家庭的一员。

---

① 杜维明：《文明对话的语境：全球化与多样性》，《史学集刊》2002 年第 1 期。

二

全球化的辩证法表明，全球化与本土化均不是纯粹、单一概念，而是处于既相互对立又相互依存的辩证联系中。它一方面强调人类在走向全球化的过程中所达成的普遍性的价值理念与文化共识，另一方面更重视由不同文化所创造的文明资源的独特价值。全球化的辩证法为我们提供了开放性理论视野，有助于我们辩证地理解人类文化的趋同性和差异性，从而建立一种更为科学、客观的文化认同观。其一，人类文化尽管千差万别，但遗传基码说明人类几乎都是由同一材料构成的。人类不仅和其同类，而且和动物、植物、树木、岩石构成了一个联系的整体，不同的肤色、种族、语言、文化传统、宗教归属、教育背景，都无法削弱人类的共性，因而，人类行为、思想、情感、心理的类似性，世界不同民族文化所折射出的一些共同性的内涵，全球文化所表现出来的相通性，为人类多元文化的认同提供了基本前提。没有人类文化对人这一大概念所达成的普遍性共识，文化认同无从谈起。其二，全球文化更表现为一种丰富的、各具特色的多元文化特征。人类文化的多元性体现了不同民族、地域文化的丰富性特征。跨越多元文化的认同意味着用一种更为理性、客观的态度审视不同文化之间的差异性，把各种文化体系看作一个始终处于动态、开放、兼容并蓄的辩证运动过程。

纵观人类文明发展史，全球化实际上是人类不同族群的文化逐渐冲破各自封闭的地域阻碍而走向相互融合、交汇的世界化大潮之动态运动过程。早在19世纪40年代，马克思、恩格斯就深刻揭示了全球各民族文化在世界经济一体化的影响下所必然走向世界化的趋势，几乎在同一时期（甚至更早一些），在文学领域，德国文学家歌德曾预见民族文学在现代算不了很大的一回事，世界文学的时代已快来临。歌德在宣告世界文学时代的来临时，首先是基于对不同民族文学所表达的思想情感类同性的感悟。一本在中国尚不太出名的明代传奇《风月好逑传》，竟使歌德感悟到了中西文学所表达的思想感情的惊人的类似性。在《歌德谈话录》中，他的一番有感而发的议论，成为佐证人类文学趋于世界化的经典话语："中国人在思想、行为和感情方面几乎和我们一样，使我们发现他们是我们的同类人。""世界永远是一样的，一些情景经常重现，这个民族和那个民族一样过生活，讲恋爱，动情感那末某个诗人做诗为什么不能和另一个诗人一样呢？生活的情景可能相同，为什么诗的情境就不可以相同呢？"①

　　人类文化表现的某种趋同化反映了生活在同一地球上的人类某些共性特征。尽管人类隶属于不同的族群，但又归属于人类这一大概念之下。人类具有类似的生命形式（从出生到成长、衰老、死亡）和体验形式（欢乐与痛苦，团聚与分离，希望与绝望，爱与恨等），这决定了人类在对自我、他人、自然、社会及宇宙的体悟和感知上的相通性。马斯洛认为，各种族文化可以有千差万别，但最终结果似乎是相同的，驱使人类的若干始终不变的、遗传的、本能的需要，即生理需要、安全需要、归属和爱的需要、尊重的需要、自我实现的需要成为人类自下而上阶梯式的共同追求的生命目标。荣格的"集体无意识"理论则进一步从心理学角度揭示出不同民族心理趋同的规律。在他看来，在"个人无意识"的深层先天存在着"集体无意识"，"它与个性心理相反，具备了所有地方和所有个人皆有的大体相似的内容和行为方式。换言之，由于它在所有人身上都是相同的，因此它组成了一种超个人的心理基础，并且普遍存在于我们每个人身上。"②

　　世界不同民族文化所折射出的一些共同性的内涵，全球文化所表现出来的相通性，为人类多元文化的认同提供了基本前提。没有这种人类文化对人的概念认知相类同的大语境，人类之间的对话与交流便无从谈起。然而，文化的世界化趋向并非意味着各民族文化的一同化、雷同化，相反，文化的多元化更能体现人类文明发展的本质特征。人类五千年的文明史表明，正是希腊文化、中国文化、希伯来文化、印度文化、阿拉伯伊斯兰文化等诸多不同体系的文化构成了世界大文化的宝库。而在全球化愈演愈烈

---

① ［德］歌德：《歌德谈话录》，朱光潜译，人民文学出版社1987年版，第112—113页。

② ［瑞士］荣格：《心理学与文学》，生活·读书·新知三联书店1987年版，第52—53页。

的当今世界，全球化并没有遮蔽世界文化多元化的丰富性特征，相反，它促进了殖民体系的瓦解及各种"中心论"的解体。在后殖民语境下，以往的"逻各斯中心"和"宏大叙事"遭到解构，世界已不再是一个整体，而是呈现出多元价值取向，显示出断片及非中心的特征。正是全球化浪潮加快了各种多元文化交锋、冲突、融合和交流的过程，凸显了多元文化在世界大舞台的交融共生。"全球性恢复了文化的无边界性并且促进了文化表达方式的无限可更新性和无限多样性，而不是促进了同质化或杂交化。"[①]

人类文化的多元性体现了不同民族、地域文化的丰富性特征，正是不同文化所表现出来的个性化特质构成了其文化之灵魂。世界不同的文化体系丰富而多样化，它们构成了多姿多彩的世界文化宝库。各民族在审视人与世界的关系，探寻宇宙的本质，思索人的存在意义等本原性问题上，各有不同的理解与阐释方式。如不少学者曾多次论及中西思维观的不同之处，认为西方传统思维方式表现为主客对立的思维模式，作为主体的人独立于客观世界，人们认识世界就是一个对外在于主体的客观对象进行观察、分析、切割、综合的过程。而中国传统的思维方式则视主客体为一体，强调尽心、知性、知天，认为"天道"存乎人心，须从人的内心去挖掘、体察。让·杜布菲也曾比较研究过西方文化与世界一些原始民族部落文化在思维方式及宇宙观上的差异性：

> 西方文化相信人大别于万物……但一些原始民族不相信人是万物之主，他不过是万物之一而已。……西方人认为世界上的事物和他思维想象中的完全一样，以为世界的形状和他理性下规划下来的形状完全一样……西方文化极喜分析……故把整体分割为部分，逐一地研究……但部分的总和并不等于整体。[②]

不同的文化原型意象也折射出不同民族文化思维的差异性。"独角兽"

---

① ［英］马丁·阿尔布劳：《全球时代：超越现代性之外的国家和社会》，商务印书馆2001年版，第277页。

② 李达三、罗钢：《中外比较文学的里程碑》，人民文学出版社1997年版，第50页。

在西方文化传说中是一种长着美丽独角的动物，在西方一直是幸福圆满的象征，但它在中国文化中却并无特殊的意义，正如松、竹、梅等原型意象对西方文化而言毫无意义一样。再譬如龙是中国文化祥瑞尊贵的至高权威的象征，在西方文化中却被视为邪恶的敌对力量，如英国古代英雄史诗《贝奥武甫》中龙就是一代表恶势力的形象。

世界文化的多元化同时也意味着不同文化体系的巨大差异性。面对世界不同文化体系的丰富性和差异性，该如何进行文化认同，是摆在我们面前的一个重要课题。

三

全球化语境下的文化认同，需在考察文化类同与文化差异两个层面上展开，既要重视文化类同研究，即在承认人类多元文化的前提下研究、探讨人类文化中表现出来的一些趋同性的内涵，更要致力于对文化差异性的研究。否认人类文化对人的概念认知相趋同的大语境，不同文化体系就失去了对话的前提，而人类文化的多元性体现了不同民族、地域文化的丰富性特征，文化研究的最终目的还是为了探讨、审视、比较不同族群文化的诗性化特质。

然而，在全球化多元文化的交锋中，却始终存在着这样一种根深蒂固的"文化部落主义"，赛义德把它称为"本质主义的认同观"，它把本族文化视为一种纯粹、本真、静止、绝对的本质存在，以一种狭隘民族主义的情绪，把其民族族性绝对化、本质化。如占据西方主导叙事的西方文化优越论，它认为西方文化包含着最合理的行为模式和思维模式，应普及应用于全世界。在解构此种西方文化主义霸权的同时，东方国家的一些知识分子却又强化了另一种本质主义的文化与族性观念，不自觉地陷入对本土文化的绝对维护中。他们实际又在确立一种新的本土性与全球性，东方与西方，第三世界与第一世界的二元对立的思维模式。此种"本质主义的认同观"旨在维护本族文化的纯粹性，它必然会造成文化认同中的狭隘文化观，其结果只能是导致各文化体系之间不相容与敌意的紧张关系。为此，一些学者提出重建文化认同。在当今全球化语境中，各民族文化之间的互动与杂交成为世界文化发展的态势，任何一种诉诸纯粹、本真、静止、绝对化的民族文化认同都是不可思议的。他们主张在阐释文化认同时，要打破这种本质主义的、绝对的主体性观念与认同观念，取而代之以流动的主体性、多重自我和复合身份的概念。尤其要抛弃把一个民族的族性绝对化、本质化的狭隘的民族主义情绪，用一种更加开放与灵活的态度来思考认同问题。故我们要持一种更为理性、客观的文化认同观，要始终把各种文化体系看成开放性的文化体系。没有任何一种文化体系永远处于静止不变的同一状态中，若对其进行封闭，与其他文化隔离，必然会导致其发展的滞缓。为此，哈贝马斯主张用一种"非我的""陌生的"眼光，使不同的文化"互为主观"，这样就跳出了原有体系的自我设限。杜威·佛马克对多元文化的理解也是沿此思路展开的。他认为，多元文化主义（multi-culturalism）这一术语隐含着一种元视角，这种元视角有助于我们借助他元文化超越我们自身文化之局限。这些学者的建设性意见对我们建构一种更为理性、客观的文化认同观具有很大的启发性，我们应该看到在世界文化资源中，每一种文化体系都是独特的个性存在体，都有其对世界及人类生活方式独到的阐释和理解，但任何文化体系都不是绝对的、完善的，都有其局限性。因而建立科学的文化认同就是以更开阔的视野来打破文化本位主义，促进各种异质文化体系的兼容并蓄。

全球化视野为我们提供了一种更为科学、理性的文化认同理路。在全球化的推进过程中，世界各族群文化日益从与外界隔离的状态走向了与他种文化的交融与汇合，并在这一融合过程中不断获得文化新质。我们在全球化语境中审视各族群文化，就是要跨越不同文化体系的差异，以一种开放的文化认同观，来审视各种文化体系，从而既能探寻到一些人类文化、文学的基本规律，更能从深层次上挖掘出不同民族文学的丰富性特质。

（原载于《山东社会科学》2004 年第 5 期）

论全球化视野下的文化产业发展战略

文化产品作为一种特殊商品，兼有一般商品和精神产品的双重属性。文化产业在世界经济迅猛发展的背景下应运而生，成为当今世界具有巨大市场发展潜力的一个重要经济领域。一方面，文化渗透于经济发展中，以提供文化产品或文化服务的方式直接参与经济的运行；另一方面，产业化经济促进了人类精神产品的相互交流，为传播世界不同的文化的交流搭建了平台。在当今世界经济愈来愈趋向一体化的背景下，世界各民族、各个国家的文化产业也不可避免地融入了全球化的态势中，在这一发展过程中，该如何更好地处理全球化与本土化、国际化与民族化的关系，不但事关世界文化产业是否能够得到健康发展，也决定着每个国家文化产业发展的成与败。

全球化（globalization）是近年来中外学术界讨论的一热门话题，它被用来描述世界各国在经济、科技、文化等领域相依共生的状况。麦克卢汉用"地球村"这一隐喻形象地描述了世界各个角落作为整体的地球一个不可分割的组成部分，世界呈现出一体化这一当代全球风貌。特别是近一个多世纪以来，随着遍及全球的货币资本、信息技术、人力资源在全球范围内空前的流通，全球化语境已构成了现代人需时时刻刻面对、无法逃遁的生存环境。故罗纳德·阿克斯特曼说："全球化的这些过程，要求我们重新给出生活于其中的社会世界的概念。"[1]

---

① 王宁、薛晓源主编：《全球化与后殖民批评》，中央编译出版社 1998 年版，第 78 页。

一

　　20 世纪 70 年代以来，世界各国在现代性的推演过程中逐渐进入了一个"全球化"时代，主要表现为以国际金融、跨国公司一体化为典型特征的全球资本主义体系逐步取代了落后的、封闭的帝国主义体系，与经济一体化同步的是西方的一些经济发达国家，特别是美国运用其领先发展的优势，以强大的经济、资本实力为后盾，试图以西方或美国文化作为普世文明，强制性地向非西方国家输出自己的政治文化、商业规范、文化习俗、价值观念及生活方式，在全球化与本土化关系上，表现为把单一的西方或美国模式确立为全球化模式，并试图以之来取代、遮蔽其他异质文化。有些学者甚至用"文化全球化"或"文化帝国主义"来描述这种美国强势文化产业雄霸世界文化产业的境况。

　　文化产业是传播文化价值观及影响文化心理和行为的一个重要媒介。联合国教科文组织曾对"文化产品"这一概念从"文化商品"和"文化服务"两个层面进行过界定，其中着重强调了文化产品是一种"传播思想、符号和生活方式的消费品，它能够提供信息和娱乐，进而形成群体认同并影响文化行为"①。从中我们看到文化产业在传播文化价值观及影响文化行为上所起的重要作用。

　　冷战时代结束后，美国逐步确立了其作为一个文化产业大国的地位，世界文化在全球化浪潮的推演下愈来愈呈现出"美国化"的趋势。譬如，美国前商务部高级官员大卫·罗斯科普曾自豪地宣布："对美国来说，信息时代对外政策的一个主要目标必须是在世界的信息传播中取得胜利，像英国一度在海上居支配地位那样支配电波。如果世界趋向一种共同的语言，它应该是英语；如果世界趋向共同的电信、安全和质量标准，那么，它们应该是美国的标准；如果世界正在由电视、广播和音乐联系在一起，

---

① 张玉国：《国家利益与文化政策》，广东人民出版社 2005 年版，第 269 页。

节目应该是美国的；如果共同的价值观正在形成，它们应该是符合美国人意愿的价值观。"①

而在现实层面上，我们看到美国流行音乐产业、广播电视产业、动漫产业与出版产业在全世界范围内均处于世界遥遥领先地位。美国的音乐唱片发行在国际市场上的占有率超出20%的份额，美国的出版业也令人瞩目，仅在2000年，美国图书销售额就达253.2亿美元，占同年世界图书销售总额的30%。在传媒业方面，美国拥有世界上最强大的广播电视及报刊产业集团，控制着世界网络媒体的发展趋势。而美国电影产业自1987年起就占据了整个世界电影市场的50%以上的份额，这种状况一直延续到今天。美国还试图通过电影文化产业控制世界电影文化产业的市场。譬如，1946年，二战后的法国为重建经济被迫与美国政府签署了一项10亿美元的贷款协议，在这项协议的附加条款中，美国要求法国重新向好莱坞开放其电影市场。美国前总统胡佛曾这样评价美国电影之于美国经济和文化的重要性："既作为直接的商业贸易出口，也代表一般美国商品和美国生活方式的强大的影响力。"② 美国文化产业不仅攫取了世界各国丰厚的文化产业利润，而且在文化价值观等层面对世界各国进行着"软"控制。

由上观之，美国在当今文化产业中正在试图制造一种文化"全球化"，那么这种全球化是否就是一种"美国制造"的全球化？美国产业文化究竟能否代表一种文化"普世主义"？答案显然是否定的。全球化并不简单意味着单质化的美国化模式，全球化包含着由诸多本土文化构成的复合多元文化，过分强调全球文化产业的美国化只能把世界产业文化引向一种单一的文化模式，这是对世界文化多样性和丰富性的扼杀。

---

① 李怀亮：《当代国际文化贸易与文化竞争》，广东人民出版社2005年版，第139页。
② 同上书，第114页。

二

如果说美国在文化产业发展中一直以一种积极、进攻的姿态来引领全球文化的美国化，那么以法国和加拿大为代表的一些国家则走向了另外一条积极抵制美国文化产业入侵、固守本土文化的道路。它们多年以来一直以"文化主权"的名义来抵制美国的文化入侵，并竭力弘扬民族文化、扩大民族文化影响力。

法国是坚决维护本土文化纯洁性的一个典型国家。首先，在语言上极力捍卫法语在法国的权威性，曾于1994年通过杜蓬法，禁止在各类电视、电台节目及公告、广告中使用外语，对违反杜蓬法者实行罚款。其次，在文化产业方面，更是采取了一系列措施来保护本土文化免受美国文化的侵袭。譬如在法国的呼吁下，1989年欧盟国家制定了《无国界的电视》，颁布了音像产品播出的配额制度，按音像作品播放配额规定，40%的时间必须播放法国作品，60%的时间可以播放其他国家的作品。而配额制度的实质则包含限制的含义，归根结底是为了保护法国和欧洲的视听作品的制作和播放。在1993年的关贸总协定乌拉圭回合谈判中，法国坚持"文化不是一般商品"，提出了"文化例外"这一概念，以抵制美国所提出的把自由贸易的范围扩大到影视等文化产业领域的提案。

此外，加拿大目前也制定了相关文化产业法，要求本国电视台必须提供60%的加拿大节目，广播电台必须提供30%的加拿大节目。加拿大政府还颁布法令限制电影发行领域的外国投资；韩国政府也采取了增加国产电影放映时间的办法以控制美国电影的播映。

法国、加拿大和韩国在文化产业的全球化和本土化取向中均选择了后者，面对全球文化美国化的蔓延趋势，为了捍卫本国文化主权，它们纷纷采取种种措施，甚至通过立法的形式来抵制美国文化的侵袭，尤其是法国对美国文化几乎采取了坚决抵抗的态度，由此走向了片面固守本土文化的另一端。而文化本身则不断处于开放和变化之中，不可能是封闭的、静止不变的，若一味强调文化的纯粹性而对外来文化实行封锁，则会走向一条狭隘的民族主义道路，也不利于文化产业的健康发展。如上文所述，全球化并不意味着文化的一元化，相反，"全球经济一体化与全球文化多元化，二者在'二律背反'中呈现出一种非和谐的历史对称性。"① 实际上，全球化一方面表现出本土化差异的存在，另一方面又表现为本土化的流动与交换。为此，亨廷顿在1996年补充自己的"文明的冲突"理论时，认为历史上文化时尚一直是从一个文明传到另一个文明。一个文明中的革新经常被其他文明所采纳。在17—18世纪，西方世界曾非常崇拜中国文化和印度文化，而自19世纪以来，在中国和印度，西方文化又逐渐变得流行起来，而且这一趋势至今还在延续。

　　故全球化是一个复杂、对立的统一体，是国际化和本土化的统一，是单一性和多样性的统一，美国以强权文化垄断世界文化产业市场，片面强调全球单一文明，试图在全球以美国式文明普遍模式来取代、遮蔽世界其他国家本土文化的做法是不可取的。而法国为了维护文化主权，在文化产业发展中一味固守本土文化、排斥外来文化的态度同样是不可取的。特别是在当今国际化的时代背景下，任何一种本土文化都不能隔绝与其他文化的交流与糅合。正如上文所提及的赛义德的"本质主义的认同观"理论所阐释的，这种片面维护本土文化的纯粹性的做法，实际上是一种把其民族族性绝对化、本质化的狭隘民族主义的表现，也不利于本土文化的发展与创新。总之，在文化产业的全球化与本土化问题中偏执于任何一端都是对文化多样性这一概念的背离。

　　联合国教科文组织在2001年的《文化多样性共同宣言》中，很好地阐释了文化多样性的重要意义："时间和空间的变化产生了不同的文化形式，这种多样性包含在众多社会和群体的独特的文化个性之中，而人类社会正是由这些社会和群体组成。作为交流、创新和创造的源泉，文化多样性对人类的重要性正如生物多样性对自然界的重要性。在这种意义上，文化多样性是人类的共同遗产，它的重要性应该被认识到并加以保护和促

---

① 胡智锋主编：《影视文化前沿》，北京广播学院出版社2003年版，第164页。

进，以造福于当今和子孙后代。"① "文化多样性"概念的提出，与上文杜威·佛马克"多元文化主义"的理论视角是一致的，它们均强调人类文化的多元化和差异性，把不同文化之间的交流、对话置于重要的位置，认为多元、互存的不同地域、民族文化的相互交流和影响，是人类文化发展和创新的源泉，"多元文化主义"和"文化多样性概念"的提出对在文化产业中更好地处理全球化和本土化之间的关系提供了有益的理论支撑。

<h1 style="text-align:center">三</h1>

在文化产业中全面、客观地把握全球化与本土化的辩证关系至关重要，在发展策略上应着重从以下两个方面入手：其一，发展文化产业要具有开放的全球化意识和国际化视野，应按照文化产业的市场运行法则积极、主动地参与全球文化产业的交流和互动。其二，须大力发展具有民族文化特色的文化产业，以切实提高国家文化产业的核心竞争力。

商品属性是文化产品的重要属性之一，是能够真正实现文化产品精神属性带来产品增值的价值，是文化产业发展的重要内驱力。文化产品若只具有精神资源优势，不能有效转化成资本优势，其精神价值属性就像一块璞玉一样不能得到充分实现。正如文化产业研究学者胡惠林所指出的那样："文化产业只是人类社会发展到市场经济阶段，在市场经济条件下，以市场经济的方式和机制再生文化资源的一种途径和动力机制，而不是相反。"② 联合国教科文组织则从"工业标准"的角度定义文化产业，认为："文化产业就是按照工业标准，生产、再生产、储存及分配文化产品和服务的一系列活动。"③ 在此，"工业标准"指工业生产的社会化、专业化、程序化和规模化等特性，它包括文化产品生产、再生产、传播与消费等各个环节，是工业化社会的产物。

---

① 张玉国：《国家利益与文化政策》，广东人民出版社 2005 年版，第 71—73 页。
② 胡惠林：《文化资本：现代文化产业和谐发展的能源形态》，《探索与争鸣》2007 年第 1 期。
③ 黎元江：《关于发展文化产业的十个问题》，《光明日报》2001 年 8 月 25 日。

　　当今世界经济全球化、一体化愈加强化了文化产业的市场化、标准化、专业化和规模化的运作趋势，在这种情形下，任何国家若要加快发展文化产业，必须具有开放的国际化视野和全球化意识，按照世界文化产业市场的经济运行规则来积极、主动地开拓国际市场，使本土文化资源借助资本资源的媒介最大限度地实现其价值。

　　新中国成立后，我国曾一度采取闭关锁国的政策，文化产业的发展几乎是一片空白。自改革开放以来，我国的文化市场空前繁荣，图书、报纸、期刊、音像制品、电子出版物及电影、电视、摄影、雕塑等文化产品丰富多彩，而且有些文化产品在国际上也产生了一定的影响，这一切成绩的取得若没有改革开放市场经济条件下产业化方式的运作是难以想象的。而目前，我国的文化产业仍处于起步阶段，我国尽管是文化资源大国，却是文化产业小国，文化资源的优势远没有被转换成文化产业优势。我们一方面要进一步解放思想、更新观念，树立全球意识和国际视野，制定我国开拓文化产业国际市场的战略，采取各种有效措施拓宽国际市场；另一方面要充分认识文化产品的商品属性和文化产业的市场化运作规律，借鉴、学习美国发展文化产业较为成熟的产业化经营理念和经验，加快社会主义市场经济体制的改革，做到与国际市场接轨，为我国文化产业的发展搭建更好的经济平台。

　　但文化产品的精神属性决定了文化产品不是一般的商品，它是一种具有独特"价值内容"的文化商品，"价值内容"在文化产业中占有重要地位，不同国家的文化产品因其本土文化"价值内容"的不同而呈现出丰富性，而在全球化商业浪潮经济利益的驱使下，文化产业的本土文化"价值内容"也日趋变得单调、贫乏，正如1999年欧盟文化部长非正式会议在讨论欧洲文化产业发展的框架性合作计划时所担忧的那样："商业压力和由此而来的内容贫乏，而不是文化的多样性，是存在于我们这个日益发展的、由数字电视造成的广播时代自身中的固有威胁。可靠而高水平的公共服务应该是欧洲的竞争优势所在。保存欧洲人的文化认同至关重要。如果没有有价值的内容，技术的未来发展是没有意义的，这是新千年的最大挑战。"①

事实证明，欧盟和亚洲的一些国家采取了一系列措施发展具有民族文化特色的文化产业，以凸显文化产业中的本土文化"内容价值"，很好地促进文化产业经济效益的增长。如法国从第四个五年计划开始，正式把文化列入五年计划之中，把文化遗产保护始终列在首位，曾先后颁布了旨在保护文化遗产的《保护及修复历史遗迹法》《古迹保护法》《遗产捐赠与继承抵偿法》等各项法规文件，并于1984年首创文化遗产日，对文化遗产的保护和开发使法国成了全球旅游胜地，从而很好地促进了旅游产业的发展。亚洲的日本和韩国走在了文化产业发展的前沿，这与它们所采取的一系列"文化立国"策略和政策是分不开的。1996年7月，日本文化厅正式提出《21世纪文化立国方案》，对"文化立国"战略进行了详细阐释，并把21世纪作为日本依靠本国的文化资源与文化优势开始新一轮发展的世纪。韩国政府继日本之后也于1998年正式提出"文化立国"战略，将文化产业作为21世纪发展国家经济的战略性支柱产业加以优先发展，并且提出"韩国文化世界化"的口号，将韩国文化推向全球，韩国文化的发展由此步入了新纪元。

上述各国文化产业发展的成功经验值得我们借鉴。我国的文化产业要走向世界，必须走文化产业化、市场化的道路，采取国际化的文化产品生产、传播方式，这是文化产业全球化的必然要求。但同时我国文化产业的发展却又必须立足本国文化，在激烈的世界文化产业竞争中，中国文化产业要努力打造具有中国特色的文化产品和民族文化品牌，使中国的文化产业在世界产生愈来愈深远的影响。

中国是一个拥有五千年文明史的文化古国，历史、哲学、文学艺术等文化资源积淀丰厚，历史文明为我们留下了大量的文化典籍、文学艺术精品、文物古迹和民间文化瑰宝。丰富的文化资源为我国文化产品走向世界提供了很好的条件，也奠定了我国文化产业发展的巨大潜力。

---

① 张晓明、刘钢：《文化产业与信息产业合流》，《中国文化报》2001年2月14日。

中国传统的历史、哲学、文学艺术文化博大精深，如何充分发掘其思想资源，借助现代文化产业的力量进行文化普及，是我们当前面临的一个重要课题。《百家讲坛》栏目策划的成功为我们探求了一条在文化产业中运用现代传媒和市场化运作策略传播传统文化的路子，其系列节目《刘心武揭秘红楼梦》《易中天品三国》《汉代风云人物》《明亡清兴六十年》《于丹〈论语〉心得》《于丹〈庄子〉心得》《王立群读史记》等相继推出，《百家讲坛》的收视率节节攀升，影响日益扩大，在社会上掀起了"红楼热""三国热""论语热"。《百家讲坛》栏目的成功得益于两个因素：一是传统文化的生命力，二是产业化运营方式。当然，它也受到了诸多非议和责难，存在媒体炒作、市场追捧过度、学术质量尚待提升等问题。另外，《三国演义》《红楼梦》《水浒传》等中国传统文学名著也多次被搬上荧屏，在国内乃至国际上产生了一定影响，世界上许多国家竞相购买这些影视剧的播放权，这些文化产品产生了极好的社会效益与经济效益。

同时，我国是个多民族国家，各个少数民族都有自己独特的民族文化，如服饰、习俗、音乐等，这些特色鲜明的民族文化也是中国文化资源必不可少的组成部分。近年来，《云南映像》《印象刘三姐》《丽水金沙》等既有民间艺术特色又有市场需求的文化产品也产生了重要影响。

这一切成功的经验使我们进一步思索该如何真正从我们的传统文化中汲取文化资源，对中国传统哲学、历史、文学艺术作品、少数民族文化进行现代性诠释，提炼出具有独特价值的中国文化内核和元素，借助产业经济的平台，转化成影视、传媒、动漫等文化产品，打造出一批具有国际竞争力的民族文化精品，从而实现中国文化产业的腾飞。

综上所述，在文化产业中全面、客观地把握全球化与本土化的辩证关系至关重要，偏执于任何一端的文化产业取向都是对文化多样性的背离。科学的文化产业发展策略是既要积极参与全球文化产业的交流和互动，又要大力发展具有民族文化特色的文化产业，以切实提高民族文化产业的核心竞争力。

（原载于《青岛农业大学学报》2008 年第 4 期）

试论深生态学视域下的海洋伦理观[*]

    21世纪被称为海洋的世纪，世界主要发达国家相继在《联合国海洋法公约》的框架下，制定和完善了国家或区域的海洋战略，海洋开发和保护在国家发展中的战略地位空前提高。然而，随着我国经济的飞速发展，海洋开发力度的加大，大规模、高强度的不当海洋开发加速了海洋环境和生态的恶化，加剧了海洋环境灾害发生的频度，直接威胁海洋资源的可持续利用。面对日趋严重的海洋生态危机，反思人类凌驾于海洋之上、一味向海洋攫取利益的狭隘的海洋观，重新审视人类与海洋的关系，建立人与海洋和谐共生的深层海洋伦理观至关重要。

    在西方，自20世纪中叶以来，随着经济和科技的发展，环境遭到了很大的破坏，保护环境的运动此起彼伏。全球性的生态环境的恶化促使西方环境主义者对环境问题进行了更深层面的哲学思考，从20世纪70年代起，西方的环境运动不断深化，逐步从具体的环境保护，转向关注整个生态系统的平衡，提倡保护生态物种的多样性，探究导致环境问题的政治、经济、社会、文化等因素。在这种背景下，深层生态学理论应运而生。它坚持以生态系统为中心的整体论，反对浅生态学所持的人类中心主义的立场，主张从整个生态系统的利益出发，把人类和自然界看成一个相互依赖、相互联系的有机整体。认为人类和非人类生物具有内在的均等价值，主张保护生态物种的多样性和丰富性，以实现人类与自然万物的和谐共

    * 此文系中国海洋发展研究中心项目"深生态学视域中的海洋资源开发与保护研究"（AOCOUC20110）阶段性成果。

生。深生态学的理论内涵对于建构深层海洋伦理观，正确处理人与海洋和谐共生的关系，解决我们目前面临的日趋严重的海洋生态危机，促进海洋开发和保护的良性、可持续发展具有重要的理论和实践意义。

一　深生态学作为一种环境伦理哲学

近半个世纪以来，世界环境保护运动此起彼伏，深生态学理论也应运而生。顾名思义，深生态学是与浅生态学相对应的，是 20 世纪 70 年代以后西方社会出现的一种生态中心论的环境保护理论，最早由挪威生态学家阿伦·奈斯提出，后经由美国的比尔·迪伏、乔治·塞逊斯塞及澳大利亚的沃里克·福克斯等学者的丰富和发展，最终成为一种影响深远的生态理论思潮。深生态学坚持以生态系统而不是人类为中心，主张从整个生态系统的利益出发，实现人类与自然的和谐共生。这种深生态学理论的产生是基于一种非人类中心主义的"生物圈平等"和"自我实现"哲学原则。

1. 深生态学环境伦理哲学理念

深生态学（deep ecology）这一概念由挪威著名的生态学家阿伦·奈斯于 1972 年首次提出，后来逐步发展成为一种具有深刻内涵的环境伦理学理论。1973 年，阿伦·奈斯在《哲学探索》上发表了《浅层生态运动和深层、长远的生态运动：一个概要》一文，全面阐释了深生态学以下基本理论观点：第一，反对人与环境关系中的人类中心主义的态度。主张人与环境的互相关联，认为任何有机体都是生物圈网络中的一个点，没有万物之间的联系，有机体不能生存。第二，遵循"生物圈平等原则"。认为这一原则的重要性在于摒弃一切为了实际需要的杀戮、掠夺和压迫。生态工作者必须予以深深尊重乃至敬重任何生命形式。对生态工作者来说，平等生存和发展是最高的价值准则。第三，遵循"多样性和共生、互利原则"。认为多样性增加了更多生命形式生存的机会和可能性及丰富性。适者生存应该在互生、共存的关系中阐释，而不是强调一种屠戮、剥削和压迫的能力。第四，反对等级制。基于生物圈的平等和共生互惠的立场，深生态学反对等级制度，认为上述原则适用于所有的物种、群落和种族。第五，反对污染和资源枯竭。指出在这方面生态学家已找到了强有力的支持，但浅生态运动没有考虑采取措施的社会意义，而深生态运动要担负起伦理责任。第六，主张"复杂而不混乱"。认为生态系统中的生物之间、生物与环境之间进行着复杂而有序的物质、信息和能量的交换，构成动态平衡的有机统一体。第七，主张"区域自治和分散化"。深生态学重视生态环境保护中的"区域自我管理"及"物质和精神上的自我满足"。①

深生态学被视为一种"生态中心主义"的环境伦理观，它从整体论出发，把整个生态系统看成一个完整、有机、不可分割的整体，各个部分是相互联系、相互制约、相互依存的，缺一不可，并且生态系统的各部分是平等的，不存在谁的利益高于谁的问题；在深生态学看来，人类作为生态系统的组成部分之一，并不是高于自然界的，人类不能为了自身的利益而破坏生态系统的完整性。因之，深生态学反对单纯从人类的根本利益出发，认为自然环境的作用是为人类提供资源，并以人类的利益为终极目标这一狭隘观念。

2. 深生态学的两个"最高规范"

在提出上述深生态学的基本理论主张的基础上，奈斯进一步确立了深生态学理论的两个"最高规范"（ultimate norms），即"生物圈平等"和"自我实现"（self-realization），这两个最高规范是深生态学环境伦理思想的理论基石。

其一，"生物圈平等"规范。"生物圈平等"规范是深生态学理论的一个核心理念，其"平等"内涵是指所有生物圈里的生命形式，都拥有在"大自我"统一体中平等生存、繁荣、实现"自我"价值的权利，即在生物圈中所有的有机体和存在物，作为不可分割的整体的一部分，在内在价值上是平等的。因此，一切存在物对生态系统来说都是重要的、有价值的。

---

① Devall Bill and Sessions George, *Deep Ecology*, Layton: Gibbs M. Smith. Inc., 1985, pp. 1 - 2.

其二，"自我实现"规范。在"生物圈平等"规范的基础上，深生态学继而提出了"自我实现"规范，将人类自我价值的实现扩展至对宇宙所有生命的和非生命个体价值的认同。在奈斯看来，深生态学意义上的"自我实现"超越了现代人个体价值的实现和自我利益满足的局限性，即"小自我"意义上价值实现的拘囿，这种狭隘的社会意义上的自我价值实现很容易使人沦为庸俗世俗观的牺牲品，而深生态学则试图唤醒个体意识的进一步成长，把自我认同拓展至与非人类的自然界生物圈的更广领域，即从"小自我"的认同走向整个统一体的"大自我"的认同。而这个统一体，在比尔·迪伏和乔治·塞逊斯看来，不仅包含人类，还包含"鲸鱼、大灰熊、整个雨林生态系统、高山、河流及土壤中的微生物等"[①]，故深生态学的"自我实现"是人类精神向自然万物包括生命及非生命物认同的过程。

深生态学还认为，"生物圈平等"与总体意义上的"自我实现"是密切相关的："我们伤害大自然的其他生物便是在伤害我们的自身。没有什么分界线，每一种事物都是互相关联的。而且，若我们视自然界的存在物为有机体，我们就会尊敬所有的人类与非人类所享有的作为整体组成部分的个体权利，而不必建立一种把人类置于最高层次的种类等级制度。"[②] 为此，深生态学家们主张应以对其他物种产生最小影响的方式来生活。特别是人类在面临生存与发展的需要与保护生物圈内其他存在物平等生存的矛盾时，深生态学主张把人类的"生死攸关的需要""基本的需要"与"边缘的、过分的、无关紧要的"需要区别开来。故深生态学提出了一个十分重要的口号："手段简单，目的丰富。"它对当今社会占统治地位的物质主义消费观和发展观提出了批评，主张过一种简单而又富有意义的生活。

3. 深生态学与浅生态学的分野

奈斯更多地从与浅生态学相比较的视角提出深生态学这一概念。首先，他认为两者的差异性在于浅生态学所持的是一种人类中心主义的观

---

① Witoszek Nina and Brennan Andrew. *Philosophical Dialogues*: *Arne Nass and the Progress of ecophilosophy*, Maryland: Rowman &Littlefield Publisher, INC. , 1999, p. 67.

② Ibid. , p. 69.

点，而深生态学则认为人与自然万物处于一种相互平等的联系之中，明确反对前者所持的人类中心主义观点，主张人与环境的互相关联。不仅如此，奈斯认为即便是非生命形式也具有与人类同等的内在价值，"人类与非人类在地球上的生存与繁荣均具有自身内在的、固有的价值。非人类的价值并不取决于他们对于满足人类期望的有用性。生命形式的丰富性和多样性决定了其自身具有的价值，这对人类和非人类生物在地球上的繁荣做出了贡献。"① 为此，他提出："人类除非为了满足生死攸关的生活需要，否则没有权利削弱这种丰富性和多样性。"②

美国深生态学家比尔·迪伏和乔治·塞逊斯进一步阐发了深生态学理念与浅生态学观念的不同，他们指出，深生态学主张人与自然的和谐，浅生态学则主张人与自然的分离；深生态学认为地球的供给是有限的，浅生态学则相信资源是充足的；深生态学认为只需满足优雅、简单的物质需求即可，物质目标服务于自我实现目标，浅生态学则推崇物质和财富的增长及消费主义；深生态学主张适当的技术和非控制性的科学，浅生态学则相信技术进步和科技干预。③ 面对日益严重的生态危机，浅生态学主张必须在不损害人类利益的前提下逐渐修复人与自然及社会的关系，它认为生态危机的出现是人类社会发展过程中的自然现象，只要不断地改进科学技术、完善社会的法规制度就可以杜绝危机的再次出现。深生态学则认为生态危机的出现是现代社会生存危机的反映，"生态危机的根源在于我们现有的社会机制、人的行为模式和价值观念。因而必须对人的价值观念和现行的社会体制进行根本的改造，把人和社会融于自然，使之成为一个整体，才可能解决生态危机和生存危机。"④

总之，浅生态学坚持人类中心主义的观点，认为人类的利益高于一切，自然界是人类社会的附属存在，当自然界的利益与人类的利益发生冲

---

① Witoszek Nina and Brennan Andrew. *Philosophical Dialogues*: *Arne Nass and the Progress of ecophilosophy*, Maryland: Rowman &Littlefield Publisher, INC. , 1999, p. 8.

② Ibid. .

③ Devall Bill and Sessions George, *Deep Ecology*, Layton: Gibbs M. Smith. Inc. , 1985, p. 69.

④ 雷毅:《生态伦理学》，陕西人民教育出版社 2000 年版，第 152 页。

突时，自然界必须牺牲自身的利益从而服从人类的利益，自然界是为了人类的存在而存在的，自然界本身并没有内在价值，这就否定了自然界的本体存在特征。

由上观之，深生态学自产生之初，就坚持整体性的原则，即把人类和自然界的一切存在物视为一个相互依赖、相互联系的整体。深生态学的核心观念是生态中心主义，它以整个生态系统（包括整个自然界及其一切生命和非生命体）的利益为目标，认为所有的生命体和非生命体都是平等的，且具有内在的价值，故奈斯把深生态学视为一种关于生态和谐或平衡的哲学，"它是一种生态哲学，而不仅仅是生态学。生态学是一种运用科学方法进行研究的有局限的科学，而哲学理念是深生态学的根基。深生态学的内涵更为丰富，它不仅仅是关于污染、资源和人口的一种事实，更重要的是一种价值观"①。

二　深生态学对确立深层海洋伦理观的启示意义

深生态学理论的兴起，源于自然生态危机的凸显，其着眼点则是对人类生存困境的深层考量。深生态学突破了生态危机现象学的苑囿，认为生态危机暴露出的是一种深层的社会危机、人性危机和精神危机。深生态学试图构建新的生态文明尺度和文化伦理取向，这对我们思考如何重新定位人类与海洋的关系，反思浅生态学以人类中心主义为价值导向的一味攫取海洋资源的弊端，确立人类与海洋为有机联系体的深层海洋生态伦理观，促进海洋开发和保护的良性、可持续发展具有重要启示意义。

1. 我国海洋伦理学观念的局限性

20 世纪 80 年代，我国首次提出"海洋经济"这一概念，到了 21 世纪，海洋经济和海洋开发的地位不断提升，目前已经上升到国家战略地

---

① Witoszek Nina and Brennan Andrew. *Philosophical Dialogues: Arne Nass and the Progress of ecophilosophy*, Maryland: Rowman &Littlefield Publisher, INC. , 1999, p. 8.

位。然而，随着我国经济的高速发展，海洋开发力度不断增大，大规模、高强度的不当海洋开发加速了海洋环境和生态的恶化，加剧了海洋环境灾害发生的频度，破坏了海洋生物物种的多样性，影响了海洋资源的可持续利用。"以海洋的统治者自居、以征服海洋为己任，贪得无厌地向自然索取，依靠牺牲海洋生态环境谋得发展，走上了一条高投入、高消耗、低效益的发展道路。而当前生产力水平远超过去任何时代，人与海洋的不和谐也比过去任何时代都要严峻和复杂。"① 故目前我国海洋开发与保护存在不平衡的状态，主要表现为以海洋开发为主，海洋保护并不对等，究其根源是一种浅生态学的海洋伦理观在作祟。

长期以来，由于对海洋开发及保护海洋生态环境认识上的片面性，传统的向海洋攫取资源、谋取经济利益、征服和利用海洋的人类中心主义海洋观一度占据主导地位。由于区域及个人利益的驱动，在海洋利用、开发活动中存在着严重的重开发轻保护的观念与行为。无度、无序、无偿开发海洋资源的现象突出，出现了过度捕捞近海鱼类、过度利用可养殖海域、大规模围海造地、海洋污染严重等诸多海洋开发问题，严重破坏了海洋生物的生态环境，造成了不少海洋生物种群濒临灭绝的危害。

在海洋环境方面，《2013 年中国海洋环境状况公报》显示，近岸典型海洋生态系统健康状况不容乐观，处于亚健康和不健康状态的海洋生态系统高达77%。2014 年 1 月，国家海洋局发布第 21 期海洋环境信息。监测数据显示，在所监测的 156 个陆源入海排污口中，有 78 个入海排污口向邻近海域超标排放污水，超标排污口占到监测总数的一半。海洋开发若失去人文价值的关怀，缺乏对海洋深层的敬畏、尊崇意识，就会对人类和海洋的可持续发展带来极大的挑战。

2. 我国海洋生态观的逐步深化

面对生态日益严峻的新形势，我国政府在生态问题的认识上不断深化，逐步超越了早期的"谁开发，谁保护，谁污染，谁治理"的理念，逐渐发展形成了"生态文明"的理论。"生态文明"一词在中国出现较晚，

---

① 李全坤、朱焰：《建设和谐海洋面临的挑战及其选择》，《生产力研究》2007 年第 10 期。

1984 年，著名生态学家叶谦吉最早使用了这一概念；1987 年，刘思华提出了"社会主义生态文明"的概念，之后，"生态文明"理论研究也逐渐展开。"生态文明"概念的提出，"表征着人与自然相互关系的进步状态"①。党的十七大报告中，第一次提出了"建设生态文明"的理念；党的十八大更进一步指出："面对资源约束趋紧、环境污染严重、生态系统退化的严峻形势，必须树立尊重自然、顺应自然、保护自然的生态文明理念。"这标志着人与自然关系认识的一次巨大飞跃，也是执政理念的重大转型。从"可持续"发展到"生态文明"理念的提出，体现了我国对生态问题认识的深化。

就海洋生态这一理念，在 20 世纪 90 年代，《中国海洋 21 世纪议程》制定了"建设良性循环的海洋生态系统，形成科学合理的海洋开发体系，促进海洋经济持续发展"② 的国家海洋战略目标，并明确提出"把海洋可持续利用和海洋事业协调发展作为 21 世纪中国海洋工作的指导思想"③，首次在国家海洋"战略目标"层面提出"可持续"发展的理念；而如何从浅生态学视野的局限中进一步解放思想观念，确立深层海洋生态伦理，则标志着对人与海洋关系认知深度的进一步提升，其意义更为重大，这也是本论文的研究重点所在。

3. 深生态学对确立深层海洋伦理观的重要启示意义

深生态学不仅在理论上具有创新性，确立了"生物圈平等"和"自我实现"重要原则，尖锐批评了浅生态学的偏颇和弊端，而且提出了一系列价值准则和指导行动的纲领。深生态学认为观念和政策的改变至关重要，观念的改变在于欣赏生命的质量和内在价值，而不是一味追求更高的生活标准。生命质量要进行根本提升则需要改变政策，这影响到经济、技术和意识形态结构的改变。它继而呼吁认同深生态学观点的人们承担起行动的责任，直接或间接地致力于完成这个根本性的转变。④ 深生态学的上述主

---

① 俞可平：《科学发展观与生态文明》，《马克思主义与现实》2005 年第 4 期。

② 《中国海洋 21 世纪议程》第一章第七条。

③ 《中国海洋 21 世纪议程》第一章第十二条。

④ Witoszek Nina and Brennan Andrew. *Philosophical Dialogues*: *Arne Nass and the Progress of ecophilosophy*, Maryland: Rowman &Littlefield Publisher, INC. , 1999, p. 8.

张对确立深层海洋伦理观的重要启示意义如下。

其一，超越浅生态学一味追求单向度的海洋开发而忽视海洋资源保护的短视观念。由于受人类中心主义利益的驱使，目前我国海洋开发和利用的态势还只是停留在浅生态学的层面，更多关注短期经济利益，往往只注意到眼前海洋资源的使用价值，而忽视了人与海洋密切相关的整体利益和长远利益，在开发和利用海洋资源的过程中，虽也意识到对海洋开发、利用过度会造成一定的海洋生态环境恶化，但只是主张在不损害人类利益的前提下逐渐修复人与海洋的关系。这种先发展后治理的理念是一种本末倒置的思维方式。究其原因，归根结底是人类对海洋环境开发与保护的认知还处在浅生态学的层面上，浅生态学只关心环境退化的症候，如海洋污染和资源的逐渐枯竭这些现象问题，而不会进一步去追问这些环境危机产生的根源，也就是缺乏价值观层面上的深层认知。故只有深生态学才能从根本上解决海洋生态危机问题。

其二，按照深生态学的"生物圈平等"理论，我们在开发和利用海洋资源时应该秉持人类发展和海洋资源保护同等重要的理念，人类与海洋处于同一个大的生态系统之中，是一个相互依赖、相互联系的整体，拥有着共同的未来和命运。人类不应该凌驾于海洋之上，更没有权利去破坏海洋内部生态系统的平衡。资源丰富的海洋不是仅仅为了满足人类的需求而存在的，它同样是许多其他的陆地及海洋生物的至关重要的栖息之地。人类对于海洋无休止的开发和污染使它们赖以生存的空间受到破坏，这是大大有违环境伦理学的理论原则的，最终也会反过来影响人类整体生活质量。

其三，深生态学推崇的环境伦理终极规范——"自我实现"原则为我们处理人与海洋的关系提供了有益的价值准则和行动指南。深生态学强调的"自我"并不是狭义上的、个体意义上的"自我"，而是一种范围更广的"生态自我"，它重视的是所有存在物的善或利益。因之，奈斯提出用"大写的自我"代替传统意义上的"自我"，他从尊崇所有的生命形式价值的立场出发，提倡"最大限度的自我实现"。而"最大限度的自我实现"不是任由个体生命欲求的恶性膨胀，而是将所有的生命形式放置在同一个平台之上，在平等、公正、资源共享的原则下，让它们的价值和潜能得到最大限度的发挥。具体到人与海洋的关系，这种"自我实现"原则，不仅包括人类合理开发、利用海洋资源既定目标和利益的达成，而且更重要的是减少人类过度活动对海洋造成的破坏，从而使得海洋生态资源及海洋生物物种的多样性得到最大限度的保护，只有这样才能实现人类与海洋和谐共存的"双赢"。

三　基于深生态学视野的深层海洋伦理观确立对策

鉴于海洋对我国的重要战略意义，在海洋经济不断加速发展的情况下，构建海洋生态文明，建立符合深生态学理念的海洋生态文明的长效机制，尤为重要。目前摆在我们面前的两个重要课题即是：其一，如何在深生态学的理论视域下，转变人们对海洋认知的偏误，改变浅生态学以人类利益为根本价值取向的狭隘海洋发展观，以确立人与海洋和谐共生的深层伦理观。其二，如何正确处理好海洋生态环境保护与经济发展的关系，以促进海洋资源保护和开发的可持续性发展。为此，在观念认知改变和实践层面应该立足于以下几个方面：

1. 借鉴深生态学理念，切实树立深层海洋伦理观

以深生态学理论为指导，重新审视和定位人与海洋的关系，逐步确立"非人类中心主义"的深层海洋伦理观，从海洋保护和发展的战略高度，转变一味强调对海洋开发与利用的旧观念，走保护海洋资源的生态良好的可持续发展道路。所谓海洋生态文明，主要是指在海洋意识、海洋产业、海洋行为、海洋环境、海洋文化和海洋制度等方面，统筹协调，和谐发展，全社会应牢固树立海洋生态文明意识，切实将保护与开发并重的方针，贯穿于社会发展和海洋生态文明建设的全过程。"生态文明是人类文明发展到一定阶段的产物，是反映人与自然和谐程度的新型文明形态，体现了人类文明发展理念的重大进步。"① 只有牢固树立深层海洋伦理观，才

---

① 张高丽：《大力推进生态文明　努力建设美丽中国》，《求是》2013 年第 24 期。

能真正把海洋生态文明的建设落到实处。

2. 充分发挥宣传、科研、教育、培训、涉外交流等媒介传播深层海洋伦理观

由于浅生态学人类中心主义和功利主义思想的影响，目前我们对海洋开发在认识上还存在很多偏误，认为海洋资源就是为了人类的发展而存在的，只注重眼前海洋资源的使用价值和经济价值，而忽视甚至没有认识到海洋资源的内在价值及对人类繁衍长久的福祉。在人与海洋的关系上，认为人可以凌驾于海洋之上，人与海洋之间存在一种统治与被统治的关系，对海洋资源进行掠夺式开发，以致危及人类的持续发展。而修正这种观念非一日之功，需要通过政府引导、媒体宣传和学校教育及涉外交流等各个渠道来实施。

政府、媒体和学校在宣传人与海洋休戚相关、尊重海洋生命内在价值、保护海洋物种丰富性等深生态学海洋观上负有义不容辞的责任。政府要起到引导作用，培育公民海洋生态保护意识。媒体则要加大社会宣传力度，促进海洋生态保护理念在受众中的大力传播。学校教育应发挥其积极作用，成为宣传保护海洋资源和生态的阵地，以切实提高全社会公民海洋保护意识。此外，在涉外交流中，有意识地借鉴、学习发达国家的海洋保护与开发相关理论、观念及具体措施也非常重要。

3. 建设符合深层海洋伦理观的海洋经济发展和行政管理模式

基于深生态学的理论指导，在海洋经济运行方式上，要转变海洋经济发展思路，改变传统的单纯追求海洋经济增长的战略和政策，把对海洋生态环境的有效保护置于与经济发展同等重要的战略地位。"传统发展观之所以步入了困境和危机，从发展自身的逻辑来看，它所关注的只是'如何能够发展'和'如何发展得更快'，而忽视了'应当怎样发展'和'为了什么而发展'这个目的论、价值论问题。"[1] 深生态学也反对一味追求"大"的发展理念，而更关注整体生命质量的提升。为此，在发展海洋经济时，应坚决摒弃长期以来形成的高消耗、高污染、低效益的粗放扩张型海洋经济增长方式，在保护好海洋生态资源的前提下，促进海洋经济发展

---

[1] 俞树彪：《和谐海洋的哲学视阈》，《经济论坛》2008 年第 15 期。

质量和效益的提升。

在海洋管理层面，应改变传统的海洋资源与环境的陈旧管理模式，加强对海洋生态保护的有效管理。政府相关职能部门应将海洋有序开发与改善海洋生态环境政策并举，特别是要履行对海洋资源开发和生态平衡保护的科学规划、组织、调控等宏观管理职能。管理模式应从以前过分重视海洋经济效益向保护海洋生态资源方向转化，并制定相关细化政策、条例，协调海洋合理有序开发及海洋生物多样性保护之间的平衡。

4. 制定和完善符合深层海洋伦理观的海洋生态保护政策法规

关于海洋生态保护，中央提出"要确定和守住不再破坏生态平衡、不再影响生态功能、不再改变基本属性、已受损的生态系统不再退化的'四不'开发底线"。如何坚持这一"底线"，建立海洋保护和开发的长效机制，最根本的还是要依靠观念指导下的法律。在现有法律的基础上，应进一步构建和完善海洋资源有序开发与生态保护科学、合理的法律体系。政府要尽快建立健全国家海洋法律，完善海洋综合管理法规中有关海洋污染防治和海洋生态资源保护方面的法律法规，起草体现可持续发展战略思想的相关海洋生态保护法规和条例，为海洋资源的合理开发利用与海洋生态保护提供法律依据，与此同时，也要加强对破坏海洋环境行为的惩处力度，切实提高人们保护海洋生态的法律意识。

鉴于目前海洋生态危机愈演愈烈的现状，我们必须从意识层面深化对海洋生态环境保护的认识，转变人类主宰海洋、统治关系的人类中心主义观念，以深生态学所秉承的"生物圈平等"和"自我实现"原则为理论指导，确立人与海洋生命和谐共生的深层生态伦理观，把人类和海洋视为密切相关的"生命共同体"，促进海洋资源开发和保护的良性、可持续发展，从而从根本上解决海洋生态危机问题。

（原载于《东方论坛》2014 年第 5 期）

论后殖民主义视野中的"寻根"文学

任何文学现象的产生都有其固有的内在发展理路，就如詹姆逊所言，任何话题都是应"需求"而产生的。对于"寻根"文学，许多人都从不同角度、不同层面进行了论述，本文拟从后殖民主义文化思潮的角度，探求"寻根"文学兴起与衰退的深层次原因。

一

后殖民主义是个言人人殊的概念。一般说来，它主要是指当今一些西方理论家，如赛义德、斯皮瓦克、巴巴等人，对殖民地写作话语的研究，是一种理论学术话语，正如乔纳森·哈特早已指出的，是"对欧洲帝国主义列强在文化上、政治上及历史上不同于其旧有的殖民地的差别（也包括种族之间的差别）的十分复杂的一种理论研究"①。但这是仅就其狭义方面讲。严格说来，后殖民主义首先和主要的是指一种文化思潮，而不仅仅是一种理论批评方法。作为一种文化思潮的后殖民主义，它从研究宗主国与殖民地国家之间的文化话语权力关系入手，揭露帝国主义对第三世界国家的文化霸权主义的实质，并旨在探讨"后"殖民时期东西方文化之间的新型"对话"关系。所以，后殖民主义表现出了明显的解构西方文化权力话语神话，倡导多元文化之间对话、互渗、共生格局的文化理路。正是在这

① 王宁：《二十世纪西方文学比较研究》，人民文学出版社 2000 年版，第 32 页。

个意义上，后殖民主义才自 20 世纪 70 年代末以来，逐渐成为一种影响世界的文化思潮。

后殖民主义因其表现出的激进的政治批判性，对第三世界知识分子具有广泛的吸引力。后殖民主义的最基本也是最重要的理论方法是解构主义，其消解中心、解构权威的命题，与第三世界知识分子的文化心理十分契合。作为一种文化思潮，后殖民主义最具特征性的理论术语是赛义德的"东方主义"和杰姆逊的"第三世界文化"的概念。杰姆逊呼吁第三世界文化要超越西方文化"中心"论思想的影响，成为一种具有内在特质的独立文化形态，真正进入与第一世界文化"对话"的空间，从而从根本上消解和打破第一世界文化的中心性和权威性，进而确立自我文化"身份"，展示第三世界文化的独特魅力和价值，以及在世界多元文化格局中的位置。①

其实，对于西方知识分子来说，西方文化优越论的观念是根深蒂固的，他们对第三世界文化的歧见同样是根深蒂固的。赛义德在他的富有挑战性的《东方主义》一书中批评道，"东方主义"只不过是一个"想象的地理和表述形式"，是一个站在西方文化立场上"创造"出来的带有无法克服的偏见的"异己者"，是"一种永恒不变的东方精神的乌托邦"。"东方主义"在其最本质意义上，是西方殖民者从制约东方的立场出发"建构"出来的一种政治教义，目的是将东方纳入西方中心的权力结构。也正是在这个意义上，赛义德说，"东方主义"只是西方人的一种"建构"的结果，"东方主义的所有的一切都与东方无甚关系，东方主义之所以具有意义完全是取决于西方而不是东方本身"②。

基于这种根深蒂固的歧见和无法克服的偏见，西方知识分子不能对第三世界国家的文化作出正确的价值判断，于是，他们就把自身的意识形态"编码"在整个文化机器上，通过各种途径强制性地输向第三世界国家，进行文化殖民活动。而处于边缘地位的第三世界文化，面对这种强制性的

---

① 王岳川：《二十世纪西方哲性诗学》，北京大学出版社 1999 年版，第 483 页。
② 王宁：《后现代主义之后》，中国文学出版社 1998 年版，第 93 页。

输入，他们的传统文化正面临着一种新的威胁和挑战，母语在流失，自身传统文化和意识形态受到很大冲击，从而造成"文化原质的失真"。面对这种文化殖民主义，广大第三世界知识分子也从保持自身民族文化的立场出发，迅速调整文化策略，应对西方文化"入侵"。20世纪80年代中期，我国文坛上崛起的"寻根"派文学，即是我国敏感的知识分子面对西方殖民主义文化思潮作出的一种"反应"。

二

法国学者朱莉亚·克里斯多娃在她著名的《关于中国妇女》一书中，曾经充满激情地写道："在中国有不可思议之处……一个高度发达的文明毫无错综情结地进入了现代世界，同时又保持了并非用异国情调的说法就可以解释得了的独属于自己的逻辑。"她甚至不无羡慕地说，中国古老文明是处于"无时间之前"的另一种文化。① 但是，中国文化发展史明确地告诉我们，自1840年鸦片战争以来，古老中国封闭日久的大门在帝国主义列强的坚船利炮的逼迫下被迫打开，由此，中国社会开始了"被迫现代化"的过程。中国古老文化也由此逐渐丧失了这种"独属于自己的逻辑"，而渗入异族文化的血脉。面对这种事实上的文化"殖民化"过程，正如美籍华人周蕾所言，中国人再也无法墨守一个静止不动的传统而生存下去，他们开始过着一种"不纯洁"的、"西方化"的中国人的生活，甚至他们"看"中国的方法也无可避免地打上了那种西方文化的烙印。"西方化"已成为深烙在中国人身上的不可磨灭的主体的一部分。中国文化结束了长达几千年的"单质"时代，进入一个"合金"阶段。自那时起，中国的知识分子在面对西方文化和我们民族传统文化时，第一次有了一种无法说清的"焦虑"心态，长期以来围绕"西体中用"而展开的激烈论争，就是这种"焦虑"心态的明证，就在这种论争中，暴露了中国传统文化在面对西方

---

① 张京媛主编：《后殖民理论与文化批评》，北京大学出版社1999年版，第324页。

文化冲击时的矛盾心态，和中国知识分子对中国文化现代化的一种心理"预设"。

有的学者指出，20 世纪以来，中国文化经历了两次集中的"殖民化"（实际上是"被殖民化"）过程，一是五四时期，二是新时期。特别是新时期以来，伴随着经济上的对外开放，中国人从日常生活方式到社会价值观念，社会生活的各个层面都以前所未有的方式迅速"西化"，甚至出现了许多唯西方马首是瞻的"香蕉人"（外黄内白），面对这种剧烈的社会文化转型，敏感的中国知识分子对自身的文化处境和古老民族的"文化身份"产生了更加深刻的"焦虑"。应该说，"寻根"文学的兴起，是中国敏感的知识分子，面对传统文化被"殖民化"过程的"焦虑"心态的再一次呈现。

"从某种意义上讲，不论是在现代社会还是在古代社会，人们的自我意识都是从反面发展起来的。"① 刘心武早在"寻根"文学刚刚兴起时，就非常敏锐地指出，"寻根"意识的产生，是中国知识分子目光向外的结果，是"深受当前西方新潮影响的一种反应。"② 我们无法确证刘心武所说的"新潮"是否就是后殖民主义文化思潮，但是我们可以从"寻根"作家的言论中得知，无论是韩少功、阿城，还是李杭育、郑万隆等人，对当代外国文化、文学思潮都表现得相当敏感，在这种敏感中，我们可以明显地感觉到，在面对西方文化的冲击时，他们所表现出的那种强烈的反叛情绪和"焦虑"心态。有的论者指出，"寻根"文学正是在东西方文化大冲撞、大交汇的总体背景中，"此一时代的人们在被动的局面中，所做的主动反应"③。

韩少功在他的那篇著名的、几乎可以看作是整个"寻根"文学的"宣言"的《文学的"根"》中，对青年作者"眼盯海外"，甚至连"品位不怎么高的《教父》和《克莱默夫妇》，都会成为热烈的话题"的现象，深

① 张京媛主编：《后殖民理论与文化批评》，北京大学出版社 1999 年版，第 27 页。
② 刘心武：《从"单质文学"到"合金文学"》，《作家》1985 年第 7 期。
③ 季红真：《历史的命题与时代抉择中的艺术嬗变——论寻根文学的发生与意义》，《当代作家评论》1989 年第 4 期。

表不以为然。"寻根"作家有一个"共识",那就是"五四"使中国传统文化发生了"断裂"。韩少功尖刻地认为,"五四"以后,中国文学向外国文学学习,"结果带来民族文化的毁灭,还有民族自信心的低落"①;阿城在《文化制约着人类》这篇文章中说,五四运动"较全面地对民族文化的虚无主义态度,加上中国社会一直动荡不安,使民族文化断裂"②;另一"寻根"作家郑义也认为,"五四""有隔断民族文化之嫌"。"寻根"作家们认为,只有在"彻底的清算和批判之中,萎缩和毁灭之中,中国文化也就可能涅槃再生了"③。"寻根"作家正是从这样一种文化逻辑出发,来进行他们的"寻根"文学创作的。

"寻根"作家从这种反"殖民化"的文化立场出发,断言"文学有根,文学之根应深植于民族传统文化的土壤里,根不深,则叶难茂"④,因此,"寻根"作家们都不约而同地对古老的传统文化,特别是那些"至今未纳入规范的民间文化"表现出浓厚的兴趣。阿城的《树王》表现了一种古老的"天人感应"的神秘文化,"树王"肖疙瘩的突然死亡和几百年古树被砍伐之间的神秘关系;王安忆的《小鲍庄》一开头就是"七天七夜的雨,天都下黑了",竭力发掘的是古老文化的"一种宿命的力量";韩少功的《爸爸爸》也写了一些奇异的民俗,如把老鼠烧死后把尸灰泡在水里喝,两个村子"打冤",把冤家的尸体和猪煮在一起吃掉,表现了一种巫术文化。"寻根"作家们都在对传统文化的发掘中,努力"揭示一些决定民族发展和人类生存的谜"。应该说,"寻根"作家的这种过分"焦虑"的心态,使他们在作品中尽情展示中国传统文化"景观"的同时,也丧失了对中国传统文化的清醒的理性价值判断。

---

① 韩少功:《文学的"根"》,《作家》1985年第4期。
② 阿城:《文化制约着人类》,《文艺报》1985年7月6日。
③ 韩少功:《文学的"根"》,《作家》1985年第4期。
④ 同上。

三

"寻根"文学自产生之日起，就注定了其无法克服的"悖谬"的窘境。一方面，它对中国文化"被迫现代化"表现出的反叛情绪，显示了它明显的后殖民主义的批判性；而另一方面，它对中国古老文化表现出的过分的迷恋和沉醉，又使它陷入了无法自拔的文化上的本土主义。

"寻根"作家们在创作之始，都怀有一种高度的民族文化的自觉意识，表现出了可贵的理性自觉精神，这一点从他们各自的"宣言"中可以清楚地看到。阿城在他的《文化制约着人类》这篇文章中写道："中国文学尚没有建立在一个广泛深厚的文化开掘之中。没有一个强大的、独特的文化限制，大约是不好达到文学先进水平这种自由的，同样也是与世界文化对不起话的。"① 在这里，阿城表现出了一种要与世界文化对话的自觉意识，"寻根"作家们正是从这种文化自觉意识出发，来"建构"他们的小说文本的。

"寻根"作家在他们的小说创作中，努力表现中国古老的民族文化，甚至他们的一些小说成了一种单纯的民族文化的"寓言性文本"，从而损伤了小说的艺术之美，一个潜在的动机，就是通过这种努力，来反叛和解构西方文化对我们民族文化的"殖民化"进程，从而保持我们传统文化与西方文化"对话"的资格。但恰恰就是在这种充满高度理性自觉的反叛和解构之中，"寻根"作家们不自觉地走向了他们愿望的反面——他们"建构"起了自己的"东方主义"。"寻根"作家们在试图破除西方人"制造"的"异己者"形象时，自己又"虚构"了一个新的西方人眼中的"他者"形象，丰富了西方人的视野。

自从公元前 2 世纪西方大旅行家贺拉德斯和亚历山大国王漫游东方以来，西方人就开始了他们对"欧洲以外的那片无限大的土地"——东

---

① 阿城：《文化制约着人类》，《文艺报》1985 年 7 月 6 日。

方——不知疲倦的"建构"过程。正如赛义德所言，对西方人来说，东方总是"像"西方的某个方面，"东方"作为一个"虚像"，无时无刻不活跃在西方人的想象中。日本学者竹内好也说，"东方"之所以成为东方，就是因为它被包含到了欧洲之中，"东方也只有处于欧洲中才能实现"。对于这样一个丧失了自我评价尺度的"东方"，"寻根"作家们是持强烈的批判态度的，但是"寻根"作家们所没有料到的是，作为解构西方文化中心论的文化策略而建构起来的小说文本中所呈现的"独属于"中国古老文化的事物，也无可避免地仅仅是作为西方话语的否定形式而存在着，从而仍旧是"他者"的形象，无法真正地与西方文化"面对面地相遇"。

"寻根"文学作为一种文学现象已经沉寂，但是"寻根"作家们面对我们民族文化"被现代化"的过程所表现出的深沉的历史情怀和果敢的文化策略，却值得人们永远记取和评判，供后来人长久地"阅读"。

（原载于《临沂师范学院学报》2002年第1期）

道德理性与当代情爱小说

　　情爱因其丰富、复杂和多样性的内涵，成为中外文学永恒的话题之一，它不仅折射着时代精神，反映诸多社会问题，而且使我们得以深入窥测人类精神世界之奥秘，探究人性之复杂。从某种意义上说，情爱文学的书写可以被视为衡量文学创作偏枯与兴盛的晴雨表。新时期以来，中国当代文学进入了一个空前活跃的繁盛期，情爱描写也成为其中最引人注目的一道风景线，它成为窥测人性的一个最直接的窗口。自此切入人性的深层，必能深化文学研究。目前，关于当代情爱文学的研究多侧重于对其外在表现形态及写作模式的分析上，本论文则把当代情爱文学纳入道德理性的视野中，旨在探讨当代作家情爱理性观的嬗变。

　　所谓道德理性，简言之，即各种形态的道德规范之价值尺度。自近代社会以来，价值观的问题成为哲学的核心。在探寻人类与外在世界之间各种关系，对这些关系作出价值判断时，世界不同的文化建构了不同的价值体系。"儒家文化"规约着中国传统伦理道德，它素以群体为重，认为个体命运由群体命运所决定、所支配，因而中国传统的道德观体现的是一种"尊礼""尊群"的价值理念，反映在两性关系上，则将情欲纳入礼制体系，所谓"存天理，灭人欲"便成为天经地义。西方文化自古希腊起则关注人的自然属性，文艺复兴时期弥漫着"我是人，人的一切特性无所不有"的人本思潮，此后尼采的"超人"、海德格尔的"此在"、萨特的"自由"都高举人本主义的大旗，将个人的价值看得高于一切，表现在性爱方面，则是高举、张扬性的美好和自由。

　　中国是一个封建文化传统悠久的民族，以个性为前提的人本主义道德理性曾长期遭到以扼杀个性为特征的封建专制文化的压制。五四时期，西方现代人本思潮作为与中国传统文化迥然不同的异质文化，为中国新文学注入了新的因子。进入新时期以后，随着中国国门对外敞开，西方现代人本思潮再次如潮水般涌入，冲击着人们原有的价值观。当代作家作为体察时代变化的最敏锐的群体，很快把这种变化反映在作品中。他们大多从过去"尊礼""尊群"的传统价值理念中跳出，用现代的"尊己""尊个体"及"尊性""尊女"等价值理念来张扬人的主体性、个性。总的来说，渗透在当代情爱文学作品中的是一种现代情爱价值观。而晚生代作家因没有传统文化的包袱，思想更开放，把"尊己"发展到"恋己"，把"尊性"发展为"泛性"，通过所谓"身体"把性的自由、随意夸大到了极致。中国当代情爱文学所折射的就是这样一条道德理念嬗变的历程。

一

　　新时期初期，贾平凹、古华、邵振国等作家站在历史与时代的十字路口，无法完全去除中国传统文化在他们头脑中留下的烙印，但对时代的敏锐感受力又使他们无法抗拒西方现代人本思潮的影响，在作品中便表现了这两者的冲突。贾平凹在他 20 世纪 90 年代的《废都》《白夜》《土门》《高老庄》等长篇小说中淋漓地张扬了性的魅力，但在他早期的作品中，却更多地表现了对传统道德理性的尊崇及皈依。贾平凹的早期作品《天狗》多处描写了主人公天狗对师娘那种朦朦胧胧的性爱意识的萌动，但当师娘主动投入他的怀抱时，他却表现得异常冷静和理性。天狗在性与爱、情与理之间徘徊之后走向了对传统的回归与认同。邵振国的《麦客》中俊俏的水香与她的情人麦客同样处于这种矛盾之中，她最终在感情的压抑中走向了道德的完善。在 20 世纪 80 年代初期的情爱文学作品中，这种"发乎情止乎礼"的模式，反映了一部分作家对传统"尊礼""尊他"道德理念的认同。

　　弗洛伊德曾说："健康正常的爱情，需要依赖两种感情的结合——我们可以这样说，一方面是两心相悦的挚爱的情，另一方面是肉感的性的欲。"① "挚爱的情"是两性结合的一个情感的纽带，只有由深挚的感情维系的两性关系才是最持久的。"尊情"成为新时期初期爱情题材小说的一个共同主题，这在女性作家的作品中表现得最为突出。对爱情的精神守望，构成《爱，是不能忘记的》《最后的停泊地》《永远是春天》及《东方女性》等小说的共同基调。张洁在其代表作《爱，是不能忘记的》中提出了"只有以爱情为基础的婚姻才是道德的"这一新的情爱道德理念。鲁彦周的《天云山传奇》因讴歌了真挚、纯洁的爱情而深深感染了读者，而他的另一篇小说《流泉》则表达了对纯真、诚挚的爱情丧失的一种痛惜。欲望化主题贯穿于王朔早期小说《顽主》《浮出海面》《动物凶猛》《许爷》《一半是火焰，一半是海水》《橡皮人》等大部分作品中，但这些作品仍为纯情留下了一片明净的天空。其系列小说，都塑造了纯情的少女形象，她们的冰清玉洁与充满欲望、喧嚣的尘世形成一种鲜明的对照。另外，这一时期以婚外恋、离婚为题材的情爱文学作品，如苏童的《离婚指南》、皮皮的《比如女人》等都探讨了爱情在两性关系中的重要位置。

新时期的张炜、张承志、刘醒龙等作家表现出对"灵"的境界敬仰的价值趋向。"灵"在他们眼里是至高无上的，是他们超越世俗、追求崇高的精神境界的目标。张炜是当代文坛中一个实力派作家，其代表作《古船》《九月寓言》及《柏慧》等营造了一种远离尘世、与天地自然亲近的氛围。他小说中的人物，面对当前商品经济的喧嚣，总喜欢回到清新的自然中，在远离社会的荒原野地守望人类的家园。因而，张炜的小说更欣赏得自天地自然之精气的人性之灵，在情爱观上推崇"至灵"。张承志、刘醒龙的作品同样体现了唯灵至上的价值趋向。

如果说新时期即20世纪70年代至80年代初期，作家们仍徘徊在传统道德理念与现代理念之间，并且在一定程度上表现出对传统"尊礼""尊情"道德理念的依恋，那么到了80年代中期，作家的价值观从总体上来说则发生了很大变化，表现为一种开放的现代情爱理念。

---

① 《中国当代情爱伦理争鸣作品书系》，今日中国出版社1995年版。

二

自新时期以来，作家首先觉醒的就是个性意识。20 世纪 70 年代末 80 年代初，中国的思想解放运动使人道主义在文学中开始恢复，文学是人学命题被重新肯定，尊重生命个体的个性、欲望、尊严成为文学写作的一个中心话题。特别是进入 80 年代中期后，西方现代的各种文学、哲学思潮不断涌入，冲击着人们传统的道德理念。作家们以现代人的眼光重新审视历史和现实，以一种大胆怀疑、否定的态度对传统伦理道德进行无情的抨击，越来越多的作家在作品中表现出了一种现代、开放的情爱观。他们强调个人的价值和幸福是首位的，其情感、欲念应该得到尊重和满足；性爱是美丽、健康的，它是富有人性的象征，应该得到张扬，对其压抑和摧残是不道德的，是非人性的。"尊己"与"尊性"成为当代情爱文学中的核心理念。

当代作家把遵从个体情感的自由、自主，把个体在爱情、婚姻中的幸福感放在首位。许多当代情爱文学作品宣扬了"尊己"的价值理念。如方方的《桃花灿烂》中的父亲在经历了 20 年没有感情的婚姻后，才意识到个人幸福在生活、情感中的重要性，毅然决定和母亲离婚。他宣称："我只是做了一个人基本应该做的，丝毫不出格。"这实际上体现的是作家方方对"尊己"的现代情爱观的一种倡导。

文学既是人学，就离不开对人自身的审美观照，对复杂的人性进行纵深的揭示。如果写人不写其性，是不能全面表现人的。恩格斯把爱情称为性爱，把性爱的最高形式——热恋称为性的冲动，就是把人的自然属性作为爱情的起码条件。弗洛伊德认为，性欲在诸本能中最重要、最活跃，它与生俱来，按照快乐原则寻求满足。既然写爱情，就很难避开性心理、性意识的介入。当代作家摆脱了传统的道德眼光，从生命本体价值层面去肯定。这样，性便在当代文学殿堂中占据了重要的位置。

古华的《爬满青藤的木屋》、张弦的《被爱情遗忘的角落》及邵振国的《麦客》等作品是新时期以来较早涉入性问题的小说。这些作品几乎都以悲剧形式描写了人的性的觉醒、萌动、不可遏制，肯定了人的自然本能需求的合理性。这一部分作品在酝酿期为真正意义上的涉性文学的出现做好了准备。20世纪80年代中期，随着作家文学观念的更新、对人类自身认识的加深、视野的开阔，当代作家在性描写上普遍表现出一种勇敢无畏的探索精神，涌现出一大批有很大影响的作家及作品，其中有乔雪竹的《荨麻崖》、杨克祥的《玉河十八滩》、邹志安的《睡着的南鱼儿》、周大新的《汉家女》、铁凝的《麦秸垛》、刘震云的《罪人》及王安忆的"三恋"等。在上述作品中，作家们或以现代性爱理念对传统的性伦理、性道德进行了质疑、批判及重新评估，或从性的视角来探测人的生命和情感的丰富性和复杂性。如王安忆的"三恋"小说为我们建构了一个性与爱交织而成的"伊甸园"，形象地展示了人类在性爱的"本我""自我""超我"中的复杂心理。

在新时期情爱文学中，女性作家的创作颇丰。女性作家以其特有的细腻、敏感、重感情的女性视角，细致入微地呈现了女性在两性关系中独特的生理、心理及情感感受，充分展现了女性对性爱的体验。新时期以来，随着个性意识的不断张扬，女性意识也随之显出极强的主体性。个性意识的觉醒使女性作家在作品中力图颠覆男权社会对女性的性歧视，从而从本体意义上恢复女性生命个体的价值和尊严。张辛欣的《在同一地平线上》、张洁的《方舟》、王安忆的"三恋"等都表达了这种"尊女"的立场。

20世纪80年代中期至90年代初期，是现代情爱理念逐渐确立并走向成熟的时期。作家们在"尊己""尊欲""尊女"的情爱宣言中，张扬的是生命个体的个性、欲望及尊严，是最富有人性的道德理念。

三

进入20世纪90年代，晚生代作家群体更倾向"私人化"的写作。邱华栋在《城市的面具》自序中的一段话，是对这一类作家的写作背景的一个很好的总结。他说："对于我，以及像我一样出生于'文化大革命'开始以后的一代人来说，我们没有太多的历史记忆……而我们和我的同代人也就生活在这样一个经济化的社会中。没有多少'文革'记忆的我们，当然也就迅速沉入到当下的生活状态中了。"正是这种没有思想包袱的创作背景使新生代作家在创作时无所顾忌，在情爱文学的写作中走得愈来愈远。

20 世纪 90 年代，情爱文学书写的一个最突出的特征即是赤裸裸的性描写。在这一时期的作品中，爱情已经隐退，充斥纸张的是性的展示。在晚生代的一些作家那里，性则与毒品一样，成为他们笔下"新新人类"生活里一件随手拿来的东西。在朱文的《我爱美元》、韩东的《障碍》、卫慧的《上海宝贝》、棉棉的《糖》等一大批新生代作品中，爱情的神圣性被质疑，传统的道德伦理更是受到了讽刺。小说中充斥的是赤裸裸的性爱场面和性爱游戏。主人公之间不谈爱情，所有的不过是性欲的狂热与发泄。20 世纪 70 年代出生的作家生活于更本体的感性之中，更直接面对性本身。棉棉的《九个目标的欲望》《一个矫揉造作的晚上》及《香港情人》，朱文颖的《夜上海》《霸王别姬》，卫慧的《像卫慧一样疯狂》，魏微的《一个年龄的性意识》，杨蔚的《紊乱》等"表现出了一种与此前的小说完全两样的'性状态'：更自我，更感性，更随意，纵情、自恋、颠倒、虚无、感伤、紊乱，细节上的绵密细致，透露出冲动的、情欲的、绝望的、迷茫的气息"①。

晚生代的女作家甚至将 20 世纪 80 年代"尊己""尊女"的情结发展成为一种自恋式的书写，自恋式的情调充溢着《长恨歌》《情爱画廊》《玫瑰门》《一个人的战争》《双鱼星座》《私人生活》《左手》《丹青引》等作品中。这种自恋式的情爱态度，发展到极致，一味沉湎于女性狭小的世界，甚至表现为变态心理。

应该说，晚生代作家在文学创作中真实地写出了个人的生活经历与感受，反映了一部分当代年轻人的生活状态，但他们在作品中带着玩味、欣

---

① 刘保昌：《在爱与欲之间》，《人文杂志》2001 年第 3 期。

赏的口气，把性的自由、随意、无度夸大到了极致。这固然能释放人的本能，使人获得更大程度的自由和解放，但其无边无际的性泛滥道德理念，使人沉溺于感官享乐中，没有生活目标，没有精神寄托，陷入颓废、自虐、堕落中而不能自拔，易把读者引向动物般行尸走肉的生活状态。这实际是一种颓废、消极的性爱观，与健康的现代情爱道德理念是背道而驰的，是一种"伪现代性"的性泛滥道德观。正如一位批评家所指出的那样，真正的情爱应是一种唤起人们心灵深处震动与战栗的巨大力量，真正的性爱文学应是一种对性爱的诗意的追寻与揭示，它应在文学与读者之间建立起一种永久的感怀与期盼。

我国当代情爱文学的书写经历了从传统"尊礼""尊群"的道德理念到现代"尊己""尊情""尊性"观念的转变，契合了世界"人本"思潮尊崇个体价值，遵从个体生理、精神需求的现代理念，但我们也要防范"伪现代性"的性泛滥道德理念。

（原载于《当代文坛》2006 年第 6 期）

跨文化视野中的王蒙小说解读
——《坚硬的稀粥》与《活动变人形》新论

林语堂在《我的话·杂说》中曾说，"两脚踏东西文化，一心评宇宙文章"，他希望自己能够拥有一种胸怀中西文化的宽广视野，在中国当代作家中，王蒙同样具有这样一种胸襟和眼界。

近代以来，中国一直处于西学东渐的时代语境下，在西学强势文化的夹击下，中国文化何去何从，中西文化孰优孰劣，成为近现代诸多学者、大家所关注的一个焦点问题。自改革开放以来，在新的历史时期，各种西方文化思潮又蜂拥而至，对中国文化造成了巨大的冲击。在这样一种文化背景下，王蒙作为一位对现实具有深邃洞察力的当代作家，同样非常关注中国文化在西学愈演愈烈的全球化背景下该如何发展的问题，并在他的一些作品中表现了中西文化相互交汇、融合、碰撞、冲突的发展状况，对如何审视、看取中西文化，如何构建当代中国文化等问题，提出了他的独到见解和看法。

一

首先让我们回顾一下近代以来关于中西文化之争这一命题产生的历史和文化背景。鸦片战争以降，中国关闭了几千年的大门被西方列强国家强行打开，西方文化如潮水般涌入，由此拉开了关于中学与西学、本土文化与外来文化、传统文化与现代文化之争的序幕。而在关于中西文化的争辩中，存在着以下三种评判态度。

首先，文化激进主义者认定中国是一个"精神上患病的民族"，其病因是中国传统文化，认定中国传统文化是中国在近代世界格局中处于困境的根源，是中国走向现代化的障碍，中国传统文化在道德上是罪恶的，在历史发展中是有害的，认定中国传统文化是"已死的东西"，其基本特征是"陈腐而邪恶的"，中国社会要进步，就"非走西方文明的路不可"，比较有代表性的现代学者有李大钊、陈独秀、鲁迅等人，李大钊认为"中国文明之疾病已达炎热最高之度，中国民族之命运已臻奄奄垂死之期"，中国文明与西方文明相比，已全面处于"屈败之势"，必须"根本扫荡"。①

陈独秀与他的《新青年》同仁认为，只有政治制度上的变革远远不够，要使中国改变面貌，必须在文化上来一个全面革新，于是发动五四新文化运动，提出"拥护德先生和赛先生"的口号，他曾明确指出："要拥护那德先生，便不得不反对礼教、礼法、贞节、旧伦理、旧政治。要拥护那赛先生，便不得不反对旧艺术、旧宗教。要拥护德先生又要拥护赛先生，便不得不反对国粹和旧文学。"② 就是说，中国不仅应该学习西方的工业化、科学精神、民主政治，而且要按照西方模式，对民族文化进行一番彻底清除。鲁迅持同样的观点，他将数千年中国历史概括为"吃人"，在《青年必读书》中，鲁迅说："我以为要少——或者竟不——看中国书，多看外国书。"③

而文化保守主义者则固守中国传统文化，认为中国文化是国粹，为人类文明提供了理想的范式，甚至过分迷恋中国封建文化糟粕的一面。较有代表性的人物有林琴南、刘师培、章士钊和辜鸿铭等。如辜鸿铭对中国古代的纳妾、缠足等恶习竟然大加赞赏，他曾这样解释说："中国的'妇'字，本来就由一个'女'和一个'帚'两部分构成。古代中国人把妇女称作一个固定房子的主人——厨房的主人，这种真正的女性理想———切具有真正而非华而不实文明的人们心中的女性理想，无论是希伯来人，还是

---

① 参见李大钊《东西文明根本之异点》，《言治季刊》第 3 期。
② 陈独秀：《本质罪案之答辩书》，《新青年》第 6 卷第 1 号。
③ 鲁迅：《鲁迅全集》第 3 卷，人民文学出版社 1991 年版，第 12 页。

古希腊和罗马人，本质上都与中国人的女性理想一样。"①

从上面我们看到，无论是文化激进主义还是文化保守主义，这两种倾向都表现为一种各执中西一端的"一元化"价值取向，都有其片面性和极端性。

而在中西文化的看取上，还存在第三种多元整合的文化观，即认为中西文化各有所长，又各有所短。有融通、互补的必要。如林语堂曾说他的头脑是西洋的产品，而心却是中国的。王蒙在中西文化问题上同样持一种多元整合的文化价值取向，一方面，他以一种积极、开放的态度接纳西方文化，认为西方文化所内含的科学、民主、平等、自由、文明的理念是中国传统文化所缺失、所亟须借鉴的一种现代文化资源，另一方面又依然推崇中国传统儒家文化，对其充满自信和自豪感，认为中国文化作为一种古老、悠久、独立、完整的人类文明形式，其伦理观念仍具有其独到的生命力和价值，对现代西方文明仍有借鉴意义。这种开放的价值理念决定了王蒙在中西文化问题上所持的一种辩证、审慎态度，他认为无论是对西方文化的接纳还是对东方文化的推崇都不能走向极端化。而如果各执一端将会导致各种矛盾和悲剧的产生。他的小说《活动变人形》和《坚硬的稀粥》深刻揭示了这一点。

《坚硬的稀粥》和《活动变人形》表现了在中西文化立场上的文化激进主义和文化保守主义两派力量的较量、斗争，以及他们固守一方的偏颇所带给我们的思考。《坚硬的稀粥》中的瘦高挑儿子、《活动变人形》中的倪吾诚是文化激进主义的两个代表性人物，他们对中国文化全盘否定，认为西方文化优于中国文化，主张实行全盘西化。《坚硬的稀粥》中的爷爷、奶奶及徐姐等，《活动变人形》中的静宜、静珍则属于固守中国传统文化的保守主义者。她们是中国传统文化的捍卫者，对西方文化则持一种反感、排斥、厌恶甚至坚决抵制的态度。由于中西文化在生活方式、价值观和行为取向上存在着矛盾、冲突、对立等诸多差异性，固守此两种文化的上述两派力量又缺乏融会贯通的变通思维，致使他们的斗争愈演愈烈，并

① 辜鸿铭：《辜鸿铭文集》（下），黄兴涛等译，海南出版社1996年版，第72页。

由此酿成了他们的矛盾冲突甚至人生悲剧。下文拟从文化符码的角度进一步进行阐释。

文化是人类的一种符号化的思维和行为方式，德国哲学家卡西尔曾说"人是符号的动物"。文化是由一系列可感知的符号单元组成的完整系统。不同的文化因所使用的符号不同，从而产生了世界文化的多样性。王蒙在《坚硬的稀粥》和《活动变人形》中很好地使用了一些典型的中西文化符码，表现了文化激进主义者和文化保守主义者在中西文化立场上的各执一端及冲突与矛盾。

《坚硬的稀粥》和《活动变人形》处处表现了中西文化的对立、冲突。而小说的巧妙之处则在于王蒙擅长运用现实生活中的各种符号代码来指涉、隐喻深层的内涵。首先，我们看到这两部作品当中提到了多种食物的名称，这些食物名称的内涵并非仅仅指向表层意义，而是带有较深的隐喻意味。这些食物可以分为两大类，一类是传统中国食物，如稀粥咸菜、烤馒头片、炸酱面、鸡蛋挂面；另一类是西方人饮用的食物，如鱼肝油、黄油火腿、干酪、金枪鱼、小牛肉、苹果派、冰激凌等。我们姑且以稀粥和鱼肝油这两个中西饮食文化的典型符码为个案，来具体分析一下小说的文化偏激主义派和文化保守派所持的不同文化立场。

二

《坚硬的稀粥》的开头首先介绍了"我们家"的家庭成员，包括爷爷、奶奶、父亲、母亲、叔叔、婶婶、我妻子、堂妹、妹夫和"我那个最可爱的瘦高挑儿子"，还有一个虽是非正式成员，却是举足轻重的人物——徐姐，主要负责家庭的膳食工作。本来这个大家庭几十年来一直处于超稳定状态。"我们一直生活得很平稳，很团结"，"几十年来，徐姐给我们准备好了早餐：烤馒头片、大米稀饭、腌大头菜"。但随着形势的变化，"新风日劲，新潮日猛"（此处有着现实生活的背景，当时中国进入了20世纪80年代改革开放的新时期，西方文化开始大量涌入中国），这个大家庭变得不平静起来。起因是家庭的膳食改革。"我那个最可爱的瘦高挑儿子"首先把批判的矛头指向稀粥这一传统饮食，他首先从营养学的角度，论证了一番稀粥只能供给人体碳水化合物，而不能供给充足的蛋白质的道理，之后义愤填膺地声讨了稀粥之于中国人的危害："稀粥咸菜本身就是东亚病夫的象征！就是慢性自杀！就是无知！就是炎黄子孙的耻辱！就是华夏文明衰落的根源！就是黄河式微的征兆！"瘦高挑儿子把中国落后于世界的原因归结于稀粥文化，认为它是导致中国人在各个领域落后于西方国家的罪魁祸首。显然，稀粥在此已不单单是一种普通的食物，而成为一种文化的符码，瘦高挑儿子用一种决绝否定的态度表明了他对稀粥误国误民的看法，从而也表明了他在中西文化上所持的文化激进主义立场。

而小说中的文化保守主义者徐姐、奶奶、爷爷则视稀粥为安身立命之宝，在实行膳食改革废除稀粥三天之后，小说用了一个夸张的词组"全家震荡"，描绘了改吃西餐后全家人身体的极度不适：徐姐得了中毒性肠胃炎，奶奶患了"非甲非乙型神经性肝硬化"，爷爷得了便秘，堂妹患肠梗阻，堂妹夫牙疼烂嘴角，妻子饭后呕吐。看来，失去稀粥的滋补，他们的生活发生了紊乱，身体功能遭到了严重破坏。粥已成了他们的立身之本。

梁漱溟先生曾说，"文化是生活的样法""文化，就是吾人生活所依靠的一切"。稀粥对于中国人而言，犹如长江黄河源远流长，历经岁月沧桑、朝代更迭，而长盛不衰。稀粥的产生与中国古代农业社会人们日出而作，日入而息的生活方式有一定的关系，大多数老百姓终年辛勤劳作，仍食不果腹，能够使他们世代绵延、生存下去的是微薄的土地所产的谷粟，因之用谷粟熬成的滚烫的稀粥，对于老百姓而言就不但是生命之源，而且是严寒的冬日一种温情的、熨帖的精神寄托。而中国文人对粥尤有一种深厚的情结。苏东坡在品尝了用豆浆和无锡贡米熬的粥后，写诗云："身心颠倒不自知，更让人间有真味"；明代诗人张方贤在他的《煮粥诗》中也说："莫言淡薄少滋味，淡薄之中滋味长。"稀粥在中国文人的笔下，已被赋予了清淡而悠长的含义，甚至成为一种固守本真的情操。

由此我们看到，在《坚硬的稀粥》中，稀粥的价值尽管遭到了瘦高挑儿子的彻底否定，但人们的生活终究离不开它。"鲍鱼来了又去了，海参上了又下了，沙拉吃了又忘了，只有稀饭和咸菜永存。"以至于曾一度对稀粥也持有偏见、对西方文明神往的堂姐夫，在终于如愿以偿出国深造后，写信告诉大家在国外最常吃的还是稀饭咸菜，因为稀饭咸菜带给他们的是"亲切怀恋之情"，使他们在苦闷时想到"温暖质朴的家"，并且慨叹道："有什么办法呢，也许我们的细胞里已经有了稀饭咸菜的遗传基因。"这也是稀粥坚硬力量的所在。作为一种中国传统文化的符码，稀粥已像遗传因子一样被植于中国人的细胞，不但成为中国人的一种饮食习惯，而且成为一种情感的慰藉。在其中寄予了温情、亲切、质朴、清淡而悠远的情结。

至此，王蒙已表明了他在中西文化上的态度。他认为，以稀粥为文化符码的中国传统饮食，是不能轻易被否定的。它有着古老的历史渊源，蕴含着独特的中国文化的温情、亲切、质朴、清淡而悠远的哲学，这也正是中国传统文化的独特内涵所在。所以小说结尾的安排也是寓意深远的。爸爸的一位英国朋友到家中做客，要求他们拿出具有古老传统和独特魅力的饭，他们招待他的是稀饭和咸菜。小说中这样写道：

> "多么朴素！多么温柔！多么舒服！多么文雅……只有古老的东方才有这样的神秘的膳食。"英国博士赞叹着。我把他称赞稀饭咸菜的标准牛津味儿的英语录到了"盒儿带"上，放给瘦高挑的儿子听。

结尾看似是稀粥占了上风，有东风压倒西风之势，但我们同时看到，在新风新潮即西方文化不断涌入中国之后，中国人的饮食生活、价值理念不可避免地发生了变化，出现在饭桌上的是鸡、鸭、鱼、肉、蛋、奶、糖与稀饭共存互补的局面。这也是中西文化交融互补、相依共存的写照。故在这篇小说中，王蒙一方面强调稀粥所隐喻的中国传统文化的坚硬力量及其永久生命力所在，但另一方面也主张对西方文化应持一种开放、接纳的态度。他认为，中国文化不应该是一成不变的，面对西方文化它应该具有海纳百川的胸襟和气度，但在中西文化的融合过程中，有一个根本点不能动摇，即中国文化不能失掉其古老、独特的文化之根。

三

在《活动变人形》中，王蒙继续思索关于如何看取传统文化与现代文化及中西文化的问题。小说描写了人生的种种悲剧。它表面叙述的是一个男人和三个女人斗争的故事。这种斗争是如此惨痛，以致最后的结果只能是两败俱伤。他们的纠纷，固然有经济的原因、性格的原因，但纷争的背后折射的深层问题依旧是文化的冲突。

《活动变人形》中同样包含着鱼肝油、活动变人形、童话书、温度计等诸多文化符码。从一定意义上说，它们都指向与中国传统文化相对的现代文明的层面。《活动变人形》是一本日本玩具读物。"像是一本书，全是画，头、上身、下身三部分，都可以独立翻动，这样，排列组合，可以组合成无数个不同的人图案。所以叫'活动变人形'。"这种活动变人形玩具，是倪吾诚在当铺当掉了他的瑞士表给孩子买的礼物。当时，他先买了鱼肝油，后买了这一礼物。这两种礼物分别代表倪吾诚在孩子身上所寄予的两种期望。他希望鱼肝油能使孩子们变得身体健壮，而"活动变人形"则能够丰富孩子们的精神生活。故"活动变人形"代表一种更为先进的、更具智慧的现代文明生活。小说中倪吾诚多次慨叹中国人童年生活的贫乏，"男孩子只能拨拉着自己的小鸡巴玩"。所以，倪吾诚在为孩子们买下了这样一个代表"东洋人的先进和智慧"的玩具后，希望他们也能够享受到像西洋或者东洋的孩子一样的文明生活。而且小说在描写"活动变人形"时多次使用了"色彩鲜艳""五彩绚丽""五颜六色"这样一些修饰词。这样一些词汇寓指这一玩具代表一个五彩斑斓的世界，与孩子们生活的单调、乏味的现实世界截然不同。而倪吾诚一生的向往和追求，就是他和孩子们，更确切地说是所有的中国人都能够拥有、享受到的这种现代文明和智慧。所以倪吾诚宁肯当掉自己的瑞士手表，去给孩子买鱼肝油和"活动变人形"，表明了他对现代文明的一种执着的态度，并且"他希望他也相信下一代能生活的更加文明、高尚、善良、幸福。起码他们应该生活得更加健康和合理。"但除了指向一种更先进、更富智慧的现代文明的内涵外，"活动变人形"这一文化符码，从更深的层面上看，还传递着"变的哲学"的意味。

小说在解释"活动变人形"这一玩具的玩法时，多次提到它的头、身体、腿的部位的自由组合和变化自如：

> 一本《活动变人形》帮助倪藻认识到，人是由五颜六色的三部分组成：戴帽子的或者不戴帽子或者戴与不戴头巾之类的玩意儿的脑袋，穿着衣服的身子，第三就是穿裤子或穿裙子的，以及穿靴子或者鞋子或者木屐的腿脚。而这三部分是活动可变的。比如一个戴着斗笠的女孩儿，她的身体可以是穿西服的胖子，也可以是穿和服的瘦子，也可以是穿皮夹克的侧扭身子。为什么身子侧向一边呢？这也很容易解释，显然是它转过头来看你。然后是腿，可以穿灯笼裤，可以是长袍的下半截，可以是半截裤腿，露着小腿和脚丫子，也可以穿着大草鞋。这样，同一个脑袋可以变成许多人。同一个身子也可以具有好多样脑袋和好多样腿。原来人的千变万化多种多样就是这样发生的。只是有的三样放在一起很和谐，有的三样放在一起有点生硬，有点不合模子，甚至有的三样放在一起觉得可笑或者可厌，甚至叫人觉得可怕罢了。哎，如果每个人都能自己给自己换一换就好了。

这一段关于"活动变人形"的描写，表面看来是对这一玩具的玩法及其奇妙处的赞叹与欣赏，而实际上则寓意深远。"活动变人形"最本质的特点就是变化，通过头、身子、腿、衣服及人体姿态的自由组合，像魔方一样可以千变万化，有无穷的组合，从而不断地变换出各种各样的人。因而，它在深层意义上指向了一个关于"变"的辩证法的哲学观。如果说王蒙在《坚硬的稀粥》中通过稀粥这一文化符码表达了关于"不变"的哲学观，认为中国文化的根基、民族性的东西不能随意动摇，在《活动变人形》中，则又通过"活动变人形"这一文化符码，阐明了"变"的哲学观，即认为没有任何一种文化会永远处于纯粹之中，而是必然要和其他文化相互融合、相互补充，除旧纳新，不断发展。特别是对于中国文化而言，固然它有着五千年灿烂的独特的文明，但也背负上了沉重的封建文化的负荷，在向现代化转型期间，必须以一种开放的姿态来吸纳世界其他特别是西方现代文明的合理内核。

但是，在《活动变人形》中我们却看到了坚决抵制现代文明，固守中国封建文化的保守派。他们是中国封建文化的捍卫者，身上残留着许多封建文化的痼疾，对现代文明、西方文化则持一种反感、排斥、厌恶甚至坚决抵制的态度。他们的行为举止、价值观念都趋向封闭、保守的文化心态，与"活动变人形"这一文化符码所指向的"变"的哲学精神背道而驰。

小说中提到的倪吾诚身边的亲人几乎都是这一类型的人。譬如倪吾诚的母亲，在察觉倪吾诚迷恋现代先进文化后，曾一度试图用鸦片和手淫麻痹他的身心，以达到让他远离现代文明的目的。倪吾诚的舅父和表哥等，同样过着一种典型的蒙昧、落后的封建土财主生活——抽大烟、娶小老婆、斗纸牌、提笼养鸟、随地吐痰。倪吾诚的岳母同样坚决捍卫她随地吐痰的正确性，此事引发了她与倪吾诚的第一次矛盾。因为在倪吾诚看来，这是一种极不卫生、文明的行为。而倪吾诚与姜赵氏的这次冲突最终以姜赵氏的"掼茶壶"（茶壶是倪吾诚为来京的岳母特意准备的一个礼物）和倪吾诚的下跪求饶告终。但经历这次事件之后，倪吾诚对姜赵氏所践行的这样一种落后的、不文明的生活方式深恶痛绝："他对这里的诸种肮脏、龌龊、野蛮和恶劣的痛恨增强了许多倍。他对之的抨击增加了许多倍，他的学习欧洲人的文明习惯的热烈信念坚定了许多倍。"小说还详细描写了姜赵氏无事乱翻东西、鼓捣煤球炉、修脚及刷尿壶的种种怪癖，这实际上是落后的中国封建文化的沉病在她身上的积淀。

静珍既是封建文化的可怜的牺牲品，又是这种文化的一个坚决捍卫者。她年纪轻轻就守寡，立志终身不嫁，对倪吾诚建议她再嫁深表愤恨，认为是对自己守志的莫大侮辱。她一生一直生活在一个绝对封闭的自我世界中，心灵受到极大的扭曲，她每天梳洗的"早课"及骂誓，都是个性长期处于压抑状态中的一种变态的反映。静宜同样是一个心态守旧、封闭的封建旧文化的维护者，因而与处处以西学为生活信条和行动范式的倪吾诚永远处于矛盾、冲突中。"他和静宜的矛盾是无法调和的，他讲英美，她认为全是狗屁。""每当他讲英文，静宜总觉得比听野猫叫还可厌和晦气。他的外文使她反胃。而每当静宜唱戏的时候，他的嘴也撇得吓人。"静宜虔诚地信奉封建文化的种种规矩、信条，她极端封闭的心态在与倪吾诚"刮泥疙瘩"的冲突中表现得淋漓尽致。在她的眼中，这些泥疙瘩是元宝的象征，所以她极力反对倪吾诚铲掉它们。这在接受了现代文明科学、卫生观念洗礼的倪吾诚看来，"简直是神经病。简直是妄想狂。这就是五千年文明古国的文明"。于是，"此后再也不想触犯众多的小元宝。吃饭的时候，就把许多高贵的欧洲文明的篇章，堆放在小元宝上"。分别代表东西方文明的"小元宝"和"许多高贵的欧洲文明"就这样被奇妙、荒诞地并置于一起。

从上文的分析中可以看出，王蒙对固守封建文化、拒绝接受外来文化，特别是西方现代文明的种种缺乏变通的文化心理进行了辛辣的讽刺和严厉的抨击。他希望人们都能像那灵活自如、自由变幻的"活动变人形"一样，具有变通的思想、开放的心态。因而，王蒙通过"活动变人形"这一文化符码表达了"变"的哲学观："同一个脑袋可以变成许多人。同一个身子也可以具有好多样脑袋和好多样腿。原来人的千变万化多种多样就是这样发生的。""哎，如果每个人都能自己给自己换一换。"

但每个人究竟应该怎样"给自己换一换"？小说中的倪吾诚转换的最彻底，完全着上了西洋人的行头，成了一个西洋化的"活动变人形"。与静宜等固守封建文化所截然不同的是，倪吾诚走了一条全盘西化的路子。他是一个彻头彻尾的西方文化的迷恋者。由于从小上洋学堂，接受了梁启超、章太炎、王国维等人宣扬的先进思想，对中国封建文化中"缠足"的野蛮，"拜祖宗牌位"等愚昧事宜深恶痛绝，并采取了种种极端行为向其发起挑战。及至在欧洲留学接受了欧风美雨的熏陶，他对西方文化的崇尚达到了无以复加的地步。应该说，他推崇现代西方文化的文明、科学、个性、幸福等价值理念，是应该得到肯定的，这正是中国传统文化所缺失的、亟须借鉴的文化资源。"他是那么样地希望幸福、希望高尚和文明"，尽管他的自然科学知识有限,"但他总是怀着近乎贪婪的热情倾听别人谈科学"。而他更渴望一种现代爱情,在静宜生下倪萍后,他发表了一通现代爱情演说,认为中国人的婚姻是"非人性的、野蛮的、愚蠢的,甚至是醒醍的",并认为他和静宜的婚姻同样是"没有任何的爱情也没有任何的文明"。他像一个堂吉诃德式的英雄那样坚持不懈同一切愚昧落后的封建文化做斗争,并通过洗澡、喝咖啡、吃鱼肝油、买温度计和童话书等行为践行现代文明的生活方式。

然而在小说中,倪吾诚完全变成了一个西洋化的"活动变人形",一个彻头彻尾的"香蕉人"。他这种向西方文化一边倒的转换,是否就是可取的?小说给出的答案是否定的。"只是有的三样放在一起很和谐,有的三样放在一起有点生硬,有点不合模子,甚至有的三样放在一起觉得可笑或者可厌,甚至叫人觉得可怕罢了。"可以说,倪吾诚在接受了西方文化,进行了转换之后,变成了一个上文所提到的"生硬的""不合模子的""甚至可笑""可厌"的"活动变人形"。他对西方文化及现代文明的接受可以说是囫囵吞枣,食而不化。因而,他呈现在读者面前的是一个对现实没有清醒认识,全盘接受并盲目生搬硬套西方文化的一个可笑又可怜的"香蕉人"。在倪吾诚的眼中,西方的东西就是先进的、文明的、高贵的:"欧洲,欧洲,我怎能不服膺你!只看看你们的服装,你们的身体,你们的面容和化妆品。你们的鞋子和走路(更不必说跳舞了)的姿态,你们的社交和风习。"对他来说:"接近外国字母也是快乐和骄傲的。""一想到欧洲人,一想到欧洲国家的语言,一想到诸种难懂的名词,一想到永远清洁高贵得一尘不染的史福冈的西服和大衣,他就觉得快乐、升华、升仙。"倪吾诚对西方文化达到了一种顶礼膜拜的程度,对西方文化缺乏任何理性批判意识,甚至认为欧洲爆发的两次惨绝人寰的世界大战,也是值得称道的:"即使战争席卷到了那里,法西斯主义正在吞噬一切,然而那里毕竟有热烈的活人。"至此,倪吾诚对东方文化的全盘否定和对西方文化的盲目肯定已走向了一个彻底的极端。因而,倪吾诚的转换是不可取的。

只有在倪吾诚的儿子倪藻身上,这种转换才达到了一种和谐的状态。与父亲倪吾诚一样,倪藻也生长在传统文化的土壤上并受到了西方文化的影响与重铸。倪藻身上有王蒙很浓的气质、思想，因而与倪吾诚全盘接受、盲目追随西方文化所不同的是，倪藻能以辩证的眼光清醒地看待中西文化及其关系，而不再是一个"不合模子"的人。可以说，倪藻是对其父的继承与超越。

《活动变人形》的开头即以语言学副教授倪藻作为中国学者访问欧洲某著名港口城市 H 市参加学术活动拉开了这部小说的序幕，它从倪藻出国写起是很有意味和巧妙性的。小说中写道："这就是'出国'……它似乎给你一个机会超脱地飘然地反顾，鸟瞰你自己、你的历史和你的国家……"小说用了整整一章的篇幅叙述了倪藻在国外的种种感受。倪藻在欧洲 H 市几天的访问、旅行，使他在"走到世界，来到外国后"处处以一种比较、审视的眼光对中国和欧洲的情况一一做对比分析。这是一种自觉的中西文化比较意识。一方面，倪藻对中国依然在世界上处于落后地位，某些中国人文明素质较差因而被欧洲人所瞧不起的事实感到忧愤，他慨叹："我们的堂堂的中国究竟什么时候才能跻身于发达国家行列？"另一方面，他在父亲的异域好友史福岗的家中看到了中国传统文化的复苏："致远斋"匾、"守深如执玉"和"积善胜遗金"的对联、"忍为高"的字幅、齐白石的溪水画与兰花、郑板桥的"难得糊涂"的拓片，以及史福岗太太身着中式便服，惋惜北京被拆除的牌楼和向往四合院生活，等等，上述种种符码都指向中国传统文化，小说借史福岗太太的一番话表达了他们对中国文化的迷恋和推崇："史先生整天跟我研究这个，他佩服中国，他佩服中国文化，他说这是全世界头一份的，谁也比不了的文化，它有它的道理……"在史福岗夫妇这一对坚定的中国文化的信仰者和维护者身上，倪藻看到了中国文化的生命力所在。

中国文化在现代化进程中应该怎样转换？中西文化究竟孰优孰劣？在评判价值取向上，究竟应该持有什么样的科学、理性的态度？王蒙在《坚硬的稀粥》和《活动变人形》这两部小说中致力于探索、思考这些困扰一个世纪以来中国人的重大问题。在《坚硬的稀粥》中，他通过稀粥这一文化符码，表达了应该坚守民族文化本位的"不变"的哲学观，认为中国的文明是"古老的、完整的、统一的"，中国文化在走向现代化的进程中，不能丧失其民族文化的本位。另一方面，在《活动变人形》中，他又通过活动变人形这一文化符码阐释了"变"的辩证法，犀利剖析、批判了以静宜为代表的文化保守派面对现代文明所折射出的封闭、缺乏变通的封建文化心态，同时，对倪吾诚缺乏理性批判态度，全盘接受并生搬硬套西方文化给予了善意、辛辣的讽刺。在思考传统文化与现代文化、中西文化之间的关系这些重大问题时，这一观点在《活动变人形》中借史福岗之口再次得到了明确的阐释：

> 我相信未来的中国肯定会回到自己的民族文化本分上来，不管形态发生什么变化，只有站在民族文化的本位上，中国才能对世界是重要的。今后的几十年，中国也许会变个天翻地覆，但只要中国是中国，它的深层，总保存着一些不变的实质性的东西。您看着吧，老兄，不论是日本人还是军阀还是革命家，谁也改变不了中国自己的文化传统。

小说中一个久居欧洲的中国人史福岗在此表达了对中华文明之恋，慨叹古代的其他文明都成了历史的遗迹，只有中国的文明是古老的、完整的、统一的，她有自己的独特性，独特的完整性和独特的应变能力。甚至小说描写贝蒂小姐因受中华文化的熏陶而具有了中国式的朴素，这都是东学西渐之影响。由此可以看出王蒙先生的辩证中西文化观。

（原载于《名作欣赏》2008 年第 9 期，内容有增补）

民族性与现代性成功"对接"的典范

——重读《李有才板话》

赵树理在中国现代文学史上享有较高的赞誉，他的作品得到了较充分的肯定已是不争的事实。他写的《小二黑结婚》《李有才板话》《李家庄变迁》《三里湾》等作品，由于用新颖、独特的民间文学的形式最具代表性地反映了中国农村的社会变革，而被誉为时代的"纪念碑"，其创作也曾一度被提升到"赵树理方向"。然而，自 20 世纪 80 年代以来，随着人们思想观念的解放和各种西方新思潮、新理论的涌入，一些学者开始对文学史上的一些定论提出质疑。其中，戴光中的《关于"赵树理方向"的再认识》及郑波光的《赵树理艺术迁就的悲剧》两篇文章对赵树理文学作品的意义和价值进行了否定，认为"从小说发展的主流着眼"，赵树理的小说是一股"逆流"，"从文学的观念和艺术的水准衡量"，赵树理的创作较之五四的前辈们是一个"倒退"。就此看来，对赵树理作品的评价目前存在两种极端的倾向，一是过分褒扬，另一种则是过分贬斥。这两种态度都不是一种科学、客观的评价，都是对赵树理的一种简单化、表面化的理解。若深化对赵树理的认识，还是要立足于他创造的文本，深入解析其文本世界。

《李有才板话》是赵树理的代表作之一。它写了太行山区的一个阎家山村，在新政权未真正深入农村工作的实际前，基层组织被地主恶霸所控制，村民因而深受其害。后来在县农会主席老杨同志的领导下，村里建起了民主政权，村民的利益得到了切实保护。这是这篇小说呈现给读者的表层意义。实际上，它还存在着许多"意义空白"，就小说的主题结构而言，它表达了多层次的内涵，如对主观主义和官僚主义的抨击，对自私狭隘、因循守旧的封建小农意识的剖析，对封建血亲家族排他性本质的揭露，对"畏官""迷官"等中国传统文化的奴性和惰性的批判，对新时代新生活的颂扬等等。这是这篇小说向我们展示的第二个层次。若更深入地对文本的意义进行探析，我们还会发现第三个层次，即《李有才板话》真切生动而又比较完整地保存了中国农村社会转型期的原生状态，此其一。其二，赵树理在这篇小说中，用洋溢着浓郁的民间语言气息的民族文学形式表达了民主、平等、文明等现代理念，创造了民间形式与现代观念成功"对接"的现代小说典范。尽管赵树理的作品从表面看来与政治联系紧密，艺术表达形式还有待突破，但其意义价值已超越了一般意识形态的概念化表达的局限，在思想内涵和审美旨向上均呈现出丰富性。

赵树理在谈到《李有才板话》的创作意图时曾说："那时我们的工作有些地方不深入，章工作员式的人多，老杨式的人少，应该提倡老杨式的做法，于是我就写了这篇小说。"① 《李有才板话》作为一部"问题小说"，也许最初的创作动机确如赵树理在上文所言，但这部作品却不是对农村现实和问题的一种简单化和概念化的表达，它保存了历史的生动性和鲜活性，使人有逼近历史的现场感。《李有才板话》就是这样一部能使我们真切地感受到"过去事情的新鲜感"的历史文本，它真实而深刻地展示了处于变革时期的中国农村复杂的社会现状，再现了新生政权与封建宗法制共存状态下农村的政治经济结构及农民在历史转折期复杂的文化心理状态。

小说中的故事发生在太行山区一个叫阎家山的村子，赵树理在文章的开头是这样描述这个村子的："阎家山这地方有点怪：村西头是砖楼房，中间是平房，东头的老槐树下是一排二三十孔土窑。……西头都是姓阎的；中间也有姓阎的也有杂姓，不过都是些在地户；只有东头特别，外来开荒的占一半，日子过倒霉了的杂姓，也差不多占一半，姓阎的只有三家，也是破了产卖了房子才搬来的。"村子从西到东分布的三种房屋类型——砖楼房、平房及土窑分别代表着三种不同的经济阶层。很显然，拥

---

① 赵树理：《当前创作中的几个问题》，《火花》1959 年第 6 期。

有地产的阎家户处于这三个阶层的上层。而杂姓，特别是无地的杂姓则处在底层。黄修已在《赵树理的社会学批评》一文中指出，赵树理的作品"相当深刻地描绘中国封建农村的社会基本组织形态"，"还写了血亲观念和乡土观念在农村中具有黏结力"①。这种家族观念的狭隘、保守、排外一旦和个人私欲结合起来，就会形成一种具有很强破坏力的恶势力。《李有才板话》就真实再现了阎家山村以阎恒元为首的这样一股地方恶霸势力。他们依靠封建血亲家族的力量，垄断权力，打击排挤外来户。由于当时民族战争和阶级斗争的交叉重叠，那里的局势非常复杂。阎恒元在抗战以前年年连任村长，垄断着村里的大权。正如李有才在快板中所唱的那样："村长阎恒元，一手遮住天，自从有村长，一当十几年。年年要投票，嘴说是改选，选来又选去，还是阎恒元。"《李有才板话》故事发生的背景是在抗战以后，我们从小说中得知，当时共产党已在县里建立了新政权，各乡村都在其管辖之下。按理说，这时的阎家村该是另一番天地了，而实际上小说中所描写的阎家村仍处于抗战前的状态中。唯一的区别是阎恒元不当村长了，但他仍在幕后操纵村政权，实行独裁统治。后来继任的村长喜福（阎恒元的侄子）也是如出一辙："抗战以后这东西趁着兵荒马乱抢了个村长，就更了不得了，有阎恒元那老不死给他撑腰，就没有他干不出来的事，屁大点事弄到公所，也是桌面上吃饭，袖筒里过钱，钱淹不住心，说捆就捆，说打就打，说叫谁倾家败产谁就没法治。"在所谓的"模范村"里，我们看到的依然是抗战前贫富悬殊，村民们被剥夺了基本生存权、人权的现状。一方面，阎恒元大肆侵占田地（村里人押给的地就有八十四亩）、剥削雇工（他还常年雇着三个长工）、囤积私产（在山上他还有六七家店铺）；另一方面，则是老槐树底下以李有才为代表的贫民住在土窑里，把地押给了阎恒元，处于一贫如洗的境地。就像李有才常好说的两句俏皮话所描述的那样："吃饱了一家不饥，锁住门也不怕饿死小板凳。"他们所处的经济地位决定了他们毫无人权可言，小说有一段写到因李有才戳穿了阎恒元的把戏，村长广聚对他

---

① 参见严家炎等主编《中国现代文学论文集》，北京大学出版社 1986 年版。

大发脾气，说他"造谣生事""简直像汉奸"，竟下令把他赶出阎家山："即刻给我滚蛋！永远不许回阎家山来！不听我的话我当汉奸送你！""汉奸"本来特指为日本人卖命，出卖民族利益的人，在此广聚竟滥用手中职权，把敢于反抗阎恒元恶霸统治的李有才冠以"汉奸"的罪名。赵树理就这样真实地描绘了在老杨同志未到阎家山之前村里的政权结构、经济行为乃至人们的生活方式都没有因新政权的建立而有丝毫改变的事实。其中的原因，除了封建地主善于伪装、过于狡猾外，一个更重要的因素是章工作员的主观主义工作作风。赵树理在新政权建立之初就敏锐地发现了主观主义和官僚主义的问题，表明了他对我们党及农村问题认识的深刻性。小说中写到李有才在章工作员主持村里民主选举前还先到山上去放牛，小顺提醒他别误了事，李有才答道："章工作员开会，一讲话还不是一大晌？误不了！……不论什么会，他在开头总要讲几句'重要性'啦，'什么的意义及其价值'啦，光他讲这些我就回来了！"及至在会上动员阎家山村民给村长喜福提意见，大家揭露了他的种种罪行，小说又描述道："章工作员气得瞪大眼，因为他常在这里工作，从来也不会想到有这么多的问题。"最终还是阎恒元的侄子阎广顺被选为村长，因为阎恒元在背后给他拉了很多选票。最具有讽刺意味的是，在"丈地"一章中，侵占村中三百多亩地的阎恒元通过巧做手脚，地只被丈成一百一十多亩。而阎恒元所出的丈地的诡计竟被章工作员视为一种好办法，阎家山因而还被评上了"模范村"。赵树理在他的多篇小说中都抨击了这种不深入了解农村实际情况的官僚主义作风所带来的危害，揭示出它已成为阻碍新时代发展的绊脚石。

在《李有才板话》中，赵树理不仅用冷静的现实主义笔触真实勾勒了抗战初期阎家山的原生态，而且进一步表现了农民处在新旧交替时期的种种复杂心态。老秦是这篇小说中刻画得较为成功的一个人物，他对老杨前后态度的变化，流露出小生产者轻视劳动、既畏官又崇官、狭隘自私的封建小农意识。赵树理在小说中还通过对另一个角色陈小元的塑造，进一步剖析了这种可怕的小农意识在小字辈身上的延续。小元是在老槐树底下长大的小字辈，后来他"架起胳膊当主任"，让民兵给他担水、砍柴、锄地，自己既过不惯原来的生活，在思想情感上也看不起老槐树底下的村民们。当然，小说更着重表现的是另一种试图摆脱封建束缚、追求新生活的新型自主人格及乐观心态。这不仅体现为以李有才为代表的老一辈敢于大胆揭露阎恒元的封建宗法统治的平民反抗意识，更体现为以小明、小福、小顺为代表的新一辈所萌生的追求平等、民主的现代意识。

赵树理在这篇小说中就这样为我们提供了一个中国基层社会转型期，保持了历史生动性和丰富性的感性文本。他在后来写的《也算经验》中谈道："有些很热心的青年同事，不了解农村的实际情况，为表面的工作成绩所迷惑，我便写了《李有才板话》。"①《李有才板话》确如赵树理所言，写出了中国社会变革时期农村的"实际情况"，使我们仿佛可以触摸到历史的体温。

赵树理所创造的作品意义还不止于此，它们更独特的价值在于其用独特的民间话语形式表达了现代理念，《李有才板话》即是民族形式与现代意识完美结合的典范。在这篇小说中，我们真正感受到了毛泽东所提出的"新鲜活泼的为中国老百姓所喜闻乐见的中国作风和中国气派"的民间文学原汁原味。研究者们在赵树理独创了新颖的、大众化的艺术形式这一点上达成了共识。但有些人，却用现代西方小说的模式来规范赵树理所使用的民间话语叙述方式，过多地强调其局限性。固然中国传统的民间文艺在叙事模式上、结构框架上还有待于进一步突破，以克服其封闭性和凝固性的弊端，学习西方小说的优长，更好地表达现代人更复杂的情感和心理，但这种民间文艺契合了中华民族长期积淀的特殊的文化心理，也有其独特的审美价值。

赵树理在谈到中国现有的文学艺术时，认为它有三个传统。一是中国古代士大夫阶级的传统，二是五四以来的文化界传统，三是民间传统。其中文艺界、文化界多数人主张以第二种为主，他却认为应该提倡第三种传统。五四时期，在"平民文学"旗帜下崛起的白话文学，是文学开始走向人民大众的一个具有根本性意义的文体变革尝试，它是中国文学具有真正

---

①　赵树理：《也算经验》，载赵树理《和青年作者谈创作》，湖南人民出版社 1983 年版，第 22—23 页。

现代化美学形式的开端。然而，五四文学所使用的话语系统，多是知识分子的"白话"。因此，当时左联就提出了文学的大众化问题。而这时的大众化文学倡导与实践中的作家主体与大众生活、大众艺术的疏离与情感的隔膜，加之主观性极强的理想化浪漫情绪，使这时期的左翼文学并没有成为大众化的文学。赵树理的文学选择，既避免了五四文学的学者化倾向，又走出了 20 世纪 30 年代"左"翼文学以表现工农斗争为旨要而缺乏真正体验与情感，不谙真正大众文学形式的局面，创造了从思想观念到艺术形式皆与大众划一的大众化文学。

在《李有才板话》中，赵树理第一次使用了一种取自民间又超越了其原生态的、富有独创性的话语体系。赵树理的语言是真正口语化的，甚至像日常生活中老百姓经常说的大白话。但这些大白话，到了赵树理的笔下，就"有了生命，发出了光辉"。如在这篇小说中，这种大白话式的语言随处可见。小说对阎恒元的儿子阎家祥的外貌特征是这样描写的："这人的相貌不大好看，脸像个葫芦瓢子，说一句话夹十来次眼皮。不过人不可以貌取，你不要以为他没出息，其实一肚肮脏计，谁跟他共事也得吃他的亏。"简单、平易的几句话就把阎家祥丑陋的外表和不端的品行刻画得入木三分，用语虽平实，却又耐人寻味，具有深刻的话语蕴藉的特点。民间话语就像一条流动的河，因不断使用而时时保持一种新鲜和活力。这也是赵树理的小说，虽打着时代的烙印，但语言却给人一种清新感的原因。如小说里的"以后把他团弄住"这句话，"团弄"一词即是地道的老百姓用语。这个词使人联想起坏人们如何把干部团团围住，与群众隔离开来，以捉弄、起哄他们，既形象又简约。又如赵树理用"抛砖头话"以表示一种冷嘲热讽、挖苦讽刺的话，也是借鉴了民间语言的智慧。但赵树理并非机械摹写群众语言，而是对其进行精心的选择、提炼。在语言的艺术性、通俗性上，赵树理的语言达到了很高的境界，为创造、发展现代白话文学语言做出了特殊的贡献。

《李有才板话》的叙事结构，既继承了传统民间文学的一些形式，如作者站在全知方位，按故事的发展从头到尾纵向叙述，注重人物表现及动作过程，结尾常以大团圆结束等，还打破了一些固定的模式，呈现出现代小说的特征。在这篇小说中，赵树理独具匠心地用"板话"的形式来布局安排故事，他为了使每个章节的标题更富于表现力，摒弃了旧小说对句工整的"回目"，而是使用长短不一的单句，甚至一个短语、一个词汇，如"有才窑里的晚会""打虎""好怕的模范村""恒元广聚把戏露底"等。这些标题形象地概括了每一章节的故事内容。同时我们注意到，这些章节已不只是按传统小说故事发生的时间顺序来编排，而是随空间地点的转移来灵活组织其顺序，更多地体现为现代小说的结构。此外，小说采用"大故事套小故事"模式，由一连串故事构成连贯情节，在情节流动中"按扣子、设悬念"，呈现出一种西方戏剧化结构模式。这都表明此小说所具有的现代小说的特征。

赵树理小说的现代性特征，更直接地表现在其所蕴含的现代理念上。在《李有才板话》中，老杨同志就是一位体现民主、平等、法治等现代观念的化身。他来到阎家村，以现代理性，启发了老槐树底下的新、老字辈追求自身解放、争取自由平等人权的现代意识。赵树理本人就是新时代、新文化的产物。他没有固守在那贫瘠的土地上，而是适时地接受了新时代新文化的洗礼，跳出了原有的文化圈子。他写过新诗、新小说，接受过五四文学的陶冶，参加过反军阀的学生运动，进过监狱，闯荡过江湖，饱尝过生活的艰辛，最后被卷进革命的漩涡，在解放区长期从事革命工作。中国革命虽未能彻底消除民族精神的痼疾，但毕竟带来了新的文化气息，赵树理正是在从事实际革命活动的过程中，逐渐获得了民主与科学的现代思想意识。这就为他反观原来的文化生活，深入剖析那种生活的种种弊害，获得自觉的农民文化的批判意识，创造出开放的多层面的图式结构，提供了极为有利的思想条件。老杨同志在一定程度上是赵树理的化身。他来到阎家村，和贫民同吃、同住、同劳动，虽然身为县农会主席，但以完全平等的姿态与老百姓相处。当老秦称他是"县里的先生"时，他说："不要这样称呼吧！哪里是什么'先生'？我姓杨，是县农救会的！你们叫我个'杨同志'或者'老杨'都好！"他就用这种官民平等的观念去启蒙农民落后的封建思想意识。不但如此，他还身体力行，亲自跟小福去场里打谷子，在场子里什么都通，被大家称为"一把好木锨"。与大家在一起劳动时，他充分发扬民主，让大家畅所欲言，从群众中直接获取了阎恒元及喜福村长谋取私利、欺压百姓的"押地、不减租、不赔款、不民主"的四条罪证。而在与他们斗争时，与章工作员使用的捆绑式的武力方式相反，老杨采取的是组织农救会说理、法治的形式："依我说，咱们明天先把农救会组织起来，就用农救会出面跟他们说理。咱们只要按法令跟他说，他们使的黑钱、押地、多收了人家的租子，就都得退出来。他要无理混赖，现在的政府可不像从前的衙门，不论他是多么厉害的人，犯了法都敢治他的罪！"在此老杨所用的"说理""法令"等字眼都属于现代观念的范畴，他在组织农民同地主恶霸作斗争时，不使用武装暴力，而用诸如"说理、法令"等新观念去启蒙百姓，以帮助他们摆脱陈腐、落后的封建小农意识，确立真正的民主、平等、法治等现代理念。从这个意义上说，《李有才板话》是一部蕴含着深刻的现代理念的现代小说。

自五四以来的中国新文学都在探索文化现代化的问题。当时的文化巨匠们置身于那个特定时代的文化语境中，建构着各自的文化方案。胡适、陈独秀、鲁迅大都以西方的文化价值尺度为标准，以进化论为武器，坚持新优于旧，对传统文化全盘否定，态度之决绝，前所未有。他们所创作的文学作品，无论在艺术形式上还是在思想内涵上，都表现为与西方文学的趋同。但追求文化的现代化是否都得以牺牲民族文学为代价？赵树理独特的文化选择告诉我们，还应该有另一条路子。今天，我们正处于文化全球化的语境中，如何在全球化的时代潮流中使我们的民族文化、民族文学得以个性化的保存，同时又能使之实现创造性的转化以表达现代思想是一个重要的文化策略。赵树理对民间文化的重视，表现了他对中国民族文化坚定的自信心。赵树理以新颖、独特的民族文学形式，生动地表现了处于社会转型期的中国农村社会结构的原生态和农民深层的文化心理，弘扬了民主、平等、进步、法治等现代理念，这是他对中国新文学的独特贡献，由此决定了他在中国现代文学史上的特殊地位。

（原载于《青年工作论坛》2003 年第 1 期）

《长谷》压抑主题阐释

约翰·斯坦贝克是美国著名小说家，他是美国第六位获得诺贝尔文学奖的作家。他一生著作颇丰，作品题材广泛，形式多变，触及诸多主题。在美国 20 世纪 30 年代的文坛上他表现尤为活跃，他的大部分享有盛名的作品是在这十年完成的。在国内学术界，学者们注意到了这一时期他创作的《愤怒的葡萄》《胜负未决》《人鼠之间》等反映重大社会题材的中长篇小说，关于这几部作品的评论较多，而对他的另一类作品，即描写个人生活的小说关注不多。在这些作品中，故事的社会背景被淡化，斯坦贝克着重写的是个体生命所遭受的挫折和面临的困境，反映现实个体生命的普遍命运，表现压抑主题，这集中体现在他的短篇小说集《长谷》中。这部短篇小说集表现了斯坦贝克"自由个性"的哲学思想与对现代人生存状态和精神情感状态的理性思考。

自 14 世纪以来，以关注人的尊严、个性、价值与命运为主要内容的西方人文精神一度成为文学表现的主题。但是随着现代工业革命的推进，与科学和技术一并发展起来的理性至上主义逐渐代替了对人的情感和本能的关注，人性也逐步走向异化的一面。正如阿尔多诺所说："资本主义社会对人的解放潜能的压抑与消解，使人们陷入工具理性的主宰之中，独特的个性与特殊性消失殆尽……对客观世界的主观支配导致通过物化来达到主体的支配，对外在自然的支配进一步导致了人的内在自然的支配，最终导致对社会的控制与支配。"① 特别是第一次世界大战的爆发，使现代西方人

---

① ［德］霍克海姆、阿尔多诺：《启蒙辩证法》，重庆出版社 1990 年版，第 117 页。

仅存的一点"信心"和"美好理想"也荡然无存，进一步加深了他们对西方文明的没落感与幻灭感。一战后的美国在经历了短暂的经济繁荣之后，终于爆发了历史上最严重的经济危机。在十年大萧条期间，工厂停业，银行倒闭，物价飞涨，大批农民流离失所，失业与贫困给美国人民带来了深重的灾难，工业与金融等社会异化力量无情践踏人民的权利、尊严与自由，压抑一度成为一种时代特质，斯坦贝克的《长谷》就是对这一时代精神的阐释。在《长谷》中，斯坦贝克通过具体事件和一系列具有"土地般本色"的人物揭示了压抑这种可怕的封闭力量是如何扼杀人的自然本性和情感需求以至使人走向异化的主题。本文着重以《长谷》中的《菊》《紧身甲》《白鹌鹑》和《小红马》等具有代表性的作品为例，阐释斯坦贝克的压抑主题及其不同的表现形态。

在其著名的短篇小说《菊》中，斯坦贝克开篇是这样描述"长谷"的："萨利纳斯峡谷笼罩在浓厚的灰色绒布般的冬雾之中，上与天空下与世界完全隔绝了。浓雾像扣在周围山巅上的锅盖，把偌大的一个山谷变成严丝合缝的一只铁锅。"① 这里，浓雾环绕下的萨利纳斯山谷可以看作一个大的象征，它预示着将要在其中展开的故事的整体氛围——一种完全与世隔绝的封闭与压抑状态。在《长谷》中，斯坦贝克还用了其他的象征物，如《白鹌鹑》中的花园，是一个奴役女主人公玛丽·特勒心灵的象征，《紧身甲》中那个套在男主人公彼得·兰德尔身上的紧身甲则是另一个显而易见的象征物，彼得靠它的支撑维持着体面的身份，却不得不忍受它对自己身体上和精神上的压迫，摒弃他作为自然人的合理欲望和正常情感，成了它的牺牲品。此外，《菊》中的篱笆，《紧身甲》中的那张巨大的胡桃木双人床，同样是封闭的象征。在《长谷》中，斯坦贝克用这些大大小小的象征物来暗示那种无处不在的压抑氛围，人置身于这样一种封闭状态中，其悲剧性故事的发生也是顺理成章的。

在这些故事中，斯坦贝克论及压抑的各种表现形态：在《菊》《紧身

---

① ［美］约翰·斯坦贝克：《斯坦贝克选集：中短篇小说选一》，人民文学出版社1983年版，第358页。

甲》《白鹤鹑》和《蛇》中，斯坦贝克强调性压抑给他的主人公们带来的变异行为；在《菊》和《小红马》系列故事中，斯坦贝克还揭示了另一更深层次的压抑——人们精神世界所受的某种既定观念的控制；而在《菊》和《小红马》故事中，他又表现了狭小的生活空间给主人公们所带来的压抑感。

一　性压抑

表现性压抑给人们生活带来的悲剧是《长谷》的重要主题之一。美国著名评论家罗伯特·E. 斯皮勒在《美国文学的周期》中曾这样评论斯坦贝克的作品："斯坦贝克艺术的最终落脚点是原始性。他在这一点上显示出属于最丰硕的美国文学传统。斯坦贝克对人类行为背后的动物动机感兴趣并借助它创造出了一个他能用来补偿他所了解的丑恶世界的假想世界。"[①] 像许多现代作家一样，斯坦贝克也格外关注性的问题。在他看来，蓬勃旺盛的性欲是人性健康的标志，而性欲衰竭则是一种病态的表现。在《长谷》诸多故事中，斯坦贝克揭示了性压抑这种可怕的异化力量是如何扼杀人的自然本能，使人沦化为异物，或变态，或走向自我毁灭。

《菊》中的爱丽莎·爱伦出现在我们面前时几乎隐匿了她的女性性别。在花园干活时，"她头戴一顶男人戴的黑帽，帽檐儿低低地挡着眼睛，脚穿一双粗笨的厚底鞋"[②]。此处细节的描写隐喻性地暗示她的性意识处于抑制状态。接着，我们看到下面的文字："她那成熟、秀丽的脸庞不时现出一种急切的神情，甚至她使用剪刀时的动作也似乎过于急切、过于用力。

---

① ［美］罗伯特·E. 斯皮勒：《美国文学的周期》，王长荣译，上海外语教育出版社 1989 年版，第 228 页。

② ［美］约翰·斯坦贝克：《斯坦贝克选集：中短篇小说选一》，人民文学出版社 1983 年版，第 359 页。

与她那充沛的精力相比，菊茎显得太纤弱，太不堪一击了。"① 这里所特别强调的爱丽莎"充沛的精力"包含着她一部分性能量，这种性能量不能在正常的性关系中释放，只能转移到日常生活中做家务、侍弄花草之类事情上，而这对她来说似乎太容易了，更多的精力无处释放。与修补匠邂逅后，他那魁梧、高大的身材和善解人意的话语使她的性意识逐渐复苏。在交谈中，她"由于激动乳房高高挺起。"② 修补匠离去后，她来到澡堂，"用一块浮石用力擦洗小腿、大腿、腰、胸和胳膊，直到把全身皮肉擦得发痛、变红为止。身体擦干后，她站在卧室中的一面大镜子前仔细端详自己的身体。她缩进腹部，挺起前胸，转过身，回头瞅着自己的背影"③。这里的细节描写同样耐人寻味，爱丽莎受到压抑的性欲只能通过这种几乎是虐待身体般的方式找到一个小小的宣泄口。然而，这种刚刚苏醒的性本能随即又萎缩回去，见到丈夫后，"爱丽莎身子挺直，脸绷得很紧"④，她的表情又变得凝固、僵硬，这反映了她和丈夫性关系中的一种紧张状态。故事的结尾，我们看到爱丽莎坐在车上，觉察到受了修补匠的欺骗，又无法和丈夫沟通，只能"像老妇人那样虚弱地哀哀哭泣"⑤。连这哭泣也表现得如此压抑。

《紧身甲》中农民彼得长期受到遏制的性欲使他发生了人格分裂。这位被当地青年视为楷模的农民，"身材高大粗壮""腰板挺得笔直，腹部像士兵那样紧缩进去"⑥。在小说中，彼得健壮的体魄被强调的同时，他的妻子爱玛的瘦弱、多病也被极力渲染："人人都认为像她这样骨瘦如柴的女人至今还活着简直不可思议，尤其是当她经常生病卧床的时候。她体重只八十七磅，虽然才四十五岁，一张褐色的脸已像老妇那样布满皱纹。"⑦

---

① ［美］约翰·斯坦贝克：《斯坦贝克选集：中短篇小说选一》，人民文学出版社 1983 年版，第 359 页。

② 同上书，第 366 页。

③ 同上书，第 368 页。

④ 同上书，第 369 页。

⑤ 同上书，第 370 页。

⑥ 同上书，第 409 页。

⑦ 同上。

在这里，身体强健的彼得和体弱多病的爱玛身体上的不平衡状态寓意他们之间性的不和谐，而"爱玛没生过孩子"① 则是这种不和谐关系的进一步说明。一方面，彼得必须和妻子维持一种没有性的婚姻关系；另一方面，他又有正常人的性欲需求。矛盾冲突的结果是他一年四十七周扮演一个好丈夫的角色，只一周除外。这一周，他要到旧金山"办事"，所谓"办事"就是白天喝得酩酊大醉，晚上逛妓院。一年里他必须有这么一周把紧张的神经放松，把压抑的性欲发泄，在妻子死后的那个夜晚，彼得拆掉了缚在腰上的紧身甲（此项举动为妻子所迫），又把自己灌醉。那天夜里，他尽情向邻居宣泄自己压抑已久的情感，他宣称自己要种四十亩豌豆（这在他妻子活着时根本不被允许）："不论什么我都要多多的，我要四十亩颜色和香味，我要乳房大得像枕头的肥女人！告诉你！我感到饥饿，我什么都想要，而且要多多的。"② 这里彼得所感到的饥饿，固然也可以指精神生活的困乏，但他身体上的饥渴更显而易见。豌豆花鲜艳的色彩和醉人的香味、乳房大得像枕头的胖女人代表直接的感官刺激。然而彼得的悲剧远远没有结束，那天夜里，尽管他宣称很多事情需要改变：他要干自己喜欢干的事情，他不再戴紧身甲，还冒险种了四十亩豌豆，他要把家里的挂钟换成闹钟。但他依然生活在妻子的阴影之下，依旧受坟墓之中她的控制，他向邻居抱怨说："她并没有死。""有些事她不准我做，为了种豌豆的事她整整折磨了我一年！"③ 他没有带回什么肥女人管家，挂钟依旧沉闷地响着，彼得还打算安上妻子生前就想要的电灯。在故事的最后，我们看到彼得依然醉倒在每年一次的旧金山之行中，重复着以前的生活。彼得长期受抑制的欲望就这样使他发生了人格分裂，戴着双重面具生活。

性压抑带给爱丽莎的是无声的哭泣，带给彼得的是人格的变异，给《白鹌鹑》中的哈里·特勒带来的则是毁灭性的暴力行为。当哈里抱怨妻子完全沉湎于花园之中，夜晚睡觉把房门关紧，把他拒之门外时，他自然

---

① ［美］约翰·斯坦贝克：《斯坦贝克选集：中短篇小说选一》，人民文学出版社1983年版，第411页。

② 同上书，第417页。

③ 同上书，第424页。

正常的性需求也就被拒之门外。这种长期积聚的性压抑在达到一个极点时终于以暴力的形式释放出来，哈里用气枪打死了一只白鹌鹑，而这只白鹌鹑被妻子视为完美的自我的化身。

《蛇》的故事同样揭示了性压抑使人行为变态以至采取暴力行动的主题。它是《长谷》中最简单的一个故事，描写了一个妇女在一天夜里访问一个海洋生物实验室并买了一条雄性响尾蛇，并坚持用实验室里的一只老鼠喂它。在目睹了这位妇女全神贯注于蛇吞食老鼠的过程之后，生物学家恶心得要吐。这个故事的背后同样有深层的寓意，表达了性压抑导致暴力的主题。

二　观念控制

斯坦贝克所揭示的压抑主题的另一种表现形态则为人受某种既定观念的控制，异化为观念的牺牲品。这种观念，在《菊》中表现为"既定的角色"，在《紧身甲》和《约翰尼·贝尔》中为"体面"，而在《白鹌鹑》中则为"完美"。

前面我们谈到了爱丽莎的悲剧，她的悲剧并不仅仅是一个缺乏和谐的性关系的悲剧，她更大的挫折感来自精神生活所受的桎梏。在试图分析造成她精神生活悲剧的原因时，玛瑞琳·米切尔认为爱丽莎被"囚禁在社会对男女性角色的限定中，而她又试图与这种女性局限进行奋争"[1]。苏姗·西苓洛则进一步指出，"中产阶级，以它所强化的性的、精神上的、社会的约束束缚了爱丽莎"[2]。Hayashi 在《菊》开头的几个段落里，我们看到正在花园山上干活的爱丽莎四次频频低头张望在他们家院子里谈一笔出售小公牛生意的丈夫和另外两个商人。"他们三人站在拖拉机库房前，每人

---

① Mitchell Marilyn L., "Steinbeck's Strong Women: Feminine Identity in the Short Stories", *Southwest Review*, 61(Summer 1976), p. 306.

② Tetsumaro Hayashi, eds, *Steinbeck's Short Stories in The Long Valley: Essay in Criticism*, Muncie: Ball State University, 1991, p. 3.

都把一只脚蹬在那辆福特森牌小拖拉机的车帮上。"① 此处细节描写暗指爱丽莎敏锐地意识到了男性的特权地位。爱丽莎同丈夫在一起时只扮演了一个妻子的角色，没有自我感。她和丈夫在一起谈话时，总是不自觉地遵循他的话语模式，尽管他是一个谈吐一般的人。当他称赞爱丽莎侍候的菊花苗是"一批壮实的新苗"时，她就附和说"这批新苗明年会长得很壮实"②，当他夸奖爱丽莎侍候花草有点本事时，她也只是应答道"我确实有一套本事"③。甚至他建议到城里饭馆里吃饭时，她的回答也只是一个"好"字。④ 在这里，爱丽莎的角色就是别人的妻子，她没有独立的自我感。而与修补匠相遇后，她则在瞬间由"别人的妻子"转变为真正的自我。她对修补匠用诗一般的语言解释她那双会侍弄花草的手："我也只能告诉你这种感觉而已。每当你掐掉不想要的花骨朵时，好像有一股力量直通你的指尖，你瞧着自己的手指掐去花骨朵，它们好像知道该掐去哪些，你感觉它们知道。它们不停地掐呀掐，绝掐不错。手指头好像和花秧连在一起了，你明白吗？"⑤ 在那短暂的时刻，她似乎变了一个人，她完全释放了自己，语言充满了个性化、独创性。但这种自我感在见到丈夫后就像海市蜃楼一样转瞬即逝，她又回到现实中既定的妻子角色的限定中。

《紧身甲》中的彼得所受的观念操纵则为"体面"。他必须遵从妻子要他做一个"体面"人的意志，为此付出的代价就是每天戴着紧身甲，牺牲了身体的舒适而忍受网状异物紧身甲的束缚，从而牺牲他随心所欲的自然本性，在大众面前充当楷模。而在《约翰尼·贝尔》中，霍金斯姐妹作为镇子上的"贵族"代表备受人们的尊敬。但其中软弱的一位妹妹和一个中国人同床共枕怀了孕。在那个加利福尼亚小镇上，中国人是一个遭人藐视的种族，于是霍金斯姐妹所极力维持的"体面"与实际的行为产生了冲

---

① ［美］约翰·斯坦贝克：《斯坦贝克选集：中短篇小说选一》，人民文学出版社1983年版，第358页。

② 同上书，第359页。

③ 同上书，第360页。

④ 同上。

⑤ 同上书，第365页。

突。冲突的结果是为了维持"体面"的地位，那位妹妹上吊身亡。

《白鹌鹑》中的玛丽·特勒则是一个受"完美"观念控制的人物，她的整个生命都集中在创造一个完美无瑕的花园上。她甚至在选择丈夫时提出的问题不是"这个人会喜欢这样一个花园吗"，而是"这花园会喜欢这个人吗"。她的丈夫哈里完全成了她"完美"观念的牺牲品。他开了一家贷款代办处来养家糊口，却要忍受她的攻击，因为她认为他所从事的生意是不道德的。他完全顺从她的花园计划，不得不放弃自己想养一只狗的愿望，因为狗会毁掉花木。他听任自己晚上被锁在卧室外。一只偶尔飞到园子里的白鹌鹑则成了玛丽心目中另一个完美的偶像。她对它如此喜爱，当一只猫威胁到这只鸟的安全时，她竟命令哈里毒死这只猫，最后哈里失手打死了白鹌鹑，彻底打破了她执着于"完美"观念的梦幻。

三　空间限定

《长谷》压抑主题的第三种表现形态则为空间限定。斯坦贝克在《长谷》中的许多故事中还表现了狭小的生活空间给主人公们带来的束缚及他们渴望冲破这种狭小生活天地的局限而体验更广阔生活的愿望。

《菊》中的爱丽莎是个天性聪颖的女子，她用灵巧的双手培植出了美丽的菊花，她对美有很高的感悟力。但命运却把她囚禁在长谷中一个偏僻的农场，那种无处不在的压抑感笼罩着她的生活。就像她丈夫亨利所说："在农场住久了咱们都变得太压抑、太沉闷了。"① 与修补匠邂逅后，她望着他慢慢离去的篷车，低语道："那边真亮，那儿有发光的东西。"② "那儿""那边"指修补匠驾着马车云游四方的生活，那是一种爱丽莎渴望经历的生活。爱丽莎这样描述这种生活："在漆黑的夜里——呵！星星射出锐利的光芒，周围静静的。呵，突然你越飞越高，好像每颗尖尖的星星都

---

① ［美］约翰·斯坦贝克：《斯坦贝克选集：中短篇小说选一》，人民文学出版社 1983 年版，第 370 页。

② 同上书，第 368 页。

射进你的身体。热热的，烫烫的——但很舒服。"① 正如苏珊所分析的，这里马车可以被看作草原大篷车的一个隐喻，它"暗示了与爱丽莎生活天地迥然不同的世界——一个西部的神话，一种自由，一个永远开拓进取的灵魂，一种自给自足。"② 但命运注定了爱丽莎只能做一个被关在笼子里的女人，默默忍受着农场那压抑、沉闷的生活。《小红马》系列故事中的少年乔迪同样渴望冲破狭小的生活空间的局限而去体验外部世界更广阔的生活。乔迪也生活在萨利纳斯谷地——一个远离大都市的偏僻农场。离他们家最近的农场需要走一个多小时的路程。没有兄弟、姐妹，乔迪大部分时间是和几个成年人一起度过的。他和周围世界的唯一联系就是学校。这种狭小的生活空间和单调的生活样式使正在成长的乔迪非常羡慕其祖父年轻时的壮举——他曾率领一伙人跨越大草原一直往西前进，直到被大海阻挡。在乔迪眼里，祖父是个了不起的英雄，祖父真正吸引他的是摆脱狭小生活地域的局限而不断开拓新生活的那股劲儿。乔迪对他生活之外的世界的好奇和渴慕尤为表现在《大山》中他和父亲的对话中。他问父亲离他们很远的大山那边是什么，父亲告诉他是绵延不断的群山，最后一直到大海。乔迪又问那些神秘的山上有什么，父亲告诉他说除了悬崖、岩石和干草没有什么。但乔迪却神往地说能到那里看看该有多好。这些神秘的大山对乔迪来说代表着外面世界的全新生活，表明他渴望摆脱狭小生活空间的限定而体验更广阔的生活的愿望。

综而述之，斯坦贝克《长谷》中的这些故事，写了笼罩在人身上的各种压抑和束缚，他认为这是一种非人道的封闭力量，它扼制了人的自然本性的需求，禁锢了人的精神生命的自由发展，导致人走向异化。总之，他认为人的精神生命应丰富多样，自由而不受任何禁锢。人必须挣脱一切外在的束缚和压抑，解放强化其合理欲望，才能达到最有活力、最有能量的状态。斯坦贝克的"自由个性"哲学思想无疑是和 14 至 16 世纪文艺复兴时

---

① ［美］约翰·斯坦贝克：《斯坦贝克选集：中短篇小说选一》，人民文学出版社 1983 年版，第 366 页。

② Tetsumaro Hayashi, eds, *Steinbeck's Short Stories in The Long Valley*: *Essay in Criticism*, Muncie: Ball State University, 1991, p. 5.

期以人为本的艺术信仰，19 世纪浪漫主义倡导个性解放的文学宗旨，以及 20 世纪现代主义反对工业机械压抑人性的艺术信条一脉相承的，也是每个具有道德感、责任感的作家对人类本质的思考。

（原载于《山东师范大学外国语学院学报》2001 年第 1 期）

第二编
中西文学关系研究

沈从文与福克纳小说中
"神"与"上帝"的指涉意义

　　宗教是人类文化的重要组成部分，在人类文明中占有重要地位，宗教和哲学一样，都处于人类文化的核心位置，代表着人类文化的深层结构。而宗教在一定意义上讲，就是一种特殊的价值信仰哲学体系。朱光潜曾这样阐发宗教与哲学对文学而言的重要性："诗虽不是讨论哲学和宣传宗教的工具，但是它后面如果没有哲学和宗教，就不容易达到深广的境界，诗好比一株花，哲学和宗教好比土壤，土壤不肥沃，根就不能深，花就不能茂。"① 尽管朱光潜在此谈的是诗与宗教、哲学的关系，但诗也可以泛指更广义的文学。因此，在跨文化的比较文学研究中，如果绕开不同文化中的宗教因素，对于文学的理解和诠释就很难达到更深的层面。

　　关于沈从文和福克纳小说的比较研究，以往的研究者常从乡土文化的视角切入，本文将尝试从宗教学的角度来探讨。具体来说，从分析两位作家作品中"神"与"上帝"的指涉意义入手，诠释其内涵的差异性、相通性及其文学理想建构之间的内在联系。沈从文的作品带有一种浓厚的泛神论色彩，"神"字成为他诉诸文学理想的一个关键词汇。福克纳的思想则受到了基督教很大的影响，"上帝"在他的作品中被赋予了神性品格，成为我们理解其作品主旨的一个核心概念。

---

　　① 朱光潜：《中西诗在情趣上的比较》，载《中国比较文学研究资料》，北京大学出版社1989年版，第219页。

一

沈从文不是一个像福克纳那样严格意义上的信教者，但他的作品却渗透着一种强烈的泛宗教情感。这主要表现为他在小说中偏爱使用带有浓厚宗教意味的"神"这一词汇，为此他自称为泛神论者。美国的沈从文研究专家金介甫在《沈从文传》中曾谈及沈从文的泛神论思想，指出"1940年他才明确提出了泛神论（1980年又再次提出）。"① 确实如金介甫所言，沈从文在他20世纪40年代的作品，如小说《看虹录》《摘星录》和系列散文，诸如《水云》《生命》《烛虚》《潜渊》中均探索了生命、神、爱与美等抽象的问题，而"神"与"泛神"等字眼成为这个时期的作品中频频出现的词汇。特别是在《水云》《潜渊》等哲理性散文中，他多次公开表露过自己"泛神的思想"② 和"泛神情感"③。其中《水云》是他对先期创作的总结，集中阐释了他的文学审美理念，文中弥漫着一种浓郁的泛神论情绪。他这样写道：

> 失去了"我"后却认识了"人"，体会到"神"，以及人心的曲折，神性的单纯。墙壁上一方黄色阳光，庭院里一点草，蓝天中的一粒星子，人人都有机会看见的事事物物，多用平常感情去接近它。对于我，却因为常常和某一个偶然某一时的生命同时嵌入我印象中，他们的光辉和色泽，就都若有了神性，成为一种神迹了。④

其实，早在20世纪30年代沈从文创作的小说《凤子》中，这种泛神论思想已表露无遗。在小说中，"神"字出现了几十次。最早出现的一处

---

① ［美］金介甫：《沈从文传》，符家钦译，时事出版社1991年版，第221页。
② 沈从文：《沈从文全集》第12卷，北岳文艺出版社2002年版，第123页。
③ 同上书，第32页。
④ 同上书，第120页。

是在夕阳下的海边，一个嗓音低沉的中年男子对一个叫凤子的女人慨叹道："你瞧，凤子，天上的云，神的手腕，那么横横的一笔！"① 这位中年男子（其实是沈从文的代言人）被一种不可言传的海边夕阳西下的美所感动，这种美唤起了他强烈的宗教情感："先前一时，林杪斜阳的金光，使一个异教徒也不能不默想到上帝。"② 他因之惊叹道："一切都那么自然，就更加应当吃惊！为什么这样自然、匀称、和谐、统一，是谁的能力？……是的，是自然的能力。但这自然的可惊能力，从神字以外，还可找寻什么适当其德行的名称？"③ 从上面的引文中可以看出，沈从文的泛神论思想带有典型的自然崇拜的情结。正如沈从文在《水云》中所指出的："这是一种由生物的爱与美有所启示，在沉静中生长的宗教情绪，因之一部分生命，就完全消失在对于一些自然的皈依中。"④

　　从泛神论产生的历史渊源来看，这一术语是爱尔兰哲学家约翰·托兰德在其《泛神论》一书中首先使用的，认为整个宇宙万物皆有神性。在16—18 世纪的欧洲，以斯宾诺莎为代表兴起了一种自然主义泛神论哲学思潮，它不认同基督教的一神论观点，而是把神等同于自然，认为神存在于自然界的一切事物中。尽管没有确凿文献证明沈从文是否真正受过斯宾诺莎思想的影响，但"神即自然"的艺术主张构成了沈从文泛神论思想的一个非常重要的方面。在他看来，自然具有一种内在的神性，他被这种神秘的力量所吸引，认为在其背后似乎有一位巧夺天工的至高设计者在创造着大千世界的神奇与瑰丽，而这位创造者即是自然。正如《凤子》中王杉古堡的总爷对他的城里朋友所解释的那样："我们这地方的神不像基督教那个上帝那么顽固的。神的意义在我们这里只是'自然'，一切生成的现象，不是人为的，由他来处置。他常常是合理的、宽容的、美的。"⑤ 由此我们看到，沈从文偏爱用"神"字来诠释一切自然界的事物和现象，并对其怀

---

① 沈从文：《沈从文全集》第 7 卷，北岳文艺出版社 2002 年版，第 88 页。
② 同上。
③ 同上书，第 89 页。
④ 沈从文：《沈从文全集》第 12 卷，北岳文艺出版社 2002 年版，第 120 页。
⑤ 沈从文：《沈从文全集》第 7 卷，北岳文艺出版社 2002 年版，第 123 页。

有一种虔敬的宗教情感。他在自然界的每一个角落里都感受到了"神"的存在，他感念万物有灵，认为大千世界，生命表现形式虽有万种形态和风仪，但每一种生命形态，仿佛有神迹和神性寄寓其间。

而沈从文认为，在湘西世界中这种神性保持最为完整，因为唯有在远离都市喧嚣的湘西世界，人们才生活在一种和自然更为接近的状态下，唯有在此，"神"才能按自然的规律安排、支配着人们的生命。而且沈从文的泛神论思想在很大程度上受到湘西楚巫文化的浸染和影响，湘西楚巫文化中弥漫着一种崇尚万物有灵的泛神主义气息。在湘西文化中，神被普遍信仰着。在湘西人看来，自然万物都带有神性或灵性，已不是非生命的存在物形式。而且神在楚文化中更大程度上被拟人化了，它更多代表了一种自然神或人格神。神成为湘西人诉诸愿望、倾诉情感、寻求心理平衡的对象。沈从文曾在散文集《湘西》中特别提到湘西人这种神秘的泛神崇拜。他说："大树、洞穴、岩石，无处不神。狐、虎、蛇、龟，无物不怪。"①这种泛神论信仰固然带有远古巫鬼文化信仰的原始性，反映了湘西人一种自发、朴素的认知世界的方式，却赋予了自然以内在的灵性和神性，代表着一种独特的敬畏自然、尊崇自然的感知、理解世界的视角。

与沈从文在作品中偏爱使用"神"这一词汇相似的是，福克纳在其小说中则频频提及"上帝"。他的小说弥漫着浓郁的基督教色彩。尽管他的作品强烈抨击了加尔文教中的上帝，把他刻画成一个心胸狭隘、摧残人性、充满种族偏见的形象，但在福克纳的心目中，他始终高度认同《圣经·旧约》中的上帝形象，以及它所体现的神性道德品格。

福克纳一生对《圣经》极感兴趣。他曾无数次向人们提到，《圣经》是他反复阅读的书籍之一，而且他格外喜欢《圣经·旧约》，他在小说中常用英文的主格 He 或宾格 Him（第一个字母为大写）来表达对《圣经·旧约》中上帝形象的景仰。

与沈从文所持的"神即自然"的泛神论信仰所不同的是，福克纳的宗教情结带有典型的基督教神秘主义特点，认为宇宙万物（包括自然、人

---

① 沈从文：《沈从文全集》第 11 卷，北岳文艺出版社 2002 年版，第 400 页。

类）是由上帝所缔造的，上帝是万物和人类存在的内因。它不但创造了被沈从文称为"神"的自然界之各种瑰丽、奇妙的景观，而且向大自然馈赠了肥沃的土地让其生长花草树木、果蔬，同时让飞禽走兽活跃于其间，还让海里也滋生各种鱼类和生物，使自然界呈现出一派生机盎然、鸢飞鱼跃的景象。在小说《熊》中，他热情颂扬了上帝创造自然万物给人类带来的恩泽：

> 在这片土地上，在这个南方，他为南方做那么多的事，提供树林使猎物得以繁衍，提供河流让鱼儿得以生长，提供深厚肥沃的土地让种子藏身，还提供青翠的春天让种子发芽，漫长的夏天使作物成熟，宁静的秋天让庄稼丰收，还提供短促、温和的冬天让人类和动物可以生存……①

在福克纳的心目中，自然同样占有重要的位置。《福克纳传》的作者杰伊·帕里尼认为，福克纳"对大自然的情感持久而弥笃"②。他在评价福克纳最早的作品诗集《大理石牧神》时说："他的诗独特而美丽的一点在于它们表达了诗人对大自然的忠诚情感。"③ 美国福克纳研究专家罗博特·潘·沃伦盛赞福克纳笔下的自然具有"不可磨灭的美"，他认为"自然给人的活动和激情的背后张上一幅彩色幕布"，"有的富有抒情的美（《村子》里那段母牛插曲中的草地），有的富有亲切的魅力（《村子》中'花斑马'故事里试验的场面），有的阴森中包含着威力（《野棕榈》中'老人'的故事里的河流），有的庄严肃穆（《熊》中的森林）。"④ 但自然所具有的"这种不可磨灭的美"，在福克纳看来，终归是上帝创造的，是上帝伟大力量的外在显现形式。正如艾克·麦卡斯林在《三角洲之秋》中所说："上帝创造了人，他创造了让人生活的世界，我寻思他创造的是如果

---

① ［美］威廉·福克纳：《去吧，摩西》，李文俊译，上海译文出版社1996年版，第269页。
② ［美］杰伊·帕里尼：《福克纳传》，吴海云译，中信出版社2007年版，第57页。
③ 同上。
④ 李文俊：《福克纳评论集》，中国社会科学出版社1980年版，第57页。

他自己是人的话也愿意在上面生活的那样一个世界……"①

因之，福克纳的作品渗透着一种强烈的崇拜造物主上帝的基督教情结，这种宗教情绪与沈从文把自然奉为神明的泛神论情结有着很大的不同。沈从文倾心一朵花、一个微笑、一块石头所显示的神之圣境，认为它是自然的力量使然。但在福克纳看来，这一切皆为上帝所创造，他认为人和万物同源自上帝，共生共养，上帝不但是人的生命的缔造者，也是宇宙自然世界万物的创造者。换言之，上帝是人和世界之所以存在的根本，从中可以看出两位作家对"神"和"上帝"的不同理解：沈从文推崇"神"字背后所体现的自然的价值，认为自然万物皆有神性；福克纳则敬畏"上帝"创造宇宙万物的神奇力量及给人类所带来的恩惠。然而他们的宗教情结并不仅仅停留于此，在更高层面上，沈从文和福克纳还试图借助"神"与"上帝"来表达道德和美学上的理想诉求。

二

宗教与道德是密不可分的，宗教问题的探讨最终要回归道德层面。康德对道德和宗教的关系曾做过深入的思考。美国西雅图大学神学与宗教学系教授陈佐人在其《康德与基督教》一文中认为，"康德经常从哲学的角度，来探讨宗教与道德的问题"，"对于康德来说，人、道德与宗教实在是具有不可分割的关系。"② 他分析了康德著名的三大批判学说，认为在《纯粹理性批判》中康德质疑了一些证明上帝存在的观点，因为上帝的存在超越了人的经验知识的范围，所以既不能证明上帝的存在，亦不能否定其存在。但陈佐人继而指出，在《实践理性批判》中，"康德认为我们虽然不能以理性来证明上帝的存在，但人对上帝的信仰，却可以在实践内获得验证，人以理性实践善行，便自然要求上帝的存在"③。从上面的分析中我们

---

① ［美］威廉·福克纳：《去吧，摩西》，李文俊译，上海译文出版社 1996 年版，第 331 页。
② 转引自 http：//blog. sina. com. cn/joshua 2005。
③ 同上。

可以看出，虽然康德探讨的是上帝的信仰与道德的问题，但他实际上阐释了宗教与道德之间的关系。

在沈从文和福克纳的小说中，"神"和"上帝"的意义指涉也折射出强烈的道德诉求意识。尽管沈从文与福克纳的宗教情结存在着上述诸多差异性，但我们看到，其小说中的"神"和"上帝"的意义指涉最终目标指向的还是人类的道德层面。在两位作家对"神"和"上帝"之意义诉求背后，折射出他们对完美人性及道德品格的建构。

在沈从文的小说中，"神"字的内涵并不仅仅停留在"神即自然"这一点上，在一个更高的层面上，"神"字被他诠释为"爱"字。同样在《凤子》这部小说中，王杉古堡的总爷（沈从文的另一个代言人）和城里人讨论科学和自然神学的问题，认为不必为科学的发达会使神"慢慢地隐藏、消灭"而担心，认为神在人们感情中所占的地位，"除了它支配自然以外，只是一个抽象的东西，是正直和诚实和爱：科学第一件事就是真，这就是从神性中抽出的遗产，科学如何发达也不会抛弃正直和爱，所以我这里的神又是永远存在不会消灭的"[1]。如上文所论及，沈从文把生命看成泛神论的精灵，他认为生命对一切人都有份，它无处不在。但很少有人能超越生活去感知生命之神性，而这种生命神性又不是神秘莫测、虚无缥缈的。在沈从文看来，追求人性的善与爱，即"正直与诚实的爱"是人之生命神性的一个重要表现。因此，沈从文作品中"神"字之内涵从更高层面上理解就是一种素朴、正直的爱。就爱而言，它又是一种善的形式。当有人问及沈从文为什么要写作时，他回答道："因为我活到这个世界有所爱。美丽、清洁、智慧及对全人类幸福的幻影，皆永远觉得是一种德行，因为使我永远对它崇拜和倾心。这点情绪同宗教情绪完全一样。这点情绪促我来写作，不断地写作，没有厌倦，我将在各个作品各种形式里，表现我对于这个道德的努力。"[2] 爱成为沈从文创作的永恒动力和源泉。

沈从文的代表作《边城》可以说为我们提供了这种素朴爱的范本。在

---

① 沈从文：《沈从文全集》第 7 卷，北岳文艺出版社 2002 年版，第 124 页。
② 沈从文：《沈从文文集》第 11 卷，花城出版社 1984 年版，第 34 页。

边城这个几乎被世人遗忘的"世外桃源"中，充满着质朴、温馨的爱。沈从文曾谈到他创作此小说的目的是描写"几个愚夫俗子，被一件普通人事牵连在一处时，各人应得的一分哀乐，为人类'爱'字作一度恰如其分的说明"①。《边城》正是通过抒写青年男女之间的情爱、祖孙之爱、兄弟之爱、邻里之爱来表现生命的神性的。

沈从文描写湘西生活的其他一系列作品，如《阿黑小史》《三三》《萧萧》《边城》《长河》《雪晴》《湘西散记》等，无一例外也颂扬了众多乡村生命中的那份纯净、质朴的爱。而在他以浪漫手法写成的《月下小景》《龙朱》《媚金·豹子与那羊》等小说中，爱的神性光彩更是被渲染得淋漓尽致。那些女子的美丽、纯情、善良，那些男子的正直、旷达、雄强，都是人的生命神性的投射。即便是从湘西社会下层的水手、士兵，乃至土匪、娼妓身上，沈从文也发现了生命的神性和美丽，因为他们的爱皆是真诚的，因之对他们充满了一种"不可言说的温爱"②。

如果说沈从文在"神"字上赋予了爱的道德内涵，把爱提升为神之更高境界，福克纳则在上帝形象的重塑中，强化了其所体现的仁爱、同情、怜悯、宽容等超越性道德品格。在圣经文化中，上帝是宇宙间具有最高权能、智慧、仁爱、圣洁、公义等美德的至高无上的神，是最高德行的体现者。福克纳不但认同《圣经·旧约》关于世界和人类起源的解释，认为上帝是自然万物和人的缔造者，而且坚信上帝为人类确立了应该遵循的道德准则。在小说《熊》中，他直接提及了《圣经·旧约》中《创世纪》开篇"上帝创造天地"和"照自己之像造人"的故事，并借此故事阐发了更深的道德寓意：

> 因为他在《圣经》里说到怎样创造这世界，造好之后对着他看了看说还不错，便接着再创造人。他先创造了世界，让不会说话的生物居住在上面，然后创造人，让人当他在这个世界上的管理者，以他的

---

① 沈从文：《沈从文文集》第 11 卷，花城出版社 1984 年版，第 45 页。
② 沈从文：《沈从文全集》第 8 卷，北岳文艺出版社 2002 年版，第 57 页。

名义对世界和世界上的动物享有宗主权，可不是让人和他的后裔一代又一代地对一块块长方形、正方形的土地拥有不可侵犯的权利，而是在谁也不用个人名义的兄弟友爱的气氛下，共同完整地经营这个世界，而他所取得唯一代价就只是怜悯、谦卑、宽容、坚韧及用脸上的汗水来换取面包。①

这段文字是小说中的主人公麦卡斯林在决定放弃祖父老卡罗瑟斯传给他的土地和其他财产的继承权时所说的一番话，实际上麦卡斯林就是一个隐藏的作家代言人。在此，福克纳试图用上帝造物、造人的故事来说明这样一个事实：土地和财产是仁慈的上帝的馈赠，人类没有对土地和财产的永久宗主权，而人类只有彼此像兄弟般友爱，共同经营这个世界，像上帝那样具有怜悯、谦卑、宽容、坚韧等精神品格，他们才配享有上帝的恩赐。

这一观点在其后的小说中再次得到强调，麦卡斯林认为，即便是美洲国家的诞生、哥伦布发现新大陆这一事实，也应归功于上帝："直到他仅仅用一个鸡蛋便让他们发现一个新世界，在那里，一个人民的国家可以在谦卑、怜悯、宽容和彼此感到骄傲的精神中建立起来。"② 显而易见，此处的"他"指上帝，而福克纳强调上帝赐予人类新大陆是有条件的："这片新大陆是他出于怜悯和宽容特地赐给他们的，条件是他们必须怜悯、谦卑、宽容与坚韧。"③ 因而福克纳借上帝创造世界和人类的故事，启发人们思索的不仅仅是如何对待土地、财产这些上帝馈赠物的问题，而更重要的是人类应该如何培育完美的道德品格的问题。他认为，上帝为人类树立了完美的道德范式，他的慷慨、仁慈、博爱、谦卑、宽容等神性品格为人类树立了典范。而人类既然是上帝按自己的样子造出来的，也应该彼此相爱，秉承上帝的谦卑、怜悯、宽容、牺牲等神性精神品格。

费尔巴哈认为宗教是人的本质的反映，上帝是映照人的一面镜子。福

① ［美］威廉·福克纳：《去吧，摩西》，李文俊译，上海译文出版社1996年版，第240页。
② 同上书，第242页。
③ 同上。

克纳的诸多作品还通过强化《圣经》中上帝对世人审视的目光，映射了现实生活中的南方人的种种道德缺陷。在《我弥留之际》中，福克纳广泛使用了《圣经》中的原型话语，其中对上帝的指涉文字随处可见，上帝成为审视小说中人物行为和内心思想的一面"镜子"。在科拉独白片段中，作为一个虔诚的基督徒，她曾两次说："上帝可以看透人心。"①此话是大有深意的。正是在上帝目光的审视下，本德仑一家各色人物人性的弱点才得到了淋漓尽致的剖析。安斯的自私、贪婪和浅薄、庸俗，艾迪对亲人缺乏关爱的自我封闭、对丈夫的背叛和对人生所持的虚无价值观，以及他们的儿女各种各样的表现和动机，都通过运送艾迪棺材这一中心事件暴露在上帝的目光之下。

同样，在小说《熊》中，福克纳借上帝审视的目光剖析了南方历史中蕴含的原始罪恶和人性的贪婪、丑恶，他认为，南方人的苦难甚至南方人的暴行和不义都在上帝的见证下："因为他从无所不包的原始的绝对中赋予他们以形体，从那时起就在观察他们，在他们各自崇高与卑劣的时刻……"②而福克纳所强烈谴责的南方人的暴行和不义，则主要表现在他们对待黑人的态度上："他看见了那些奴隶贩子的阔绰的后代……对于他们来说尖声咒骂的黑人是另一个族类，另一种标本，就像是旅行家装在笼子里带回家的一只巴西金刚鹦鹉，而正是这些人，在温暖的、不漏风的会堂里通过要实行恐怖与暴行的决议……"③麦卡斯林后来在翻阅自己家族中的账簿时，发现了隐藏在祖父财富背后对黑人血淋淋的罪恶。

而无论是上帝对美国南方"人心的看透"，还是对美国南方历史罪恶的审视，都无法阻止南方人的堕落，福克纳的其他作品如《喧哗与骚动》《圣殿》和《八月之光》，分别描写了凯蒂的失贞，杰生的唯利是图，谭波尔的堕落和金鱼眼的凶残，以及克利斯默斯的暴力，认为造成其小说主人公悲剧的根源在于他们失去了对上帝的信仰从而走向了道德的沦丧。从一定意义上说，福克纳的南方故事重现了艾略特的荒原主题，它展现的是上

---

① ［美］威廉·福克纳：《我弥留之际》，李文俊译，上海译文出版社1995年版，第72页。
② ［美］威廉·福克纳：《去吧，摩西》，李文俊译，上海译文出版社1996年版，第268页。
③ 同上书，第269页。

帝之死的一幅幅荒原景象。随着南方人的信仰和价值体系的彻底崩溃，他们面临着前所未有的生存危机和精神危机。故福克纳在日本谈到《寓言》这部作品时尖锐地指出："如果耶稣在 1914—1915 年再度降临，他就会再一次被钉死在十字架上。"① 这表达了他对一战后的西方现代社会上帝被人们所摒弃的现实的清醒认识。这也就不难理解福克纳的小说所塑造的一系列扭曲、变形的耶稣形象的人物：《圣经》中那个至善至美的上帝之子耶稣的形象被"置换变形"，或退化为智力低下的白痴（如《喧哗与骚动》中的班吉），或成为对现实失去感知力、为自己母亲打造棺材的木匠（如《我弥留之际》中的卡什），或堕落为一生苦苦寻求自我身份而不得的杀人犯（如《八月之光》中的乔·克里斯默斯）。

尽管福克纳认为上帝会被人们所抛弃，但又坚信上帝不会放弃对人类应负的责任，上帝是人类的拯救者。小说《熊》中的一段对话寓意深远：

> 于是他再一次转身面向这片土地，他仍然有意拯救这片土地，因为他已经为它做了那么多的事情——于是麦卡斯林说"什么？"于是他说"——他仍然对这些人负有责任，因为他们是他创出来的——"于是麦卡斯林说"转回来对着我们？他的脸朝着我们？"于是他说。②

"他的脸朝着我们"这句话意味深长，它表明上帝对南方人还没有绝望，他在南方人身上还寄予了希望，因为他发现爱的温暖的火苗依旧在南方燃烧。小说写到南方人的妻子和女儿在黑人生病时为他们煮汤，并送到黑人所住的臭烘烘的小屋，在黑人病重时还把他们搬到大宅照顾、护理。正是这些白人女子对黑人无私的爱，"让炉火一直燃烧直到危机过去"③。这种爱的火苗的燃烧使福克纳看到了重建人类道德的信心。因而福克纳借麦卡斯林之口表达了对上帝和《圣经》终极道德意义的思索，上帝向世人

---

① Merywether James B. and Millgate Michael, eds. *Lion in the Garden*. Random House, 1968, p. 178.
② ［美］威廉·福克纳：《去吧，摩西》，李文俊译，上海译文出版社1996年版，第271页。
③ 同上。

提供了一个完美的道德样式，上帝身上处处体现的是慈爱、公正、平等、同情、怜悯、牺牲的品质；而南方这块土地既埋藏着苦难、暴行、不义与罪恶，又萌生着爱、同情、仁慈和怜悯的种子。

因为受圣经文化的影响，福克纳所宣扬的爱，是一种带有浓郁基督教气息的爱，这与沈从文所倡导的"爱的宗教"的内涵有着很大的不同。沈从文倡导的爱是一种合乎自然人性的素朴的爱，它体现了自然的人性之美。这种素朴的人性，历来为中国道家所推崇。老子主张"见素抱朴，少私寡欲"①，而庄子则诠释"素朴"为："同乎无欲，是谓素朴，素朴而民性得矣。"② 沈从文从这种素朴、自然的人性中见出了神性，这种信仰源于他的泛神论思想，与前文所分析的"神即自然"的观点有着密切联系。像西方主张回归自然的文学家卢梭、歌德和华兹华斯等人一样，沈从文认为自然具有永恒的精神价值，自然具有一种提升人的精神境界与道德价值的力量。从尊崇自然价值，沈从文继而转向尊崇自然的人性。如席勒在《论素朴的诗与感伤的诗》一文中所归纳的那样，人在自然状态下所表现的人性就是素朴。因而，沈从文把自然的价值和自然人性提升至神之境界，这与福克纳对神性的理解有着很大的不同。福克纳认为神性主要体现在上帝的超越性精神品格上。人作为上帝的创造物，是上帝按照自己的样子创造出来的，应该力求实现人性向神性的提升，培育仁慈、谦卑、怜悯、牺牲等神性品格。在《没有被征服的》中，主人公白亚德·沙多里斯的父亲沙多里斯上校被人杀死，南方旧传统要求以血还血，南方人的荣誉感要求他去杀死凶手，为父报仇。但福克纳在小说中并没有安排白亚德复仇，而是让他遵从了更高的信仰，那就是上帝的教导："你不能杀人。"他认为"以牙还牙"的旧信条应该让位于以爱与原谅为核心的基督教精神。

① 《老子》第十九章。
② 《庄子·马蹄》。

三

饶有趣味的是，沈从文与福克纳在对上述精神品格热烈的宗教诉求中，还阐释了它们与美之间的关系，这实际上印证了宗教、道德与美之间的关联性。这与康德的观点非常相似。康德在研究了宗教和道德的关系后，继而探讨了宗教与美的关系。陈佐人教授指出，在《判断力批判》一书中，康德"提出了著名的'美是道德的象征'的定义，因为他发现人在鉴赏美感的同时，往往产生对永恒不朽的感受，此种穿透现象界的判断，十分类似道德对理性的超越，由此康德便点出了美学与道德的关系"①。

同样，在沈从文的文学理念中，宗教（神）、爱与美三者也是紧密相连的。在散文《烛虚》中他写道："我过于爱有生一切。……在有生中我发现了美，那本身形与线即代表一种最高的德性，使人乐于受它的统制，受它的处治。"② 他进而指出："这种美或由上帝造物之手所产生，一片铜，一块石头，一把线，一组声音，其物虽小，可以见世界之大，并见世界之全……人亦相同。一微笑，一皱眉，无不同样可以显出那种圣境。"③ 在沈从文看来，美与善是人的生命存在的更高层次，它超越了只追求动物式生存的生活的层面，这种趋于神的境界只有在康德所说的忘却自我、无功利目的状态下才可能达到。

然而在现实生活中，正像福克纳对南方堕落满怀失望之情一样，沈从文对中国都市的现状也是忧心忡忡。因为他看到，在现实世界中，特别是在都市生活中，"某种人情感或被世物所阉割，淡漠如一僵尸，或欲扮道学、充绅士、做君子，深深惧怕被任何一种美所袭击……像这些人对于'美'，对一切美物、美行、美事、美观念，无不淡然处之，竟若毫无反

---

① 转引自 http：//blog. sina. com. cn/joshua 2005。
② 沈从文：《沈从文全集》第 12 卷，北岳文艺出版社 2002 年版，第 23 页。
③ 同上书，第 23—24 页。

应"①。沈从文把这些人称为"阉寺性的人"，认为他们既没有美的情趣，也缺乏爱的情感，在精神状态上始终是个阉人。所以他强调："我们实需要一种爱与美的新宗教，来煽起更年轻一辈做人的热诚，激发起生命的抽象搜寻，对人类明日未来向上合理的一切设计，都能产生一种崇高庄严感情。国家民族的重造问题，方不至于成为具文，为空话。"② 因而在沈从文看来，爱与美既是神性的呈现形式，又是生命的本质属性；培育爱与美的情感，不仅可以真正实现生命的意义，而且能重塑被金钱和权势腐蚀的日渐退化、衰微的民族品格。

而福克纳也把上帝所体现的神性品格与爱和美视为一体。他认为上帝的博爱、怜悯、同情、忍耐、牺牲等精神品格揭示的是心灵的真理，而心灵的真理是美的最高境界。故麦卡斯林在《熊》这部小说中不断思索上帝与《圣经》带给人类的启示，他认为人们应该用心灵来接近上帝，用心灵来读《圣经》："因为那些为他写他书的人写的都是真理，而世界上只有一种真理，他统驭一切与心灵相关的东西。"③ 而这种心灵的真理，它具有永恒的美，它将永世长存。小说有这样一个耐人寻味的细节描写：麦卡斯林诵读了济慈的《希腊古瓮曲》的几行诗："她消失不了，虽然你也得不到你的幸福"，"你将永远爱恋，而她将永远娇美。"④ 作为孩子的艾萨克问他诗中是否讲的是一个姑娘的事情，麦卡斯林却说："他讲的是关于真理的事。真理只有一个。他是不会变的。……勇敢、荣誉和自豪，还有怜悯和对正义和自由的热爱。它们都与心灵有关，而心灵所包容的也就变成了真理，我们所知道的真理。"⑤ 济慈在希腊古瓮身上寄予了对永恒的古典艺术美的向往，而福克纳借济慈的《希腊古瓮曲》把希腊古瓮所体现的永恒的美引申至"心灵的真理"，并且认为它永远不会消失。

需要指出的是，沈从文和福克纳小说中"神"和"上帝"的内涵意义

---

① 沈从文：《沈从文全集》第 12 卷，北岳文艺出版社 2002 年版，第 32—33 页。
② 沈从文：《沈从文文集》第 11 卷，花城出版社 1984 年版，第 379 页。
③ ［美］威廉·福克纳：《去吧，摩西》，李文俊译，上海译文出版社 1996 年版，第 243 页。
④ 同上书，第 283 页。
⑤ 同上。

虽然在深层次上指向美，然而两位作家对美的诠释有着很大的不同。沈从文对自然持有一种独特的泛神论情感，他对神奇瑰丽的自然所蕴含的外在结构形式之美有着深切的感悟。在《潜渊》中，他这样阐释道："美固无所不在，凡属造型，如用泛神情感去接近，即无不可以见出其精巧处和完整处。生命之最大意义，能用于对自然或人工巧妙完美而倾心，人之所同。"① 从对"美物"的鉴赏，他进而主张培养"美行"及"美观念"。而福克纳则更注重美的精神品格的培育。正如他在诺贝尔获奖词中所指出的："我相信人不仅仅会存活，他们还能越活越好。他是不朽的，并非因为生物中唯独他具有永不枯竭的声音，而是因为他有灵魂，有能够同情、牺牲和忍耐的精神。"② 他认为作家的职责就在于写出这些东西，并提醒人们记住"勇气、尊严、希望、自豪、同情、怜悯和牺牲，这些是人类历史上的光荣"③。

　　以上考察了沈从文与福克纳小说"神"和"上帝"的意义指涉及其文学理念之间的关系。"神"字被沈从文赋予了自然、爱与美三个层面的意义，它实际上是沈从文作品主旨的三个重要维度。而福克纳作品强化了上帝形象的指涉意义，则对人类培育仁慈、怜悯、同情、宽容等道德品格有着重要启示意义。尽管两位作家来自中西不同的文化背景，但他们经由不同的宗教信仰的路径，最终还是走向了对人类道德和美学终极目标的诉求。归根结底，他们的文学作品诉诸的是一种共同的艺术追求，即对真善美的呼唤。

（原载于《中国比较文学》2009 年第 3 期）

---

① 沈从文：《沈从文全集》第 12 卷，北岳文艺出版社 2002 年版，第 32 页。
② ［美］威廉·福克纳：《福克纳随笔》，李文俊译，上海译文出版社 2008 年版，第 122 页。
③ 同上书，第 123 页。

沈从文、福克纳小说的"神话—原型"阐释

夏志清在评价沈从文所描写的湘西世界时曾指出："沈从文并没有提出任何超自然的新秩序；他只肯定了神话的想象力之重要性，认为这是使我们在现代的社会中唯一能够保全生命完整的力量。"① 美国著名作家威廉·福克纳描写的约克纳帕塔法世界也常被视为美国南方的神话，福克纳研究专家马尔科姆·考利认为，福克纳的作品具有双重意义："第一，创造了密西西比州的一个县，它像神话中的王国……第二，他使约克纳帕塔法县的故事成为最边远的南方的寓言和传奇，活在人们的心中。"② 在此，"神话"这一概念被赋予了新的内涵，意指文学作品中深层次的、具有象征和隐喻意义的体系。从一定意义上说，沈从文建构了一个"神之再现"的湘西神话世界，他的湘西小说像是一曲关于"神之再现"的颂歌，而福克纳的约克纳帕塔法神话故事，则描绘了一幅神性已逝、人性走向堕落的"神之解体"画卷，其间也穿插着"神之复活"的场面。

加拿大著名人类学家诺斯罗普·弗莱提出了神话—原型批评理论，这一理论用"神话"与"原型"这两个核心概念对文学的本质性特点进行了全新的阐释和研究。一方面，他认为原型是文学的一种隐含的象征结构形式，认为"对原型的研究是从整体上对文学象征的研究"③。另一方面，他用神话这一载体来概括文学作品中所存在的普遍的原型结构模式。用弗莱

---

① 夏志清:《中国现代小说史》，刘绍明等译，香港中文大学出版社 2001 年版，第 162 页。
② 李文俊编:《福克纳的神话》，上海译文出版社 2008 年版，第 21 页。
③ [加] 诺斯罗普·弗莱:《批评的剖析》，陈慧等译，百花文艺出版社 1998 年版，第 125 页。

的神话—原型批评理论来考察沈从文和福克纳的小说世界，会发现沈从文和福克纳的作品分别表现了神的故事的不同阶段，勾勒了不同的神话原型模式结构和人物类型。从小说原型模式结构上看，沈从文的湘西世界着重表现的是神的诞生和恋爱的神话，而福克纳的约克纳帕塔法天地展现的则是神之解体和死亡的故事。沈从文的湘西神话为我们重塑了一个个充满感伤的青春气息和浪漫传奇色彩的爱情故事，这些故事以湘西苗族人生活为背景，超越了现实的、形而下的湘西生活，富有形而上的原型神话意义。那带有原始、神秘色彩的苗族人居住的山寨和古城堡，好像是一个充满自然情趣、温馨浪漫的伊甸园，而故事中的主人公则像天神或天使一样具有超凡脱俗的美貌和品德，展现了完整、圆满和优美的神性生命。比较而言，在福克纳的约克纳帕塔法神话中，我们看不到象征神之诞生、充满青春气息的爱情故事，相反，他的作品通过隐喻神之受难与死亡，宣告了神之解体时代的来临。与沈从文在湘西神话中所营造的优美、静谧，充满田园气息的诗意氛围所不同的是，福克纳的约克纳帕塔法神话中充满着"喧哗与骚动"，呈现出一派荒诞与混乱的场面，沈从文小说中那热烈、纯真的神之恋爱故事在福克纳的作品中荡然无存，映现在读者眼前的是一幅幅触目惊心的爱的荒原图景，小说中的人物丧失了正常的爱之情感和爱的能力，连接两性之爱的纽带被割断，取而代之的是扭曲、畸形、变态的两性关系，其间充斥着性暴力、自虐和梦魇。这种差异性集中体现在沈从文和福克纳作品对人物类型的刻画上：沈从文湘西小说中的主人公大多是超凡脱俗、具有神性品格的形象；福克纳作品所塑造的角色大都失去了神性生命的光环，在身体上和精神上呈现出萎顿、异化甚至堕落的态势。

在小说《凤子》中，沈从文借王杉寨古堡敬神谢神的仪式，慨叹"神之存在，依然如故"。事实上，沈从文所创作的湘西作品，即为我们创造了一个"'神'尚未解体的时代"的鲜活的湘西神话，它为神在湘西民间文化的诞生、重现唱了一首赞歌。沈从文的湘西小说可以分为两类，一类是具有超现实的、梦幻般色彩的湘西神话，如《龙朱》《媚金·豹子与那羊》《神巫之爱》等；另一类是湘西背景凸显较清晰，具有较强写实性的小说，如《边城》《长河》《木木》《萧萧》《阿黑小史》。

《龙朱》《神巫之爱》《媚金·豹子与那羊》三部作品均发表于1929年，其时沈从文正寓居在繁华的上海，但他对都市生活表现出的不是积极的认同，而是强烈的反感和憎恶。沈从文认为"神之一字"在都市文明中已不复存在，于是他把关注的目光投向了湘西。《龙朱》等小说中的背景设置都不太明晰，都是虚构的苗族青年男女恋爱的故事，却带有普遍的神话原型意义。男主人公集相貌和品德之美于一身，具有象征青春和俊美的太阳神阿波罗的风貌和《圣经·雅歌》中所罗门王的威仪风采。女主人公兼有爱与美之神阿佛洛狄忒美丽、青春、感性的气质和《圣经·雅歌》中书拉密女的痴情和坚贞，她们用"美的身体和美的歌声"演绎了一个个热烈、执着、疯狂的爱情神话。

《龙朱》的开头在描写白耳族苗族人出美男子时，直接把他们比作阿波罗神："仿佛是那地方的父母全曾参与过雕塑阿波罗神的工作，因此就把美的模型留给儿子了。"龙朱作为白耳族族长的儿子，则是"美男子中之美男子"。《神巫之爱》中的神巫"威仪如神，温和如鹿，而超拔如鹤"，就连族总见到他时也惊叹："年轻的人呀，如日如虹的丰神，无怪乎世上的女人都为你而倾心，我九十岁的老人了，一见你也想作揖。"《媚金·豹子与那羊》中的豹子在唱山歌时对媚金自夸"豹子的美丽你眼睛曾为证明"。同时，这些男性主人公在品德方面也堪称典范，龙朱在白耳族人眼中甚至成了不可超越的神，神巫具有"完美的身体和高尚的灵魂"，豹子是"凤凰族相貌极美又顶有一切美德的一个男子"。这些男主人公的形象，还带有《圣经》中的所罗门王的原型。尽管沈从文不是基督徒，但与《圣经》有不解之缘。在他早期创作的短篇小说和后期的哲理文章中都引用了《旧约》《新约》中的语句，从中可以看出基督教对他的影响。在上述三部作品中，不仅出现了与《圣经·雅歌》类似的祷词和喻象，而且直接以所罗门王的形象来刻画龙朱、豹子和神巫的性情和品性，如盛赞龙朱"美丽强壮像狮子，温和谦顺如小羊，是人中模型，是权威，是力，是光"；《媚金》中豹子在媚金的眼中"如太阳光明不欺"，他的热"如太阳把我融化"等等。

福克纳小说中的男主人公与沈从文上述作品中的男性角色有很大的不

同，他们是尘世生活中的凡夫俗子，在体魄上他们不仅失去了雄健和阳性之美，而且出现了"生理和心理上的萎缩"状态，甚至呈现出异化和变态的症候，他们或退避到一个自我封闭的世界，失去了行动的方向和动力，或在精神上堕落、蜕化。具体来说，福克纳小说中所描写的男主人公可以分为以下几个类型：一是理想幻灭、逃避现实的怯懦者，代表人物有《喧哗与骚动》中的昆丁父子，《圣殿》中的霍拉斯，《八月之光》中的海托华牧师等；二是自私自利、邪恶阴险、灵魂堕落的恶魔，代表人物有《喧哗与骚动》中的杰生，《圣殿》中的金鱼眼、弗莱姆，《我弥留之际》中的安斯等；三是一些映射耶稣基督的人物，他们虽带有耶稣的影子，但与《圣经》中那个无所不能、至爱至善的神之子耶稣的形象已大相径庭，他们以扭曲、变形的耶稣形象出现，严重背离了耶稣基督所体现的至善和全能的精神，因此福克纳借这类人物形象讽喻了神之子的死亡和退化。

美国南方有着崇尚骑士的传统，福克纳笔下所描写的庄园世家曾出过许多具有骑士品格的种植园主，但时势的变迁和唯利是图的工商资本主义势力摧毁了旧日他们赖以生存的经济基础，庄园主及其后裔从物质到精神上都被彻底摧毁，他们已不能适应新的生活，甚至丧失了活下去的信心和勇气，对往昔家族荣誉和尊严的追忆成为他们逃避现实生活的精神鸦片，昆丁父子、霍拉斯和海托华均对现实世界流露出厌倦之情，沉溺于一个虚构中的贞洁、优雅、浪漫的南方贵族神话中，执着于寻求一个远离现实尘嚣的虚幻的精神世界，他们的梦想又无时无刻不被冷酷的现实世界所打破，他们既无力重整乾坤、肩负起光复传统的重担，又缺乏与现实力量抗争的能力，与具有英雄气质、雄悍刚强的康普生祖辈相比，他们是耽于幻想、逃避现实、软弱无力的退化的一辈。

《喧哗与骚动》中的昆丁被夹在传统重荷和冷酷现实的夹缝中，陷入极度的矛盾冲突中。一方面，占据他的精神世界的是那些受挫的鬼魂和他们喋喋不休的怨气，这预示着他的出生和成长注定要受这些鬼魂的控制；另一方面，他在像一个勇敢的骑士那样拼命维护凯蒂的贞洁和南方荣誉的行动中，最终被证明是一个失败者。生活在祖先鬼魂阴影和康普生先生虚无主义价值观的双重围困中的昆丁是痛苦不堪的，也是软弱无力的。他的精神中缺乏内在的活力，以及康普生祖辈那种骑士做派的强悍和血性，他已失去了与现实抗争的勇气和能力。这注定了他试图重建南方神话价值体系的失败。

《八月之光》中的牧师海托华和昆丁一样逃避现实，生活在一个沉溺于回忆先辈荣耀的梦想世界中："他布道时手舞足蹈，他所宣扬的教义里充满了奔驰的骑兵、先辈的光荣和失败"；"他似乎把宗教、奔驰的骑兵和在奔驰的马上丧生的祖父混在一起，纠缠不清，甚至在布道坛上也不能区别开来。而且也许在他家里，在他的个人生活里，这些事儿也搅成一团。"① 在小说的最后，海托华牧师终于从梦境中醒了过来，认识到他远离生活和民众所犯下的错误："是我做得不对……说不定是道德上的罪恶"，"我知道整整五十年来我甚至还没有变成人"。②

与昆丁和海托华牧师一样，《圣殿》中的霍拉斯也是一个追求理想、追求完美世界而逃避现实世界的人物，他首先出现在小说《沙多里斯》中，是一个深受古希腊文学和欧洲浪漫主义文学影响的青年。在《圣殿》中露面时，霍拉斯已是一个43岁的成年男子，他是以一个逃离者的身份出现的，他企图逃离的是令他感到窒息、乏味的婚姻牢笼。他的妻子是一位庸俗、乏味的女子，代表着无聊、平庸的现实世界，而十年来霍拉斯一直生活于这样一个世界中，每个星期五他都要遵照妻子的嘱托去火车站为她搬回一箱虾，小说里写道："我觉得仿佛跟着我自己上火车站，站在一边，看着霍拉斯·班鲍从火车上拿下那只箱子，拎着它走回家，每走一百步就换一下手，我跟在他身后，心里想，这里埋葬着霍拉斯·班鲍，埋葬在密西西比州一条人行道上一连串逐渐消失的臭烘烘的小水滴里。"③ 霍拉斯每周五被妻子派去取虾的行为暗示了他受控于一种代表程式化的琐碎、无聊生活力量的限制，而霍拉斯的生命就埋葬于其中。霍拉斯在和妻子生活了十年后终于选择离家出走，但小说的结尾，霍拉斯重新回到妻子的身边，这证明霍拉斯和昆丁一样软弱，缺乏改变自己命运的勇气和力量。正如霍

① ［美］威廉·福克纳：《圣殿》，陶洁译，上海译文出版社1997年版，第44—45页。
② 同上书，第348页。
③ ［美］威廉·福克纳：《八月之光》，蓝仁哲译，上海译文出版社2004年版，第14页。

拉斯在小说的开头对鲁碧所说的那样："我没有勇气：我身体里没留下勇气。整台机器都在，可就是开动不起来。"①

福克纳的作品还塑造了另一类男主人公，他们完全走向了英雄的对立面，是一类阴险毒辣、自私冷漠、个性扭曲的恶魔，代表人物有《喧哗与骚动》中的杰生、《圣殿》中的金鱼眼弗莱姆，以及《我弥留之际》中的安斯等等。杰生自私冷酷、贪婪狠毒，这一性格特征反映了新兴工商资本主义唯利是图的本性。金钱成了他做事的唯一法则，金钱使他失去了做人起码应具备的人性和亲情。《圣殿》中的弗莱姆同样是一个外表庸俗丑陋，性格贪婪自私、卑琐下流、道德败坏的人物，带有斯诺普斯家族卑琐冷酷、不顾一切道德准则、千方百计往上爬的性格特点。《我弥留之际》中的安斯除了具有上述两人的性格特点，还多了几分滑稽可笑的色彩，就像一个在舞台上表演的小丑，把自己性格中的虚伪、自私、冷漠、贪婪的弱点暴露无遗。

沈从文和福克纳所塑造的女主人公也迥然相异。在沈从文的神话世界中，女主人公被赋予了超凡脱俗的神性品格，她们不仅具有美的身体和美的歌声，而且具有率直、舒展的个性，开放的性观念，旺盛的情欲。《神巫之爱》中的花帕族女人在表达和追求爱情上表现出了超乎寻常的大胆和热烈。小说的开头以浪漫、抒情的笔触描写了湘西云石镇砦门外大路上，一群身着花帕青裙、打扮得像花一样的年轻美貌的女子守候神巫来临的情景。她们都渴望能够得到神巫的爱情，"在云石镇的女人心中，把神巫款待到家，献上自己的身，给这神之子受用，是以为比作土司的夫人还觉得荣幸的"。于是神巫每到一处便有女人拦路欢迎，更有"野心极大的女人"在窗边吹笛、唱歌。"花帕族的女人，在恋爱上的野心等于猓猓族男人打仗的勇敢。"及至神巫在村里做法事时，花帕族的女子们最大的愿望即是能够"使神巫的身心归自己一件事"。

与沈从文小说中所描写的一系列美丽善良、忠贞不渝、具有神性品格的天使般的少女截然不同的是，福克纳的小说是一部关于女性堕落的神

---

① ［美］威廉·福克纳：《八月之光》，蓝仁哲译，上海译文出版社 2004 年版，第14页。

话。像伊甸园中的夏娃被魔鬼撒旦引诱失去了往昔的纯真一样，福克纳小说中的诸多女性如凯蒂、谭波尔等打破了南方淑女冰清玉洁的神话而走向堕落。福克纳曾指出：《喧哗与骚动》这部小说，描写的是"两个堕落的女人，凯蒂和她的女儿的一出悲剧"。凯蒂的堕落始于性，性是贯穿福克纳小说的一个重要因素。与沈从文极力渲染、颂扬青年男女出于自然本性、冲破世俗束缚的酣畅淋漓的性爱观不同，福克纳对性持一种基本否定的态度，他把性视为一种使人堕落的邪恶的力量。在《喧哗与骚动》中，他把凯蒂的性堕落问题放在首要的位置上，不但班吉认为性破坏了凯蒂曾带给他的安全感和宁静感，昆丁更是把凯蒂的性纯洁视为与南方的荣誉、他的生命同等重要的事情。尽管他对凯蒂的性活动采取了一种不可理喻的、近乎专制的抵制态度，但他和班吉一样，认为凯蒂只有永远保持童贞，才能维系他对一个圣洁、本真、完美世界理想的幻想，所以他采取各种行动和措施，企图使凯蒂能够与性所代表的邪恶的现实世界隔绝开来，永远保持纯洁。最终在凯蒂失去贞操后，他的精神支点也随之轰然倒塌，他只能以自杀来告别对他来说已失去意义的世界。

如果说凯蒂是一个堕落的天使，《圣殿》中的女主人公谭波尔则是一个彻头彻尾的堕落了的恶魔。《圣殿》的译者陶洁在这部小说的序言中曾总结、梳理了研究者对谭波尔形象的不同观点和看法，同时指出研究者们有一点达成了一致，即谭波尔的本质是邪恶的，邪恶、堕落和淫荡构成了谭波尔性格中的主导因素。具有讽刺意味的是，她的名字"Temple"的意义是神殿，身为法官的父亲之所以给她取这样一个名字，是试图在她身上寄予对贞洁的南方淑女的期待，而在"Temple"的名字铸成的这座"神殿"中却隐藏着人性中的一切龌龊、邪恶、淫荡和空虚的弱点，谭波尔成了一个彻底堕落的现代女性。

综上所述，神话原型批评理论为我们探悉沈从文和福克纳的艺术世界提供了一个新的阐释视角。随着现代文明进程在都市和乡村世界的推演，沈从文日渐意识到现代文明对湘西神话纯粹性的侵袭和破坏，在他所写的其他一些湘西小说及都市小说中转向了对"神之解体"主题和结构模式的叙述。福克纳对人类的未来依旧怀有信心和希望，他后期的小说一改前期作品低沉、忧郁的基调，回荡着神之复活的快乐旋律，他所塑造的另一类形象，如《喧哗与骚动》中充满爱心的迪尔西，《圣殿》中忠贞不渝的鲁碧，《八月之光》中自然、纯真的莉娜，和善良、富有奉献精神的邦奇，给他的小说带来了缕缕光明的色调，他们的出现预示着神的再生，也象征着福克纳所坚信的"勇气、尊严、希望、自豪、同情、怜悯和牺牲"① 精神的不朽。

（原载于《齐鲁学刊》2009 年第 5 期）

---

① ［美］福克纳：《福克纳随笔》，李文俊译，上海译文出版社 2008 年版，第 123 页。

生态学视野中的沈从文与福克纳

　　在 20 世纪世界文坛上，沈从文与福克纳是两位具有深刻国际影响的文学大师。他们生活在不同的地域、文化背景下，审美理念及艺术表现形式必然会呈现出巨大的差异性。但若把其纳入现代生态学的视野来蠡测，我们会发现这两位作家的作品中蕴含着极为丰富的崇尚自然、敬仰生命、推崇健康、淳朴的精神价值的生态理念。他们在对文明与自然、物质与精神关系的思索上，表现出类似的价值取向。对现代文明，他们均持一种本能的厌恶和憎恨，相反，则认同自然的价值与崇尚自然的人性；他们对物质主义都采取了一种激进的反抗与抨击的态度，而推崇纯洁、质朴的精神。对自然价值及精神价值的提升也正是现代生态学所倡议的基本立场。以生态学的视野来审视沈从文与福克纳，可以进一步深化对两位作家的研究。

　　现代生态学产生于反思现代文明所造成的人与自然、物质与精神割裂的背景之下。与现代工业文明价值观相反，现代生态学所持的是一种自然生态价值观。它主张宇宙、自然和人类社会的有机统一关系。这种统一并非如传统价值观，把人类社会的发展看得最为重要，以人的实际利益作为价值的衡量尺度，而是要求人类超越工业文明的狭隘利益观，以一种系统、整体论的眼光，承认并尊重自然界中的各种生命及非生命体所具有的内在均等价值，以达到人与自然的协调发展。因而，它是与现代工业文明价值观迥然不同的一种崭新的理念，它把自然的价值提升到与人类的发展同等重要的位置，反对物质主义无视甚至任意掠夺自然价值的态度，反对现代文明过分注重物质发展所造成的人性异化。

　　在世界文学，尤其在 20 世纪世界文学的大潮中，同样涌动着一股回归自然、反文明异化的潜流。作为深刻洞悉人类本性及精神需求的文学家们，面对喧嚣、物欲横流的现代工业社会，在对自然、田园、故乡的书写中，寻求拯救现代文明的精神良药。沈从文与福克纳，作为20世纪世界文学中有影响的作家，是这股回归浪潮中具有代表性的作家。沈从文一生痴迷自然，思索人与自然的关系。在沈从文那里，回归自然的主题，达到了现代文学所能达到的高度和广度。在福克纳笔下，自然是伟大的，人对自然的正确态度应该是爱，与他的伟大融为一体。这种回归并不是一种简单的对自然的认同，海德格尔认为，回归意味着重新修正人与自然的关系，而在舍勒看来，它也是人类精神的一次自我超越，"人类必须再一次把握那种伟大的、无形的、共同的、存在于生活中的人性的一致性，存在于永恒精神领域中的一切精神的同契性，以及这个第一推动力和世界进程的同契性"①。

　　强调自然对人类的价值和意义是生态学的核心主题。沈从文和福克纳的作品则很好地表达了这一生态学的核心理念。沈从文小说精神结构的核心就是以自然作为抨击都市文明的尺度，从而建立一种"优美、健康而又不悖乎自然的生命形式"。因而，贯穿于沈从文创作中的是对自然人性的追寻和探索。福克纳同样认同自然价值，反对现代机械文明对自然所采取的疏离、掠夺的态度，以及所造成的人性异化，并呼吁建立一种体现自然法则诸如"勇气、荣誉、希望、自豪、同情、怜悯"等精神力量的"心灵的真理"。但由于处于不同民族、文化背景下，沈从文和福克纳审视自然的视角又必然存在着一定的差异性。沈从文对湘西自然风物的认同更多地带有中国古代文人寄情于自然山水的雅士情结，而福克纳则把代表着自然界的大森林及生活于其中的"老班"——熊一类的动物尊为圣灵，表达了典型的西方式的对自然及其生灵膜拜的情结。再者，沈从文更侧重于从抽象的层面上思索人与自然的关系，而福克纳则具体展示了人对森林及其生灵的蹂躏，揭示了没有爱的一味开发、掠夺自然必然会遭到自然报复这一

---

① ［德］马克斯·舍勒：《资本主义的未来》，罗悌伦等译，生活·读书·新知三联书店1997年版，第231页。

生态主题。从这个意义上说，福克纳的思想与现代生态学的主张更接近。下文拟具体从自然生态、社会生态和精神生态分析沈从文与福克纳创作的相似性与差异性。

一

在沈从文与福克纳的作品中，自然占有重要的位置。他们甚至把自然提升到神与人的地位，这表现出他们对自然崇敬、膜拜的态度。在沈从文的《凤子》中，古堡的总爷对到矿区勘探的城里工程师说："我们这个地方的神不像基督教那个上帝那么顽固的。神的意义在我们这里只是'自然'，一切生成的现象，不是人为的，由他来处理，他常常是合理的，宽容的，美的。"因而，神在沈从文的眼中不再带有玄妙、神秘的色彩，它就是自然。同样，福克纳借艾克·麦卡斯林这一人物，在《三角洲之秋》中说："他创造了世界，让人生活在那里面，我想他创造的世界，正是他想要在那里面生活的世界，假如他是人的话。"在上文中，无论是沈从文还是福克纳，都用"他"来称谓"自然"，而不用没有生命的"它"，"自然"被提升到与人平等的地位，这也是现代生态学的一个基本价值取向。

沈从文和福克纳的作品，均向我们呈现了一个趣味盎然、鸢飞鱼跃的生态世界，这是一个充满生机和活力的世界，在这个世界中，人的心灵与花草树木、虫鱼鸟兽、山川湖海、日月星辰相感应，从大自然中汲取爱与美的源泉。

在沈从文建构的自然生态世界中，水的清澈、云的诡秘、山的挺拔、雾的朦胧、风的轻盈构成了湘西自然世界流动的旋律。在《从文自传》中，他说："我的教育全是水上得来的，我的智慧中有水气，我的性格中仿佛一道小小河流。"云的姿态在他的笔下也是千变万化、姿态迥异的。他把风比作祖母或母亲的手，温柔地抚摸着他的脸庞，"还温柔地送来各种花朵的香味，草木叶子的香味，以及新鲜泥土的香味"。湘西特殊的地理、气候孕育了独特的动植物。其中有"被严霜侵染，丹朱明黄，耀人眼

· 104 ·

目"的橘柚，河中"大如人"的鱼，"如龙蛇昂首奋起"的林中松杉，还有绿得像"大毡菌"似的草坪，"正努力从地下拔起的草"，"同火那么热闹开放"的桃花。在沈从文的湘西世界，这样美妙的景色随处可见。如《月下小景》中有"松杉挺茂嘉树四合的山寨"，"月光淡淡地洒满了各处，如一首富于光色和谐雅丽的诗歌"，"薄暮的空气极其温柔，微风摇荡大气中，有稻草香味，有烂熟的山果香味，有甲虫类气味，有泥土气味。一切在成熟，在开始结束一个夏天阳光雨露所及长养生成的一切。一切光景具有一种节日的欢乐情调"。沈从文在评论闻一多的《死水》时说："一首诗，告诉我们不是一个故事，一点感想，应当是一片霞，一园花，有各种各样的颜色与姿态，具各样香味，作各种变化，是那么细碎又是那么整个的美，欣赏它，使我们从它那超人力的完全中低首，为那超拔技巧而倾心。"① 沈从文的作品为我们展示了一幅鸢飞鱼跃、趣味盎然的自然生态图景。

福克纳的约克纳帕塔法小说所描写的自然背景也非常鲜明生动。罗博特·潘·沃伦盛赞"任何小说中的世界在物质形象上都比不上这个神话般的县那么生气盎然"。福克纳认为自然具有"不可磨灭的美"，在他的笔下，在不同的时间、不同的季节，自然风物呈现出千姿百态。沃伦还详细分析了福克纳作品生动、鲜明的自然形象。他认为，"自然给人的活动和激情的背后张上一幅彩色幕布"，有时它富有抒情的美，（如《村子》中母牛插曲中的草地），有时富有亲切的魅力（如"花斑马"故事里试验的场面），有时阴森中包含着威力（如《野棕榈》中"老人"的故事里的河流），有时则庄严肃穆（如《熊》中的森林）。②

深层生态学认为，生态系统的每一存在物都具有内在均等价值，即便是非生命物体，如山脉与河流，也有其内在价值。在沈从文与福克纳的作品中，我们同样可以看到这种深层生态理念的形象化表述。

在他们的笔下，自然界的动植物，不再被看成一种非人类的存在物，

---

① 沈从文：《论闻一多的死水》，《沈从文文集》第 11 卷，花城出版社 1984 年版，第 151 页。
② 参见李文俊编《福克纳的神话》，上海译文出版社 2008 年版，第 60 页。

而是被视为具有内在价值的生命个体。沈从文的《凤子》中，宁静的杉树，被誉为树中之王，它"常年披上深绿鸟羽形的叶子作成一种向天空极力伸去的风度"，杉树被赋予了人的品格，"那种风度是那么高，同时还那么高不可企及"。即便是树中并不名贵的杨栗树，也是一派"倔强朴野的气质，闪着乌金色的光泽"。而在福克纳的著名短篇小说《熊》中，多年被追逐杀害的大熊则被描写成一个爱与崇敬的对象，它身上似乎有一种灵性，它显得那么神圣、伟大，像慈祥的上帝出现在森林中。在猎人眼里，这头老熊"是一个从已逝的古老年代里残留下来的顽强不屈、无法征服的时代错误的产物，是旧时蛮荒生活的一个幻影，一个缩影与神话的典型"。它不仅是熊，是"熊司令"，他为自己争取到了只有一个人才配享有的名字。福克纳的另一部小说《村子》，还写了一个名字叫艾克·斯诺普斯的低能儿与一头母牛朱诺之间深厚的感情。小说中几次写到朱诺"那温暖的、巨大的、湿润的乳房"，从那里，"那强劲的、取之不尽的生命汁液不断从生命深处涌出"。而备受世俗白眼的艾克在母牛朱诺那里得到的不仅是甘甜的乳汁，更是一种女性的、温暖的东西。他也因此把朱诺看成心目中的女王，用他那笨拙的手，为她编织花环。小说把艾克这一生活中的低能儿写成最接近自然的人，而世俗社会中的成功者弗莱姆——一个冷酷无情的新兴资产阶级的代表人物，则被刻画成一个自然的对立物。

即便是同样表现自然生态，沈从文与福克纳审视的视角也存在着差异性。沈从文更多展示的是自然生态美丽、茁壮的一面。对他来说，他印象中和回忆中理想的湘西世界，是一个充满生命"茁壮美"的世界，这是湘西自然风物世界中生物形象的特质，这生命的"茁壮美"与湘西人在同样的环境下形成的生命的发展性和进取精神是一致的，而与他生活的污浊、恶劣的城市世界形成鲜明对照。沈从文的价值取向即是以与自然契合作为衡量尺度。而福克纳则在表现自然美的伟大之外，还同时呈现了自然并不让人感到赏心悦目的另一面。沈从文笔下最美好的春天，则被福克纳描述为："一切都同时来临，杂乱无章，毫无次序：果子、花朵与树叶，色泽斑驳的牧场，鲜花盛开的树林，以及从冬眠中被推开的犁头推成一个个黑长条的田野。"他在《我弥留之际》中说："所有的一切，天气也好，别的也好，都拖延得太长。像我们的河流，也像我们的土地：混浊、缓慢、狂暴；这使得南方人的生活也那么不能平静、郁郁寡欢。"福克纳认为，"这就是南方的症结所在"。在此，"天气""河流""土地"不再被视为美的载体，而是现实世界混乱和狂暴的隐喻性象征。因而，福克纳笔下的自然生态呈现出两重性。

二

从沈从文与福克纳作品所表现的社会生态视角来看，它们在以自然作为批判现代文明的价值尺度上，表现出相当程度的一致性。在沈从文所呈现的湘西世界和都市世界、福克纳所展示的沙多里斯和斯诺普斯两极世界中，我们发现他们都极力肯定代表自然价值的前者，否定体现物质文明的后者。

沈从文和福克纳同处于农业文明向近现代工业文明过渡的历史转折期，正是社会处于大动荡的变革时期。他们对现代文明在情感上都有一种本能的反感和憎恶，认为现代人对物质利益的过分追求，扭曲了自然的人性，造成了人的阉割或人性的异化，他们不约而同地把目光投向自然，以期在未被文明污染的自然中找到疗救现代文明的方案。

沈从文所建构的湘西世界是他艺术创作的源泉，也是他抗拒现代都市世界的一个理想境界。而这一"湘西世界"的典型特征是它的自然化特质。在沈从文创作的诸多小说和散文《湘行散记》中，对自然神的膜拜与信仰成为湘西文化的普遍性观念。与之相一致的是以敬神谢土、人与自然契合为内容的社会风俗系统的形成。这种自然化的人生形式是沈从文最为推崇、最为向往的理想化的人生形式。他在谈到《边城》的写作动机时说，他在《边城》中所要表现的是"一种人生形式"，"一种优美、健康、自然而又不悖乎人性的人生形式"。这种"优美、健康、自然而又不悖乎人性的人生形式"，就是一种合乎自然生态的人生形式。自然的人化产生了对自然神的信仰，而湘西人在对自然神的信仰中，也呈现出自然化的特质。湘西小说创造了一系列代表湘西自然人格的形象。而这些代表了湘西自然人格的形象所体现出的人格魅力就是他们"情感的素朴和观念的单纯"。因而，他们之间的人际关系极为简单、纯朴。人与人之间的交往更重义而非利。在《长河》中，橘子在当地"只许吃不肯卖"，而在《船上岸上》中，卖梨子的妇人因为我们多付给她钱，趁我们不备，又多添给我们一堆梨。在《柏子》中，即便是吊脚楼的妓女，更看重的也是与水手之间的情和爱，而不是利。湘西小说的两性关系更是一种与自然生命形式相适应的自然人生形式。在《龙朱之恋》《神巫之恋》和《媚金之爱》中，我们看到了两性关系在未遭到金钱与权力扭曲下的自然性和纯洁性。在《雨后》《采厥》《媚金·豹子与那羊》《月下小景》中，这些动人的爱情小说，合乎自然、顺乎人性的自然情欲得到了尽情渲染，爱情被视为一种自然、热烈的、灵肉融合的生命燃烧。

由金钱和权力所支配的反自然的都市社会生态则是沈从文猛烈抨击、讽刺讥笑的对象。他把现代都市文化培养出来的"有教养"的城市人称为"阉宦似的隐形人格"，萎靡、虚伪是他们的共性。在唯利是图、自私庸俗的市侩人生观支配下，他们的情感、生命力被金钱和权势所压制，日趋萎顿。沈从文认为这种生命形式是只有生活，而没有"生命"的"阉割"，对一切美，皆毫无反映，漠然处之，是一种丧失生命爱与美的生活方式。在《八骏马》《焕乎先生》《或人的太太》《某夫妇》等小说中，沈从文均展示了这种萎靡、困顿的都市社会生态图景。

而福克纳的作品也展示了代表自然力量的沙多里斯，以及代表现代机械文明的斯诺普斯两个世界的矛盾冲突。其中，福克纳所肯定的是前者，是那些生活在沙多里斯世界里与自然性情接近的人们，因为在他们身上体现了大自然所要求的"勇敢、谦逊、忍耐、牺牲"等法则。他欣赏他们身上表现出来的纯洁、质朴的本性，他们之间融洽的关系，以批判代表商业社会的斯诺普斯唯利是图，把人变成机器附属品、破坏自然的弊端。斯诺普斯是福克纳猛烈抨击的对象，他们代表了现代机械文明唯利是图的物质主义者。其中《圣殿》中"金鱼眼"式的人物以他们失去人性成为现代文明的象征。在小说中，福克纳把"金鱼眼"描写成两只眼睛像两个橡皮球，是"一个具有冲压过的铁皮那种邪恶的肤浅的品质的假货"，这个人

"赚了钱不知怎么花，也没处花，因为他既没有朋友，也没有结识过一个女人"。因而"金鱼眼"式的人物是一个失去了人性的金融资本主义社会的存在物。而其失去人性的一个突出标志，就是他们对自然所采取的疏离、仇视、掠夺式的态度。福克纳认为，那些对自然抱着错误态度的人们是纯粹的开拓者，他们虽然可以得到对所攫取东西的使用权，却不真正拥有它。福克纳通过这类人物讽喻现代机械文明对自然所采取的敌意态度导致的人性异化。

沈从文与福克纳同样对现代文明持否定、批判态度，但沈从文更侧重于从反自然的人性角度来反思现代都市文明的弊端，认为现代都市人远离自然，过于追求私利，其人性萎靡、困顿皆是由于违背自然所成，其生活是一种反自然的异化状态。沈从文对现代文明的批判，主要立足于此。福克纳抨击美国现代文明的矛头，则直接指向现代文明对自然的掠夺和蹂躏。他认为，美国现代工业文明的发展，是以破坏森林和杀戮异己创造出来的，是丑陋和堕落的，是把人类自己朝毁灭方向上推。他认为，现代文明"是朝着资本主义对全人类有价值的东西进行掠夺式的毁灭的方向走去"①。在《森林三部曲》中，借艾萨克之口，他曾痛心地说："他糟蹋的森林、田野，以及他蹂躏的猎物将成为他的罪行和罪恶的后果与证据。"因而福克纳更侧重于从批判人对自然无节制的开发、掠夺这一现代生态学的视角，抨击现代文明的弊端，从这个意义上说，福克纳的观点更贴近现代生态学的主张。

沈从文与福克纳各自在作品中描写了特定地域人们的生存状态，但他们更为关注的是人类的精神状态问题。沈从文把培养理想的人性作为自己一生追求的目标。在他看来，最美的精神生态是一种"优美、健康、自然而又不悖乎人性"的精神状态。福克纳也通过他的作品，一直在进行道德探索，试图找到代表"勇气、荣誉、希望、自豪、同情、怜悯"等精神力量的理想道德范式。对人类精神生态的反思和重构，使沈从文和福克纳站在人类文化的制高点上，对人类的本体性存在进行更深层次的思考。

---

① 李文俊编:《福克纳评论集》，中国社会科学出版社 1980 年版，第 154 页。

三

沈从文所推崇、敬仰的人性，是一种自然化的人性，这种人性质朴、纯洁、雄强而富有生命活力，是一种生命自由、伸展的自在状态。对人性问题的思索可以说是贯穿沈从文作品的一条主线。沈从文终生把培养理想的人性作为自己创作的宗旨，他说："这世界上或许有想在沙基上或水面上建造崇楼杰阁的人，那不是我。我只想建造希腊人性小庙。选山地作基础，用坚硬的石头堆砌它。精致、结实、匀称，形体虽小而不纤巧，是我理想的建筑。这神庙供奉的是人性。"① 而沈从文所追求并倡导的人性，是一种与自然相契合，呈现着活泼的自然本性的人性，是一种健康、单纯、真挚、纯朴的人性。无论是在《凤子》《神巫之爱》《龙朱》《月下小景》等描写远古湘西神秘美丽爱情的故事中，还是在反映真实湘西农村生活的《边城》《长河》《柏子》《雨后》《阿黑小史》《采蕨》《旅店》等小说中，我们随处可见媚金、豹子、滩佑、翠翠、夭夭、柏子这些秉承自然造化的"自然人"。他们同自然风物一样单纯、质朴，跃动着生命的活力。他们"是光、是热、是泉水、是果子、是宇宙的万有"。他们大都诚实拙朴、勇敢健壮、生命力旺盛、敢作敢当、不虚伪、不矫饰，体现的是一种自然、健康、具有生命活力的精神生态。

与湘西人自然化的健康人性相反，沈从文笔下都市人的精神状态则是反自然的、病态的。他们"懒惰、拘谨、小气，全部都是营养不足、睡眠不足、生殖力不足"的生命萎靡者，他们的生活是一种违反了自然法则、生态失衡状态下的人生形式。他们表现出一种处于异化状态的精神生态。

如果说沈从文一直致力于从湘西世界寻求完美的人性，福克纳则试图在美国南方传统中找回"人类古老的优秀品质"。在他著名的诺贝尔文学奖获奖演讲中，他拒绝接受"人类末日的说法"，而是满怀信心地宣布：

---

① 沈从文：《沈从文文集》第 11 卷，花城出版社 1984 年版，第 42 页。

"我相信人类不但会苟且地生存下去，他们还能蓬勃发展。人是不朽的，并非在生物中唯独他留有绵延不绝的声音，而是人有灵魂，有能够怜悯、牺牲和耐劳的精神，而作家的职责就在于写出这些东西，提醒人们记住勇气、荣誉、希望、自豪、同情、怜悯之心和牺牲精神，这些是人类昔日的荣耀。"① 与沈从文所追求的自然人性不同的是，福克纳更推崇"忍耐、怜悯、同情、牺牲"等这些人类优秀的道德品质，更强调人类摆脱、超越动物性欲求的道德升华。

福克纳通过他的诸多作品，向我们展示了从传统向现代转型历史时期美国南方人的种种精神生态。其中，《圣殿》中的金鱼眼，《斯诺普斯三部曲》中的弗莱姆，《喧哗与骚动》中的杰生体现了商业社会拜金主义者的冷酷无情、自私自利。《喧哗与骚动》中的昆丁，《押沙龙，押沙龙》中的洛莎小姐，《纪念爱米丽的一朵玫瑰花》中的爱米丽则陷入了另一类精神状态，他们沉迷于传统世界或自我世界而不能自拔，以自我麻醉来逃避现实世界。而福克纳最为欣赏的则是像迪尔西、朱迪斯、斯蒂文士、拉特克利夫等具有"古老的优秀品质"的人物，因为在他们身上，真正体现了人类最卓越的精神生态，即福克纳反复强调的"勇气、荣誉、希望、自豪、同情、怜悯和牺牲"等体现了自然法则的价值观，一种他所说的"心灵的真理"。在《熊》中，麦卡斯林诵读了一段五节诗："她消失不了，虽然你也得不到你的幸福，你将永远爱恋，而她将永远娇美。"作为孩子的艾萨克问他诗中是否讲的是一个姑娘的事情，麦卡斯林却说："他讲的是关于真理的事——荣誉、自豪、怜悯、正义、勇敢和爱。"福克纳把真理比喻为一个永远年轻、娇美的姑娘，并且认为它永远不会消失，体现了他探索永恒的精神力量的信心。

在中国现代文学史中，沈从文的作品曾被冠以落后、守旧之名，他的湘西小说因为无法被整合到一个以"革命"为主题的文学式结构中而长期处于被遗忘和忽视的状态。而福克纳也因其过分强调美国南方传统的价值观、同情南方人的命运而被视为保守者。沈从文与福克纳成为20世纪世界

---

① 李文俊编：《福克纳评论集》，中国社会科学出版社1980年版，第255页。

文学"回归自然"与"回归传统"浪潮中的代表性作家。这种"向后看的历史意识"曾一度被认为是一种保守和退步。但我们今天以现代生态学的眼光来看，或许能得出一个相反的结论，这一回归的姿态也许更是一种超前的眼光，它主张人与自然的和谐、统一，以使生命获得最大限度的自由、舒展；强调恢复传统中与自然同质的、最具有生命力的精神力量以拯救现代文明所造成的人性的偏枯和愚钝。从这个意义上说，它提供的方案是对现代文明偏颇的超越，这也正是当今现代生态学所要倡议的立场，它也会成为 21 世纪一个充分展开的话题。

（原载于《东岳论丛》2003 年第 7 期，被《中国现代文学研究丛刊》2004 年第 2 期收录为目录索引，内容有增补）

后现代视野中的沈从文与福克纳小说

后现代主义是一种在西方 20 世纪后半叶曾产生了广泛影响的社会文化思潮，其中"后现代性"问题，成为后现代主义的一个核心命题。但从广义上看，"后现代性"并不仅仅是一个时间性概念，而体现了一种新的理论价值取向，这表现在它与现代性的分野上。"后现代性"表面看来与"现代性"仅一字之差，表示的却是对现代性的背离、转向、超越和竞争性互补。正如我国学者王岳川所指出的那样，后现代的"后"字意义有两重，一是要超越和压抑现代主义本身，二是表明时代的线性发展已使现代主义过时。①

后现代主义对现代性的批判首先表现在它对现代文明的畸形发展所导致的现代性内涵蜕变的反思上。它认为启蒙以来的现代思想以人类全体、以自由为目标，然而社会以单一目标为旨归就会产生对异端的压制和摧残。理性对社会的总体设计，造成了操纵和压制个体的意愿与行为的结果。在物质领域表现为人与社会、人与人之间、人的思想与机能都被物质化、一体化；在精神领域则造成了人的道德沦丧、人性泯灭以及精神的单调、空虚这一现代性的严重问题。

其次，在理论层面上，在对现代性的解构中，后现代主义反对（否定和超越）现代性所支持的中心主义、一元论和决定论，而倡导非本质主义、多元论、不确定性和差异性。利奥塔号召："让我们向整体性开战；让我们成为那不可表现之物的见证人；让我们继续开发各种差异性并为维

---

① 参见王岳川《后现代主义文化研究》，北京大学出版社 1992 年版。

护'差异性'的声誉而努力。"① 而另一位后现代主义的代表人物德里达则运用解构的方法批驳了逻各斯中心主义，通过颠覆现代性关于中心与边缘的二元结构模式，指出二元模式的次序不是固定不变的，中心优于边缘的地位是虚假的。并且，他通过解读文本，强调意义的多向性、不确定性，颠倒结构的中心和边缘的关系，消除结构中一切确定和固定的东西。

正是在这样一种后现代理论视野中，我们看到了沈从文与福克纳所共同呈现出的一种对现代性的反思。本章运用后现代的理论主要从以下三个角度对两位作家进行比较：其一，现代性之反思。其二，对边缘文化的关注。其三，偶然性与不确定性这两个后现代的变量函数在两位作家文本中的凸显。

一　现代性之批判

沈从文与福克纳不约而同地表现出一种对以现代性为特征的现代文明强烈的厌恶与反感的姿态，这不是乡下人守旧的心态，而是体现了超前的眼光。在现代工商文明初露端倪之时，他们就敏锐地看到了现代性的负面影响，从而表达了对现代性的一种批判性反思和质疑，这无疑是一种后现代的眼光。

沈从文与福克纳都对以现代性为特征的现代文明极为反感，他们均采取了批判、抨击的姿态。他们都多次声称自己的农民身份，以乡下人身份自居，其中暗含了他们对现代城市文明的抵触情绪。"乡下人"就字面意义来看，包含一种与现代文明对立的意味。沈从文和福克纳始终以一个乡下人的心态来审视现代文明，这种审视使他们与现代文明始终保持一种距离，对以现代性为特征的时代主流文化保持一种本能的疏离。现代商业文明是建立在以利益、功利为原则的组织结构中，它追逐物质利益与现代生活的舒适与奢华，但也因此把现代人引向对物欲的单向度的追求中而导致

---

① 刘放桐：《后现代主义与西方哲学的现代走向》，《国外社会科学》1996 年第 2 期。

精神蜕化、道德滑坡。沈从文与福克纳对现代文明的负面作用的批判和反思主要立足于此。

沈从文在都市世界里，洞见的不是文明与进步，而是人性的茬弱、生命力的萎缩、都市上流社会的堕落与无耻，以及各色都市人的无聊、空虚、浅薄、庸俗、愚蠢。沈从文始终以一个"愤怒青年"（金介甫语）的姿态面对都市生活，他对代表现代文明的都市上流社会的批判是严厉和尖刻的。同沈从文一样，福克纳也非常憎恶现代工商文明在内战后南方的崛起和对南方的侵袭。在他的第一部以约克纳帕塔法为题材的小说《沙多里斯》中，他把沙多里斯家庭的主要变故归咎于现代科技。拉贝亚特猝死在被老贝亚特称为"毒蛇"的汽车里。小贝亚特开快车事故不断，最后死在飞机上。现代文明带给沙多里斯家族的是其家庭成员接连不断地死于现代科技的代表物汽车、飞机等事故中，这实际上反映了福克纳对现代文明的批判与嘲讽态度。

对道德退步的二律背反现象的揭示上，他们均在作品中揭示了现代文明进程中所引发的人的精神蜕化问题。

沈从文以他独特的"乡下人"视角，发现了经济进步与道德倒退之间的深刻矛盾，洞察了现代都市文明对人性的侵蚀，以及由此导致的人性扭曲，进而对之予以猛烈抨击。沈从文认为，金钱所支配的城市世界的人生形式，扭曲了人性，形成了现代城市所独有的生命形式："阉寺型"人格，它是城市绅士阶级的典型性格，虚伪和生命力萎靡是这种由现代城市文化培养出的"阉宦似的隐性人格"的共性。

总之，沈从文尖锐地揭示出现代都市人在唯实唯利、自私庸俗的市侩人生观支配下，情感为权势萎缩，个性被财富压瘪和扭曲，生命力因只满足于追求物质享受而日渐萎靡、退化的事实。

福克纳在他的约克纳帕塔法世系小说中，同样鞭挞了沉溺于物质主义追求，而丧失一切道德准则的南方新兴资产阶级。这类新兴资产阶级来自两个阵营。其中一个阵营是南方社会的穷白人，另一阵营则是北方人。穷白人本来处于南方社会的底层，由于善于钻营和投机取巧，在社会中的地位不断上升。福克纳对这一类人充满厌恶之情，把他们刻画成邪恶、无知、冷酷残忍、为物质利益所驱使而不惜做出极端损人利己之事、毫无道德感的人物。《喧哗与骚动》中的达尔顿·艾米斯、《圣殿》中的"金鱼眼"，以及福克纳的诸多小说中反复描写的"斯诺普斯们"，都是这类穷白人的形象。《喧哗与骚动》中，引诱凯蒂走向堕落的是一个叫达尔顿·艾米斯的穷白人，拐走小昆丁的同样是一个打着红领结的戏班里的"穷白人"。另外，福克纳的一些短篇小说，则着重刻画了穷白人的代表性人物"斯诺普斯们"为了追逐钱财，而坑蒙拐骗，甚至杀人放火的恶劣行径。《烧马棚》中的斯诺普斯就是这样一个为了一己之利而无恶不作的穷白人形象。小说深刻揭露了资本之中蕴含的残酷本质："是多少愤恨、残忍、渴望，才哺育出这样一腔血？"对物欲的渴望和追逐，导致了斯诺普斯们的疯狂和残忍。其他小说如《花斑马》《黄铜怪物》同样讽刺了弗莱姆·斯诺普斯的狡诈阴险、唯利是图。后来福克纳在长篇小说《村子》中再次把这些关于弗莱姆·斯诺普斯的发迹史的故事搬了进去，以讽刺现代新兴资产者的唯利是图、冷酷无情。斯诺普斯主义现已成为一个英语词汇，用来指称那些为追逐物质利益而不惜使用任何手段，不顾及任何道德准则的人。

上文主要从三个方面分析了沈从文与福克纳对现代文明的批判，但同时我们看到，由于沈从文与福克纳生活在中美两个不同国家，其现代化的发展存在着相当大的时间差，从而决定了他们对现代性反思角度的差异性。沈从文生活的时代，是现代文明在中国的发展还很不充分的时期，沈从文主要从人性扭曲的角度批判现代文明，侧重于对现代文明发展前期所暴露的负面性的抨击，而福克纳则对现代文明发展后期由工具理性所导致的人性堕落及人的本质的失落现象进行了深刻的反思。

在 20 世纪上半叶，现代文明在中国正处于初始发展阶段。而对于从湘西世界奔向现代都市寻求现代文化的沈从文来说，他所看到的更多不是现代文明带来的文明与进步，而是都市文明对人性的扭曲。在他的一系列都市小说如《绅士的太太》《八骏图》《大小沅》《岚生同岚生太太》《来客》《有学问的人》《如蕤》中，沈从文展示了一幅幅生活于现代都市的人们道德衰败和人性扭曲的连轴图卷。从世俗的观念看，这些衣冠楚楚的绅士淑女，是社会的"中坚"，"社会一物是由这些人支持的"（《烛虚·潜渊》）。沈从文却在这些所谓的代表都市文明的上层人物身上，透过他们的"聪明"见出其"虚伪"，透过他们的"文明"见出其"肮脏"，透过他们的"稳重"见出其"庸鄙"。《岚生同岚生太太》中夫妻之间的关系完全消耗在毫无意义、平庸无聊的心机算计里。《某夫妇》里的某绅士为了弄钱，竟让自己的妻子接待男客，而且要"既不上当又能得到钱"，其结果是"赔了夫人又折兵"。《绅士的太太》里所展示的上流社会的生活，也不过是在打牌、调情、贿赂、瞒骗等无聊的事情上消耗生命。《八骏图》里的教授们也无一不因顾及文明道德而压抑其自然欲望。总之，沈从文对现代性的批判主要立足于此。

而福克纳却着重于从现代性发展后期的工具理性压抑、束缚人性的角度对现代文明进行反思与批判。由于西方现代化的进程要远远超前于中国，福克纳生活的时代，现代性的发展已充分展开，处于发展的成熟期，它暴露的现代性的弊端也非常突出，故福克纳深刻揭示了现代工具理性桎梏人的自由个性，现代人过分追求物质利益，以至导致人性堕落及人与人之间关系恶化等弊病。上面已谈到，福克纳认为现代文明直接催发了没有任何道德准则、唯利是图的斯诺普斯们的产物，现代文明使他们变成只满足于追求物质利益的单向度的空心人，故福克纳喜欢用冷冰冰的、没有任何情感和思想的机械物形象来比拟现代工具理性对人性的压抑。《圣殿》中的"金鱼眼"及福克纳诸多小说中的斯诺普斯们都是这样的人物。此外，福克纳还深刻洞见了现代人性的堕落及人与人之间关系的恶化。在《喧哗与骚动》《圣殿》《我弥留之际》等小说中，他都深刻揭示了现代社会的精神荒原状况及人的本质的失落。

二 对边缘文化之关注

后现代性主义反对中心主义，强调差异性，主张多元论。后现代精神的一个核心内容，即表现为解构中心、重视边缘的解构意识。沈从文与福克纳的作品正体现了这种后现代主义精神。在解构、批判现代性所代表的主流价值观的同时，他们不约而同地把关注的目光投向为主流文化所压制和摧残的边缘文化。苗人与黑人在湘西和南方世界中一直是弱势群体，长期以来，他们一直遭受主流文化的迫害，沈从文与福克纳的作品均反映了这两个弱势群体遭受主流文化压制的事实。沈从文在谈到自己的家乡凤凰城时，认为它是一个"古怪的地方"，这一小镇的诞生，"只由于两百年前满人治理中国土地时，为镇抚与虐杀残余苗族，派遣了一队戍族屯兵驻扎，方有了城堡与居民"。这个仅有三四千人口的"边疆孤城"的四周，竟有"五百左右的碉堡，二百左右的营讯"。而这些碉堡与营讯，竟是为了解决退守一隅常作"蠢动"的边苗"叛变"而设的。

沈从文童年时期亲身经历的一次苗人谋反惨遭杀害的事件，更是在他的脑海中留下了永久的烙印。这次事件记录在《从文自传》中的《辛亥革命的一课》中。沈从文以稚子之心体会到了这场杀戮的残酷与愚蠢，这使他对苗人的处境有了更切身的了解。沈从文对苗族人的命运和特殊遭际深表同情。

同沈从文笔下的湘西世界的苗民一样，美国南方的黑人同样是一个被迫害的弱势群体。在南方贵族文化主流价值观中，黑人只是白人的工具、商品和财产，与牲畜无异。罗莎小姐（《押沙龙，押沙龙》）眼中的黑人是"一群恶性十足的野鬼"，是"半驯化的跟人一样直立行走的野兽"，在《去吧，摩西》中，一个白人警官竟这样诽谤黑人："他们简直可以说是一群可诅咒的野牛。"在白人贵族眼中，黑人不但没有独立的人格、没有主体意识，而且简直是牲畜、商品，是供人享乐的物体，是满足性欲的工具。

然而，沈从文和福克纳却发掘了苗人与黑人身上独特的精神品格和文化资源。沈从文笔下的苗人与福克纳描写的黑人都具有纯朴、正直、勤劳的优秀品格。

在《阿丽思中国游记》中，沈从文把苗族塑造为一个天真朴实的民族。苗族人具有孩童般的心灵，他们单纯，不懂权术，被汉人讥笑为"无知"和"呆"。但沈从文却认为他们的文化空白，恰恰构成了他们的道德优势。

　　在他的另一部小说《龙朱》中，沈从文以敬仰之情把白耳族中苗族人族长的儿子龙朱塑造成一个"人中模型"，"是权威，是力，是光"。他还追溯自己的家族与苗族的关系，一方面以此为荣，另一方面却慨叹自己久居于都市，所秉承的苗族人身上一些优秀的品格逐渐被现代都市文明所吞噬。"血管里流着你们民族健康的血液的我，二十七年的生命，有一半为都市生活所吞噬，中着在道德下所变成虚伪庸懦的大毒，所有值得称为高贵的性格，如像那热情，与勇敢，与诚实，早已完全消失殆尽，再也不配说出是出自你们一族了。"沈从文以处于边缘地位的苗族文化来反拨处于主流地位的汉民族都市文化，他认为汉民族主流文化"虚伪庸懦"，在道德上劣于具有"热情、勇敢与诚实"等高尚精神品格的苗族文化。他自愧自己长期生活在都市，灵魂久被汉文化的都市生活所侵蚀，苗族人所给予他的勇敢、热情的血性已荡然无存。

　　沈从文所表现的苗民的精神气质与汉族人有很大不同。苗族人具有乐观开朗、自由开放、不重物质的精神气质。他们较少受人为的道德观的约束，养成了一种个性自由无羁、率性而为的种族特征。尽管平日耕作劳苦，在节日及农闲时，苗族人通过举行庆祝活动和宗教典仪，尽情狂欢和娱乐，放纵自己的情感。苗族妇女的地位要比汉族妇女地位高，她们较少受各种成规的约束，在性关系和日常交往中享有更多的自由。因此，欧洲的传教士把苗族人描写成比汉族人更加富有感情，更加直率，可塑性更强的民族。沈从文所塑造的湘西人，在很大程度上是以苗民为原型的。他力图通过艺术创作发掘苗族人的开放、自由、质朴的性格之优长，为重塑汉族人民族品格注入新鲜血液。

　　沈从文从苗族人身上看到了汉族人所缺乏的生命力和道德，并且在他们更为开放、率真的民族性格中发现了更契合人性的生活方式和精神气质，特别是苗族人自由、浪漫、开放的性爱文化，为他的艺术创作提供了丰厚的土壤。沈从文小说中所表现的男女之间大胆、自由的性爱关系成为他作品的一个显著特点。在中国汉民族性道德极为刻板、僵硬的体制下，沈从文艺术世界中所表现的开放、自由的性爱观使他与20世纪中国现代文学史上的其他乡土作家迥然相异。其中，苗族特殊的性爱文化对他产生的影响很大。

福克纳也在揭示黑人所遭受的种族歧视与迫害的同时，不但重塑了黑人的形象，而且挖掘了黑人身上所具有的真诚、善良、纯朴等优秀品质。在这些南方社会边缘人身上，福克纳甚至看到了新的希望。

福克纳塑造了数以百计的黑人群体。尽管他有时把黑人写成滑稽、可笑的人物，也曾嘲笑过他们，可他塑造了一系列"好黑鬼"形象。这一人物系列中有《喧哗与骚动》中的迪尔西、《没有消失的》中的卢万妮娅、《沙多里斯》中的爱尔诺娜与《去吧，摩西》中的莫莉，他（她）们共同的性格特点是正直、忠厚、诚实、勇敢、吃苦耐劳。在这些黑人人物中，《喧哗与骚动》里的迪尔西可以说是一个典范。福克纳曾说："迪尔西是我所喜爱的人物之一，因为她勇敢、大胆、慷慨、温柔和诚实，她永远比我勇敢和诚实和慷慨。"① 他后来在为这部小说写的"引言"中说："迪尔西代表着未来。"《喧哗与骚动》并不仅仅是一个关于康普生家族分崩离析、走向解体的故事，它是关于整个南方道德的寓言故事。它象征着旧南方传统道德的衰微和新兴资产阶级道德的邪恶。而康普生家中的黑人奴仆迪尔西在这个四分五裂的，缺乏爱、温情与幸福的家庭中，却在"维持着一切"。与冷酷无情、自私自利、缺乏母性的康普生太太形成鲜明对比，迪尔西在受尽歧视与凌辱的凯蒂及小昆丁母女，以及可怜的白痴班吉等人身上，倾注了母亲般的慈爱。她还具有鲜明的是非观念、疾恶如仇，在同杰生的恶行做斗争中，她毫不畏惧，表现出非凡的勇气。在康普生家庭道德沦丧，处于四分五裂的情形下，她用人类伟大的良知苦苦支撑着一个破败的世界。无疑，福克纳在她身上寄寓了一种道德力量，寄寓了正直、诚实、勇敢、慷慨、温柔等优秀品格，而福克纳把这些优秀品质赋予一个黑人身上，表明了他对一再遭到扭曲的黑人形象的重构。

我们看到，沈从文与福克纳对苗族人和黑人这两个弱势群体寄予了很大的同情，修正了他们被扭曲、被误读的形象，并挖掘了他们独特的精神

---

① Meriwether James B. and Milligate Michael, eds. *Lion in the Garden*, New York: Random House, 1968, p. 224.

品格和文化资源。然而，由于沈从文具有平民意识，福克纳则具有贵族思想，这使他们在对苗族人和黑人的情感倾向上又有差异性。

而福克纳的思想中则带有贵族意识。尽管他对黑人遭受歧视和迫害的处境深表同情，也发掘了黑人独特的道德品格，但由于他的白人贵族身份，他对黑人的审视态度就不是平视，而是俯视。他强烈谴责种族制度，却不主张废除奴隶制度，试图用一种美好的主仆关系来取代奴隶制的残忍。因而，他塑造了一系列黑人忠仆形象，所有这些黑人的特点都是顺从、忠诚，对于那些不安分守己、渴望自由的黑人，他则把他们刻画成"坏黑鬼"的滑稽形象予以嘲笑。

三 "偶然性"与"不确定性"

后现代性理论的一个根本特征是反对本质主义，它认为在所谓本质的背面，站立的是偶然、机遇、运气和莫名其妙的荒诞性。其次，差异性是后现代性的另一律令。差异打破了一切绝对性和统一性，差异让事物返回事物本身，从而避免了对事物评定的所谓权威和绝对标准。在阅读沈从文的作品时，我们时而感到一抹浓重的宿命论色彩，偶然性作为一个不速之客，经常光顾他的诸多小说，从而使小说中人物的命运、故事的情节发生逆转。而福克纳的作品则表现为主题的不确定性。他的重要作品如《押沙龙，押沙龙》《喧哗与骚动》《我弥留之际》都具有这种特点。在这些作品中，福克纳没有强加给小说一个权威的声音或一个统一的意义，相反，小说中的人物不仅独立于作者的意识，而且每个人的"声音不仅相互平等"，而且"保持着他们的独特个性"。偶然性与不确定性，这两个后现代性的变量函数，分别在沈从文与福克纳的作品中凸显出来。

沈从文的生活充满了传奇色彩。他的一生见过太多美丽生命的毁灭和千奇百怪的毁灭方式，命运的偶然性和随之而来的沉痛伴随着沈从文走过了他的生命历程，以至于他在七十岁生日时发出了"浮沉半世纪，生存亦偶然"的感怀。① 沈从文的作品更是凸显了命运的偶然性这一命题。他在对人生进行思考时，其哲学观中带有浓厚的东方宿命论色彩。沈从文自己解释说："这或许是属于我本人来源古老民族气质上的固有弱点，又或许只是来自外部生命受尽挫伤的一种反映现象。"在他的诸多作品中，偶然性的突转成为诸多生命的毁灭形式，人的命运在这种无形的偶然性大手的操纵下，似乎丧失了理性把握与控制的力量。这种宿命观在许多研究者看来带有消极的宿命论色彩。但如果我们把其放在后现代的理论视野中来审视，便发现它或许更符合历史的本真状态。福柯认为，对于人类和知识而言，人不是最常见也不是最古老的存在体，人只是近期的一个知识的发明，人的出现，人的产生及有关人的全部概念和知识体系只是在漫长的历史长河的某些瞬间诞生的，他只是偶然性的产物。那么这种漫长的历史也是片断式的、不可预料的、断裂的，历史充满着机遇与偶然性。从这一角度来看，沈从文对这种人生偶然性的揭示，更契合历史的原生态。

从沈从文开始小说创作的 20 年代中后期，他的作品就零星地以不同的方式表达了对命运无法把握的悲哀情绪。在这些回忆性的小说如《黎明》《堂兄》《记陆涛》中，正文部分多写"生"之鲜活强健，补记部分则写"死"之偶然与莫名其妙。堂兄被错杀，水性很好的陆涛被偶然淹死，而叔远的死因尚未交代。这种补记总是如此简洁有力地凸显出生与死的反差与死亡的偶然性。

此外，沈从文创作的其他作品如《初八那日》《石子船》《媚金·豹子与那羊》《边城》与《八骏图》也频频表现了偶然性所带来的命运的无常，偶然性在沈从文笔下似乎成了主宰人物命运的一只无形的手。

在 20 世纪 40 年代的思想性小说和哲理散文中，沈从文进一步表达了他对偶然性这一命题的思考。《水云——我怎样创造故事，故事怎样创造我》是沈从文关于创作与生命的一个注释。在其中贯穿着两种对立声音：一个是"对生命有计划有理性有信心的我"，而另一个则是"宿命论中不可知的我"。但在思考感性与理性，偶然与必然，不可知与可知等问题时，

---

① 沈从文：《沈从文文集》第 10 卷，花城出版社 1991 年版，第 359 页。

他认定前者似乎更具有左右人生的力量，沈从文同一时期创作的类似作品还有《烛虚》《潜渊》《长庚》《生命》《七色魇》等，其中无不交织着命运与理性，偶然与情感，听天由命与奋斗意志的冲突。

如果说偶然性成为沈从文作品中的一个变量函数，那么福克纳作品的另一个变量函数则为不确定性。与沈从文作品文本意义的单一性相比，福克纳作品的一个突出特点就是其意义的不确定性。这种不确定性使他的小说呈现出多元性和复杂性。福克纳的几部主要作品均表现出这种特征。

传统的小说，都试图给作品一个终极的意义，作品被视为一个有机的艺术整体，有一个统一的意义。福克纳的小说则表现出对这种统一意义的质疑和解构。这实际上也是后现代主义理论的一个基本精神。

譬如《押沙龙，押沙龙》这部小说围绕着斯德潘家族的兴衰史，通过小说中沙罗小姐、康普生先生、昆丁、史里夫等人对它的叙述展开。这样一个故事，不像传统小说那样按照故事发展的来龙去脉展开叙述，而是通过小说中的几个人物根据自己的情感因素、价值取向和各自不同的理解从不同的角度来解释、推测、解读，他们甚至用自己的想象来虚构出一些情节。在这部小说中，没有压倒一切的权威声音，每个叙述者的声音都是平等的，而且独立于作者的意识，作者也没有强加给作品一个权威的声音。

以上分别从"现代性之批判""对边缘文化之关注"及"偶然性与不确定性"三个层面比较分析了沈从文与福克纳作品中所呈现出的后现代性特征。我们看到"后现代性"并不仅仅是一个发生在现代性之后的时间性概念，而是体现了一种对现代性的批判、转向和超越。由此也就不难理解，尽管沈从文与福克纳生活、创作的年代距后现代主义思潮盛行的当下语境有很长时间段上的差距，然而其作品却体现了一种后现代精神，这也是他们作为伟大作家的超前性之所在。

（原载于《中国海洋大学学报》2005 年第 4 期）

试论沈从文与威廉·福克纳小说中的
文化特质及价值评判

　　中国作家沈从文与美国作家威廉·福克纳是20世纪产生了广泛世界影响的两位文学大师，他们都是终生耕耘着自己故乡的土地，通过表现故土生活而走向世界的作家。他们笔下的文学世界蕴含了迥然相异的中美地域文化与民族文化特质，深厚的地域与民族意识使两位作家把关注点投向中西本土文化的根基处，从中汲取宝贵的精神资源，并在此基础上对本土文化的价值进行了进一步的反思。

　　美国作家威廉·福克纳一生绝大部分时间都生活在美国南方小镇奥克斯福，并以这个小镇及周围地区作为自己所虚构的约克纳帕塔法世界的蓝本。美国南方的土壤、历史与文化养育了福克纳，耕耘在"约克纳帕塔法"那块"邮票般大小的土地"上，他在思索南方问题，乃至整个人类问题。他也因之在诺贝尔授奖词中被誉为"南方伟大的史诗作家"。

　　从一定意义上说，在现代文学史上，沈从文之所以成为一个"另类"作家，并因此赢得了世界声誉，一个重要的原因在于他通过文学开辟了一个新天地"湘西世界"。"湘西世界"和由此建构的价值观、情感倾向及独特的艺术呈现，成为中国现代文学史上一个具有丰富特质的文学存在体。

　　下文将具体分析"湘西世界"和"约克纳帕塔法"世系所呈现的中西地域文化与民族文化的特质及沈从文与福克纳对其文化特质的价值评判。

一　"湘西楚巫文化"与"南方庄园文化"

一个作家的养育之地是其创作之根基，反过来讲，作家则是地域文化的产物。任何一位成功的作家莫不是从一个特定的地域与时代出发，来反映生活的真谛。

沈从文多次谈到，他秉承的是一种南方楚巫文化的熏陶。楚文化充溢着原始的活力、狂放的意绪和自由奔放的热情，把人带入了一个充满奇异想象、神话传说、巫术观念的神秘世界，故沈从文的作品弥漫着一种浓郁的南方楚巫文化色彩。福克纳作为美国南方文学的集大成者，其作品深深打上了美国南方文化的烙印。他欣赏南方贵族文化所表现出来的优秀人文主义传统及优雅、浪漫的气质，敬仰他们富有开拓性、进取性、英勇、坚毅的精神品格。但对这种贵族文化所背负的沉重的历史负担和隐含的非人道异化力量则予以强烈的谴责和抨击。这两种文化源自中美两个国家不同的地区，各自受中美不同的社会、历史的影响，带有鲜明的地域文化特色，其差异性甚大。大致来说，这种差异性主要表现在以下两个方面。

1. "泛神论"与"加尔文教"

湘西楚巫文化和美国南方文化都强调对神或上帝的信仰，主张人与神或人与上帝之间的沟通，但在上述两种文化之中，两者之间的关系却迥然不同。中国楚巫文化的根基是"泛神论"，即信仰万物有灵，认为人与神之间可以相互沟通、交汇，乃至相互愉悦。因而，神在楚文化中被拟人化了，它更多代表一种自然神。神与人之间的关系是平等的，神生活在人们中间，人与神相悦，神成为湘西人诉诸愿望、倾诉情感的对象。这种宗教不仅可以使湘西人的心灵与情感得到平衡，而且形成了他们重个性、爱自由、重情感的个性气质。而美国南方庄园文化则建立在加尔文教的基础之上，与楚巫文化所洋溢的鲜活的"泛神论"迥然不同的是，在加尔文教中，上帝被置于高高在上、窥视人间罪恶的地位，是一种冷冰冰、至高无上的权威的象征，因此形成了南方文化的原罪情结。正是在这样的宗教文化氛围中，美国南方人的生活与情感遭到了压抑与摧残，个性自由遭到了遏制。

沈从文在《湘西·凤凰》中介绍凤凰城人们的宗教信仰时，曾提及楚文化的泛神观对凤凰人的影响。他说："大树、洞穴、岩石，无处不神。狐、虎、蛇、龟，无物不怪。神或怪在传说中美丑善恶不一，无不赋以人性。因而人与人相互爱悦，和当前道德观念极端冲突，便产生人和神怪爱悦的传说。"在湘西文化中，人神不但保持一种平等的关系，而且人神相互愉悦，人的情感在与神交会之中得到极大的宣泄。

而在美国南方，清教主义，特别是以加尔文教为核心的新教是支撑美国南方的社会、政治、文化，控制南方人思想与生活的一股主要力量。加尔文教强调人生来都是有罪的，人们必须依靠上帝不断摆脱心中的原罪，压制内心欲望，摒弃任何享受和娱乐。而南方在内战中的失败更是促成了各种新教在战后的发展。尽管福克纳信奉基督教，但他却强烈谴责南方的加尔文教，抨击其摧残人性的非人道本质，这反映在他的许多作品中。

2. 民间文化与贵族文化

楚巫文化是一种来自民间的文化，它带有民间文化特有的原始、自然、活泼的色彩，而南方庄园文化则是一种贵族文化，它强调庄园主的绝对权威地位，具有僵硬、反自然、强调等级制、专制残暴等特点。

楚文化带有清新、自然的民间文化特色。由楚巫宗教及与它共生的奇风异俗所形成的楚巫文化带有瑰奇、自然、原始性的色彩。楚巫文化固然因其占卜、神游、求女、祭祖等宗教仪式行为而具有神秘性，但从根本上说，它反映的是一种典型的民间文化诉求。湘西人之所以娱神，是因为他们感到人世有所不足，或是对生老病死的慨叹，或是对人间所思所爱不得，因而求之于神，故娱神的祭歌及庆典是湘西人民一种朴素愿望的倾诉和宣泄。

楚巫文化的民间性特点在湘西世界所弥漫的浓郁的乡风民俗中得到充分表现。在沈从文的湘西小说中，酉水岸边的吊脚楼、碾坊、碧溪岨的竹簧、白塔、渡船，以及逢年过节舞龙、耍狮子、燃放烟火、龙舟竞赛，无不带有神秘与浪漫的乡风民俗色彩。《边城》中几次写到端午节的热闹场面：妇女、儿童的额角上用雄黄蘸酒写"王"字，赛龙船敲的高脚鼓"用牛皮蒙好，绘有朱红太极图"。《长河》中用很大的篇幅写当地农民日常生活的禁忌和四时八节的习俗。《龙朱》里苗族人"男女结合，在唱歌庆大年时、端午时、八月中秋时及跳舞刺牛大祭时，男女成群唱，成群舞，抓住自己的心，放在爱人面前，方法不是钱，不是貌，不是门阀，也不是假装的一切，只有真实热情的歌"。

而福克纳所表现的南方庄园文化则带有贵族文化的特点。它带有浓厚的贵族等级观念，认为作为庄园主的贵族对妇女、子女及奴隶具有不可动摇的权威。南方文化是建立在庄园经济基础上的，而庄园经济主要是以家庭为基本单位组成的一种社会结构形式，作为庄园主的父亲同时又是家庭的主宰者，福克纳的许多作品均表现了南方名门望族的衰败。在更深层次上，这些家族的败落也标志着旧南方和旧秩序的解体。而福克纳在揭示其分崩离析的原因时，认为这种衰败来自家族内部的腐朽，其根源则在于作为庄园主与家庭主宰者的父亲非人道的行为。福克纳的诸多小说塑造了一系列专制、凶狠、冷酷无情的父亲形象，他们集中体现了南方贵族文化的父权制特征。在这些作品中，笼罩在家庭中，特别是加尔文家庭中的，是一种强大的父性权威的阴影。它的力量是如此之大，以至它具有摧毁整个家庭及左右家庭成员幸福的能力。如《八月之光》中乔的外祖父道克·汉斯·乔的继父麦克伊琼，《献给爱米丽的一朵玫瑰花》中爱米丽的父亲，《押沙龙，押沙龙》中的斯德潘等，他们是老上校及沙多里斯一类形象的进一步展开，是南方旧贵族的一系列群体形象。他们一个共同的性格特征即表现为反人性的专制与残暴。

种族制则是南方贵族文化孕育的另一怪胎，它集中体现了南方贵族文化的专制和残暴。奴隶制这个早已被人类文明抛弃了的东西，在近代又被殖民者在美洲大陆复活，成为现代社会的毒瘤。奴隶制对美国的影响是巨大的，它不仅直接导致了美国内战和后来大规模的社会冲突和动乱，而且对美国的经济、文化及美国人的道德价值观都有间接的影响，尤其是它为美国南方文化打下了一个耻辱的烙印。生活在南方文化这样一种特殊环境中，福克纳对种族制文化现象具有敏锐的洞察力，他对种族制表现了极大的愤慨。几乎他的所有约克纳帕塔法作品都不同程度地涉及黑人或种族问题，他的诸多小说，再现了一幕幕黑人在南方社会中备受歧视、奴役和迫害的非人般的生活情景。《押沙龙，押沙龙》中的斯德潘在市场上买奴隶时"像他买其他牲口——马和驴和牛——一样精明"。在《沙多里斯》和《喧哗与骚动》等小说中，我们看到主人随意打骂黑人是家常便饭，更有甚者，黑人还一再遭到追捕或在私刑中被活活烧死。《八月之光》《干燥的九月》《去吧，摩西》和《坟墓的闯入者》都描写了疯狂而令人恐怖的私刑场面。

短篇小说《殉葬》用讽刺的笔调描写了作为曾遭受欧洲殖民者血腥屠杀的土著居民印第安人，竟也学起白人蓄起了奴，甚至竟残忍到用黑奴陪葬。福克纳在小说中一针见血地指出："都叫白人给败坏了。"一句话点出了万恶之源。种族主义观念是如此具有腐蚀性，连纯朴的印第安人也深受白人的影响沾染上了蓄奴的恶习，并比白人有过之而无不及，福克纳对种族主义文化的讽刺可谓叹为观止。在他关于沙多里斯、康普生、斯德潘和麦卡斯林四大家族没落的重要作品中，探讨种族问题对这些家族毁灭性的影响，成为这些小说一个共同的主题。

因此，与来自民间的自然、活泼的楚文化所截然不同的是，美国南方的贵族文化则表现为专制、残暴，是一种僵硬、冷酷的文化。更进一步说，楚文化是一种张扬个性、具有强旺的生命意识、富于人性的文化，而南方庄园文化则是一种摧残个体自由、扼杀生命情感欲望的反人性文化。

二 "天人合一"文化与"个人主义"文化

考察两位来自不同国度、不同文化语境下的作家，我们不但要关注他们与地域文化的关系，而且要把他们放在中西民族文化大背景下来蠡测、审视，以发掘他们作品所折射的深厚的民族文化内蕴，这是我们比较其作品文化特质之非常重要的一环。

　　与五四主流作家、学者对传统文化所采取的单值性批判的文化价值取向所不同的是，沈从文在更大程度上表现为对中国传统文化的亲和与接纳。特别是因秉承了中国传统文化"天人合一"的影响，他的作品与当时主流文学诉诸民主与反封建的主题有着很大的不同。作为西方 20 世纪文学中最具影响力的作家之一，福克纳深受西方传统文化的影响和熏陶，他的作品有力地表达了西方传统人文文化的精华。他在作品中反复表达、倡议的自由、平等、个性、博爱、勇气、怜悯、同情等价值理念，也是西方传统人文文化的核心理念。福克纳曾广泛阅读了他所能得到的各种西方文学、艺术、哲学、宗教、心理学、历史、法律、地理乃至生物和医学等各学科领域的书籍，从人类历史上的优秀文化遗产及当时的各种思潮中汲取精神养分。

　　但在西方传统文化价值观中，对福克纳影响最大的是个人主义人道主义思想。当福克纳被问及属于什么流派时，他回答说："我想说，并且我希望，我唯一属于的，我愿意属于的是人道主义流派。"① 在福克纳的定义中，人道主义除了具有西方传统人文文化中的博爱、自由、平等等普通含义外，还具有非常特殊的内涵即"个人主义"。"个人主义"，也就是关于个人价值的观念，是他的人道主义思想的一个非常重要的方面。在福克纳看来，个性就是人性的表现，他甚至表示要做个人主义的"传道士"。

　　福克纳的个人主义价值观，固然与南方传统文化重视个体价值的影响有关，但更是建立在广阔的西方文化背景之上。在西方文化史上，自古希腊以来个体价值就得到肯定，经由文艺复兴人文主义思潮的发扬光大，个人主义逐渐成为西方文化传统极为重要的组成部分。而在美国，特别是在以爱默生为代表的超验主义运动之后，几乎所有美国的人道主义思想及与之相关的哲学、教育、文化、文学、艺术都带有明显的个人主义特征。因而，福克纳的个人主义思想深受西方文化，特别是美国传统文化的影响。

　　福克纳之所以对南方贵族文化表现出相当程度的怀恋和认同，一个重

---

① Jellieffe Robert, ed., *Faulkner at Nagano*, 4th ed., Tokyo：Kenkyu sha, 1966, p. 95.

要原因在于他看到了南方旧贵族身上所闪烁的开拓进取、独立自主的个性主义精神品格。福克纳在家族小说中塑造了一系列以其曾祖父"老上校"为原型的南方庄园主的形象。福克纳不仅以"老上校"为原型塑造了约翰·沙多里斯上校这个人物，而且在斯特德家族、麦卡斯林家族和康普生家族中塑造了一系列具有开拓性、个性独立、有雄心、有魄力、意志坚强的南方旧贵族形象。

在短篇小说《高大的人们》中，福克纳借小说中的一个人物之口，尖锐地指出现代文明发明了"字母、规章和方法"，但现代人却为这些"字母、规章和方法所束缚"，"已经学会了怎样悄悄抽去骨头和内脏还能活下去"（比喻失去了独立自主的个性）这一事实。与现代人日益失去个性相反，小说中描写的乡下人麦克勒姆一家所表现出来的个性独立的精神品格令人钦佩，福克纳因之对他们充满敬意，把他们尊称为"高大的人们"。麦克勒姆一家却相信"一个人有权利、有自由根据自己的条件和愿望决定干什么"，他们认为政府无权干涉他们经营农场的自主权和独立性。在这些地位低下的乡下人身上，福克纳表达了对他们独立品格的敬意。麦克勒姆一家像他们所热爱的大地一样纯朴、坚毅，具有古老民族的一切美德，是一群人格独立的"高大的人们"。正是有这些人的存在，福克纳坚信人类最终会寻回现代人所失去的独立个性。

因而，受西方文化，特别是美国文化的影响，福克纳特别强调个人主义价值观，这构成了他思想中的一个核心内容。他的所有作品都表达了对个性价值的肯定和对扼杀、摧残个性的强烈谴责和抨击。

三 "湘西世界"和"约克纳帕塔法天地"文化价值评判

以上从地域文化和民族文化的角度分别分析了沈从文作品中的湘西楚巫文化与福克纳小说中的南方贵族文化的典型特点，我们从中可以看出，沈从文发掘了湘西楚文化中蕴含的独特的精神资源，他对湘西楚巫文化持一种积极认同的态度，他欣赏这种自然、质朴、弥漫着天人合一气息的湘西文化；而福克纳对南方庄园文化则持辩证的评判态度。一方面，他肯定这种文化所蕴含的"勇敢、荣誉、骄傲、怜悯、爱正义、爱自由"等人类古老的道德力量和体现的个人主义价值观；另一方面，又批判了建立在奴隶制之上的南方庄园文化所蕴含的摧残人性的道德危机。

沈从文对湘西独特文化资源的发掘是有深远意义的。长期以来发源于先秦孔学的儒家文化构成了中国的主体文化。由孔子确立的先秦理性精神铸就了中华民族的基本性格和文化心理结构。儒家的"实践理性"带有诸多的道德束缚和理性约束，严重压抑了人性的自由舒展和个性的发展，而楚文化以其原始自然的气息把远古的原始活力和野性充分保存和延续了下来。沈从文于20世纪上半叶在文坛上的崛起，他通过充分表现被遮蔽和被遗忘的湘西文化，而复兴楚文化的生机和活力，并以此向处于僵硬、衰败状态的汉儒主体文化发起挑战。从这个意义上说，沈从文复兴湘西楚巫文化的意义是深远的。

但湘西文化毕竟是一种带有原始性的农业文化，有其蒙昧、落后的一面，沈从文对它却缺乏科学的理性批判精神，沈从文对湘西文化基本持一种认同的态度，尽管他也偶尔提到湘西世界的生命形式"终归单调"，但他始终认为湘西世界因保存了"生活的素朴""情感的单一"和"环境的牧歌性"而优于城市文明，乡村人在道德上优于都市人，与虚伪、怯懦的城市人相比，湘西人具有更健全、质朴、富有活力的生命形式。他试图以湘西文化拯救正在走向衰败的汉儒文化，以复兴中华民族文化。对湘西文化的过分偏爱使沈从文对其审视缺乏清醒的理性批判精神，他对湘西文化所包含的原始性、蒙昧性，甚至是野蛮性等负面因子也加以颂扬，正如有的学者所指出："在这种时候，他以自己的逻辑，连同蒙昧一起颂扬着原始性，让和谐宁静与清静无为抱雌守虚联系在一起，把奴性的驯良与纯朴忠厚一并作为美德。"①

与沈从文对湘西文化几乎全然肯定所不同的是，福克纳对美国南方的贵族庄园文化则采取了一种辩证的审视视角。他对旧南方表现出一种爱恨

---

① 王路编：《沈从文评说八十年》，中国华侨出版社2004年版，第378页。

交织的复杂矛盾情感，他看到了它的两重性。他既敢于正视并大胆暴露南方庄园文化"恶"的一面，同时对南方传统文化的一些优秀精神品格又非常推崇和留恋。

福克纳的思想中具有南方传统文化中普遍存在的尊严感，他敬仰优秀的南方庄园主身上所表现出来的英勇、尚武、忠诚的骑士精神，崇尚他们所表现出来的自尊感、荣誉感及特立独行的个人主义精神，更为推崇他们身上所体现的"勇敢、荣誉、骄傲、怜悯、爱正义、爱自由"等传统精神品格。

福克纳之所以对南方庄园文化表现出相当程度的认同和留恋，是因为他痛感于南方新兴的资产阶级的唯利是图、道德沦丧和缺乏信仰，而试图从南方传统文化中发掘出一些富有生命力的精神资源，为现代社会提供一种精神借鉴。在旧南方贵族沙多里斯们身上，他看到了南方现代社会所缺乏的一种传统精神品格，一种南方传统文化中具有生命力的道义力量。

在理智上，福克纳又清醒地洞察了南方社会的各种问题和罪恶，并在作品中予以犀利、尖锐的批判和抨击，这使他同所热爱的故土，所描绘的对象保持一定的距离，从而使他的评价更客观，暴露更为深刻。正如霍夫曼所指出："一个伟大作家同他周围的世界总是处在某种对立之中，我们从未发现伟大的作家在他们的环境中感到舒适惬意，关系和谐。"① 福克纳对南方文化的热爱和批评，他对南方爱恨交织的心情形成了其作品的丰富性、复杂性和多元性。

尽管存在着上述诸多的差异性，但我们看到，作为伟大的人文主义作家，无论是沈从文对湘西楚文化的认同还是福克纳对南方庄园文化的批判，都表达了一个共同的价值取向，即对人性自由的张扬，对摧残、压抑人的情感欲望等异化力量的强烈谴责和批判。

（原载于《中国海洋大学学报》2008 年第 1 期）

---

① 肖明翰：《威廉·福克纳研究》，外语教学与研究出版社 1997 年版，第 112 页。

福克纳与新时期小说思潮关系研究①

福克纳是一位20世纪西方现代派文学承上启下的作家，一方面他的创作受到了艾略特、乔伊斯、柏格森、萨特等象征主义、表现主义、意识流、存在主义思想的很大影响，另一方面又对拉丁美洲以马尔克斯为代表的魔幻现实主义文学产生了重要影响。从一定意义上讲，以福克纳为代表的西方现代派作家对莫言新时期作家的成长和创作不但起了触媒和引领的作用，而且在深层面上激发了其在文学观念和艺术表现手法上的创新和突破，下文拟以福克纳和新时期小说作为切入点，主要通过考察新时期三种主要小说思潮——"寻根小说思潮""新历史主义小说思潮""先锋小说思潮"的文学创作主旨和艺术表达形态，蠡测福克纳对中国新时期小说观念变革和艺术形式创新的影响。

20世纪70年代末以来，随着世界哲学、文艺思潮的涌入和外国作品译介的传播，中国禁锢已久的思想闸门被打开，新时期文学在与世界文化、文学的相互碰撞、渗透和交融下，整体风貌发生了根本性变化，探讨世界文艺思潮及国外重要作家与新时期文学的关系因之成为比较文学研究的重要课题。新时期文学涌现出一大批在国内外具有一定影响力的作家，特别是莫言被授予2012年的诺贝尔文学奖这一标志性事件代表着中国当代文学创作达到了被国际认可的高度。而事实上，福克纳对莫言等新时期作家的成长和创作确实起到了触媒的作用，当代作家莫言、余华、苏童、贾

---

① 此文系国家社科基金一般项目"威廉·福克纳对中国小说的影响研究"（批准号：13BWW007）阶段性成果。

平凹、王安忆、郑万隆、吕新、张抗抗等都曾论及福克纳对其创作的启发，譬如莫言坦言在思想和艺术手法表现上受到外国文学极大的影响，其中对他影响最大的两部著作是福克纳的《喧哗与骚动》和加西亚·马尔克斯的《百年孤独》，福克纳在邮票般大小的故乡书写中所创造的文学天地激发了莫言创建"高密东北乡"文学共和国的梦想，而福克纳让他的小说人物闻到了"耀眼的冷的气味"，丰富、拓展了莫言小说"超感觉"和印象主义的艺术表现手法；余华尊崇福克纳为"师傅"，声称是福克纳教会了他心理描写；贾平凹认为福克纳等西方现代派作家作品"有大的境界和力度"，表现了"博大的生命意识"。总之，在外国作家中，福克纳对中国新时期文学产生了非常重要的影响，尤其是福克纳极具地域文化特色的"约克纳帕塔法"文本及其全新的现代主义文体实验形式对新时期小说在文学观念和艺术表达形式上产生了直接或间接的辐射、影响及渗透作用。

一　福克纳与新时期寻根小说

一个作家的养育之地是其创作之根基，反过来讲，作家则是地域文化的产物。福克纳多次提及他的创作与美国南方的关系，"从《沙多里斯》开始，我发现我自己的像邮票那样大的故乡土地是值得好好写的，不管我多么长寿，我也无法把那里的事写完……它为别人打开了一个金库，却为我创造了一个自己的天地。……我喜欢把我创造的世界看作是宇宙的某种基石，尽管那块基石很小，如果它被拿走，宇宙本身就会坍塌。"① 福克纳在此所说的"天地"，即为他大多数作品的地理背景——一个虚构的位于美国密西西比州的约克纳帕塔法县。他也因描写这块"像邮票那样大小的故土"而蜚声世界文坛。

就中国新时期文学观念的变革而言，重新认识和解决文学创作中的

---

① Meriwether James B. and Michael Millgate, eds., *Lion in the garden*, New York: Randon House, 1968, p. 255.

"写什么"和"怎么写"是两个核心的要素。从一定意义上说，福克纳的约克纳帕塔法文本对新时期小说"写什么"产生的重要影响在于以"世界文学"的视镜激发了新时期作家的现代民族意识和寻根情结，使其认识到文学之根只有深植于民族文化传统的土壤，并对其优劣进行现代性的审视和反思才能走向世界。

寻根文学对文学民族化的探寻和追求正是立足于从民族文化根基上进行挖掘和表现，1985 年韩少功率先在一篇纲领性的文章《文学的"根"》中指出："文学有根，文学之根应深植于民族传统的文化土壤中"，寻根文学的另一位重要作家阿城也认为："我们的文学常常只包含社会学的内容却是明显的。社会学当然是小说应该观照的层面，但社会学不能涵盖文化，相反文化却能涵盖社会学及其他。"寻根文学这种对民族文化之根的探求和追寻，并不仅仅是一种简单意义上对传统文化的回归，如上文所言，它的产生是基于世界文化思潮，特别是各种西方现代文学思潮的影响和激发，而其中福克纳的影响功不可没。

2000 年 3 月，莫言在加州大学伯克莱校区发表的演讲"福克纳大叔，你好吗"一文中谈到他受到外国文学影响时认为福克纳是他的导师，他说："一个作家读另一个作家的书，实际上是一次对话，甚至一次恋爱，如果谈得成功，很可能成为终身伴侣，如果话不投机，大家就各奔前程。"[1] 在他和世界各地作家们"对话"及"谈恋爱"的过程中，他认为很多作家的书对他用处不大，直到最后遇到福克纳，他才找到了真正的文学"导师"。他具体谈到了 1984 年 12 月一个大雪纷飞的下午，从同学那里借到一本福克纳的《喧哗与骚动》的欣喜和感动，"我一边读一边欢喜"，"尤其是他创造的那个'约克纳帕塔法县'更让我心驰神往"。"他的约克纳帕塔法县尤其让我明白了，一个作家，不但可以虚构人物、虚构故事，而且可以虚构地理……受他的约克纳帕塔法县的启示，我'大着胆子把我的高密东北乡写到了稿纸上。决心要写我的故乡那块像邮票那样大的地方。这简直就打开了一道记忆的闸门，童年的生活全被激活了。我想

---

① 莫言：《用耳朵阅读》，作家出版社 2012 年版，第 23 页。

起当年我躺在草地上对着牛、对着树、对着鸟儿说过的话，然后我就把它们原封不动地写到我的小说里。从此我再也不必为找不到要写的东西而发愁，而是要为写不过来而发愁。经常出现这样的情况，当我在写一篇小说的时候，许多新的构思，就像狗一样在我身后大声喊叫。"① 受福克纳约克纳帕塔法文本的影响，莫言立下了自己文学创作的目标：其一，树立一个属于自己的对人生的看法；其二，开辟一个属于自己的阵地；其三，建立一个属于自己的人物体系；其四，形成一套属于自己的叙述风格。他因此在寻根文学的浪潮中创造了一个"高密东北乡"文学地理世界。

对莫言而言，他挖掘"高密东北乡"这样一个文学地理世界的寻根之旅与对包括福克纳作品在内的西方文学的借鉴和参照是分不开的，在第十七届亚洲文化大奖福冈市民论坛"我的文学历程"演讲中，他特别谈及学习西方文学对他转向中国的民间和传统写作的影响："经历过这个向西方文学广泛学习和借鉴的阶段之后，我开始有意识地把目光投向中国的民间文化和传统文化，这样做并不是对学习西方的否定，而是进一步的肯定。因为，只有广泛深入地了解西方文学的历史和现状之后，才能获得一种重新认识中国文学的参照体系，才能在比较中发现东西方文学的共同性和特殊性，才能够写出具有创新意识的既是中国的又是亚洲的和世界的文学。"② 在此可以看到以福克纳等为代表的西方作家对莫言创作立足乡土的影响作用。

2012 年诺贝尔文学奖颁奖词称颂莫言的作品"将魔幻现实主义与民间故事、历史与当代社会融合在一起"，并且指出"莫言创作中的世界，令人联想起威廉·福克纳和加西亚·马尔克斯作品的融合，同时又在中国传统文学和口头文学中寻找到一个出发点。"

口头文学是中外诸多作家创作的重要源泉，福克纳的写作受到了美国南方民间口头文化很大的影响。童年时期他就特别喜欢听别人讲故事。在家中"大地方"的门廊里，他从祖父那里听来许多关于曾祖父"老上校"的传奇和自己家族的传说。他也是家中黑人老保姆棚子中的常客，在那里

---

① 莫言：《用耳朵阅读》，作家出版社 2012 年版，第 25—26 页。
② 同上书，第 196 页。

听到了不少关于动物、鬼怪，特别是黑人、奴隶的故事。他的家乡小镇奥克斯福法院门前的广场，更是他听故事的好地方，在那里，他经常一坐就是几个小时，听老人们讲关于美国内战、印第安人及打猎的传说，后来他的许多作品都直接取材于他童年时代所听到的故事。

在一定意义上说，代代相传的高密民间口头文化也成就了莫言，在谈到他的写作经历时，莫言特别强调他童年时期在乡村"用耳朵阅读"的特殊经验对他日后创作的影响，他说自己的"写作知识基本上是用耳朵听来的"。[1] 老祖母、说书人、父亲一辈的人口口相传的传奇化的民间历史成为他创作的源泉。莫言认为"民间把历史传奇化、神奇化是心灵的需要"，对于一个作家来说，他"更愿意向民间的历史传奇靠拢并从那里汲取营养"。[2]

"民间"这一术语，是 20 世纪 90 年代陈思和在《民间的沉浮》和《民间的还原》两篇论文中首先系统提出的，它指向的是一种长期处于边缘位置、被主流意识形态所遮蔽的文化意识和价值立场。莫言以自己的故乡为摹本，建构、想象了高密东北乡这样一个具有隐喻性的生气勃勃的文学地理世界，这个文学乡土世界中既充满着苦难、纷争、灾难和死亡，也洋溢着生机勃勃的原始生命力、最本真的欲望和无所畏惧的精神及来自土地母体的坚韧、忍耐与厚爱。而源自山东高密民间的奇异、诡谲、自由、奔放的齐文化为这个文学地理世界注入了灵动性和丰富性。

在寻根文学中产生重要影响的中国当代作家贾平凹也曾谈到阅读福克纳作品所产生的认同感："我对美国文学较感兴趣，像福克纳、海明威这种老作家。看福克纳的作品，总令我想起我老家的山林、河道，而看沈从文的作品，又令我想到我们商洛的风土人情生活画面。读这两种作品都有一种对应关系，能够从中获得很多营养和启发。"[3] 在此可以看出，贾平凹主要是从乡土性这一视角认同福克纳的作品，受此启发和激励，他创作了"商州三录"等一系列充满浓郁商洛乡土风情的作品。在这些作品中，他以现代工商文明作为对比，展现了纯净乡土的可贵性。在《商州初录》中

---

① 莫言：《用耳朵阅读》，作家出版社 2012 年版，第 55 页。
② 同上书，第 57 页。
③ 贾平凹、张英：《地域文化与创作》，《继承和创新》1996 年第 7 期。

他指出："今日世界，人们想尽一切办法以人的需要来进行电气化、自动化、机械化，但这种人工化的发展往往使人又失去了单纯、清静，而这块地方便显出它的难得之处了，这里的一切似乎是天地自然的有心安排，是如同地下的文物一样而特意要保留下来的胜景！"

贾平凹在文学寻根的观察和思考中看到了现代商业文明对自然素朴乡土世界的侵蚀，福克纳在他的约克纳帕塔法世系小说中，对工商资本主义对美国旧南方庄园生活的入侵，也是怀着一种排斥、批判的态度，正如瑞典科学院院士古斯塔夫·哈尔斯特龙在诺贝尔文学奖授奖词中指出的那样，"摆在南方人面前的是工商业及其机械化、标准化的生活模式。他们对这种生活既感陌生又充满敌意……福克纳的小说深入地描写了这一过程，对这种痛苦他自身也有体验并且感觉强烈"①。福克纳的很多作品通过刻画冰冷的机械物形象表达了对与乡土性相对立的现代工商文明的批判和反思。如《圣殿》和《斯诺普斯》三部曲等诸多长篇小说中塑造了以"金鱼眼"和"斯诺普斯们"为代表的新兴资产阶级形象，其中"金鱼眼"是福克纳笔下典型的机械文明的代表人物。"金鱼眼"在小说中出场时，就是一个没有内在本质的空洞人物，小说多处描写他类似机械物的形象特征，如他的"蜡做的洋娃娃的脸"，"像两团橡胶的眼睛"，"绷紧的西服和硬邦邦的草帽使他有棱有角，轮廓分明，像个现代派的灯座"，是一个"具有冲压过的铁皮那种邪恶的肤浅的品质的"家伙，总之，通过这类机械物形象的勾勒，福克纳的作品揭示了现代工商文明对南方的腐蚀，表达了对旧南方的怀恋之情。

寻根并不必然意味着对文化之根和传统的一味肯定，如何来辩证审视、看取文化之根，发扬其优秀成分，挖掘、分析其劣根性，是衡量一个作家作品丰富性的重要标准。当福克纳在日本访问被问及是否热爱南方时，他回答道："我既爱它又恨它。那里有些东西我一点也不喜欢，但我出生在那里，那里是我的故乡，所以我仍然要保护它，即使我恨它。"② 在

---

① 潘小松：《福克纳——美国南方文学巨匠》，长春出版社1995年版。

② Jeliffe Robert A., ed., *Faulkner at Nagano*, Tokyo：Kenkyusha, 1966, p.26.

此我们可以看到福克纳对南方复杂的情感，一方面，福克纳对旧南方怀有深沉的爱，极为珍视南方社会传统的价值观念，他肯定南方文化中所蕴含的人类古老的道德力量。他不仅欣赏优秀的庄园主身上所表现出来的优雅的风度和浪漫的骑士精神，而且肯定他们所奉行的一些体现了"勇敢、荣誉、骄傲、怜悯、爱正义、爱自由"等品格的人类优秀的道德准则；但另一方面，他在理智上又清醒地洞察到南方文化的种种弊端，深刻剖析了南方文化所背负的罪恶和历史重负。他对南方社会和历史中的各种问题，特别是父权制、妇道观、种族主义等予以强烈的谴责和抨击，对南方爱恨交织的矛盾、复杂情感突出表现在他的很多作品中。

与福克纳相同，莫言在《红高粱家族》小说开篇表达了与福克纳类似的对文学地理故乡既爱又恨的复杂情感："我曾经对高密东北乡极端热爱，曾经对高密东北乡极端仇恨。长大后努力学习马克思主义，我终于悟到：高密东北乡无疑是地球上最美丽最丑陋、最超脱最世俗、最圣洁最龌龊、最英雄好汉最王八蛋、最能喝酒最能爱的地方。"① 这表明莫言意识到高密东北乡文化土壤中既有美丽、圣洁、英勇、爱等优秀成分，也同时蕴含着丑陋、龌龊、罪恶等糟粕因子。

新时期其他寻根作家同样展现了他们所审视的文学之根的两面性。在《文学的"根"》中，韩少功追问"绚丽的楚文化流到哪里去了"，在湘西的崇山峻岭中他找到了它的存在，"只有在那里，你才能更好地体会到楚辞中那种神秘、绮丽、狂放、孤愤的境界"。而在渲染、认同这种楚文化的绚丽、狂放的同时，韩少功在《归去来》《爸爸爸》《女女女》等小说中，剖析、批判了湘西荆楚文化的未开化、混沌、蒙昧等劣根性。郑万隆的《异乡异闻》系列小说，也有类似的倾向性，既表现了神秘的东北边陲风光，也展现了当地鄂伦春人的狩猎文化的原始、愚昧和残酷。

总之，福克纳的"约克纳帕塔法"文本对"寻根小说"在本土经验的表达、地域文化的挖掘和反思及民间话语的诉诸等层面上产生了深刻影响，其中最主要的影响在于以"世界文学"的视镜激发了新时期作家的现

---

① 莫言：《红高粱家族》，作家出版社 2012 年版，第 3 页。

代民族意识和寻根情结，使其认识到文学之根只有深植于民族文化传统的土壤，并对其优劣进行现代性的审视和反思才能走向世界。

二 福克纳与新时期新历史主义小说

斯蒂芬·葛林伯雷在 1982 年首次提出，"新历史主义"在美国作为文学批评方法论上的意义，认为编纂者特定的观念影响了对以往各种历史文本的编撰，使其具有和文学作品同样的虚构成分，正如美国新历史主义理论家路易·芒特罗斯所说："我们的分析和我们的理解，必然是以我们自己特定的历史、社会和学术现状为出发点的；我们所重构的历史，都是我们这些作为历史的人的批评家所做的文本建构。"《新历史主义》论文集的主编 H. 阿兰穆·威瑟教授认为新历史主义是"一个没有确切指涉的措词"。新历史主义发端于文学批评，向传统的文学史理论的权威性和一元性提出了挑战，新历史主义批评对于中国新时期文学的影响意义深远，尤其是它对新时期文学历史观点的更新上产生的影响具有颠覆性，为新时期作家在文学创作中如何想象、解读和重构历史提供了多种可能性。

寻根文学与新历史主义思潮具有千丝万缕的联系，甚至无法做泾渭分明的区分。新时期很多寻根文学作家以文化寻根为契机，在诉诸传统文化和民间文化的同时，也倾向于表现历史的个体性、神秘性和偶然性。新历史主义理论的引介，使新时期诸多作家获得了新的历史观和审美视角及叙述方式，他们以民间化、个人化、多元化的叙事方式，或解构主流意识形态的非此即彼的一元化历史观，或关注历史中边缘的人与事，认为历史存在着无数种偶然性和不确定性，也存在着无数种解读与重构的可能。这种新历史主义文学思潮与福克纳的"约克纳帕塔法"文本中对南方历史的解构具有某种不期而遇的契合性。

福克纳的长篇小说中，有近三分之二是家族小说。他的诸多作品通过形象描绘南北战争后南方庄园家族生活的衰败状况来解构旧南方历史中的非人性文化，这与新历史主义小说颠覆、解构历史的主张不谋而合。《喧哗与骚动》中康普生家族的大宅长年累月为阴沉和死亡的氛围所笼罩，到了昆丁一代手里，该家族的财产全部被变卖。《押沙龙，押沙龙》中斯德潘苦心经营的大庄园最后在一片大火中苦苦呻吟，像个"怪物似的火绒般干燥的烂空壳，烟雾正透过挡雨板扭曲的缝隙往外渗透"，大火过后只剩下"那堆灰烬和四根空荡荡的烟囱"。《去吧，摩西》中的卡洛萨斯·麦卡斯林曾被他的后代们视为一个具有超人力量和勇气的祖先，但他的曾孙契克有一天偶然在翻看家族日志时发现了这个他曾一直引以为自豪的家族，竟隐藏着如此多的罪恶。老卡洛萨斯不仅强奸了家中的黑人女仆，而且同与此黑奴所生的亲生女儿发生了乱伦关系，致使备感屈辱的黑人女仆于圣诞节时在溪中自溺而死。老卡洛萨斯灭绝人性的行为让契克对南方历史产生一种透不过气的沉重的负疚感，并下定决心抛弃沾满鲜血的祖产，自食其力。

海登·怀特曾说："如何组织一个历史境遇取决于历史学家如何把具体的情节结构和他希望赋予某种意义的历史事件相结合，这个做法从根本上说是文学操作，也就是小说创作的运作。"[1] 在 20 世纪 80 年代中后期继寻根文学后兴起的新历史主义小说，代表性的作品有莫言的《红高粱》《丰乳肥臀》《檀香刑》，苏童的《妻妾成群》《米》《1934 年的逃亡》，格非的《迷舟》，余华的《活着》《呼喊与细雨》，陈忠实的《白鹿原》，刘震云的《温故一九四二》，等等，它们在叙事模式、历史观念、话语风格方面，均表现出不同于以往历史题材小说创作的独特风貌。在创作路径上，新历史主义小说以民间视角来解读被主流意识形态所遮蔽的历史，挑战传统正史以阶级性和意识形态为主导的一元化思维模式，试图在文学意义上立足于人性的丰富性和复杂性来重新诠释历史，表现出颠覆、解构正统历史的强烈倾向性。这与福克纳在"约克纳帕塔法"家族叙述中对南方政治权力观念的解构、对人性丰富性的剖析如出一辙。

莫言在谈到《丰乳肥臀》的写作初衷时特别强调"这个小说模糊了一种阶级观点"，并说他写这部小说有一个非常明确的目的，"就是要改变一

---

[1]　张京媛：《新历史主义与文学批评》，北京大学出版社 1993 年版，第 165 页。

下过去我们那种历史小说和革命历史小说的写法"①，认为过去的革命历史小说阶级立场非常鲜明，好人和坏人之间的界线泾渭分明。"好人绝对没有任何缺点，有的话顶多是急躁冒进，绝对不会是道德方面的缺点，只是性格方面的缺点。而一旦写到坏人呢，肯定是从骨子里坏，不但相貌丑陋，而且道德败坏，可以说头顶上长疮，脚底下流脓，坏透气了。"② 事实上呢，他认为恰恰相反。在他的村子里"有两个当过八路的恰好都是满脸麻子，两个当过国民党兵的是五官端正、浓眉大眼"③。《丰乳肥臀》从解构阶级性的视角出发，站在人性的立场以还原历史的丰富性和复杂性，人性成为衡量历史真实性的一个主导性的线索。

陈忠实的《白鹿原》也是新历史主义的一部重要代表性作品。同《丰乳肥臀》类似，此小说表现了同一家庭的成员由于各自不同的生活经验而选择不同阶级路线的复杂状况。族长白嘉轩的儿子白孝文是国家政权的维护者，而女儿白灵走上了反政权的革命道路。乡约鹿子霖的两儿子则分别加入国共两党。刘震云的《故乡天下黄花》、苏童的《米》也展现了各种错综复杂力量的较量，均表现了新历史主义消解和淡化主流历史观的倾向性。

由上观之，福克纳的家族史小说及解构旧南方文化的历史观对中国"新历史主义小说思潮"倾心于家族叙述，用开放的、现代性的思维观诠释历史、文明和人性的复杂性存在着一定的同构性。

三　福克纳与新时期先锋小说

福克纳作为 20 世纪西方现代派文学的重要代表作家之一，对新时期作家的辐射和影响更体现在对其先锋意义的创作上，在深层面上激发了新时期作家在文学观念和艺术表现手法上的全面创新和突破，这在新时期先锋

---

① 莫言:《用耳朵阅读》，作家出版社 2012 年版，第 290 页。

② 同上。

③ 同上。

小说创作中表现尤为显著。

"先锋"（Avant-garde）一词最早并不是一个文学术语，它来自法文，始于法国大革命，原意是军事上的"先头部队"，后来被作为文化和文学艺术术语使用。作为一个与时间密切相关的概念，"先锋"与现代性这一概念密切相关，甚至很多学者认为"先锋派"即是现代主义，"先锋"一词不仅意味着一种前卫的艺术形式的变革，而且标志着对社会文化变迁作出的超前敏锐反应，形式的革新服务于表现主题表达的需要。

20世纪20年代以来，现代主义思潮在西方人类精神活动的各个领域延展，在欧洲文学界出现了乔伊斯、卡夫卡、艾略特、庞德、普鲁斯特、萨特、加谬、尤奈斯库等现代派作家。美国现代派文学则在20世纪二三十年代的"南方文艺复兴"中达到高峰。福克纳是美国现代派文学思潮中涌现出来的一位代表性作家。作为现代派小说文体实验的探索者，福克纳的作品大量运用了象征隐喻、意识流、多角度叙述及时空倒置等富有创新性的文学手法，丰富了传统小说的表现形式，打破了传统小说叙事结构的局限性，给读者的审美想象带来了全新的冲击。特别是他的作品在语言表达、感觉诉诸、心理描写、多角度叙述等方面对先锋小说家解决如何写的问题提供了有益的借鉴。

就中国新时期文学而言，对"先锋小说"这一术语的界定存在诸多争议，曾以"新潮小说""探索小说"等来命名，而"先锋小说"这一概念则后来泛指当时一切"与西方现代哲学思潮、美学思潮及现代主义文学创作密切相关，并且在其直接影响下的"，"其作品从哲学思潮到艺术形式都有明显的超前性的小说"。① 在当下的文学史中，这一流派主要是指在20世纪80年代中后期崛起于中国当代文坛，以前卫的姿态进行文体形式探索的一种文学派别，代表性的作家有莫言、余华、马原、格非、苏童、叶兆言、北村、孙甘露等。他们的作品侧重于在文体形式、语言表达和叙述方式上进行文体实验。

---

　① 李兆忠：《旋转的文坛——现实主义与先锋派文学研讨会纪要》，《文学评论》1989年第1期。

正如上文论及寻根派文学所谈到的，莫言之所以能够洞察到"高密东北乡"对于他的创作所起的重要文学资源意义，缘起于1984年首次阅读福克纳的《喧哗与骚动》所受的触动，感召于福克纳"不断地写他家乡那块邮票般大小的地方，终于创造出一块自己的天地"，莫言也建立了一个自己的"文学共和国"。但福克纳对他的影响不但在于"写什么"，而且在"怎样写"上，即使用何种文学语言形式进行创作。莫言不仅强调用耳朵阅读，而且倡议用鼻子写作，他在悉尼大学的演讲中风趣地说："所谓用鼻子写作，并不是说我要在鼻子里插上两只鹅毛笔，而是说我在写作时，刚开始时是无意地，后来是有意识地调动自己对于气味的回忆和想象，从而使我在写作时如同身临其境，从而使读者在阅读我的小说时也身临其境。"[①] 用鼻子写作的主张表明了莫言对气味描写的重视，而莫言之所以对气味描写特别敏感，在一定程度上也源自阅读福克纳的《喧哗与骚动》所产生的共鸣："读到第四页的最末两行，我已经一点也不觉得铁门冷了，不过我还能闻到耀眼的冷的气味。"福克纳让他小说中的人物闻到了"耀眼的冷的气味"，冷不但有了气味而且耀眼，一种对世界的奇妙感觉方式诞生了。然而仔细一想，又感到世界原本如此，我在多年前，在那些路上结满了白冰的早晨，不是也闻到过耀眼的冰的气味吗？未读福克纳之前，我已经写出了《透明的红萝卜》，其中有一个小男孩，能听到头发落地的声音。我正为这种打破常规的描写而忐忑不安时，仿佛听到福克纳鼓励我："小伙子，就这样干。把旧世界打个落花流水，让鲜红的太阳照遍全球！"[②] 从重视味觉描写，莫言拓展到强调其他感官描写的同等重要性，"其实，在写作过程中，作家所调动的不仅仅是对于气味的回忆和想象，而且还应该调动自己的视觉、听觉、味觉、触觉等全部的感受及与此相关的全部想象力。要让自己的作品充满色彩和画面、声音与旋律、苦辣与酸甜、软硬与凉热等丰富的可感受的描写，当然这一切都是借助于准确而优美的语言来实现。"[③] 莫言的小说充满各种具象、生动的感官描写，小说的

---

① 莫言：《用耳朵阅读》，作家出版社2012年版，第59页。
② 莫言：《会唱歌的墙》，作家出版社2012年版，第192—193页。
③ 莫言：《用耳朵阅读》，作家出版社2012年版，第59页。

画面感和视觉感非常突出，而且打通了各种感觉的界线，侧重于表达超感觉的印象，这在一定意义上得益于他对福克纳小说通感的领悟和融会贯通。

余华也受到福克纳很大的影响，特别是在心理描写上。在《奥克斯福的威廉·福克纳》一文中，他谈到对他产生影响的作家比较多，如川端康成和卡夫卡等，但在他的心目中，他只把福克纳尊称为师傅，"可是成为我师傅的，我想只有威廉·福克纳。我的理由是，做师傅的不能只是纸上谈兵，应该手把手传徒弟一招。威廉·福克纳就传给我一招绝活，让我知道了如何去对付心理描写。在此之前我最害怕的就是心理描写。我觉得当一个人物的内心风平浪静时，是可以进行心理描写的，可是当他的内心兵荒马乱时，心理描写难啊，难于上青天。问题是内心平静时总是不需要去描写，需要描写的总是那些动荡不安的心理，狂喜、狂怒、狂悲、狂暴、狂热、狂呼、狂妄、狂惊、狂吓、狂怕，还有其他所有的狂某某，不管写上多少字都没用，即便有本事将所有的细微情感都罗列出来，也没本事表达它们间的瞬息万变。这时候我读到了师傅的一个短篇小说《沃许》，当一个穷白人将一个富白人杀了以后，杀人者百感交集于一刻之时，我发现了师傅是如何对付心理描写的，他的叙述很简单，就是让人物的心脏停止跳动，让他的眼睛睁开。一系列麻木的视觉描写，将一个杀人者在杀人后的复杂心理烘托得淋漓尽致"[1]。余华在上述段落中详细谈到了阅读福克纳的短篇小说《沃许》对其心理描写的赞赏和认同，特别是从福克纳那里借鉴到了如何描写动态的、瞬息万变的心理。的确，在文学创作中，静态地刻画人物、描写场景还不是太难，而能淋漓尽致、入木三分地挖掘人物的内心世界，表现人物复杂多变的瞬间心理状态，实属不易。而先锋作家在开掘人物的心理世界上的突破在一定程度上与福克纳等西方现代派作家的影响有关。

传统的小说，通过全知全能的叙述，试图给作品一个终极的意义，福克纳的小说通过多角度叙述等艺术形式表现出对这种统一意义的质疑和解

---

[1]　余华：《奥克斯福的威廉·福克纳》，《上海文学》2005 年第 3 期。

构，这成为他的作品的一个显著特色。在福克纳的《押沙龙，押沙龙》《喧哗与骚动》《我弥留之际》等小说中，我们发现没有一个压倒一切的权威声音，"这不是一群在一个由作者在作品里逐渐显示出来的统一思想所照耀的统一的客观世界里的人物和命运，而恰恰是一些平等的意识和他们各自的世界的多元，他们由于某一事件聚集在一起，但同时仍然保持着他们的独立个性"①，譬如《押沙龙，押沙龙》。这部小说围绕着斯德潘家族的兴衰史，通过小说中沙罗小姐、康普生先生、昆丁、史里夫等人对它的叙述展开。这样一个故事，不像传统的小说那样按照故事发展的来龙去脉展开叙述，而是通过小说中的几个人物根据自己的情感因素、价值取向和各自不同的理解从不同的角度来解释、推测、解读，他们甚至用自己的想象来虚构出一些情节。

热奈特在其《叙事话语》一文的"引论"中对"故事"和"叙事"两个概念做了区分："建议把'所指'或叙事内容称作故事（即使该内容恰好戏剧性不强或包含的事件不多），把'能指'陈述或叙述文本称作本义的叙事。"② 此番论述内含着这样的假定，"故事"即为纯客观的事件，而使用特定视点进行表述就是叙事。由于叙述者的立场、情感及态度的不同，多叙述层相互冲突，甚至相互干扰、相互否定，从而造成叙事的模糊、朦胧性、不确定性和歧义性。在这一点上，新时期先锋小说与上述福克纳诸多作品善用多重叙述技巧来处理故事和叙述的关系如出一辙。

马原的《冈底斯的诱惑》是先锋小说叙事探索和革新的一部重要代表作。这部作品的故事有三，使用了多重叙述视角，并且形成了一种拆解式的叙事结构。首先，每一个故事都有一个叙述人，他们分别是姚亮、穷布和作为探险顾问的老作家，构成了小说故事叙述的三个叙事视角。而小说有一个全知的作者叙述人贯穿始终，在每个故事之后将故事的谜底道破。此外，小说中还有一个第一人称叙述，但很快被置换为替代叙述人姚亮。但在第一个故事的结尾，全知叙述人却反问："天哪，姚亮是谁？"在第三

---

① ［俄］巴赫金：《陀思妥耶夫斯基诗学问题》，雅迪斯 1973 年版，第 152 页。

② ［法］热拉尔·热奈特：《叙事话语新叙事话语》，王文融译，中国社会科学出版社 1990 年版，第 7 页。

个故事中穷布叙述猎熊和遇到野人的故事，但紧接着全知叙述人又予以了解构："现在你们知道了，穷布遇到的是野人，也叫喜马拉雅山雪人。这是个只见了珍闻栏的虚幻传说，喜马拉雅山雪人早已流传世界各地，没有任何读者把这种奇闻逸事当真。"综观整个小说，各个故事各自独立但又串联在一起，这种把作者、叙述者、人物糅杂混合多角度、变幻无穷的叙述方式，很好地应和了神秘莫测的故事内核，表现了西藏原始、荒凉的自然景观及神秘绮丽的独特宗教文化，从而在深层面上揭示了"西藏神话世界和藏民原始生存状态对现代文明的'诱惑'和这种诱惑的内在含义"。从此意义上说，《冈底斯的诱惑》是当代小说叙事革命的一次有益尝试。这与福克纳作品多重叙述视角的运用具有相似性。

　　综上所述，福克纳作品对新时期"寻根派小说"在本土经验的表达，对"新历史主义小说"用开放的思维观诠释历史、文明和人性的复杂性，以及对"先锋小说"的"文体革命"，或产生了一定程度的影响，或存在着一定程度的相通性，从而影响和改变了新时期小说有别于传统现实主义小说的现代性状貌，这种关系值得关注和深入探讨。

　　（此文系中国比较文学学会（CCLA）第 11 届年会暨国际学术研讨会宣读论文）

第三编
跨文化沟通与对话

论中国传统文化"和谐"理念在
跨文化交际中的意义

　　跨文化交际是一个注重交际与文化关系的研究领域，这一学科的最终目的是帮助不同文化背景的人们更好地沟通，建立和谐的人际关系。从某种程度上说，来自不同文化的人们建立一种和谐的沟通关系，对于成功实现跨文化交际有着至关重要的意义，而中国传统文化的"和谐"思想不仅能够在理论基础层面，而且能够在实践应用方面为这一领域提供新的、有价值的资源。

　　在当今时代，一方面，全球化使跨文化交往变得越来越频繁；而另一方面，激烈的文化冲突也日益频发。正如王柯平所言："在我们的瞩望中，新千年是一个充满希望的和平与发展的时代。然而与所有的期待恰恰相反，它从一开始就笼罩在恐怖主义、恐惧、仇恨、紧张、冲突和战争之中，其中还掺杂着许多其他形式的苦难和不幸。"[1] 新千年的破坏力量主要来源于对外来文化和多元化差异的敌对态度，这种情况迫切需要辩证的思想前来救援，并亟须在跨文化接触中建立一种和谐的关系。而中国传统文化中强调差异性和多样性的和谐理念，无疑是颇具启发性的。

---

　　① 王柯平:《中国文化的精神》，外文出版社 2007 年版，第 36 页。

一 中国传统文化"和谐"理念考辨

在中国传统文化中，"和谐"的概念往往被理解为一个辩证的、动态的术语。"太和"或"大同"的概念是在《周易》中被首次提到的。在冯友兰先生所著的《中国哲学简史》一书中，曾经谈道："这种和谐，不仅是指人类社会，它也渗透全宇宙，构成所谓'太和'。易乾卦《象辞》说：'大哉乾元，……保合太和，乃利贞。'"① "乾"这一术语表示宇宙运作的终极方式，被视为与自然力量相对照的一种完美的和解。正如余敦康先生在他的论文《〈周易〉的太和思想》中所阐述的："由于乾道的变化，万物各得其性命之正，刚柔协调一致，相互配合，保持了最高的和谐，所以万物生成，天下太平。"② 在《道德经》中，关于和谐的理念也有相似的阐述："道生一，一生二，二生三，三生万物。万物负阴而抱阳，冲气以为和。"③ 因此，《易经》中的"乾"和《道德经》中的"道"都被解释为原动力或宇宙的内在原理，其中包含着和谐互动的相对面，如阴和阳、明与暗、硬与软、水和火等，"太和"也因此被视为这些力量之间的动态平衡。此外，和谐理念也在《中庸》中得到阐述，"冲"和"和"是"中庸"的两个关键术语。书中提到："喜怒哀乐之未发，谓之中；发而皆中节，谓之和。中也者，天下之大本也；和也者，天下之达道也。致中和，天地立焉，万物育焉。"④ 因此，《中庸》中的和谐（或"和"）可以被视为恰当的完美状态，它着重强调适当的位置和各种元素在其中的比例。

在另一部著名的中国古籍《左传》中，晏子进一步阐述了和谐理念，他使用了一个著名的比喻："和如羹焉，水、火、醯、醢、盐、梅，以烹

---

① 冯友兰：《中国哲学简史》第 2 版，赵复三译，天津社会科学院出版社 2007 年版，第 287 页。

② Yu Dunkang, "The Concept of 'Great Harmony' in *The Book of Changes*", in Silke Krieger&Rolf Trauzettel(ed). , *Confucianism and the Modernization of China*, Mainz：v. Hase &Koehler Verlag, 1991, p. 53.

③ 老子：《道德经》，［英］亚瑟·韦利译，外语教学与研究出版社 1999 年版，第 90 页。

④ 冯友兰：《中国哲学简史》第 2 版，赵复三译，天津社会科学院出版社 2007 年版，第 284 页。

鱼肉。"① "和谐"同样是解读孔子思想的一个关键词汇，在《论语》中就出现了八次之多。作为一位圣人，孔子是良好的美德和礼仪的倡导者，"仁"和"礼"是《论语》中的两个主要概念，而终其一生，孔子都致力于完善人的道德与人格，使之成为君子（或完人）。儒家从和谐的角度解释了这两个概念。孔子认为，"仁"是"人与人之间的理想的关系"②，并强调在践行"礼"的规则中，"它这种和谐是值得珍视的"。通过强调"君子和而不同，小人同而不和"，孔子进一步拓宽了和谐思想的内涵。因此，根据孔子的观点，君子（或完人）一方面通过与人为善，另一方面通过保持自己的独立思想，从而能够达到对自身美德和人格的最大发展，这反映了孔子对个体的和谐观念的独特理解。总之，和谐是中国传统文化中的一个十分重要的概念，它体现了中国文化的最高理想，即"万物并育而不相害，道并行而不相悖。"③

二 "和谐"理念之辩证、动态阐释

上述引用的观点对和谐进行了不同的阐释，都表现出了对和谐的一般辩证与动态的认知，即强调差异、和解与创造的价值。首先，这些观点没有将和谐简单地看作一个内涵相同、统一和一致的范畴，而是特别强调了这一概念中蕴含的差异性、多样性和多元化的价值；其次，这些观点着重强调了不同事物之间的和解而非其中的对立、冲突与斗争；最后，这些观点认为，和谐能够在各种成分的转换合成过程中，为其中各方带来共同的益处，从而将其视为一种创造性的源泉。

---

① 冯友兰：《中国哲学简史》第 2 版，赵复三译，天津社会科学院出版社 2007 年版，第 47 页。

② Smith H. , *The Illustrated World's Religions：A Guide to Our Wisdom Traditions*, New York：Harper Collins, 1994, p. 110.

③ 冯友兰：《中国哲学简史》第 2 版，赵复三译，天津社会科学院出版社 2007 年版，第 286 页。

1. 差异：和谐的重要基础

当下，中国政府一直呼吁建立和谐社会与和谐世界，这一倡议对于中国及世界的健康发展都具有重大意义。然而，"和谐"这一概念常常被简化为各个方面的一致性和连贯性，在某种程度上，甚至被视为相同性和同一性。但应该认识到的是，中国传统文化孕育的差异性与多样性恰恰是和谐的基础。在《中国哲学简史》中，冯友兰先生曾引用晏子的比喻，对和谐与同一的关系作出了明确的区分：

> "和"便是协调分歧，达成和睦一致。《左传》中曾经记载，昭公二十年（公元前 522 年），齐国大夫晏婴有一段话，分析"和"与"同"的区别说："和，如羹焉。水、火、醯、醢、盐、梅，以烹鱼肉。"这些调料合在一起，产生一种新的味道，既不是醋又不是酱的味道。"同"则如同以开水作调料，或一个乐曲，只准用一个声音，并不引进任何新的味道。在中文里，"同"意味着单调一律，不容许有任何不同。"和"则意味着和谐，它承认不同，而把不同联合起来成为和谐一致。①

中国传统文化中的"和谐"理念能为跨文化交际提供丰富的资源。众所周知，跨文化交际的主要问题是处理源于不同文化背景和交际规则的差异，因此，这一理念对于理解跨文化交际中的差异至关重要，尤其是在当今的全球化时代，在中国及整个世界都被同质的商业文化威胁的今天，中国传统文化寻求差异和多样性的"和谐"理念，无疑是具有启发性的。

关于全球化的影响问题，激烈的争论仍在持续。持积极态度的一方认为，全球化可以带来诸多好处，人们得以有更多的机会去体验和欣赏来自不同国家的文化；而对全球化持消极态度的一方认为，这种过程是一种文化同一性的入侵。无论如何，正如硬币总有两面，全球化既为我们提供了跨文化交往的良好机遇，也带来了在处理文化差异时的巨大挑战。因此，在全球化

---

① 冯友兰：《中国哲学简史》第 2 版，赵复三译，天津社会科学院出版社 2007 年版，第 285 页。

过程中，对我们而言，防止同质化趋势的发展是迫在眉睫的任务。

正如上面提到的，中国目前正致力于构建和谐社会，因为和谐并不意味着一致，所以中国应该更多地听取和考虑来自人民的不同声音，不仅要看到来自"主流文化"的意见，而且要重视非主流文化发出的声音，如少数民族、弱势群体等。在对现代化的追求中，国人已然受益良多，然而，我们更应该警惕现代化带来的负面影响，应注重对多元文化，特别是少数民族文化的保护。虽然汉文化是中国的主导文化，但我们也应该确保少数民族文化的平等发展，然而，在现代化进程中，商业追求业已在一定程度上破坏了少数民族文化，例如，据某些研究人员考察，在中国东北地区，因为越来越多的年轻一代朝鲜族人选择去韩国和中国的其他大城市赚更多的钱，朝鲜本土文化正面临着毁灭的危险。

2. 和解：和谐的最佳策略

在跨文化交际过程中，寻求和谐是最宝贵的原则，因为和谐可以作为调和差异和对立的最佳策略。因此，保留分歧而避免冲突是跨文化交际中的明智之举。特别是在当前时代，世界正处于误解、紧张、冲突、恐怖主义、仇恨和战争的威胁中，求和平、求和谐、尊重文化的多样性和差异性就更有其宝贵和独特的价值。除此之外，需要采用对话、协商和合作的方式来调和文化差异，实现和谐，这是处理文化冲突很好的方法。

3. 创新：和谐的最高追求

传统文化观念中的和谐理念还强调建设性的创造力，在这种创造力的驱动下，所有部分的关系都是互动、互利的。我们将这一理念投射在跨文化交际领域中，可以看到，协调是创造性转化的动态过程，在这一过程中，不同文化通过不断发展、相互协作而完成转化，与此同时，也共同维护了自己的基本文化身份。由此可见，和谐能够促进多元文化的共存和共同繁荣，也可以实现文化的互利共赢。

回顾人类文明的历史，正是文化不断实现传播、吸收与创新的发展史。正如著名哲学家罗素在其论著《中国问题》第十一章"中西方文明的对比"中所指正："不同文明的接触，以往常常成为人类进步的里程碑。

希腊学习埃及，罗马学习希腊，阿拉伯学习罗马，中世纪的欧洲学习阿拉伯，文艺复兴时期的欧洲学习东罗马帝国。"从罗素的评论中我们可以看出，中西方文化之间的跨文化交流从未停止，而在这一进程中，东方文化和西方文化都在相互学习的过程中受益匪浅，中国学者汤一介对此分析道："罗素的这段话是否十分准确，可能有不同看法，但他说：一、不同文明之间的交流是促进人类文明发展的重要因素；二、今日欧洲文化吸收了许多其他民族文化的因素，而且包含了阿拉伯文化的某些成分。这两点无疑是正确的。如果看中国文化的发展，就更可以看到在不同文化之间由于文化原因引起冲突总是暂时的，而不同文化之间的相互吸收与融合则是主要的。"

从某种意义上说，每一种文化保持在一种封闭的状态都是非常困难的，原因在于，事实上，文化是随时变化的，变化的机制是一种文化借用另一文化从而生成一种新的文化，而和谐就包含着文化中的创新元素。以美国文化为例，美国经常被描述为一个世界上各种文化都混杂在一起的大熔炉。一位美国教授说，当被一个中国学生问到"什么是典型的美国食品"时，很难列举出一个食品名，因为甚至像麦当劳和肯德基这样的快餐也不是大多数美国人的主要选择，对大多数的美国人而言，基于家庭原因和个人喜好，他们有着各自不同的饮食选择，而美国文化的移民特征也导致了美国食物的多样性。这与中国的情况相似，自从中国在20世纪初对外开放以来，伴随着各种外来文化的涌入，中国从外面的世界学到了很多，中国文化也正在经历由农业文明向现代文明的转变过程。在这一过程中，一方面，古老的中华文明保持了传统的价值观；另一方面，也兼容并蓄了来自不同文化的价值观念。与此同时，中国文化也在对世界其他文化施加影响，世界各地的人们也因中国经济和文化受益良多。

总之，中国传统的"和谐"理念凸显了差异、和解与创造的价值，为跨文化交际提供了丰富的资源，也拓宽了中西跨文化交流的新视野。展望未来，正如王柯平教授在他的诗歌中所期许的：

东方不都是东方，

西方不都是西方，

为什么不到一块儿去。

让世界以多样的秩序

或是和而不同。①

（王梦瑶译，原载于中国大陆和美国同时发行的英文刊物《中国传媒研究》2009 年第 1 期，内容有删减）

---

① 王柯平：《中国文化的精神》，外文出版社 2007 年版，第 55 页。

中国传统文化中的时间取向的独特价值
——兼与西方文化中的时间观相比较

爱德华·霍尔曾经将非言语交际看作一个隐藏的、被忽视的维度，而现在，在跨文化交际学界，非言语交际领域愈来愈得到关注。然而，在过去，国内的非言语交际研究主要集中在身体语领域，而时间的问题往往被忽视，西方学术界对于中国传统文化时间取向的研究还没有充分的考虑。本文将尝试探索中国传统文化中的时间取向的独特价值，并兼与西方文化中的时间观念相比较。

在跨文化交际中，文化背景是关键因素，正如伍德所言："影响交际的最大的系统就是你的文化，这是所有的相互活动得以发生的环境。"① 跨文化交际中存在着众多值得研究的文化变量，时间就是其中最重要的变量之一。为此，美国时间研究学者布鲁诺用文化时间的概念来描述时间取向的文化差异：

> 文化时间取向是跨文化交际研究中的一个重要问题，因为它是反映文化的深层价值结构、生活理念和生活方式的一面镜子。尤其是传统的中国传统文化时间取向有其独特的价值观，这与西方文化中的时间观念存在着鲜明的对比。②

---

① Wood, J. T. , *Gendered Lives: Communication, Gender, and Culture*, Belmont, CA: Wadsworth, 1994, p. 29.

② Bruneau, T. J. (1977), *Chronemic: The Study of Time in Human Interaction. In J. A. Devito &M. L. Hecht (Eds.), The Nonverbal Communication Reader*, Prospect Heights, IL: Waveland Press, 1990, p. 309.

一　西方文化中的时间观

在某种意义上，时间是一个哲学命题，它与人存在的本质有着某种联系。著名古希腊哲学家赫拉克利特曾将时间比作一个玩游戏的男孩，然而，他认为，这个男孩并不是一个平凡的男孩，而是这个游戏中的权威之王。因此，根据赫拉克利特的解释，人类是从属于时间的，而时间是在控制人类生活中起主导作用的真正的世界之王。

"时间具有压倒一切的力量"这一观念深深植根于西方文明的土壤中，并体现在西方文化的方方面面。自从古希腊时期以来，时间常常被从物理方面进行考察。柏拉图将世界分为两层：现象界和理念界。他认为，现象界是虚幻的，只是绝对理念界的影子，它象征着现实的世界；而理念界是真实的，因为它代表着永恒不变的境界。虽然柏拉图贬低了现象界的价值，但他认为现象界是由时间可变的运动控制的。亚里士多德在他的著作《物理学》中，将时间定义为一个可以测量的对象，与柏拉图不同，他开始接受现象界的真实性，并进一步探讨了时间的物质性、客观性特点。

文艺复兴之后的科学家和哲学家们都遵循亚里士多德的思想，他们认为时间是一种直线运动的物体。著名的科学家，如伽利略和牛顿认为时间是一个用来计算物体运动速度的定量，这一时期的大多数哲学家，如勒内·笛卡儿和约翰·洛克也从物理领域对时间进行了解读。其中，牛顿对时间的解释最具影响力，在其著作《自然哲学的数学原理》中，他强调了"绝对时间"这一概念。事实上，对于运动中的绝对时间的物理阐释一直是西方文明的主导时间观念。

由亚里士多德和牛顿建构的对于时间的物理学阐释强调规律性、绝对性及时间的过程，在西方工业化的过程中，这些特点都得到了加强。正如芒福德所说："现代机器文明的第一个特征是它的时间规律性……从醒来的那一刻起，一天的节奏就开始以时钟敲响。时间声称，不论紧张或疲劳，无论拒绝或冷漠，人们都在不断地接近它的设定。"① 更重要的是，我们在西方文化中看到，时间通常被认为是明确的、绝对的、有价值的，甚至是用来衡量利润和成就的尺度，有许多著名的谚语都表达了时间的重要性："早起的鸟儿有虫吃"（美国谚语），"今日事，今日毕"（英国谚语），"早上浪费一小时，一天都在追逐它"（犹太谚语）。在西方文化中，时间已成为绝对的、决定性的力量，正如爱德华·霍尔所说的："西方世界的人们，尤其是美国人，往往认为时间是固定在自然界中的一种存在，环绕在我们的周围，我们不能逃避；时间是一个有史以来就存在的环境，就像我们呼吸的空气。"②

对直线运动的绝对时间的物理学阐释，加之工业文明的进步，形成了西方世界大多数国家的未来时间取向。以美国人民为例，他们特别重视未来，并且相信他们可以控制未来。

霍尔曾用"单向时间制"来描述上文所提到的西方文化中时间取向的特征，当然，单向时间取向有其自身的优点，据霍尔所说，秉持单向时间取向的人们专注于工作，认真对待时间许诺（最后期限，计划表），坚持计划，注意不去打扰别人，并遵守规则的隐私。③ 一般说来，在遵循单向时间取向的文化中，更加强调效率和及时性。

然而，我们也逐渐认识到，单项时间制也有其自身的缺点和局限性，甚至有些学者对此进行过尖锐的批评。正如基姆观察到的："生命是处于不断运动当中的，人们认为时间正在浪费或失去，除非他们正在做什么事情。"背负单向时间制重压的人们常常被时间看不到的铁腕所控制，他们的个性和自由也被严重损害。正如赖特曾一针见血地指出："这是不受抑制的、无法忍受的'chronarchy'一词，在《牛津英语词典》里找不到这个词。它的创造者应该定义它。让'chronarchy'不仅指'受时间的控

---

① Mumford，L.，*Technics and Civilization*，New York：Harcourt，Brace &World，1962，p. 269.

② Hall E. T.，*The Silent Language*，New York：Fawcett，1959，p. 19.

③ Hall，E. T. and Hall，R. H.，*Understanding Cultural Differences*：*Germans*，*French*，*and Americans*，ME：Intercultural Press，1990，p. 15.

制'，而且指通过计时使人系统化。"① 著名的中国作家和学者林语堂用另一个术语——"工作动物"，来形容一个文明程度更高的世界中的人们所面临的悲惨处境。他认为文明是一个寻求食物的问题："但是重要的事实仍然是，人类的生活已经变得太复杂了，而仅仅是直接或间接地养活自己，在我们人类活动中占了百分之九十以上。"② 赖特和林语堂所共同揭示的是，在现代工业社会中，人们越来越受到时间和物质的控制，人们的自由和个性已然受到了物化世界的极大破坏。

然而，中国传统文化的时间取向反映了对生活的不同态度，它可以帮助解决西方文化所面临的一些问题。不同于西方时间取向中强调客观性、绝对性和固化的时间，在中国传统文化的时间取向中，时间是主观的、相对的和灵活的。

众所周知，中国的文化深受儒、释、道三家思想的影响，其中，儒、道文化是本文的主要论述对象。在某些方面，这两家的思想所秉持的时间观念有所不同，然而，也有一些共通之处：它们既对时间持开放的态度，又把它视为相对的、无限的和灵活的存在。

二　儒家文化中的时间取向

几千年来，儒家思想文化在中国文化的塑造中扮演了重要的角色。正如巴里·陈·沃森指出的，"如果我们用一个词来描述这两千年来中国人的生活方式，这个词是'儒'"③。

孔子是一位倡导"仁"和"礼"的圣人，这也是他的两个最主要的思想内核，终其一生，孔子都致力于构建完善的个体德性，和国家整体的繁荣。他对生活持积极的态度，并认为时间是有价值的，是应该被好好利用

---

① Wright, L., *Clockwork Man*, New York：Horizon Press, 1968, p. 7.
② 林语堂：《生活的艺术》英文版，外语教学与研究出版社1998年版，第144页。
③ Barry W. T., Chen W. T. and Watson, B., *Sources of Chinese Tradition*, New York：Columbia University Press, 1960, p. 17.

的。据《论语》记载，有一次孔子站在河边，面对滚滚逝去的河水发出深沉的喟叹："逝者如斯夫，不舍昼夜！"① 然而，他在无尽的时间和思想的长河中保持了非常冷静的头脑，对生活也做出了积极的评价："吾，十有五，而志于学，三十而立，四十而不惑，五十而知天命，六十而耳顺，七十而从心所欲，不逾矩。"②

儒家文化另一方面的时间取向是过去时间取向，这不能简单地理解为一种保守性。孔子生活在春秋时期，这一时期礼崩乐坏，战乱频仍，因此，他非常不满现实的状况，并打算通过回顾过去，克己复礼，将周朝作为一个很好的模式实施社会改革。虽然孔子在下面的论辩中似乎指出了古代人的一些不足之处，但他真正的目的是表达对古代人的欣赏，并以此完成对他所在时代道德堕落的批判："古者民有三疾，今也或是之亡也。古之狂也肆，今之狂也荡；古之矜也廉，今之矜也忿戾；古之愚也直，今之愚也诈而已矣。"③

孔子与他同时代的其他哲学家对问题有不同的解决办法，在当时，法家思想占据主导地位，推崇严苛的法律和严厉的惩罚，而孔子则用这样的名言祭出周仪，表达自己的政治主张："周监于二代，郁郁乎文哉！吾从周。"④

孔子把周王朝的仪式看作一种继承了前代夏商文化的遗产，是一代又一代人智慧的传承，他把自己当作一个"传播者"，而不是一个"发端者"，因为他"信而好古"。⑤ 毫无疑问，孔子是一位圣人，他建立了一套独特的社会和伦理哲学体系，其思想对中华文化产生了深远的影响。然而，孔子坦率地把自己的思想归结为周礼的传承，因此，我们看到，在对待过去的时间态度上，儒家包含更多积极而非消极的内涵。由于孔子偏好"周礼"，他提出了"礼"的概念，这个词不仅指外部的仪式，也指根植于

---

① 蔡志忠：《孔子说：仁者的叮咛》，Brian Braya 译，现代出版社 2005 年版，第 79 页。
② Pan, F. E, and Wen, S. X., *The Analects of Confucius*, Jinan: Qilu Press, 2004, p. 11.
③ Ibid., p. 215.
④ Ibid., p. 25.
⑤ Ibid., p. 65.

个体生命中的优雅与文明礼仪。"礼"一直是孔子的重要教义之一。

最后，儒家文化对时间持灵活态度。在处理事务上，它强调"合适的时机"和"机会"，主张无论是国家大计，还是琐碎的家务事，都应该在一个合适的场合进行。孔子的继承者孟子发扬了孔子的思想，《孟子》一书中"拔苗助长"的寓言就是一个很好的例证，它生动地说明了在正确的场合做正确的事情的重要性："宋人有闵其苗之不长而揠之者，芒芒然归，谓其人曰：'今日病矣！予助苗长矣！'其子趋而往视之，苗则槁矣。"儒家文化中对时间的灵活处理，对中国文化产生了深远的影响，即使在现在，中国人也善于在商业、政治和日常生活中寻求处理事务的恰当时机。

总之，儒家文化中的时间取向是多维的，其过去的时间取向使其伦理内核建立在前朝传承下来的丰富的历史遗产之上，而积极的时间观念和对待时间的灵活态度同样具有启发性。

三 道家文化中的时间取向

林语堂认为，对中国人来说，仅仅有儒家文化是不够的，因为儒家"太高雅，太合理，太正确"[1]，从而在中国文化中又产生了道家文化。他还将儒家和道家做了比较说明："儒家学说通过它的礼仪和社会地位，代表着人类文化的约束，而道家强调回归自然，并不迷信人的限制和文化。"[2]

在本质上，道家思想是一种追求无限自由的、突破各种界限和限制的哲学。作为道家最有名的圣人，庄子终其一生都追求自由并且厌恶世俗名利。因为很有才华，他曾经被问及是否愿意在楚国为相，他没有直接回答，而是给楚王讲述了这样一个故事："吾闻楚有神龟，死已三千岁矣，王巾笥而藏之庙堂之上。此龟者，宁其死为留骨而贵乎？宁其生而曳尾于

---

① 林语堂：《吾国与吾民》，张振玉等译，外语教学与研究出版社 2005 年版，第 113 页。
② 同上书，第 114 页。

涂中乎?"而后, 庄子曰: "往矣, 吾将曳尾于涂中。"故事很快就有了答案——庄子说他也喜欢像乌龟一样摆动着尾巴在泥浆中自由自在地游泳, 享受没有限制的生活的快乐。他还写了另一篇关于"庄生梦蝶"的文章, 在文章中, 庄子想象自己变成了一只无忧无虑的蝴蝶, 并且发出了"不知周之梦为蝴蝶与, 蝴蝶之梦为周与"这样的疑问。事实上, 蝴蝶已成为庄子独特的自由观念的代表。①

在道家的思想中, "道"是庄子汲取了老子的主要观点后提出的最重要的概念之一, 而老子实际上是道家的创始人。老子以"道"为"天地万物之源", 而庄子以"道"为最高原则, 庄子之"道"中的生与死、美与丑、过去与现在等没有明显的界线。因此, 在道的概念的基础上, 庄子确立了他独特的相对论人生观。

就时间取向而言, 因为庄子对自由的追求和他独特的相对论的人生哲学, 所以道家主张时间的相对性和无限性。蔡志忠机智地解释道: "这是一种将人生专注于时空的无限性中以体验最丰富人生的哲学。"②

在其最为著名的作品《逍遥游》中, 庄子采用了一系列的隐喻, 试图说明他对于时间相对性的观点。下面列举了他文中一个很好的例子: "朝菌不知晦朔, 蟪蛄不知春秋, 此小年也。楚之南有冥灵者, 以五百岁为春, 五百岁为秋; 上古有大椿者, 以八千岁为春, 八千岁为秋。此大年也。而彭祖乃今以久特闻, 众人匹之, 不亦悲乎?"③

根据亚里士多德和牛顿的观点, 时间是一个绝对的物理概念, 八千年和五百年作为实际上的物质时间, 其长度肯定比一个春天、秋天或一天长。然而, 当与时间和空间的无限相比时, 它们在庄子的眼中并没有明确的分别。因此, 庄子在其整个生命中所追求的是超越各种限制的无限的自由, 这些限制或是一定时间和空间的限制, 或是来自世俗的束缚。时间对于庄子而言已不再是控制人类生活的主导力量, 而是被人类自由处理的对

---

① 参见蔡志忠《庄子说 I：自然的萧声》, Brian Braya 译, 现代出版社 2005 年版, 第 27 页。
② 同上书, 第 5 页。
③ 同上书, 第 6—7 页。

象，这将使人类享有更多的自由和轻松的时间。因此，依据庄子提出的对于时间的感知，前文赖特所提出的"chronarchy"可以轻易解释。

此外，道家的时间取向更加强调主观性，这也有助于培养中国传统文化的独特气质和悠闲的生活方式。在《生活的艺术》一书中，林语堂高度评价了"这游荡在中国的神圣的渴望"和"无忧无虑的，空闲的，幸福地走在中国的学者的幸运"，认为中国的普通人也"往往具有诗意的气质"，[①]他认为这种气质可以追溯到"道家的渊源"[②]。事实上，道家文化中无忧无虑的人生观，对中国人悠闲的生活方式产生了巨大的影响，这在中国古代诗歌中得到了很好的体现。

在著名的《汉英对照千家诗》中，就有许多诗歌生动地描绘了中国知识分子和普通百姓的悠闲惬意的田园生活图景，书中第一首题为"春日偶成"的诗就是一个很好的例子：

> 云淡风轻近午天，傍花随柳过前川。
>
> 时人不识余心乐，将谓偷闲学少年。[③]

身为伟大哲学家和诗人的程颢在写下这首诗时，已不再年轻，然而，一次春日的郊游使诗人忘记了他的真实年龄，他的心变得年轻而快乐。另一位著名的中国诗人苏轼在他的诗歌《春宵》中甚至表达了"春宵一刻值千金"的感觉。因此，林语堂表明了他对中国知识分子和诗人的随和的度日方式的欣赏，并称："最聪明的人也因他游荡得最优雅。"[④]

虽然越来越多的中国人，尤其是大城市的人们，开始有着更快的生活节奏，但在普通中国人的生活中，这种对生活的热爱仍会常常被观察到，多数普通老百姓还是更愿意花些时间和他们的朋友、亲戚或邻居聊天，享受无忧无虑的生活。

---

① 林语堂：《生活的艺术》英文版，外语教学与研究出版社 1998 年版，第 145 页。
② 同上书，第 150 页。
③ 郭著章、傅惠生等编译：《汉英对照千家诗》，武汉大学出版社 2005 年版，第 2 页。
④ 林语堂：《生活的艺术》英文版，外语教学与研究出版社 1998 年版，第 148 页。

总体看来，在传统的中国文化中存在着独特的时间价值观。儒家文化中的过去时间取向提醒我们，在人类文明和人类智慧的发展进程中文化遗产继承的重要性；道家的相对时间观则为我们提供了超越各种限制追求自由的可能性。此外，中国传统文化中时间的主观性、灵活性和相对性取向，也能够为持客观、绝对、未来时间观念的西方世界提供有意义的启示。

（王梦瑶译，原载于美国学术期刊《跨文化传播研究》2008 年第 XVII：1 期）

跨文化对话

——麦克·H. 普罗斯教授访谈录

访谈背景：

麦克·H. 普罗斯（Michael H. Prosser）教授为跨文化传播学创始人之一，美国弗吉尼亚大学及罗切斯特技术学院等院校知名教授，上海外国语大学新闻传播学院、北京语言大学英语学院、中国海洋大学、扬州大学等院校荣誉教授，曾任上海外国语大学跨文化研究中心学术委员会主席，"跨文化交际"丛书资深编辑。麦克·H. 普罗斯教授撰写、出版了近20部跨文化交际著作，包括专著《文化对话》，合著《跨文化视角下的中国人：交际与传播》（与 Steve Kulich 合著）、《中国跨文化交际》（与李萌羽合著）等，普罗斯教授还是 Ablex/Praeger，Greenwood 出版集团出版的"新千年的公民话语"丛书的编辑，这套丛书从 1998—2004 年共出版了18 本。

普罗斯教授在北美教过的学生有 8800 人，在中国教过的学生有 2300人，他在北京语言大学、上海外国语大学等高校召开的中国传播学大会上发表过 13 次主题演讲，在印度和俄国等高校也曾做过系列讲座。作为受访者，他 12 次受邀参加央视九套的"对话"节目，6 次参加上海外语频道的"说东道西"节目，多次参与中国国际广播电台的"了解名人"节目，被列入美国名人录、亚洲名人录和世界名人录。

2011 年，麦克·H. 普罗斯教授应邀赴中国海洋大学讲学，其间笔者对他做了此次访谈。该访谈主要内容有：普罗斯教授在美国积极参与跨文化交际领域学科建设和学术活动的情况；跨文化交际传授者的职责；学生批判性思维培养的重要性；东西方传统文化理念的价值；中国跨文化交际学科发展的态势及"思想全球化，行动本土化"对培养世界公民的启示意义等。

李萌羽（以下简称李）：众所周知，您是北美跨文化交际的奠基人之一，您积极参与跨文化交际领域的学科建设和教学与学术活动。比如，您启动了跨文化交际课程在美国的早期教学，协助组织了许多跨文化交际的国际会议，并且编写了大量相关书籍，您能更详尽地介绍一下您在该领域所做的重要贡献吗？

麦克·H. 普罗斯（以下简称普罗斯）：1967 年，我与演讲交际协会与国外大学见面时，就创建跨文化交际专业的事宜做了非正式的讨论。当时，我们并不确定怎样为这个专业准确地命名。20 世纪 60 年代中晚期，美国的许多大学都开始开设跨文化交际课程。我于 1970 年在印第安纳大学第一次讲授跨文化交际课程，以埃弗雷蒙德·C. 罗杰斯关于拉美革新的书作为教材。事实上，这使得这门课程更像是一门与交际和社会变革相关的课程，而不是一门跨文化交际的课程。而 1970 年，K. S. 西塔拉姆和其他人共同创立了国际交流协会跨文化与发展部。25 年前，也就是 1995 年，我和他共同主持了第一次曼彻斯特跨文化会议（曼彻斯特跨文化会议于 1995—2001 年一共举行了 6 次），以庆祝跨文化交际成立 25 年。

1971 年，演讲交际协会在印第安纳大学布朗郡州立公园举行了一次讨论会，决定将跨文化交际作为学术研究的一个独特科目加以建设。国际演讲交际协会主席威廉·豪威尔、加拿大言语交际协会主席格雷斯·雷曼、爱德华·L. 斯图尔特、埃德蒙·格伦、弗雷德·卡斯米尔、我还有我的 12 个研究生——其中最有名的是我带的第一个跨文化交际博士生威廉·J. 萨拉索塔，以及其他成员参加了这次会议。芭芭拉·孟菲尔斯、谢里·弗格森和冈萨雷斯一起讨论了未来跨文化交际的研究内容及如何去发展它这两个关键问题。

1973 年，在弗吉尼亚大学召开的马萨内会议上，我们中的 55 位与会者一起研究了跨文化交际、沟通和社会变革的学术要旨。美国海军也派出一个小代表团出席了这次会议。我写的《国家与民族间的相互交流》也在这一年出版。1974 年，在演讲交际协会、国际交流协会和国际跨文化教育培训研究协会的发起下，我们 200 个人齐聚芝加哥，以爱德华·L. 斯图尔特的"跨文化交际概要"作为学科内容建设的基础性文件，进行了探讨。会议记录已由演讲交际协会出版。1974 年，日美双边文化研究会议在日本的二本松市举行，这次会议旨在探讨两种文化交流模式的异同。我在《文化对话》一书中记录了这次会议。《文化对话》于 1982 年被译成日文。

1974 年，弗雷德·卡斯米尔成为《国际跨文化交流年鉴》的第一任编辑，在演讲交际协会和国家交际协会的赞助下，《国际跨文化交流年鉴》作为一部定期出版的年刊已发行了 25 年。1978 年，由于美国情报局的 L. 罗伯特·科尔斯的支持，我有机会在情报局为中层主管讲授跨文化交际的课程，并且担任该署副主任的顾问。随后，在 1979 年和 1980 年，我负责协调 23 期跨文化交际的全球半小时英文广播节目。

这些就是跨文化交际作为一门学科的发展。正如我在与史蒂文·J. 库里奇合编的《中国交际的跨文化视角》中指出的，19 世纪 80 年代和 90 年代见证了这一研究领域在北美及海外的成熟以及其在中国的迅猛发展。我和西塔拉姆教授一起主持了 1995 年至 2001 年在罗切斯特举行的六次跨文化交际专题会议，同时合编了两卷国际跨文化传媒的书册。1998 年至 2004 年，在亚历克斯、普雷格和格林伍德出版集团的倡议下，我成为 18 册国际跨文化传媒书籍出版的丛书编辑。从 2001 年到 2009 年，我在中国的几所高校讲授跨文化交际或国际传媒的课程，包括 2011 年在中国海洋大学的授课——这是我最近的一次教学活动。2010—2011 年，李萌羽教授和我合著了由高等教育出版社出版的《跨文化交际教程》一书，我们希望这本书能够帮助中国学生更好地理解跨文化交际的重要意义。2009 年和 2011 年，中国跨文化交际协会基于我对跨文化交际在中国的发展与研究所做的贡献授予我特别贡献奖，对此，我深感欣慰。

李：您喜欢引用苏格拉底的名言："我是一个公民，既不仅仅属于雅典，也不仅仅属于希腊，而是属于世界，"这句话对跨文化交际而言有何意义？

普罗斯：基于苏格拉底的这一理念，国际跨文化教育培训研究协会于1981 年将全球公民奖颁发给我。这使我受到了极大鼓舞。于是，我将自己最喜欢的这句不朽格言应用到我在北美、瑞典和中国的全部教学活动中。我坚信，培养学生的批判性思维，使他们形成多元化的世界观，最终成为真正的世界公民，是我们这些跨文化交际传授者的职责之所在。2010 年 6月，我在上海外国语大学跨文化交际研讨会上做了题为"参与其中：跨文化交际的学术发展历程"的发言，在发言中我谈到自己已朝着这个方向迈出了几步。

李：您经常称自己为"中美人"，在中国居住多年之后，您是如何看待自己现在的文化身份的？

普罗斯：实际上，早在 2009 年，上海外国语大学的一些硕士研究生就开始这样称呼我了。作为一名外国教授，我算不上真正意义上的中国人；形成了多元的世界观，即使我依然保持着我的美国人身份，也算不上完全意义上的美国人。旅居中国近 10 年，我从中国文化中汲取了许多积极的因素。然而，我依旧是一个全然的美国人。诚如一句戏言所言："你可以将麦克远离美国，却无法将其美国性拿掉。"我喜欢"中美人"这个说法，每当学生这样称呼我时，我都会感到很高兴。

李：您在中国执教近 10 年，已经相当了解中国文化和中国人了。那么，您从中国文化和中国人那里学到了什么呢？

普罗斯：除了我们上面提到过的那句著名的格言，苏格拉底还指出他的目标是成为一个明智、公正、诚实和善良的人。如果一个人打算接受"哲学家"这个头衔，他就会渴望成为一个这样的人。在柏拉图的《苏格拉底对话录》中，苏格拉底提到他力求获得更多知识，事实上他甘愿做一只马背上的小小的牛虻。苏格拉底与其他智者交流观点，通过对话的方式寻求真理。读了这些对话，我们确信，苏格拉底的确是早期最有智慧的思想家与哲学家之一。在中国，我把对西方哲学和笛卡尔名言"我疑故我思，我思故我在"的喜爱和对孔孟之道愈发强烈的兴趣及它们在现代中国人生活中的应用相融相交。虽然我几乎没有学过中文，但自 1949 年新中国成立以来，我一直是当代中国的认真的学生。我尽可能地大量阅读以更好地理解中国文化。在教授了 2300 名中国学生，给另外 8500 名中专生和大学生做演讲，同时为中国幼儿、小学生、中专生和大学生义务授课之后，我对中国青少年产生了特别的兴趣。在我们由高等教育出版社出版的合著《跨文化交际教程》中，我也谈到了这一点。

李：您对东西方文明分别为世界所做的贡献，尤其是像苏格拉底和孔子那样的伟大思想家对世界所产生的深远影响有什么看法？

普罗斯：其实在前面的交谈中，我对这个问题略有提及。尽管两种文明之间存在着巨大差异，但是东西方的思想、哲学和风俗传统往往是水乳交融的。中国人从西方学来了很多，认识到文明之间的异质性却还能相互借鉴取长补短是十分明智的。如今，每年光在美国学习的中国年轻人就有 10 万，或许也有同样数量的美国年轻人在学习中国的语言和文化（其中包括将近 7500 名在北京语言文化大学学习的美国学生，以及在美国、澳大利亚、加拿大和比利时等西方国家的孔子学院的中文研习班学习的学生）。可以说，这本身就对跨文化交际作出了巨大贡献。从个人的角度讲，由于不懂中文，无法用中文授课，我和许多外国专家都无法深入地了解当代中国及中国青少年。对我来说，这着实是个遗憾。

李：众所周知，在当今世界，全球化是一种发展趋势。从一方面来说，美国文化拥有最强的影响力，例如，好莱坞电影和以麦当劳和肯德基为主的快餐行业席卷了整个世界；从另一方面来看，随着经济的高速发展，中国似乎对世界发挥着越来越重要的作用。您对这种现象有什么看法？当今世界该如何实现全球化与区域化的协调发展呢？

普罗斯：马丁·雅克在 2010 年出版的《当中国统治世界》中指出，虽然中国和亚洲的现代化是以西方为导向的，这些我们可以通过对比中西方的衣着和装饰、食物、语言、权利和政策看出来。但是，实际上所谓的西化影响是亚洲国家站在自己的角度而言的。并且，他最后提出，亚洲和中国的社会应依据社会发展情况来实现其现代化。尽管我们认为麦当劳和肯德基在一些国家占有大量的市场份额，但事实上中国百胜餐饮集团在东西方比任何西餐馆都拥有更多的加盟店。所以说，最终每个亚洲国家都会采取切实可行的方式，摒弃不切实际的做法来应对全球化和区域化的问题。

李：跨文化交际自被介绍到中国以来取得了迅猛发展。您认为，与美国相比，中国在跨文化交际与研究中的优势和劣势是什么？

普罗斯：中国把跨文化交际作为一个研究领域始于 20 世纪 80 年代中期，与此同时，美国的跨文化交际已趋向成熟。但它在中国的发展非常迅速，并且正进入成熟期。如今，跨文化交际在技术和理论上都已取得了飞速进展，但是就其理论而言，跨文化交际却始终未能超越传统与现代化这两个既定语境。我认为，2008 年的北京奥林匹克运动会和 2010 年的上海世博会是中国近代史上积极的跨文化交际实践的两个标志性事件。虽然汉文化与 55 个少数民族的文化经常互动，但是也要注意与异质文化的交流。越来越多的西方人、非洲人、中东人、拉美人和亚洲其他国家的人需要去中国学习和工作。同样，也有越来越多的中国人需要走出国门，去其他国家学习和工作。一个短期旅行是文化交流的良好开端，但只有当我们长久生活在另一国家时，我们才能更好地理解其本土的文化，并且可以了解这两种文化是如何相互作用的。

李：到目前为止，您说您已经游历了世界上 64 个国家及许多城市，您似乎成为一个全球公民；您认为这种国际旅行可以帮助您开阔视野及更好地了解来自世界不同地区各种各样的人吗？

普罗斯：4 世纪希波的奥古斯丁提出："如果我们不旅行，就无法打开生命之书。"就我自己而言，在青少年时期，我就与父母一起短期地游历北美；大学毕业之后，我在欧洲进行了为期两个月的旅行；后来我和家人又进行了多次旅行。自从 2001 年来到中国之后，我又游历了日本、印度、柬埔寨、越南、泰国、菲律宾、新加坡、马来西亚、印度尼西亚、韩国、澳大利亚、新西兰、拉丁美洲和欧洲。我经常鼓励中国的青年人去办个护照，因为他们永远不知道走出国门开阔眼界的机会会何时降临到他们身上。我曾带领 7 个中国青年人走出国门，而正是这次旅行，使他们所有人几乎都获得了更加广阔的视野。我的三个孙儿都到过中国，其中有一个还去过西班牙，这为他们未来广泛的国际旅行奠定了基础。

李：您喜欢说"思想全球化，行动本土化"，这对成为一个全球公民有何启发？

普罗斯：这是一个国际化标语。要成为一个世界公民，不仅需要了解自己的国家，同时也应尽可能了解周边和海外国家。当地震、海啸或台风袭击某一国家或地区时，我们都有责任尽可能地为其提供帮助。对中国人来说，这意味着放下以往的民族伤痕，与外国人友好相处。如果我没有到中国去任教，我也许只会和那些在美出生的亚裔美国学生或者海外留学生交流，却永远无法与中国的同事和学生结下如此深厚的友谊。

李：您曾写过题为"同一个世界，同一个梦想：以跨文化交际构建和谐社会——中国跨文化交际前奏"的论文。当今世界，政治、文化和宗教的差异依然阻碍着不同国家之间的相互理解，面对这种情况，您认为我们应该怎样通过跨文化交流来创造一个和谐的世界？

普罗斯：在2001年我首次前往中国任教之际，已故的 D. 雷·海西教授给了我三条建议：第一，耐心；第二，耐心；第三，耐心。这三条建议同样适用于到海外去学习和工作的中国人。实现文化间和国家间的和谐并非易事，但是我们可以借助更多的合作和积极的关系去推动它。孔子"仁"（仁慈、友爱）的观念可以引导我们更深入地了解彼此，智慧和幸福作为实现美好生活的途径意味着我们必须共同努力寻求这种和谐。诚如一句中国谚语所言"千里之行，始于足下"。或者像人类学家玛格丽特·米德所说："更美好的世界始于有一个社区。"抑或如希拉里·克林顿所认为的"一个乡下孩子的成长需要一个村的良好环境"。而建设一个更美好、更和谐的国家、地区或国际社会，我们则需要理解并实践潘基文的观点："当今社会最大的危机在于全球性领袖的缺失，拥有全球责任感和全新世界观的公民少之又少。因此，我们需要思想全球化，行动本土化。"

（罗紫晨、吕越译，原载于《山东外语教学》2011年第6期）

语言、文化与传播

——罗伯特·圣·克莱尔教授访谈

访谈背景:

笔者于 2008 年赴美国路易斯维尔大学做访问学者期间,对传播学系的资深教授罗伯特·圣·克莱尔博士做了深度访谈。访谈内容包括语言及网络在知识传播中的重要性、中美文化喻体的差异性、中美跨文化传播学发展状况、全球化与文化传播、中美视觉传播的差异性及"文化网络"和"具身认知"等理论内涵阐释。访谈对我们从深层次上理解文化、语言、传播等问题具有很大的启发性。

李萌羽(以下简称李):罗伯特·圣·克莱尔博士,作为路易斯维尔大学传播学系的资深教授,您的研究领域非常广,您能介绍一下您的主要研究领域和学术成就吗?

克莱尔教授(以下简称克莱尔):我做学术研究的目的是洞察、探究问题,找到解决问题的途径和答案。这一种责任意味着若需要另外学习一门外语以便能够用这种语言读懂一些文献,我就要学习这门语言。我拿到学士学位时,对十一种语言已得心应手。我现在学习了二十八种语言,我将要学习的第二十九种语言将是汉语。就学术领域的内容来讲,当我试图解决一些跨学科的问题时,我将到课堂上学习其他领域的学科知识,并贪婪地阅读其他领域的书籍。我的老本行是语言学,但对自己在哲学、传播学理论、社会学、政治学、语言教育等领域的研究也颇感满意。能够在这些领域有所作为,花费了我多年的心血,但是这个探究多学科的旅程是非常值得的。

现在我正在从结构认识论和结构本体论的角度研究符号理论。我想修订符号交互作用模式，从哲学的角度研究人类认知和符号处理的过程。这是我目前正在研究的问题。

李：您建立了自己的学术网站，目前有 7 万多人次访问您的网站，这表明您的研究在网络上也产生了很大影响，您还建立了一个跨文化论坛网站，您认为网络在其中发挥了什么作用？

克莱尔：我的研究的责任之一就是复兴语言。我做因纽特文化研究而获得了博士论文，我研究了七种北美土著语言，我也因之成了讲授土著语言组织的成员。这个组织曾举办了一个讲授美洲土著语教师的研讨会，有二三百位教师参加。会后我们出版了与会成员的研讨成果，两周后我们把这一成果挂到了网上。它产生的影响是惊人的，网站的访问量达到了数百万次，访问者来自世界各地。网络加快了解决问题的速度。

我们通过网络相互学习，信息共享在当代学术研究中起了重要作用。我开设了一个个人网站，以期共享学术信息，我还创建了一个跨文化传播研究所，并在网上开设了跨文化论坛，栏目包括网络期刊、网络专题讨论、网络教材。我们正在为这些期刊、杂志争取刊号。

在一次哈尔滨的国际跨文化传播研究学术会上，一位来自伊朗的教授走上前来，说他现在在课堂上使用我发表的一些东西。我认为更多的学者应该通过互联网分享知识。按照西方思维，人们拥有对自己思想及著作的版权，这是无可非议的，因为学者创造性的劳动应该得到认可。然而问题是思想的商业化运作和控制，使得一些读者阅读一些杂志需要花费很多的钱，这把一些经济在某一水平线之下的国家的读者拒之门外。这是一个资本主义掌控知识的模式，这个模式是为少数人所操控、为少数人所服务的，因而我更赞成网络杂志的运行模式。网络杂志在知识分子中应该增加。

此外，还有另外一个原因，许多国家的文化传播方式迅速从印刷文化发展到传媒文化和视觉文化，网络杂志就是一种全新的传播范式。我的课就运用了课程管理软件，学生可以把他们的论文上传到校园网内部系统里，他们还可以把一些录音文件、电影剪辑片断、超链接、超文本的材料传上去，这是传播在未来发展的方向，互联网促成了这种新的传播范式。

李：似乎您的学术观点受芝加哥社会学派的影响很大，比如，我注意到您更倾向于从社会学的角度研究文化、语言、传播，为什么您认为社会学视角如此重要？

克莱尔：西方人喜欢把自己视为生命个体，他们喜欢这样想，他们所取得的一切成就应归功于个人努力。他们认为自己是自我造就的。这是西方思维的盲目性。事实是，每个人成功的背后通常有六七个层面的人在发挥重要作用。在亚洲文化中这一点是显而易见的。人们置身于一个由社会人组成的社会，必须在做事时考虑到他人，每个人都是作为一个社会群体成员的身份行动的。每个人具有社会自我和个体自我的双重角色。个体在更广的社会语境下所扮演的是一个和谐的角色，他要尊重同样参与社会群体活动的他人。

芝加哥社会学派在美国学界的独特处正在于此，它为美国文化提供了一种社会自我模式。欧文·高夫曼提供了一种绝妙的自我中心角色模式，他的同事们则进一步研究现代社会人的社会角色是如何扮演的。同这一研究模式相关的是德国的法兰克福社会学新学派，也是致力于探究个体是如何被社会化的，我对此非常着迷。它为人们该如何看待自我提供了洞见。但在社会结构的分析上，这一模式还没有充分展开并进行细化研究。仅仅了解人在现实中是如何被社会化的还不够，我还想知道这一结构和其他社会及语言模式之间的关系。因而，我正在从事社会文本理论的研究，以探究人们在社会中扮演的各种角色。诸多社会学的研究模式表明这些角色是确实存在的。这只是一个非常有趣的发现，用一个一以贯之的社会和文化模式阐释分析这些角色的探索之旅刚刚开始。

李：您的一本书中谈到文化喻体可以被用来概括文化系统的总体特征，你能详细阐释一下这一观点吗？

克莱尔：有许多这样的比喻，可能会有不同的阐释。比如当代美国文化中"航程"这一喻体，但它不是一个根植于美国文化的核心喻体。"成长"作为西方思维的一部分，是一个核心的喻体。"进步"这一喻体，已有三百多年的历史，它也和"成长"喻体有着密切的联系，它构成了美国人看取世界的本质内核。"旅程"或许是亚洲文化的一个喻体，却不是美国文化的核心喻体。基于此，我认为研究构成一种文化特征的主要喻体是一件富有洞察力的探索。美国文化的喻体有成长、机器、世界舞台、线性时间和欧几里德空间喻体等。

中国也有其文化喻体，我的一个博士生正在研究这一课题，他正在梳理中国主要的文化喻体，并分析它们是如何反映中国思维和文化的一些总体特征的。

李：您认为美国的传媒产业对美国当代文化有何影响？

克莱尔：传媒对美国文化的影响与社会化进程有很大关系。大众传媒在人们被社会化的过程中起着重要作用。它提供了一种社会"剧本"，告诉人们应该怎样去表演。很多人并没有意识到这些影响及它是如何改变美国文化的。一旦我能在细节方面具体阐释社会剧本理论，我就能阐明这些影响及它们是如何发挥作用的。我们现在还没有做到这一点。

李：您能评价一下美国跨文化交际研究的现状吗？

克莱尔：语言学家喜欢研究理论和思维诸系统，许多传播学者则不擅长此道，他们提出了很多研究课题，却用定量研究的方法来求证。他们并没有致力于对传播学中的一些重大的哲学层面问题的研究。我所创建的新网站试图研究这些问题。我从符号理论和探究人类交际行为中结构所起的重要作用着手。我正在构建跨文化交际模式，已经勾勒出了一个大纲，正在进一步细化研究。譬如，跨文化交际不是近期才有的现象，它始于古老帝国的商贸活动，我正在研究这一过程，梳理这一交际模式是从何时开始的，文化知识和交流风格在这些语境下是如何产生并通过文化扩散被人们所分享的。

李：似乎中国学者和日本学者在跨文化传播领域越来越活跃，您怎样评价他们对此领域的贡献？

克莱尔：在跨文化传播领域，每个国家都有一些领军人物。在日本，教授 Masanori Higa（University of the Air）是一个杰出的学者，他曾在很多国家生活过，精通西班牙语、葡萄牙语和英语。他对唤醒日本学界的跨文化交流意识作出了很大的贡献。Nobuyuki Honna（Aoyama Gakuin Daigaku）也是如此，他们都是国际跨文化传播学会非常活跃的人物，我曾经担任该学会的执行主任长达十年之久。胡纳曾致力于研究各种形式的亚洲英语，他做得很出色，但在日本之外影响不大，如果他的杂志能做成电子杂志，他的贡献能更好地得到认可。

在中国，哈尔滨工业大学的贾玉新教授在跨文化交际学理论研究领域非常活跃，他组织承办了两次非常成功的国际跨文化交际研讨会，于2007年在哈尔滨举行的国际跨文化传播研讨会的参会成员达七百多人，贾教授还指导了此领域的许多博士论文，对促进跨文化交际学科在中国的确立发挥了重要作用。贾教授现在是中国跨文化传播学会的会长。作为中国跨文化传播学会名誉会长的胡文仲教授是在领域中另一位有影响的学者，他在推动跨文化传播在中国的发展中所起的重要作用值得进一步探讨，因为他的贡献远远不止这些。

美国罗得岛大学的陈国明教授现在是国际跨文化交际学会的执行主任，他是又一位致力于推动中国跨文化交际学研究的学者。他同广州的同行学者们协力做了很多工作，以期把中国此领域的研究推到最前沿。

最后，我们还应该提到上海外国语大学跨文化交际研究中心的顾力行和普罗斯教授，两位教授与上述所提及的学者们齐心协力，共同推动了跨文化传播学在中国的发展。

中国学者所创建的跨文化交际领域的诸多研究模式非常好。但中国学者所需要做的是使他们的学会向国际化方向发展，能够主办重要的国际期刊。重要的不仅仅是质量问题，而且要得到国际认可。

李：目前全球化的趋势愈演愈烈，您如何看待全球化对当今世界文化与传播的影响，以及各种全球化理论？

克莱尔：全球化并不是新事物，全球文化传播的过程一直在持续。有两个全球化范式值得一提，首先，文化传播和影响的速度令人吃惊。这部分归因于现代文化之间的大规模信息传递和商品交换。其次，目前学者们所提出的现代性范式过于狭窄，基本限于经济模式，对目前全球化的进展展示的是一幅不平衡的图景。它忽略了一种新的全球文化现代性的发展，这种新模式受多种力量的影响，譬如经济范式、全球经济贸易、现代化的建筑、高速公路、便利的交通、空中旅行等。我目前正致力于研究文化现代性。

李：视觉传播越来越受到人们的关注，您能谈一谈它为什么重要吗？在传播中它起什么作用？

克莱尔：在西方文化的思维观中，逻辑在语言哲学中起着重大作用。逻辑建立在演绎推理的基础上，这就是在推理中为何有大前提、小前提及结论。人们认为这种理性思维的模式在解释人类如何思考方面行之有效。这是一种类推推理，人们首先假定某些概念、想法、形式、模式是一种来源，通过类同推理推导出一种新的东西。譬如，以太阳系为例，人们根据其他行星围绕太阳环行这一模式推导出在原子系统内电子环绕核子运行的模式。类推思维的重要性在于它是人们解决问题的主导模式。然而，视觉思维同言语类推在很多方面不同。在视觉思维中，人们构建了一个认知空间，并且在这个空间内组织、安排物象的空间位置，这也正是视觉类推的源泉。在西方思维观中（特别是罗道夫·阿赫姆模式中），人们以视觉空间的正方形的中心为视点，其他物象围绕这一中心平衡、对称分布。西方视觉艺术家们熟知这一创作模式，将其运用于视觉作品创作中。问题是，并不是所有文化都采用这种罗道夫·阿赫姆模式，很多文化中视觉空间是垂直从右到左安排的。跨文化传播中的视觉传播是一个新的研究领域，这也是我为此着迷的原因。

李：您能介绍并评析一下"文化网络理论"吗？

克莱尔：系统论告诉我们，任何事物都不是孤立的，都是和更大的网络连接在一起的，系统内的各因子相互作用。目前大多数从事文化研究的学者都没有这种系统论意识，也没有意识到人类系统和非人类系统有着本质的不同。在商业、广告和大众传媒领域，这两个系统常常是合并在一起的。这向理论构建提出了挑战。文化网络理论是这种范式研究的开端，它把文化视为一个系统，并试图描述这个系统内各组成部分如何相互作用。除此之外，它还探讨富有创造力的各系统如何增生扩散出新系统。这适用于人类系统和非人类系统。学者们应该致力于系统理论研究，以构建出更好的人际传播和跨文化传播的范式。

李：您还有一个研究方向，称为"具身认知"，您能详细解释一下这一研究领域吗？

克莱尔：所谓"具身认知"是指人的大脑并不局限于头盖骨之内，而是和整个身体相连。大多数语言学家从语言学范式中推断出生物学信息，而真正需要做的是从中突围出来。我们需要做的是研究人们如何在生理上发声和接受视听信息，并根据此信息建立一个语言学的范式。目前语言学家对语言生理学层面的研究还主要是推断性的，缺乏对生理学的探究深度。目前我正在和医学院的同事们着手从生物学、生理学和化学的角度向外探究，以寻求语言学理论范式。

李：越来越多来自不同国家的访问学者到您的跨文化传播研究所，在您的指导下工作，您如何评价他们的访问？

克莱尔：我们彼此相互学习。我们在一起共事，分享见解，从各自的思想库中探究美妙的见解，所以并不是指导与学习的关系。我们各有自己擅长的专业，但在其他领域却像个幼稚的孩子。譬如一个出色的语言学家，对系统论或社会学理论有可能知之甚少。我们在一起共事，可以相互学习，这正是访问学者来此的意义所在。

（李萌羽译，原载于《中国海洋大学学报》2010 年第 4 期）

福克纳研究在美国

——罗伯特·W. 罕布林教授访谈

访谈背景:

罗伯特·W. 罕布林是美国东南密苏里州立大学外语系教授、福克纳研究中心第一任主任。他共出版了 14 部福克纳研究著作（合著）、三部诗集。其福克纳研究代表著作有：《福克纳：布罗德斯基收藏本理解指南》（五卷本，与路易斯·丹尼尔·布罗德斯基合著，密西西比大学出版社 1982—1988 年版）、《威廉·福克纳百科全书和福克纳研究指南》（与查里斯·P. 皮克合著，绿林出版社 1999、2004 年版）、《福克纳教学：途径与方法》（与斯蒂芬·合恩合著，绿林出版社 2000 年版）、《21 世纪中的福克纳》（与安·J. 阿贝迪合著，密西西比大学出版社 2003 年版）、《威廉·福克纳批评指南：福克纳生平及著作文学参考文献》（与 A. 尼古拉斯和迈克尔·高雷合著，档案出版公司 2008 年版）、《福克纳和台湾》（与梅勒尼·斯贝特合著，东南密苏里州立大学出版社 2009 年版）。

2008 年 12 月，本书作者赴美国东南密苏里州立大学福克纳研究中心做学术访问，对罕布林教授就美国诺贝尔文学获奖作家威廉·福克纳进行了专题访谈，在访谈中，罕布林教授首先介绍了美国东南密苏里州立大学福克纳研究中心及其对福克纳研究的贡献，继而探讨了美国福克纳研究状况、约克纳帕塔法神话体系的重大主题，福克纳作品中所涉及的过去观、种族观、男女主人公的塑造及其短篇小说和诗歌的价值等诸多问题。在访谈的最后，罕布林教授评析了福克纳的文学成就和中国的福克纳研究，本访谈为英文稿，由本书作者翻译成了中文，希望能对国内福克纳研究有所启发和借鉴。

李萌羽（下文简称李）：从 20 世纪 30 年代威廉·福克纳被介绍到中国开始，中国读者和学者便对福克纳表现出很大的兴趣。特别是 80 年代以来，中国学术界对福克纳的研究持续升温，福克纳成为中国学者最为关注的西方作家之一，研究成果不断涌现。然而，中国目前的福克纳研究也存在一些局限性。中国学者大多依据译介过来的福克纳作品做研究，而目前翻译过来的只是福克纳的代表性作品，他的其他作品很少有人问津，且中国学者对福克纳西方研究学术成果的了解也不够全面。因此，非常有必要架起一座中西福克纳研究的桥梁，尤其是把美国福克纳研究的学术成果介绍给中国学者是一件非常有意义的事情。罕布林教授，今天下午，在福克纳研究中心，我想就福克纳创作和美国福克纳研究的情况做一个专题访谈，希望您能和我们的学者和读者分享这方面的信息，以及您多年研究福克纳的心得，下面我有一些问题要向您请教。

罗伯特·W. 罕布林（下文简称罕布林）：谢谢！我期待着和你交谈。

李：谢谢！首先，您能介绍一下美国福克纳研究的现状吗？

罕布林：美国系统的福克纳学术研究始于 20 世纪 50 年代，在福克纳获得诺贝尔文学奖之后，至今福克纳研究在美国依旧很热。我想其中的一个原因是福克纳的小说具有开放性，可以从不同的批评角度探究。最初的美国福克纳研究在很大程度上受到新批评理论的影响，侧重于从作品的结构、形式、语言运用等方面进行文本细读分析，早期还有大量的研究关注福克纳作为一个美国南方作家的特殊性，探究他的作品致力于发掘美国内战和战后重建的悲剧性文化遗产等特质。近年来，福克纳研究的视角主要有种族、性别、后殖民主义，甚至环境批评，等等。人们也许会认为，这么多年过去了，福克纳研究会出现衰退的情形，但事实不是这样。即便是在今天，在福克纳获得诺贝尔文学奖六十年之后，平均每年还会有一百多部福克纳研究著作和论文发表。因此，福克纳仍然被视为美国最伟大的作家之一，当代美国学者依然孜孜不倦地致力于福克纳作品研究。

李：您能更具体地谈一谈美国福克纳研究的著名学者及他们的代表

作品吗？

罕布林：早期最有影响的福克纳研究学者是马尔科姆·考利，1946 年他出版了《袖珍福克纳文集》，文集序言是一篇开山之作。第一部福克纳研究专著是哈利·坎贝尔和罗奥·福斯特于 1951 年出版的《威廉·福克纳：批评性评价》，或许早期最好的著作是克林斯·布鲁克斯在 1963 年出版的《威廉·福克纳：约克纳帕塔法县》，早期其他优秀的福克纳研究者还有理查德·P. 亚当、迈克尔·米尔盖特、梅尔文·伯克曼、欧嘉·威克利、沃尔特·史拉托夫、哈亚特·H. 瓦格纳和欧文·豪。目前出版福克纳研究著作最多的学者是诺埃尔·鲍克，他的研究涵盖了几乎所有福克纳作品的文本解读、心理学分析和主题探析。

另一位杰出的当代批评家是菲利普·温斯顿，主要研究福克纳作品中的种族问题。撒迪乌夫·戴维斯也曾探讨过福克纳作品和种族的关系。约翰·T. 欧文的《成双和乱伦：重复和复仇》是最好的心理分析学著作。两位历史学家，乔尔·威廉姆森和唐·柯南道尔对福克纳的作品做了详细的历史文本分析。明罗斯·格温、黛博拉·卡拉克、萨利·佩奇、大威·威廉斯主要从女性角度研究福克纳，刘易斯·戴伯尼研究福克纳作品中的土著美国人，詹姆斯·凯若泽和 Theresa 唐娜为福克纳 1942 年后的作品的质量辩护，这些作品曾遭到早期评论家的贬低。后殖民主义批评家如黛博拉·考恩、马克·弗里斯曾探究福克纳作品对加勒比海和拉丁美洲作家的影响。我的福克纳研究中心同事克里斯多佛·瑞格从生态学和环境批评的角度阐释福克纳的作品。最重要的福克纳诗歌评论家是朱迪斯·森西巴，在其著作《福克纳艺术的起源》中分析了福克纳诗歌对其小说的影响。布鲁斯·卡文、吉恩·菲利普斯、路易斯·丹尼尔和我主要研究福克纳的电影作品。第一部内容较为翔实的福克纳传记是约瑟夫·布劳特纳撰写的，出版于 1947 年。其后，弗雷德里克·卡尔、大卫·明特、斯蒂芬·欧茨、理查德·格雷（英国人）和杰伊·帕瑞尼都出版过福克纳传记。我向大家特别推荐的是布劳特纳的传记，这部传记如实记载了福克纳的生平并包括帕瑞尼撰写的福克纳作品的评论。

李：就我所知，你们中心在福克纳研究中起了很大的作用。作为中心的主任，您能介绍一下你们中心在福克纳研究中所做的贡献吗？

罕布林： 因为有布罗茨基的收藏，我们中心得以成立。从 1978 年开始，我和路易斯·丹尼尔·布罗茨基合作了 10 年之久，在 20 世纪 80 年代我们一起写书和文章，举办展览和讲座，1988 年他作出决定，把他私人收藏的福克纳资料放到这里，现在我们研究中心已成为世界四大福克纳作品收藏中心之一，其他三个中心分别是弗吉尼亚大学、密西西比大学和得克萨斯大学收藏中心。自布罗茨基先生把他私人收藏的福克纳资料放到这里来的那天起，我们就把这些资料向所有福克纳研究学者开放。我们很高兴能够接待不但是来自美国，而且是来自世界各国如中国、日本、朝鲜、加拿大、英国、法国、德国和罗马尼亚的学者，欢迎他们参阅这些资料并从事福克纳研究。所以很难把中心和布罗茨基收藏分开。很荣幸能够和布罗茨基先生合作了三十年之久。因为有他和他的收藏，我才得以和诸多学者一起研究福克纳，我真是感到莫大的荣幸。

我们还有一个网站，帮助那些不能亲自到这里访问的学者。我们很高兴能够通过互联网提供福克纳研究资料，譬如照片、复印的书信、扫描的文件及网上所进行的问题解答。我们很高兴能在此接待访问学者，也很乐意运用现代互联网技术给来自世界各地的人们提供帮助，因为毕竟很多人因经济和其他原因还不能够到这里来。所以网站建设是福克纳研究中心很重要的一个工作。我希望此访谈发表后能够有更多学者了解我们中心和网站。不管是通过互联网联系还是在此接待访问学者，我们都很高兴能够帮助学者们从事福克纳研究。

李： 现在让我们转向讨论福克纳作品。众所周知，福克纳创造的约克纳帕塔法世系常被视为一个旧南方的神话，同时也是一个现代社会的神话，您是怎样看待这一神话体系的？

罕布林： 福克纳的约克纳帕塔法小说植根于南方的奥克斯福，所以它是以真实世界为摹本的。福克纳生于斯长于斯，因而他的作品反映这个地方的生活就很容易理解。但约克纳帕塔法要远大于奥克斯福，或密西西比，或美国，它是现代人生活状况的神话再现，是福克纳对人性、人类的社会结构、宗教、种族及所有这些事情的文学艺术呈现。它是一个了不起的成就，是一种具有伟大想象力的创造。美国文学还没有类似的体系。

李：是的，它确实很独特。那么您认为在约克纳帕塔法神话体系中蕴含的主题有哪些？

罕布林：福克纳的小说的主题不计其数，你可以发现很多主题。其中一个显性主题就是过去对现在的影响，就像他的小说主人公加文·史蒂文斯所说的那样："过去从来没有死去，它甚至没有成为过去。"在美国南方，奴隶制、美国内战和重建、穷人争取公平和正义，有许多过去因素影响着现在。福克纳作品伟大的主题之一就是表现他的主人公如何处理过去和现在的关系。就历史而言，有很多过去的东西值得我们去珍惜、敬仰和保存，但也有很多过去的负面的东西需要我们抛掉、改变和超越，以便能够继续前行。就像我们的个人生活，有很多让人感到不愉快、悲剧性的事件，我们必须把它们抛到一边，继续前行。我想福克纳的很多作品揭示了其主人公有必要摆脱过去，走向现在和未来这一主题。有时过去可被视为具有积极意义的遗产，因为传统中有我们必须保存和珍视的东西，但是很多过去的因子已成为一个负担、诅咒，比如奴隶制度，因而表现过去和现在的紧张关系是福克纳作品的重要主题之一。

在作品中，福克纳还表达了对联邦政府、北方、性别、女性的角色、种族、社会等级、宗教、战争、穷人和富人的矛盾关系等诸多问题的看法。马克思主义者会觉得福克纳的书很有趣，因为福克纳的作品经常表现穷人——无论是白人还是黑人——的生存困境及他们与经济体制的抗争，这种体制把他们远远抛在后边，不给他们任何机会。因而，福克纳的小说还表现了社会阶级的冲突。但是我认为展现过去和现在的冲突是福克纳小说的一个核心主题。

李：个人和社会的关系是美国文学和政治表现的一个重大主题，福克纳的小说也表达了类似的主题吗？

罕布林：就个体对他人、团体的责任而言，福克纳持一种传统的眼光。极端个人主义者在福克纳的小说中生活得很孤独。乔·克里斯莫斯作为悲剧性的人物是一个很好的例子。谈到个人责任，我们要谨记福克纳属于南方文学传统，没有受到决定论观点的束缚。总体而言，南方作家认为我们有必要作出负责任的选择，我们不应把失败归咎于遗传或环境因素的影响。19世纪末20世纪初，自然主义者和决定论者占据美国文坛的主导地位，譬如斯蒂芬·科恩、弗兰克·诺里斯、杰克·伦敦、Theodore 德莱赛。福克纳曾经受过这些作家的影响，但他像大多数其他南方文艺复兴的作家一样，从不愿意放弃这样一个观点：人的命运是自由选择和自由意志的结果。我们在作出自己的选择，如果我们作出了好的选择，我们就会收获幸福，我们就能在团体中生活得很快乐，我们就会有一个成功的人生。如果我们作出坏的选择，我们就要遭受痛苦并自食苦果。福克纳小说的主人公是莎士比亚式的，不是希腊式的，他们的生活遵循自由选择的自由而不是仅仅受制于命运的控制。他们通过自由选择为自己的命运负责。这种信仰使南方作家，尤其是福克纳有别于许多20世纪持决定论观点的作家。

在福克纳的作品中，自由选择、自由意志、个人责任起决定性的作用。福克纳作品的主人公或是撒旦式的，像弗莱姆·斯诺普斯、金鱼眼；或是圣人式的，如迪尔西、《八月之光》中的拜伦·邦奇。福克纳的作品中总是充满善与恶的斗争，因为人们的心灵总是处于矛盾和分离状态之中。有一种牵引力不仅把你拉向旧的、丑陋的过去，也把你拽向人性恶的一边。你必须与之抗争，你要选择什么是好的、可以接受的，尽管这很难。在这一方面，福克纳的看法与基督教相一致。福克纳生于一个基督教背景中，所以他受到《圣经》观点很大的影响。他相信在这个世界上我们无时无刻不在作出选择，若我们作出正确的选择就会通向幸福之路，作出错误的选择就会导致悲剧和不幸。南方作出了很多错误的选择：奴隶制是一个，美国内战是一个，毁坏大森林是一个。你必须纠正这些先前作出的错误的选择，为的是现在能够作出正确的选择。但你不是孤立地在作出这些选择，你是人类大集体中的一员。

李：有一种存在主义理论，它与福克纳的观点有相似之处吗？

罕布林：存在主义强调自由意志和自由选择，存在主义有一个著名的论断叫"人注定是自由的"，这种观点可以说与决定论思想相对抗。但是福克纳只是在一定程度上赞成存在主义的观点，却反对存在主义所持的对世界虚无、悲观的态度，他不认为我们的世界是荒谬的，他的人生态度更为积极。但福克纳对人的行为和历史，特别是人的自由和责任问题的看法确实与存在主义思想有很多相同之处。

李：福克纳在他的作品中揭示，南方在工商资本主义的侵蚀下发生了很大变化，福克纳怎样看待这种变化和工商资本主义的入侵？

罕布林：福克纳喜爱自然，热爱土地，他对工业化和商业化持一种怀疑的态度，但他同时又认识到应处理好这些关系。班吉生活在一个永远天真的世界中，他的心理年龄只有三岁，他也永远停留在三岁上了。但福克纳不认为班吉所代表的世界就是一个完美的世界，相反他是可悲的，他被困在某一个生命阶段，不能成长和前进，这是一种悲剧。应对挑战的正确态度是抓住旧世界中好的东西让它们和你一起前行，并把它们带到当代世界中。过去并不是一定就比现在好，反之亦然。过去有些事情可能比现在好，现在有些事情也许比过去好。因而，你必须作出聪明的选择、理智的判断。自然和工业化的关系也是这样。福克纳一直倡议保护土地、尊崇荒野、古老的界标和建筑。比如他曾竭力保护奥克斯福的旧法院，当时很多居民以进步为由想拆掉它，再建个新的。但今天当你参观奥克斯福，瞻仰宏伟的旧法院时，你就发现福克纳是对的。福克纳尊崇传统中美好的事物，他认为我们应该以它们为荣，携带它们前行，然而过去也有我们需要抛掉的东西，因为它们对我们有害。

诺埃尔·鲍克是一位杰出的福克纳研究学者，他把福克纳称为一个"夹在中间的人"。他的主人公也是如此，他们必须应对过去和现在的两极关系，这也是福克纳小说具有开放性的原因。他不会把自己的想法强加给读者，而是把问题做戏剧化的处理，让读者对作品的主旨和寓意作出自己的判断，他知道我们读者总会以不同的方式进行思索。福克纳并不赞成回到过去，班吉这一人物揭示了被过去所困的悲剧，昆丁、盖尔·海托华、托马斯·斯德潘也是如此，福克纳所塑造的沉溺于过去不能走向现在的人物都是悲剧性的主人公，同样，他笔下那些生活在现在、没有道义根基、没有过去的主人公，就像斯诺普斯们，也是悲剧性的人物。斯诺普斯们在现在和将来中苟且偷生，但他们没有人性根基，没有价值追求和道义理念，他们是无耻之徒。他们掌控权力和金钱，贪婪成性，但他们只是兽性的动物，缺乏人性，他们需要以积极的态度来面对变化。所以处理好过去和现在关系的秘诀是要寻求两者之间的平衡。福克纳塑造的最好的人物有迪尔西、拜伦·邦奇和 V. K. 拉特利夫，他们都是成功处理好了上述对立的关系。

李：种族是福克纳作品一个非常重要的因素，您认为福克纳对它持一种什么样的态度？

罕布林：几乎所有南方作家的作品都涉及种族，因此福克纳小说涉及种族问题也就不足为怪。福克纳的曾祖父拥有奴隶，因此在他的小说《去吧，摩西》中描写了麦卡斯林家族的故事，这或许就是福克纳自己家族的历史。福克纳非常同情生活在这个世界上的小人物，不管他们是何种肤色。在美国南方历史上，黑人曾饱受歧视，被视为二等公民，在公交车上他们被隔离在后面。福克纳呼吁正义、公平，《去吧，摩西》就是一个很好的例证，主张人们无论是何等肤色，都应该是平等的，都应该依照法律受到平等的对待，应该在经济、商业和政治等方面享有平等的机会。尽管如此，但我不认为福克纳在种族问题上就是一个自由主义者，我称他为一个保持中立的人。福克纳是一个南方白人，他没有活着看到民权运动和后来美国发生的巨大变化。他生活的世界迥然不同，是一个更为保守的年代。他主张黑人应该享有平等教育权利，但我不认为他会赞成社会融合。我想，若他的女儿吉尔带回家一个黑人男朋友，他会不安的。因而，我认为福克纳是一个持中立立场的人。就种族问题而言，福克纳是他时代和地域的产物。我确信如果他还活着，他会很惊讶（我想也会很高兴）地看到他的国家在民权运动五十年后有了一位非裔美国总统。福克纳认为美国种族观念发生根本性的变化，也许会需要一百年的时间。所以我深信福克纳看到美国南方在种族关系上的巨大变化会感到非常震惊。

福克纳的一些最好的小说譬如《去吧，摩西》《八月之光》都以种族特别是兼有白色和黑色双重血统的人物为表现的对象。福克纳很清楚，美国的大多数黑人都不是纯粹的黑人，他们有白人祖先。马丁·路德·金常被称为黑人，但他有部分黑人血统，部分白人血统，也有部分土著美国人血统。《八月之光》中的乔·克里斯莫斯是一个兼具白色和黑色血统的人物，但事实上，他也不清楚自己真实的身份。即便是今天，我们的历史、文化还固守那个陈腐、老套的观念，那就是即便你有一丁点黑人血统（称为"一滴血规则"），你也会被人们视为黑人。后殖民主义批评家有一个很有趣的发现，在美洲南部的加勒比海一带，混血血统不成问题，甚至人们还以混杂的祖先血统而自豪。但在美国南方历史上，一个人若有黑人血统，即便是部分黑人血统，也会受到咒骂。当然，这种观念正在发生变化，然而还在一定程度上残存在人们的头脑中。不管奥巴马多少次提醒我们他不是一个黑人，他有白人母亲、外祖父母，但仍有一些人坚持认为他是而且只能是黑人。这也是为什么当今很多学者指出种族是一种"社会结构"，也就是说，黑人是社会贴在他们身上的标签。奥巴马对他父母双方的祖先血统均引以为荣，他为自己的黑人祖先感到骄傲，同时也为自己的白人祖先感到自豪。我们不应该让他在两者中选择其一。

事实上，很多美国人是混血人种，所以把一个兼有白人和黑人血统的人称作黑人是不准确的，因为这只是他的部分身份。福克纳早已深谙此事实，所以他的作品刻画了兼有白人和黑人血统的主人公被夹在一种不允许他们具有双重血统的文化之中。这是乔·克里斯莫斯和查理斯·邦所处的境地。如果他们生活的地方不是在密西西比，譬如在加利福尼亚或者是纽约，或欧洲，当然还有加勒比海一带，或许就是在当下的密西西比，他们的肤色也不会成问题。但在当时的美国南方，福克纳深知种族还是一个至关重要的问题，一个人只要他有一丝黑人血统，就会被看作黑人。

李：您能简要评析一下福克纳塑造的男女主人公吗？福克纳的小说如何阐释阳性和阴性主义？

罕布林：福克纳作品中的主人公反映了他们生活的时代的状况。有些男主人公虐待女主人公（比方说金鱼眼），有些则相反（如拜伦·邦奇）。有些女性主人公还被传统的女性角色束缚，有些（如康普森·凯蒂）则试图向传统的女性角色挑战。福克纳的小说塑造了不同类型的男女主人公，有时他们反映了其生活年代的性别角色，有时（如康普森·凯蒂）则走向了这些角色的对立面。

诸多探讨福克纳作品中性别问题的成果不断涌现，它们不单单侧重于分析性别，而且还探究其中的异性恋和同性恋问题，如种族研究领域一样，性别研究也不断出现一些新的视角，这些研究成果受到西格蒙德·弗洛伊德和卡尔·荣格很大的影响。特别是荣格，认为我们每个人身上都兼具雌雄两种属性。也就是说，即便我们是男性，我们也需要有一些阴柔的气质，同样作为女性，我们也应具有一些男性特质。当然，在心理发展中，女性或男性特征会在我们身上起主导作用，但我们还是需要两者关系的平衡。荣格认为压抑上述其中一性就会导致神经紊乱或出现更糟糕的情形。福克纳塑造的最成功的人物如迪尔西、琳娜、拜伦·邦奇、V. K. 拉特利夫、加文·史蒂文森、艾克·麦卡斯林、卢卡斯·伯查都不是具有暴力倾向的、进攻型的，甚至具有破坏力的人物，而是很好地建立了与自我、邻居、团体之间和谐关系的人物。他们似乎是荣格理论完整人格的体现。女性主人公保留了男性阳刚的气质，男性主人公则保持了女性阴柔的特征。和上文谈到的福克纳作品的其他主题，譬如时间、个人主义和种族一样，阳性和阴性双性人格并存与和谐，才是完整的个体。因而，两性关系解决的方案不在于性别冲突和性别战争，一方胜利而另一方失败，而是保持一种和谐的双性平衡的状态。我们可以运用荣格的理论探究福克纳笔下的人物，分析一下哪些人物能够以一种健康、积极的方式处理双性和谐的关系。譬如艾克·麦卡斯林，他的性格中似乎带有阴性特征，杰生·康普生则相反，他仇视妇女，完全摒弃了柔性化的一面，他是一个彻头彻尾的阳性主义者。有些评论家在福克纳传记中找到了这位作家对性别角色看法的一些依据。若看一下福克纳儿时的照片，你会发现他长得很柔弱、漂亮，几乎像一个女孩子。福克纳蓄胡须的原因或许是他想使自己看起来更具有一些男性气质。他外表看起来缺乏一些阳性气质，这是一件烦扰他的事情，所以他撒谎说曾经上过战场，他经常去打猎，尽管他不太喜欢杀戮动物，当然他还饮酒过度。在所有这些行为中，福克纳似乎想树立一种比现实生活中更为男性化的形象。就此而论，福克纳在塑造主人公昆丁·康普生时或许夹杂着这方面的情感。按传统观点来看，昆丁不是一个具有阳刚男性气质的人物，他为自己的性别和性而苦恼，挣扎在自我内心欲望和冲动的痛苦中，最终没有找到解决这些冲突的和谐之道。昆丁只是其中的一个角色，福克纳在他的作品中塑造了多种不同的人物类型。

李：您怎样评价福克纳作为一个短篇小说家？

罕布林：很多评论家把福克纳视为一个更为出色的短篇小说家，而不是一个长篇小说家。我想马尔科姆·考利或许是第一个提出此观点的人。作为一个编撰《袖珍福克纳文集》并具有很大影响力的评论家，考利认为福克纳的长篇小说主要是在他创作的短篇小说的基础上完成的。

并且福克纳的短篇小说相对来说更易懂，而他的长篇小说更艰涩难懂。近期的评论家中詹姆士·卡洛瑟斯写了一部评价福克纳短篇小说的著作，他赞成考利的观点，认为福克纳是一个更为出色的短篇小说家，他主张人们应该多花些时间研究他的短篇小说。在排列创作各种文学体裁的作品难度时，福克纳把诗歌放在首位，其次是短篇小说，最后才是长篇小说。因此很显然，他把自己视为一个优秀的短篇小说家。我想大部分评论家会赞同此观点。

李：那么，您怎样评价福克纳的诗歌作品？似乎它们更受冷落。

罕布林：是的，确实是这样。或许这是一个遗憾，福克纳并没有充分挖掘他的诗歌写作才能就停止了写诗。福克纳创作诗歌作品时，更多的是在模仿艾略特、斯文伯和豪斯曼。大多数作家出道时都是模仿者，他们起初模仿一些文学大师，最终创作会走向独立。但是福克纳的诗歌创作没有坚持下去。他所有的诗歌作品完成于其创作的早期（即便是有些作品出版要晚一些），所以福克纳在模仿阶段就放弃了诗歌创作。我认为福克纳的诗歌很有趣，我喜欢其中的一些作品。但是他没有最终坚持下去，以证明他在诗歌领域会有怎样出色的表现。朱迪思·森斯芭深入研究了福克纳的诗歌作品，探讨了其中的主题、语言的运用、人物类型及在他小说中的再现。尽管她赞美福克纳的诗歌作品，并做了细致的研究，但她认为福克纳的诗歌只是一些习作，它们之所以有趣，主要是因为和他后期创作的伟大小说作品之间有关联性。但是关于福克纳诗歌还有待进一步研究。

同样，另一个被评论界忽视的领域是他的电影作品。很少有评论家关注这一领域，仅有几位学者在研究福克纳的好莱坞创作生涯。总的来说，评论界忽视了两个福克纳研究领域，一是诗歌领域，一是电影剧本领域，这两个领域还有许多工作可做。

李：您能从总体上评价一下福克纳的创作地位吗？您怎样看待福克纳的文学成就？他对美国作家及其他国家的作家产生了什么样的影响？

罕布林：毫无疑问，福克纳是美国伟大的作家之一，他被称为"美国的莎士比亚"，我同意此评价。在美国作家中，他的地位与麦尔维尔、霍桑、艾伦·坡、马克·吐温、亨利·詹姆斯相当。我姑且不会把福克纳称为美国最伟大的作家，尽管他经常被誉为美国20世纪最伟大的作家，然而，他被称作美国最优秀的作家是当之无愧的。我想，丰硕的福克纳学术研究成果就是一个很好的佐证，关于他的研究成果，目前有上百部研究著作、数千篇研究论文，这足以证明他是多么重要。具有讽刺意味的是，尽管他是一位伟大的作家，却不是一位通俗作家，他也永远不会变成一位通俗作家，因为他的作品很难读懂。他的书不是畅销书，因为福克纳的成功在很大程度上是在学术界，他的读者是精英读者，而不是普通读者。福克纳与艾略特的情形相似，艾略特的《荒原》就很难读懂。人们在机场候机或在公交车站牌前等车的时候不会随手拿一本福克纳的小说作为消遣，的确，阅读福克纳的作品需要一定的欣赏趣味，但毋庸置疑，他是一位伟大的作家，一个例证就是其他国家的作家对他评价很高。美国的威廉·肯尼迪、哥伦比亚的作家加夫列尔·加西亚·马尔克斯、日本的作家大江健三郎和中国的作家莫言都很崇拜福克纳，而且受到他很大的影响。

李：确实如此，很多中国作家都受到福克纳很大的影响。莫言曾经坦言福克纳的《喧哗与骚动》对他走向创作产生了直接影响。最后，您能谈一下您对中国福克纳研究的看法吗？

罕布林：我只是在中国学者来到福克纳研究中心之后才了解到近几年中国福克纳研究的情况，才知道福克纳在中国很受欢迎。但我想强调的是，我们也要向你们学习。正如我前面所谈到的，美国福克纳研究有一个很大的倾向性，就是把福克纳视为南方作家，但中国学者来到这里，告诉我你们是怎样阅读福克纳的，我从你们那里也学会了从不同的语境去阅读福克纳。在美国，我们一直给福克纳贴上南方作家的标签，但中国学者或许对美国南方历史、美国内战的详细情况不太熟悉，你们没有从南方历史的角度解读福克纳,你们从更广阔的人文主义的视角阐释他作品中的人物、语言、悲喜交加、善恶交织的主题。由于中国学者不像美国学者那样置身于南方文化的语境中,所以能更加自由地表达新观点。我们可以帮助中国作家了解福克纳作为南方作家的一面,譬如我带你们参观奥克斯福,了解他作品涉及的地理图景,旧法院啦,他的故居啦,但你们是从中国视角,而不是美国的南方视角研究福克纳,所以你们所站的这样一个立场提醒我们,福克纳的作品要远大于南方语境,具有更普遍的意义。

当然,所有伟大作家的作品都具有普遍意义。莎士比亚不仅仅属于斯特拉福,他的作品具有超越性,同样,福克纳的作品也远大于奥克斯福和美国南方。我想,阅读伟大作家的作品的正确方式是从人文主义的视角出发,而不能仅仅局限于其地域的视域。当然,福克纳曾说,你不能随便在什么地方坐下就创作出一部具有普遍意义的作品,但如果你的作品写得足够好,你又很幸运,你所写的东西将会具有超越性。来自世界另一个地方的人也许会说他也有同感。我并没有生活在这个作家的世界中,但关于子女、政府或梦想等体验也许会和那位作家相同。所以对中国学者和我而言,这是一种双向交流,我们彼此受益。我从你们那里学习了你们是如何解读福克纳的,希望你们也能从我这里学到一些东西。

李: 确实,我们需要相互学习,很高兴能和您交谈,希望中国学者和读者通过此访谈能更好地了解福克纳。

罕布林: 谢谢!

(李萌羽译,英文访谈原载于《外国文学研究》2010年第1期)

福克纳研究新视点

——克里斯托弗·瑞格博士访谈[*]

访谈背景：

东南密苏里州立大学福克纳研究中心是美国重要的福克纳研究中心之一，中心现任主任克里斯托弗·瑞格博士是著名的福克纳研究专家，其专著《被砍伐的伊甸园：南方文学中的生态和田园书写》作为美国南方文学研究具有重要影响的著作，分析了以福克纳为代表的四位美国南方作家的作品中所体现的一种"后田园"审视视角，认为这些南方作家更为强调以相互依赖、相互合作的生态学模式来取代过去更为重视个人主义和竞争性的旧田园模式，以期寻求人类和自然界、科技和荒原及城市和乡村之间的平衡，此著作被美国学者视为"美国南方研究的一个重大贡献"。瑞格博士还对福克纳和中国作家的关系颇感兴趣，曾撰写了关于福克纳和莫言比较研究的论文，提出了诸多富有启发性的观点。2015 年 7 月，本书作者因所主持的国家社科规划项目"威廉·福克纳对中国新时期小说影响研究"的需要，前往该中心进行学术访问和交流，并对瑞格博士进行了专题访谈，针对福克纳美国研究新的学术视点、福克纳创作的历史文化语境、种族、性别、宗教、现代性及后现代性、后田园牧歌主题及福克纳与中国当代作家的比较研究等话题展开了深入的交流，希望该访谈能为国内福克纳研究提供一些新的思路和视角。

* 本文系国家社科规划项目"威廉·福克纳对中国新时期小说的影响研究"（13BWW007）阶段性成果。

李萌羽（以下简称李）：非常高兴能够再次来到福克纳研究中心进行学术访问，贵中心是美国福克纳研究的四大中心之一，我因为从事福克纳研究，曾经于2008年年底慕名前来访问，搜集了很多福克纳研究资料，对当时中心的主任罕布林教授就福克纳研究做了专题访谈，还参观了福克纳故居，受益良多。时隔7年后，旧地重访，感慨良多。今天很荣幸能够对您就福克纳研究再做一个专题访谈。您能简单介绍一下您所在的东南密苏里州立大学的福克纳研究中心吗？它对美国及美国以外的福克纳研究中发挥着怎样的作用呢？

克里斯托弗·瑞格（以下简称瑞格）：我们东南密苏里州立大学的福克纳研究中心成立于1989年，由于获得了路易斯·丹尼尔·布罗茨基先生收藏的大量福克纳研究资料，此中心得以成立。布罗茨基先生是著名的福克纳收藏家，他当时是福克纳资料最大的私人收藏家，共收藏了1万多册，与福克纳研究中心首任主任罕布林教授共事后不久，他决定将所有藏品捐赠给我们大学，他想确保这些资料能够真正用于学者的研究而不是将其束之高阁。所以福克纳研究中心成立的目的在于充分利用这些研究资料，并且为全国乃至全世界的研究人员提供参考，从而促进福克纳研究。

而我们的主要工作就是接待访问学者，为前来搜集资料的人提供相关书籍和文章，特别是有关福克纳研究的论文。每两年我们还将举办一次研讨会，全世界的福克纳学者都可以在会议上展现他们在该领域内的成果。

李：据我所知，你们研究中心最近还开设了福克纳研究的慕课课程？

瑞格：是的，这是我们为促进福克纳研究，提高教学水平而开展的新项目，通过网络公开课或者慕课这种新形式来帮助人们阅读福克纳的作品。大多数情况下，人们并没有机会在教授的指导下或者通过参与课堂学习来阅读福克纳的作品，然而有时候在自己的阅读过程中难免又会遇到一些困难。所以我们开设了这些慕课来帮助人们阅读并且理解福克纳的作品。

李：2014年我收到了罕布林教授的一封关于福克纳教学慕课信息的电

子邮件，得知这个消息后我很高兴，注册、浏览了该课程，并把它介绍给我的学生们。我注意到此课程现在已进行了两个专题内容的网络教学，第一个专题内容是集中研讨福克纳的《喧哗与骚动》等几部重要作品，第二个专题内容是介绍美国南方的历史和文化。慕课中提供的资料和关于福克纳作品的评析对我们进行福克纳研究很有启发性。作为福克纳研究专家，您能介绍一下您的研究情况吗？

瑞格：好的，我个人关于福克纳的大部分研究都与生态批评有关，我的研究主要侧重于探讨自然界、环境与福克纳作品之间的关系，比如我的专著《被砍伐的伊甸园：南方文学中的生态和田园书写》中有一章，专门探讨了福克纳的小说是如何处理自然环境和人类之间关系的，我最近发表了一篇从生态批评角度分析《喧哗与骚动》的论文，也主要探讨自然环境在这部作品中的意义。

李：此研究视角在中国也很受关注，我曾经出版过一本《多维视野中的沈从文与福克纳小说》著作，其中一章也从生态学的视角分析了福克纳作品中所蕴含的重视自然价值、倡导人对森林保持敬仰之心的生态理念，还有许多中国学者使用生态批评的方法来研究福克纳的小说。

瑞格：有一位来参加会议的日本学者同样使用了生态学批评的方法进行福克纳研究。

李：您所撰写的专著名为《被砍伐的伊甸园：南方文学中的生态和田园书写》，您能解释一下"被砍伐的伊甸园"的意义吗？

瑞格：此书名有多重意义，其中之一便是作家或者他人把南方视为天堂或者伊甸园的一种历史化倾向。然而在20世纪早期，南方的自然环境以极快的速度遭到了很大的破坏，虽然整个美国都面临这一问题，但南方尤甚，主要是因为南方是乡村地区，你可以十分清楚地看到自然环境受到了何等损害，这是此书名包含的一个意义。此外，伊甸园指向的是一个想象中的完美之地。人们把过去浪漫化，认为美国南方的过去更加美好和完美，并且试图从某种程度上去找回它，尽管这只是一个虚幻之物。所以这本书使用了生态批评的方法来研究大萧条时期的四位美国南方作家：福克纳、考德威尔、赫斯顿和罗林斯。我使用了生态批评和历史批评的方法来研究大萧条在何种程度上影响了作家的小说对自然环境的书写。

李：在这本书的最后一部分，您对福克纳的《去吧，摩西》中的后田园牧歌进行了分析，能介绍一下您的主要观点吗？它是如何反映在《去吧，摩西》一书中的？

瑞格：从全书出发，我探讨了南方文学中最初的田园是如何作为城市和荒野的中间地带来呈现的。所以在较早的南方文学中，传统的田园图景以农场或者种植园作为载体，作为对抗力量保持平衡的中间地带，它某种程度上意味着天堂。但是当我们进入大萧条时代，自然环境受到了很大的破坏，农场和种植园成了问题地带，作家们审视它们的眼光也不再像以前的作家那样。即使这些新作家依然使用田园牧歌的说法，但关注的目光却从这些中间地带移到了荒野，以期获得或者希望获得一种平衡感，比如人类和自然界的平衡、科技和荒原的平衡，或者城市和乡村之间的平衡。作家们依然在试图使用田园模式来找寻中间地带的平衡，但是场所发生了转换。

李：有一种深生态学理论，和浅生态学有很大的不同，或许正如您刚刚所解释的那样，这在某种程度上接近于一种后田园牧歌式吧？

瑞格：是的，我认为生态学很有影响力，你可以发现，在20世纪30年代到40年代，南方作家更关注人与人之间、人与自然之间的合作关系、集体性行为及相互依存的关系，以至相互依赖、相互合作的生态学的模式取代了过去更为个人主义、竞争性的模式，正如我在书中所谈到的，这主要是受到了大萧条时代的影响，比如，受这个时期的一些环境灾害，如洪水、干旱、土壤沙化、大面积的树木被砍伐、棉铃象甲虫侵袭等影响。这对人们来说预示着人类与自然界的休戚相关。

李：这是研究福克纳作品的一个非常好的切入点。接下来，您能介绍一下当下美国福克纳研究的新视角吗？

瑞格：当下有许多福克纳研究的新视角，最近研究者们使用较多的新的研究视角是残疾研究，这是一个全新的领域。同时，在我们出版的书籍中也收录了一些有关残疾研究的文章，结合创伤研究理论进行研究，是近来大受欢迎的一个研究视点。文化研究视点，尤其关注大众文化与福克纳的作品所产生的诸多交集,是另一研究新视点。通常情况下,我们不会把福克纳看作一位通俗文学作家,但是的确有一些新的研究就他的作品与大众文化之间的关系得出新的成果,比如在音乐、电影、通俗文学、杂志等相关领域。今年在密西西比大学举办的福克纳与约克纳帕塔法研讨会的主题就与印刷文化有关,有许多发言都涉及福克纳是如何参与当时的大众文化的。

李: 您刚刚参加了"2015 福克纳与约克纳帕塔法"研讨会,您可以介绍一下会议的有关内容吗?

瑞格: 本次会议的议题是"福克纳与印刷文化",涌现出了大量论文。正如我所说,许多学者看到了福克纳和出版业及大众文化之间的联系,所以有些论文论及福克纳与杂志的关系,以及他是如何被大众传媒所描述的。还有与会者论及了他作品中的封面艺术,他的小说如何融入当时的"平装书革命",以及福克纳与文学出版行业重要人物的联系等,总之,研讨会谈论的内容非常丰富。

李: 您在研讨会上发言的题目是什么?

瑞格: 我发言的题目是"福克纳《寓言》小说创作的修改(订)过程研究",探讨了他对这部小说最后所作出的修正,我主要使用了一些布罗茨基收藏的资料,以证明他如何完成这部小说并作出了重要修改,在小说出版的最后关头又作出了修改。

李: 这个研究很有趣。众所周知,福克纳经常被称作美国南方作家,您如何看待美国南方在福克纳作品中的地位?

瑞格: 我认为,如果要采用历史或者文化的方法进行福克纳研究,就要建立在了解美国南方的历史和文化的基础之上,否则很难对他和文化、历史的关系有透彻的了解,因为福克纳本人就对南方历史,以及其如何在南方人及非南方人心目中呈现颇感兴趣。福克纳也致力于探讨他所处的时代面临的一些难题,尽管这些事情现在已成为历史,但对于他来说,这些都是当时需要解决的问题。但你又不能仅仅把福克纳视为南方作家,我认为和一些国际学者的交流使得我们站在超越南方作家的身份来看待他,从其他方面来审视他。

李：刚刚我们讨论了文化环境，如果我们在此之中评析福克纳的作品，除了南方文化之外，还有哪些其他的文化环境对福克纳产生了影响？

瑞格：比方说，把南方置于全球南方的视野中来研究，而不再仅仅停留在美国的南方，南美洲、加勒比海，甚至非洲及南半球的其他一些国家都可以纳入其中，研究它们和美国南方之间的关系，可以把福克纳放置于上述文化环境之中。他有一些小说涉及加勒比海，比如《押沙龙，押沙龙》，他超越了美国南方，对其他南方地区的问题均展开了探索。

我们也可以把福克纳研究置于美国文化的语境下，也可以超越南方，在整个美国文化环境中了解福克纳，因为作为一个美国作家，福克纳所探讨的许多问题不只是南方也是美国社会所面临的。他只是恰好选取了他生于斯长于斯，并且有较多了解的南方，这样他的写作内容就更为丰富、真实，但同时他也借此从总体上讨论美国文化，比如他对种族问题的探讨，并不是简单局限地谈论南方种族问题，而是从全局出发对美国种族问题进行了思考。

所以，你也可以从中发现与国际环境的关联，我认为这可以帮助我们了解为什么福克纳的作品在中国和日本也大受欢迎，因为他所谈论的问题具有普遍性，对全人类都有影响。你可以清楚地看到这一点，比如在《寓言》中，地点设置在欧洲，而不是密西西比或者美国。福克纳的其他作品也可以延伸到这样一个环境中，例如他多次谈到乡村地区的人们和农民的困境，我认为其他许多国家的人们都可以理解这一问题，这或许可以解释为什么一些中国读者认为他在谈论城乡之间的阶级差别，类似的问题依旧发生在中国，如小村镇和大城市之间的对抗，过去与当下的矛盾，许多文化都会对此产生认同感。

李：我们谈论了文化语境、全球资源这些非常有趣的话题，这让我想起了在中国也存在这样的南方作家，比如有一些学者就福克纳和苏童展开了比较研究，认为苏童是关注中国的南方的著名作家。之前我们谈论了许多福克纳研究的视角，我注意到有很多都是现代或后现代的研究视角，您能介绍一下福克纳研究中此类研究的视角吗？

瑞格：我认为，现代性的研究方法也可以说是历史性的，纵观过去的现代主义艺术运动，20 世纪前 30 年代到 40 年代是主要时期，所以学者十分关注詹姆斯·乔伊斯、弗吉尼亚·伍尔夫等现代主义作家，以及福克纳的风格、写作方式是如何与其他现代主义作家产生相似之处的。他们同时也关注现代主义的其他形式，尤其是绘画，我们知道，福克纳曾经在 1925 年去法国巴黎旅行并见到了许多现代主义画家，这对他产生了很大的影响，所以一些批评家看到了福克纳的现代主义写作和现代主义画作之间的联系，这或许是审视现代主义的主要方法，也有几本著作就福克纳与现代主义的关系进行了全面的研究。

李：那么关于后现代主义方法呢？

瑞格：我认为，后现代主义研究方法是再一次将福克纳和文化领域联系起来，虽然从表面上看并没有多大关系。所以就又可以回到我之前提出的大众文化研究方法上，是一种大众的、后现代主义研究方法，这也是福克纳经常重复利用他的写作素材的一种方式，他完成一个故事后常常再回过头提取一些相同的素材并且以不同的方式运用到将来的写作中去，这些都是后现代主义的写作技巧。

李：我对福克纳研究的心理学分析也非常感兴趣，您能介绍一下这一心理学透视法在美国是如何运用的吗？

瑞格：心理学方法在福克纳研究中很常见，特别是在 20 世纪 80 年代和 90 年代，至今仍在使用但远不如过去流行。较早使用的是弗洛伊德的方法，约翰·T. 埃尔文有一本与之相关并较为有影响力的著作，就运用了弗洛伊德的心理学研究方法，之后便出现了大量有关研究，不仅仅是弗洛伊德和拉康，还使用了许多其他现代心理学理论进行福克纳研究。

福克纳的确对无意识有较多描写，人物对所做的事情不明就里，埃尔文在他的书中提到，这是因为福克纳的主人公有非常复杂的心理，我认为有许多相关的研究，他常常通过人物的内心想法、回忆、家庭历史和背后的故事来塑造错综复杂的人物心理。所以和其他作家相比，他提供了许多可以对人物展开心理学研究的信息。

李：在 2014 年的福克纳与约克纳帕塔法的研讨会议上，您还发表了福克纳和莫言的比较研究的论文，我很高兴看到您对现当代中国作家产生了兴趣，您在这二者之间发现了什么相同点或者不同点？是什么原因让您着手这一研究？

瑞格：我认为莫言和福克纳有很多相同之处，他们都在叙述技巧上进行了新的尝试，都使用了意识流的手法，在同一个故事中进行了许多不同视角的转换，并且多次切换故事时间，从过去、现在直到当前，他们综合使用了上述方法叙述故事。我于2014年在美国学术会议上的发言特意选取了两位作家的两部小说，福克纳的《不败者》和莫言的《红高粱》。

这两部小说都是关于战争的，特别是内战，所以我对他们如何描述发生在自己家乡那片土地上的战争尤为感兴趣，并且认为有很多相似之处，他们和过去都有着非常相近的关系，比如以一种批判的眼光看待过去，试图去解释一些被他人所掩盖的真相。在我的发言中，也提到了这两部作品中所描述的来自过去的人物是如何呈现出传奇性的，而现今之人却永远无法估量这些过去的传奇人物，虽然两位作家都表现出了对过去的某种批判，但是他们都看到了当下与过去相比所存在的某种细小而微弱的意义，过去存在许多卓越而传奇的人物，以及具有神话特色的故事，但相较之下，当前则少有乐趣。我认为，这两位作家和过去都存在一种非常矛盾的情感，他们在某种程度上不喜欢过去，并予以批判，但同时又被过去所吸引。

李：正如您的论文所论及的，两位作家对过去所持有的既清醒又迷恋的态度。

瑞格：是的，的确这两种相悖的情感同时存在。

李：我发现您关于这两部作品中女强人的分析也十分有趣。

瑞格：是的，这也是另外一件非常有趣的事情。这两个故事都带有悲伤的色调，刻画了坚强的女性人物，在某种程度上她们比男性角色更擅长应对战争，一些男性人物在战争中表现得毫无荣誉感，但这两位作家都赋予了女性人物以领导者的形象，对家庭富有奉献精神，表现出了忠诚、勇敢、力量、进取等优良品质。

李：我对福克纳创作的宗教背景也很感兴趣，比如说他的作品描写了被称作"圣经地带"的美国南方，您能谈一下基督教对福克纳创作的影响吗？

瑞格：福克纳的确在一种基督教的环境下成长，在他的后半生中，他十分虔诚地信仰基督教并且常常去教堂，他对《圣经》非常了解，并使用了其中的故事形式、事物及人物类型。在他的小说中，有许多指涉都和《圣经》有关，我想，从基督教和《圣经》的角度理解福克纳是很有益的。然而，福克纳对宗教也作出了一些批评，但这并不是针对宗教本身，而是意在批评那些出于一己私利利用或误用宗教的行为，剖析了这些行为所导致的后果。福克纳非常乐于揭露基督教和宗教中的问题。

李：由于美国的历史原因，种族问题非常棘手，现在对非裔美国人的看法依旧存在争议，您认为福克纳创作中揭示的种族问题意义何在？

瑞格：福克纳对种族问题的描写从某种程度来说是具有超前性的，正如他在《八月之光》中所展现的，种族和肤色并没有联系，这部作品写于20世纪30年代早期，但这个话题至今仍然困扰着人们，同时福克纳也就这一问题作出了文化上的解释，最早可追溯到1932年的《八月之光》，我认为福克纳作品所提出的一些与种族相关的看法在今日的美国同样适用，我们今天还面临很多同样的问题，所以福克纳的作品依旧对当代美国社会具有启发性。

最近有一篇新闻报道在谈论《八月之光》和巴拉克·奥巴马的关系，包括他的个人经历及一些人和媒体对待他的方式，我认为这是与现代非常有趣的联系。

李：那么关于女性问题或性别问题呢？福克纳对女性有怎样的态度？

瑞格：这是一个非常有趣的问题，我们刚才还谈到此话题，关于福克纳笔下的女性角色及他如何展现女性人物仍然有许多争论。有些人坚称福克纳采用了刻板印象描写出了十分有局限性的女性形象；还有一部分人认为他刻画了许多女强人的角色，但这也是局限性的表现；而我认为，他这么做是为了表现男权文化之下的家长制文化，所以他向我们展现了这一现实，但并不是对此认可。他描写了女性生活的艰难，而这些困苦恰恰是男性造成的，所以现在对如何看待福克纳笔下的女性角色及他对女性的观点仍有争议。

李：在访谈的开始部分，您提到每年都有学者前来参观访问，包括中国学者和日本学者，除此之外还有其他国家的学者吗？

瑞格：在过去十年间有相当多的中国学者来此访问，我们平均每年要接待二到三位，有时候他们的访问为期数周，有时则是一整年，他们对福克纳或者是我们的文学、写作课程非常感兴趣，或者对其他领域感兴趣。我们同时也有很多日本访问学者，中心与当地一家日本的公司有合作项目，这家公司的办公地在日本，但是在我们的城市吉拉多角拥有工厂，这家公司每年都资助日本学者进行为期两周的访问，前来搜集资料或者做一些研究。

同时，我们两年召开一次的学术研讨会也吸引了来自日本、中国、加拿大、尼日利亚、澳大利亚等地的学者，也有一些法国学者来中心访问数次。我们中心的学者主要来自中国和日本，但是也有其他地方的研究者，2014 年有一位来自迪拜大学的学者进行了几周的访问研究。我们接待了许多来自世界各地的学者、研究生，学者们主要是前来搜集并使用资料，或进行一些特殊项目的研究，对于我们来说，能够接待来自世界各地的人们是一件非常棒的事情。

李：刚刚我们谈到了如此多的来自世界各地的学者，您能和我们分享一下对福克纳国际研究的观点吗？

瑞格：福克纳能够吸引来自世界各地的人们是一件很有趣的现象，在美国，有些人仅仅把福克纳看作南方作家，我认为这是一种局限性的观点，鉴于他在世界范围内如此受欢迎，就足以证明福克纳的吸引力并不是仅仅由于地域的因素，最重要的是他的作品表现的主题得到了世界的认可，比如性别、社区与个人的关系、小城镇、过去与现在的冲突等诸多问题，都能得到人们的普遍认同。

李：非常感谢您分享的关于福克纳的观点，之前提到我正在进行一个福克纳对中国现当代作家的影响的科研项目，并且拜读了一篇您的相关论文。

瑞格：是的，目前为止只有一篇，我也非常期待看到您的研究成果。

李：希望今后有机会我们能够在这一领域内展开合作并继续深入研究。

瑞格：我很期待，谢谢！

（本文由杨燕协助录音整理、翻译初稿，李萌羽修改翻译并校稿）

附录
部分代表性英文论文原文

On the Traditional Chinese Notion of "Harmony"
Resources to the Intercultural Communication

Intercultural communication is a field which focuses on the exploration of the relationship between communication and culture. The ultimate aim of the discipline is to help people from diverse cultural backgrounds communicate more effec-tively with one another and establish a harmonious relationship. To some extent, to create a harmony communication relationship among people from different cultures is of vital importance to the successful intercultural communic-ation. While the traditional Chinese thought of "harmony" can provide with the field new and illuminating resources either in theoretical basis and practical usage.

At the present time, globalization has made intercultural contact become more and more frequent on the one hand and witnessed severe cultural conflicts on the other hand. As Wang Ke-Ping pointed out: "The new millennium has been expected to be a promising era for peace and development. Contrary to all expectations, its very outset is shrouded in terror, fear, hatred, tension, conflict and war among many other forms of suffering and misery. "[1] The main cause of the destructive force in the new millennium derives from the hostile attitude towards the alien cultures and diversified differences, and this situation has called for the great necessity of dialectical thought of the differences and the urgent need of the establishment of a harmonious relationship in intercultural contact. While the traditional Chinese notion of harmony which accentuates difference and diversity is edifying.

---

[1] Ke Ping, Wang *Ethos of Chinese Culture, A Multicultural Strategy: Harmonization Without Being Patternized*, Beijing: Foreign Languages Press, 2007, p. 36.

A General Survey of the Notion of "Harmony"
in the Traditional Chinese Culture

In the traditional Chinese culture, the notion of "harmony" is often interpreted as a dialectical and dynamic term. The conception of "Supreme harmony" or "Great Harmony" (tai he) was first mentioned in *The Book of Changes (Zhou yi)*. Fung Yu-Lan in his book *A Short History of Chinese Philosophy* stated: "Harmony of this sort, which includes not only human society, but permeates the entire universe, is called the Supreme Harmony. In ' Appendix I'of the *Yi*, it is said: "How vast is the originating power of [1], Ch'ien.... Unitedly to protect the Supreme Harmony: this is indeed profitable and auspicious. "[2] The term "Ch'ien" (also translated as "Qian" ,) denoting the ultimate way the universe operates, is regarded as the perfect reconciliation of opposing forces of nature. As Yu Dunkang illustrated : "It explains that all beings find the ultimate and proper purpose of their existence by transformations of the qian path: hard and soft are reconciled and united, producing the perfect harmony by which all beings are created and on which they thrive, and bringing a state of ultimate peace to the world. "[3] The notion of harmony is also elucidated in *Tao Te Ching*: "Tao gave birth the One: The One gave birth successively to two things, three things, up to ten thousand. These ten thousand creatures cannot turn their backs to the shade without having the sun on their bellies, and it is on this blending of the breaths that their harmony depends. "[4] Hence, the conceptions of "Ch'ien" in *The Book*

---

[1] the hexagram.

[2] Yu-Lan Fung, *A Short History of Chinese Philosophy*. Tianjin: Tianjin Academy of Social, 2007, p. 286.

[3] Dun kang Yu, "The Concept of Great Harmony in the Book of Changes" . In Silke Krieger&Rolf Trauzettel(ed) , *Confucianism and the Modernization of China*, v. Hase &Koehler Verlag, 1991, p. 53.

[4] Arthur Walley. *Tao Te Ching*, Beijing: Foreign Language Teaching and Research Press, 1999, p. 90.

of Changes(*Zhou Yi)* and "Tao" in *Tao Te Ching* can be respectively interpreted as the originating power or intrinsic principle of the universe which involve the harmonious interaction of opposing forces such as ying and yang, light and dark, hard and soft, water and fire etc. "The Supreme Harmony" is thus regarded as the dynamic balance of the forces. The notion of harmony is also illustrated in *Chung yung, (or the doctrine of the Mean)* , within which *Chung* and *Ho* serve as the two crucial terms. It explains: "To have no emotions of pleasure or anger, sorrow or joy, welling up: this is to be described as the state of *Chung*. To have these emotions welling up but in due proportion: this is to be described as the state of *ho*①. *Chung* is the chief foundation of the world. Ho is the great highway for the world. Once *chung* and *ho* are established, Heaven and Earth maintain their proper position, and all creatures are nourished. "② Therefore, harmony (or *ho*) in *Chung yung*, can be perceived as the perfect state of appropriateness, which lays great emphasis on the proper position and due proportion of the various elements being involved.

In another famous Chinese ancient books called *Tso Chuan*, Yen Tzu further expounded the notion of harmony by employing the famous analogy "Seeking harmony is like making a soup. One uses water, fire, vinegar, soy source and prunes all together to stew with fish and meat. The Chef Mélanges harmoniously all the ingredients for a tasteful soup"③ . Harmony is a also a key word of understanding Confucius's thought, the term has appeared in *The Analects* for eight times. Confucius was a sage who was an advocator of good virtues and manners. And his entire life was engaged in the perfection of one's virtue and personality as a gentleman (or a perfect person) . "Jen" (humanism) and "Li" (ritual) were two main concepts in *The Analects*, Confucius particularly interpreted

---

① harmony.

② Ibid. , p. 284.

③ Arthur Walley. *Tao Te Ching*, Beijing: Foreign Language Teaching and Research Press, 1999, p. 47.

the two concepts in terms of harmony. Jen, according to Confucius, is "the ideal relationship which should pertain between individuals"[①]. And he stressed "In practicing the rules of propriety, it is harmony that is prized"[②]. Confucius had further broadened the thought of harmony by stating "The gentleman harmonizes his relationship with others but never follows them blindly (he er bu tong). The Petty man just follows others blindly disregarding any principle (tong er bu he) "[③]. Thus, in Confucius's eyes, a gentleman (or a perfect person) is a person who has accomplished the maximum development of one's virtue and personality by being kind and considerate to others on the one hand and maintaining his or her independent mind on the other hand, and this reflects Confucius's unique interpretation of the harmonious relationship among individuals. Above all, harmony is a very important conception in traditional Chinese culture, and it embodies the supreme ideal of Chinese culture that regards " All things are nurtured together without injuring one another; All courses are pursued together without collision" [④].

The Dialectical and Dynamic Interpretations of Harmony

Although the above typical views of harmony quoted are illustrated in different ways, they express the common dialectical and dynamic interpretation of harmony, which underscores the value of difference, reconciliation and creation. Firstly, they do not regard harmony as a category denoting sameness, uniformity and conformity; instead they underscore in particular the value of difference, diversity, multiplicity and plurality within the concept. Next, they lay great emphasis on the reconciliation of the heterogeneous things rather than

---

① Smith Huston, *The Illustrated World's Religions: A Guide to Our Wisdom Traditions*, New York: Harper Collins, 1994, p. 110.

② Fu En Pan, and Wen Shao Xia, *The Analects of Confucius*, Jinan: Qilu Press, 2004, p. 6.

③ Ibid. , p. 45.

④ Yu-Lan Fung, *A Short History of Chinese Philosophy*. Tianjin: Tianjin Academy of Social, 2007, p. 286.

contestation, conflict and strive among them. Finally, they conceive harmony as a source of constructive creativity which can bring mutual benefit for all in the process of transformational synthesis of various components. The interpretations of harmony in traditional culture mentioned above have offered rich revelations to the intercultural communication study.

Difference: the Basis of Harmony

At the present time, Chinese government has called for building a harmonious society and a harmonious world. The proposal is of vital importance to the healthy development of China as well as the world. However, the term "harmony" is often simplified as the accordance and consistency of all sides, or even regarded as sameness and uniformity to some extent. While the traditional Chinese culture conceives difference and diversity as the bases of harmony. Fung Yu-Lan had made a clear differentiation between harmony and uniformity by quoting Yen Tzu's allergy mentioned above:

> *Harmony is the reconciling of differences into a harmonious unity. The Tso Chuan reports a speech by the statesman Yen Tzu (died in 493 B. C.), in which he makes a distinction between harmony and uniformity or identity. Harmony, he says, may be illustrated by cooking. Water, vinegar. Pickles, salt, and plums are used to cook fish. From these ingredients there results a new taste which is neither that of the vinegar nor of the pickles. Uniformity or identity, on the other hand, may be likened to the attempt to flavor with water, or to confine a piece of music to one note. In both cases there is nothing new. Herein lies the distinction between the Chinese words t'ung and ho. Tung means uniformity or identity, which is incompatible with difference. Ho means harmony, which is not incompatible with difference; on the contrary, it results*

when differences are brought together to form a unity. [1]

As we know, the major issue of intercultural communication is to deal with the differences derived from the diverse cultures and communication regulations, Therefore, it is of vital importance to appreciate the value of difference in intercultural communication, especially at the globalization era, when China as well as the whole world are being threatened by the homogeneous commercial force, the traditional Chinese notion of harmony which appeals for difference and diversity is illuminating.

There have been heating debates on the impact of globalization, those who hold positive attitude think that globalization can bring forth many benefits since people have more chances to experience and appreciate cultures from different nations. Those who oppose to globalization argue that it turns out to be an encroachment of cultural identity. Anyway, like the coins of the two sides, globalization has provided with us the good opportunities for intercultural contacts as well as the great challenges in dealing with the cultural differences. Thus, it is very necessary for us to prevent the homogenization tendency in the process of globalization.

At the present time, as what has been mentioned above, China is engaged inthe building of a harmonious society, as harmony does not necessarily mean uniformity, China should take great considerations for the different voices of the people, not only people who come from the "dominant culture", but also people from co-cultures, such as the minority people and weak group people etc. It is true that the Chinese people have benefited a lot from the modernization pursuit, Nevertheless, as modernization requires standardization and formality, we should be more cautious of the negative effects of the modernization and pay more

---

[1]　Yu-Lan Fung, *A Short History of Chinese Philosophy*. Tianjin: Tianjin Academy of Social, 2007, p. 284.

attention to the protection of the diversified cultures and minority cultures in particular. Although Han culture is the dominant culture in China, we should also ensure the equal development of minority cultures. However, in the process of modernization, the commercial pursuit has destroyed the minority cultures to some extent. For instance, according to some researchers, the local Korean culture in the Northeastern regions of China is facing the danger of losing its own unique cultural identity with more and more young generation of Korean minority people choosing to go to south Korean as well as other big cities in China to earn more money.

Reconciliation: the Best Strategy of Harmony

In the process of intercultural communication, seeking harmony is the most valuable principle, since harmony can serve as the best strategy in reconciling difference and confrontation. Therefore, reserving differences without coming into conflict is the wisest policy in the intercultural interaction. Particularly at the present time, when the world is still being threatened by misunderstanding, tension, conflict, terror, hatred, and war, seeking peaceful harmony and showing respect for the cultural diversity and difference have precious and unique values. Besides, harmony requires the use of dialogue, negotiation and cooperation to reconcile cultural difference, which proves to be good methods in dealing with cultural conflict.

However, in today's world, cultural misunderstanding and prejudices are still the barriers which prevent people from appreciating the difference and diversity of the colorful cultures in the world. And the American professor Samuel Hungtington has ascribed the conflict to the clash of civilization. Taking China issue as an example, some western medias and governments still use their own political standpoints and cultural criteria in making the judgment. They cast sharp criticisms on the Chinese political affairs, environmental problems and even one-child policy. Particularly, the year of 2008 to China is not an ordinary year, the Chinese people's dream of holding Olympic Games will come true in August this year; however, it has undergone an uneven path. At home, the Tibetan separatists had initiated a series of turbulence events in the name of Tibetan independence and their cruel and violent actions have caused great damages to the society as well as the lives of the ordinary Tibetan people. At broad, the Olympic torch relay had encountered severe protests by either the Tibetan separatists and members of so-called international "Tibet Support" groups, Especially in Paris, the birth place of modern Olympic Games, the Olympic flames had been nearly extinguished for many times, which is a severe deviation to the Olympic concept of "one world, one dream" we have cherished. In reporting the Tibet Riots and Olympic Games in Beijing, the Western medias have showed their bias and prejudices towards the Chinese government as well as the Chinese culture. For instance, Germany television stations even presented the audience with pictures of Nepal and Indian riots as the replacements of beat-downs of Tibetan civilians by the Chinese government. Toronto newspapers openly boycott Olympic Games in Beijing, Poland has also announced to boycott the Beijing Olympics. This has raised an urgent task of reconciling the differences among diversified cultures and a great necessity of building a harmonious world as the Chinese president Hu Jintao has proposed.

To our delight, we see the world is also making its effort to approach the goal, and there has also arisen a positive force of appealing for cooperation and mutual help in the world. In the great disaster of Si Chuan earthquake, Not only the Chinese people have united as one and spare no efforts in helping Si Chuan people, but also people all over the world offer their helps by either making donations or providing other forms of support.

Creativity: The Highest Pursuit of Harmony

The traditional cultural notion of harmony also stresses the constructive creativity within which all the components are interactive and mutually beneficial. When it is applied to the intercultural communication, harmonization involves a dynamic process of creative transformation, during which the diverse cultures undergo a transformational synthesis by the means of changing and collaborating with one another but meanwhile maintaining their basic individual cultural identity. Harmony can promote co-existence and co-prosperity of diversified cultures; whereas differences foster mutual complement and mutual support. In this way, it can bring about mutual and a win-win benefit to all cultures.

In a sense, the human civilization is a history of cultural diffusion, absorption and creation. As the famous Philosopher Russell (1992) remarked in his essay Chinese and Western civilization contrasted:

> *Contacts between different civilizations have often in the past proved to be landmarks in human progress. Greece learn from Egypt, Rome from Greece, the Arabs from the Roman Empire, medieval Europe from the Arabs, and Renaissance Europe from the Byzantines.*

Russell's comment above illustrates the fact that the intercultural contact between the western and eastern culture has never ceased in human civilization and within the process both eastern and western cultures have benefited from learning from each other. As the Chinese scholar Tang Yijie (2004) analyzed:

> *Though dissents might be held on whether Russell was accurate enough on every point, two of which are undoubtedly right: 1. Contacts between civilizations are important dynamics for the progress of human civilization; 2. The European culture today has absorbed many elements from other*

national cultures, including some from the Arabian. Another observations based on the progress of Chinese culture would be even more forceful to prove that clashes of civilizations were always temporal, while mutual absorptions and convergences eternal.

Harmony involves the creation of new elements within the diversified cultures. It is very difficult for every culture to remain in a closed state, the reason lies in the fact that culture is subject to change, and the mechanism of change is caused by the cultural diffusion during which one culture borrows from another by synthesizing into a new one. Taking American culture as an example, America is often described as a melting pot within which various cultures in the world seem to blend into one another. When being asked by a Chinese student what the typical American food is, an American professor said it was hard to name one since even McDonald and Kentucky fast food are not the main foods most American choose. To most American people, they have their different choices of diets based on their families' and personal preferences, and the immigrant feature of American culture has led to the diversity of American foods which are the mixtures of various food flavors in the world. It is the same case with China. Ever since China opened its door to the outside world at the beginning of twentieth century, with the approach of diversified foreign cultures, China has learned a lot from the outside world and the Chinese culture has undergone a transformation from agricultural civilization to the modern civilization, within which it maintains its traditional values on the one hand and adopting the values of different cultures on the other hand. In the meanwhile, it continues to exert its influence on the other cultures in the world, and people all over the world have also benefited a great deal from the Chinese economy as well as culture.

To sum up, the traditional Chinese notion of "harmony" which underscores the value of difference, reconciliation and creation provides intercultural communic-ation rich resources and it has broaden a new vision for the future of

intercultural contact between eastern and western cultures as being expected by
Professor Wang Keping in his poem:

East is not all East, West is not all West,
And Why not the twain shall meet.
Let the world be in order with diversity
Or be in harmony without uniformity. ①

(The paper was first published in "China Media Research", 2009/1.)

---

① Ke Ping Wang, *Ethos of Chinese Culture, A Multicultural Strategy: Harmonization Without Being Patternized*, Beijing: Foreign Languages Press, 2007, p. 55.

The Unique Values of Chinese Traditional Cultural Time Orientation: In Comparison with Western Cultural Time Orientation

Edward Hall once regarded nonverbal communication as a hidden dimension people had often ignored and now the field of nonverbal communication has been paid greater attention in the academic circle of intercultural communication. However, at the present time, the study of nonverbal communication in China mainly concentrates on the kinesics, and the time issue is often overlooked. The study of Chinese traditional cultural time orientation in the western academic circle has not yet been taken into full account. This paper will attempt to investigate the unique values of the Chinese traditional cultural time orientation in contrast with the western cultural time orientation.

Cultural setting is a key element in intercultural communication, as Wood notes: "The largest system affecting communication is your culture, which is the context within which all your interactions take place. "[1] There are numerous cultural variables worth studying in intercultural communication, time dimension is one of the most important ones. For this reason, the American time research scholar Bureau used the concept of cultural time to describe the cultural differences in time orientation.

Cultural time orientation is of vital importance to the intercultural communication research since it acts as a mirror of reflecting a culture's deep value

---

[1]   Wood Julia T. , *Gendered Lives: Communication, Gender, and Culture*, Belmont, CA: Wadsworth, 1994, p. 29.

structure, life philosophy as well as life style. Particularly, the traditional Chinese cultural time orientation has its unique values, which has a striking feature contrast with the popular western cultural time orientation.

The Time Perception in the Western Culture

In a sense, time is a kind of philosophical issue, which has something to with the essence of human being's existence. The famous Greek Philosopher Heraclites once compared time to a boy who was playing games. However, he regarded the boy not as an ordinary boy, but the authoritative king in the game. Thus, according to Heraclites' interpretation, human beings were subordinated to time and time was the real king of the world that had a dominant role in controlling human beings' lives.

The concept of the overwhelming power of time is pervasive in the western culture, which has deep roots in western civilization. Ever since the ancient Greek time, time had often been perceived from the physical aspect. Plato classified the world into two categories: the phenomenon and noumenon, and he perceived the phenomenon world to be unreal, which was only the shadow of the absolute logos world, since it symbolized the mutable realm of reality, while he believed the noumenon world to be real, since it stood for the immutable realm of eternal form (in Greek, idea). Although Plato had debased the value of the phenomenon world, yet he considered the phenomenon world to be controlled by the mutable movement of time. Aristotle in his famous book physics defined time as a measurable object in motion, but unlike Plato, he began to accept the authenticity of the phenomenon world and further probed into the physical, objective features of time.

The scientists and philosophers after the Renaissance followed Aristotle's suit, and they thought of time as a kind of object in linear motion as well. The famous scientists such as Galileo and Newton regarded time as a certain quantity, which was used to calculate the speed of the object in motion, and most philosophers at that period such as René Descartes and John Locke also interpreted time from the physical aspect. Among them, Newton's perception of time is the most influential and far-reaching. In his famous book Natural Science he emphasized the concept of the absolute time. As a result, the physical interpretation of absolute time as the object in motion had been the main time orientation in the western civilization.

The physical interpretation of time established by Aristotle and Newton underscored regularity, absoluteness, and progress of time, and these features of time were reinforced in the process of western industrialization. As Mumford stated: "The first characteristic of modern machine civilization is its temporal regularity... From the moment of waking, the rhythm of day is punctuated by the clock. With regard to time, he claimed that irrespective of strain or fatigue, despite reluctance or apathy, the household rises close to its set hour. "[1] What's more, we see in the western culture, time is often believed to be something definite, absolute and valuable, which is even used to measure profit and achievement, and there are many famous sayings which express the importance of time: "The early bird catches the worm (the United States), "Never put off to tomorrow what you can do today "(England), "lose an hour in the morning, chasing it all day long" (Jewish culture). Time has become an absolute, determinant force in the western culture. As Edward Hall noted: "People of western world, particularly Americans, tend to think of time as some thing fixed in nature, something around us and from which we cannot escape; an ever-present part of the environment, just like the air we breathe. "[2]

The Physical interpretation of absolute time in lineal motion, together with industrialization civilization progress helps cultivate the future-time orientation in

---

① Lewis Mumford, *Technics and Civilization*, New York: Harcourt, Brace &World, 1962, p. 269.
② Edward T. Hall, *The Silent Language*, New York: Fawcett, 1959, p. 19.

most countries of the western world. Taking American people as an example, who particularly value the future and believe they can control the future.

Hall used M-time to describe the characteristics of western cultural time orientation mentioned above. Of course, M-time orientation has its own advantages, and according to Hall, M-time people concentrate on the job, take time commitment (deadline, schedules) seriously, adhere to plans, are concerned about not disturbing others, and follow rules of privacy. ① In general, M-time culture places more emphasis on efficiency and promptness.

However, it has its disadvantages and limitations, which we have become gradually aware of, and even some scholars have sharply criticized. As Kim observed (2001) : "Life is in constant motion, people consider time to be wasted or lost unless they are doing something. " ② M-time people who are under the great pressure of time are often controlled by the invisible hand of time and their individuality and freedom have been severely damaged. As what had been sharply pointed out by Wright: "This is the history of increasing, unchecked, and now intolerable chronarchy. That word is not to be found in The Oxford English Dictionary. Its coiner should be entitled to define it. Let chronarchy, then, be not merely ' rule by time', but ' regimentation of man by timekeeping'. " ③ The famous Chinese writer and scholar Lin Yu tang used another term "working animal" to describe the wretched situation in which people in a more civilized world have been confronted. He thought of civilization as a matter of the seeking food: "But the essential fact remains that human life has got too complicated and the matter of merely feeding ourselves, directly or indirectly, is occupying well

---

① Edward T. Hall, Mildred Reed Hall, *Understanding Cultural Differences: Germans, French, and Americans*, Yarmouth, ME: Intercultural Press, 1990, p. 15.

② Eun Y. Kim, *The Yin and Yang of American Culture: A Paradox*, Yarmouth, ME: Intercultural Press, 2001, p. 233.

③ Wright Lawrence, *Clockwork Man*, New York: Horizon Press, 1968, p. 7.

over ninety percent of our human activities. "[1] What Wright and Lin Yu tang revealed was that in the modern industrial society, people were more and more controlled by time and material things, and their freedom and individuality have been greatly damaged by a materialized world.

While the Chinese traditional cultural time orientation reflects quite a different attitude towards life and it can help resolve some problems the western culture is confronted with. Unlike the western time orientation that accentuates the objectiveness, absoluteness and fixation of time, the Chinese traditional cultural time orientation conceives time to be subjective, relative and flexible.

As is well known, the Chinese culture is greatly influenced by Confucianism, Taoism, and Buddhism. Among them, Confucianism and Taoism are native religions that will be the main discussion in this paper. The two schools of thoughts differ in time orientation in some aspects, however, they have some common grounds, which both hold an open-minded attitude towards time and regard it as relative, limitless and flexible.

The Time Orientation in Confucianism

Confucianism had played a major role in shaping the Chinese culture for thousands of years. As Barry, Chen, and Watson noted, "If we were to describe in one word the Chinese way of life for the last two thousands years, the word would be ' Confucian' "[2].

Confucius was a sage who advocated good virtues and manners in which "Ren" (humanity) and "Li" (ritual) were two main concepts, his entire life was engaged in the perfection of one's virtue as well as the prosperity of his state, thus

---

[1]　Lin Yu Tang, *The Importance of Living*, Beijing: Foreign Language Teaching and research Press, 2005, p. 144.

[2]　Barry W. T. , W. T. Chen and B. Watson, *Sources of Chinese Tradition*, New York: Columbia University Press, 1960, p. 17.

he maintained a very positive attitude towards life, and considered time to be valuable and to be made good use of. According to the Confucius Speaks, once Confucius stood by a river and made a deep sigh in front of the passing water: "All things that pass are just like this! Night and day it never stops. "① However, he kept a very calm mind before the endless flow of time and thought he had done quite well by making positive remarks towards the life he had spent: "At fifteen I set my heart on learning. At thirty, I could stand firm. At forty I had no doubts. At fifty I knew the Decree of Heaven. At sixty, I was ready obedient (to this decree). At seventy I could follow the desires of my mind without overstepping the boundaries (of what is right). "②

Another aspect of time orientation in Confucianism is the past-time focus, which should not be simply understood as a kind of conservativeness. Confucius lived in the spring and autumn period, a time when wars broke out frequently and there was a decline in social morality. Hence, He was very dissatisfied with the situation and intended to reform society by looking back to the past for a good model. Although Confucius seemingly pointed out some shortcomings of the ancient men in the following passage, what his real intention was to express his appreciation of the ancient men and pass criticisms upon the moral degeneration of the men in his time:

> In old days, men had three failings, which have perhaps, died out today. The impetuous of old days were impatient of small restraints; the impetuous today are utterly insubordinate. The stern dignity of old days were stiff and gravely reserved; the stern dignity today is touchy and quarrelsome. The simple men of old days were straightforward; the simple men today show themselves in sheer deceit. ③

① Tsai Chih Chung, *Confucius Speaks*, Beijing: Modern Press, 2005, p. 79.
② Pan Fu En, Wen Shao Xia, *The Analects of Confucius*, Jinan: Qilu Press, 2004, p. 11.
③ Ibid. , p. 215.

Confucius and other philosophers of his days had different approaches to the solutions of the problems. The dominant view of that time espoused by Legalists was for strict law and severe punishment, while Confucius resorted to Zhou Rituals by delivering himself of the following famous saying: "The rituals of the Zhou dynasty are inherited and developed from the two preceding dynasties Xia and Shang. How complete and elegant its rituals are! I follow upon Zhou. "[1]

Confucius interpreted the rituals of the Zhou dynasty as a cultural legacy inherited from the former dynasties Xia and Shang, which developed through generations of human wisdom, thus he addressed himself as a "transmitter" but not "an originator" because of his "believing in and loving in the ancients"[2]. There was no doubt that Confucius was a great sage who had established a unique system of social and ethical philosophy and whose thoughts had exerted a profound influence on the Chinese culture for thousand of years, nevertheless, he frankly attributed his thoughts to the Zhou Rituals. Therefore we see the past-time orientation in Confucianism contains many more positive connotations than negative ones. It is due to Confucius' preference to the "Zhou rituals" that he developed his own concept of "Li" , a term not only referring to outside rites and ceremonies but also denoting graceful and civilized manners in one's personality. "Li" has been one of the main Confucius' important teachings.

Lastly, Confucianism holds a flexible attitude towards time. It accentuates "the right occasion" and "the right opportunity" in dealing with affairs. Whatever things they might be, whether they are issues concerning big events of the state or trivial household matters, they should all be performed on a right occasion. Confucius's follower Mencius further promoted Confucian thoughts. The text, Mencius Speaks, relates the fable, "Helping rice Grow", which is a good example; it illustrates the importance of handling affairs on the right occasion. It

---

① Pan Fu En, Shao Xia Wen, *The Analects of Confucius*, Jinan: Qilu Press, 2004, p. 25.

② Ibid. , p. 65.

goes as follows: There was once a man in Song Kingdom who was terribly worried that his rice had grown slowly, he was so impatient that he went to the field to help his rice out by pulling them up a bit, the result was conceivable when all the rice died. The flexible handling of time in Confucianism has exerted a profound influence on the Chinese culture, even at the present time the Chinese people are good at seeking the right occasion for dealing with affairs in business, politics and daily life.

In short, the time orientation in Confucianism is multidimensional, its past-time focus enables its ethical core to be established upon the rich legacy passed down from the former dynasties, and its positive and agile attitude towards time is also enlighten.

The Time Orientation in Taoism

Lin Yutang thought Confucianism was not sufficient for the Chinese people since it was "too decorous, too reasonable, too correct"[1], hence arose Taoism in Chinese culture. He also made a comparison between Confucianism and Taoism by stating: "Confucianism, through its doctrine of propriety and social status, stands for human culture and restraint, while Taoism, with its emphasis on going back to nature, disbelieves in human restraints and culture. "[2]

Taoism in essence is a philosophy of perusing the limitless freedom by breaking through various boundaries and restrictions. Being one of the most famous sages of Taoism, Zhuang Zi pursued freedom in his entire life and resented worldly fame. Because of his great talent, he was once asked whether he was willing to be the prime minister of the Chu Kingdom of his time, and he did not reply directly, instead he told the two messengers sent by the king of Chu

---

① Yu Tang Lin, *My Country and My People*, Beijing: Foreign Language Teaching and Research Press, 2004, p. 113.

② Ibid. , p. 114.

Kingdom a story. It was said that there was kept in Chu Kingdom's temple the bone of a wonder tortoise which had been dead for three thousand years, and Zhuang Zi asked them a question: If they were the tortoises, would they be willing to be killed and have their bones kept in the temple, showing off their nobility or to swim freely in the mud with their wobbling tails? The messengers' reply was the latter. Zhuang Zi said he would also prefer swimming freely in the mud with his tail wobbling like the tortoise to enjoy a happy life without restriction. He further wrote another famous prose, "The Dream of the Butterfly" imaging he had turned into a carefree butterfly and wondering "Maybe Zhuang Zi was the butterfly, and maybe the butterfly was Zhuangzi"[1]. In fact, the butterfly had become Zhuang Zi's unique perception of freedom.

In Taoism, Tao is one of the most important concepts reconstructed by Zhuang Zi after he adopted the main idea put forth by Lao Zi, who was actually the founder of Taoism. Lao Zi regarded Tao as the origin of the universe while Zhuang Zi treated Tao as the highest principle of the world, in which there was no clear division between life and death, beauty and ugliness, past and present etc. Thus, based upon the concept of Tao, Zhuang Zi had established his unique philosophy of relativity towards life.

As far as time dimension is concerned, because of Zhang Zi's pursuit of freedom and his unique philosophy of relativity towards life, Taoism advocates the relativity and limitless of time. Tsai Chih Chung wisely interpreted: "It is a philosophy which takes life and hurls it into the limitless of time and space in order to be experienced to the fullest. "[2]

In his famous prose Carefree Travel of Zhuang Zi, Zhang Zi tried to illustrate his relativity view concerning time by citing a series of metaphors. Here is one excellent example of his prose:

---

① Tsai Chih Chung, *Zhuang Zi Speaks I: The Music of Nature*, Beijing: Modern Press, 2005, p. 27.
② Ibid. , p. 5.

People say that once there was a man named Peng Zu, who at 800 years old had lived the longest life ever. In contrast, there is a small bug called Zhaojun that was born in the morning and dead by nightfall. There is also an insect called the winter cicada, which is born in the spring and dies in the summer. However, in the southern part of Chu, there lived the giant wonder tortoise, to whom five hundred years was a mere Spring. And a long, long time ago, there lived the geri-tree, to which eight thousand years was a mere Autumn. The Zhaojun and the winter cicada are called ' short lives', while the wonder tortoise and the Geri-tree are called ' long lives'. To the wonder tortoise and the geri-tree, wasn' t Peng Zu just another ' short life'? People see Peng Zu as having lived a long life, but wasn' t he really just another tragic ' short life'?[①]

Considering what has been discussed above, according to Aristotle and Newton's view, time was an absolute physical concept, eight thousand years and five hundred years were real physical time, and their lengths were definitely longer than one spring, autumn or a day. Nevertheless, in Zhuang Zi's eye, there was no clear division among them when compared with the endlessness of time and space. Hence, what Zhuang Zi pursued in his entire life was the limitless freedom beyond various restraints; either they are the limitations of the definite time and space, or the bondages of a mundane world. Time to Zhuang Zi was no longer the dominant force in the control of human beings' lives, but rather the issue being freely handled at the hands of human beings, which could enable human beings to enjoy more freedom of easy-going time. Thus, in terms of Zhuang Zi's perception of time, the problem of "chronarchy" put forth by Wright above can be easily resolved.

Furthermore, the time orientation in Taoism which places more emphasis on

---

[①] Tsai Chih Chung, *Zhuang Zi Speaks I: The Music of Nature*, Beijing: Modern Press, 2005, pp. 6 – 7.

the subjectivity, relativity of time has helped cultivate the unique Chinese temperament as well as the carefree life style of the traditional Chinese culture. In his book The importance of living, Lin Yu tang spoke highly of "this divine desire for loafing in China" and "that carefree, idle, happy-go-lucky-and often poetic — temperament" in the Chinese scholars as well as the Chinese ordinary people, and he thought the temperament could be traced back to "the Taoistic Blood"[1]. Indeed, Taoism's carefree philosophy towards life has made a great impact on the Chinese carefree manner of spending time, which has been well reflected in a large number of the Chinese ancient poems.

In the famous, An Anthology of Popular Ancient Chinese Poems, there are poems here and there depicting pictures of an easy-going and idyllic life of the Chinese scholars and ordinary people. For instance, the first poem entitled, "An Impromptu Poem Composed in Spring", is one good example:

> Pale clouds and gentle breeze near midday,
> I pass the stream by the willows and flowers.
> You folks don't know my heart young and gay,
> And say I follow a lad to enjoy his free hours. [2]

When the poet Cheng Hao, who was also a great philosopher, wrote his poem, he was no longer young, however, a spring outing had made the poet forget his real physical age and his heart became "young and gay". Another famous Chinese poet Su Shi in his poem, Spring Night even expressed the feeling that "A moment of joy on a spring night is better than gold" [3]. Thus, Lin Yutang showed his great appreciation of the Chinese scholars and poets' easy-going manner of

---

[1] Yu Tang Lin, *The Importance of Living*, Beijing: Foreign Language Teaching and research Press, 2005, p. 150.

[2] Zhu Zhang Guo and Hui Sheng Fu, *An Anthology of Popular Ancient Chinese Poems*, Wuhan: Wu Han University Press, 2004, p. 2.

[3] Ibid. , p. 7.

spending time and stated that "The wisest man is therefore he who loafs most gracefully" [1].

The cult of idle life can also be observed in the ordinary Chinese people's lives at the present time although more and more Chinese people, especially people in the big cities are beginning to have a quicker life pace. Nevertheless, many ordinary Chinese people of older age still prefer to spend some time in chatting with their friends, relatives or neighbors to enjoy the carefree life.

In consideration, there are unique values underlying the time orientation in the traditional Chinese culture. The past-time focus in Confucianism reminds us the importance of the inheritance of cultural legacy developed through generations of human wisdom in the process of human civilization, and the relativity time orientation in Taoism offers us the possibility of pursuing freedom beyond various restrictions. Further more, the subjective, flexible and relative approaches of the traditional Chinese culture time orientation can provide meaningful revelations to the western world, which has accentuated the objective, absolute and future-focus time orientation.

(The paper was first published in "Intercultural Communication Studies", 2008 XVII: I and later selected by "Intercultural Communication Research" Volume 2 published by Higher Education Press in 2010.)

---

① Lin Yu Tang, *The Importance of Living*, Beijing: Foreign Language Teaching and research Press, 2005, p. 148.

A Reexamination of Perceptions of Silence in Chinese Culture

Silence as a kind of nonverbal communication is a very important field in intercultural communication, and it is generally accepted in the academic circle that silence is a positive and meaningful part in Chinese culture. However, this paper attempts to reexamine the perception of silence in Chinese culture and find out that the perception of silence in contemporary Chinese culture differs strikingly from what has been interpreted as a positive issue in the traditional Chinese culture. The findings are based on a questionnaire on silence among university students and it shows that now the Chinese people, particularly the young Chinese people prefer talking to silence in social doings.

Edward Hall once regarded nonverbal communication as a hidden dimension people had often ignored and now the field of nonverbal communication has been paid greater attention. However, at the present time, the study of nonverbal communication in China mainly concentrates on the kinesics, and silence is often overlooked. The study in the western academic circle has not taken full account of the complexities of Chinese culture's perception of silence with the passage of time, and taken it for granted that silence is always regarded as a positive issue in Chinese culture, this paper shows the perception of silence in contemporary Chinese culture have changed dramatically, comparing with what has been interpreted in the traditional Chinese culture.

Is Silence a Positive or Negative Issue?

Silence is an old topic which can be perceived either in a positive or a negative approach. As Bruneau has expounded:

For thousands of years, wise people have commented on the virtues and negativities of silence. There have been hundreds of quotations, sayings, and maxims about silence for thousands of years in Western groupings. For example: around 280 B. C. we find Epicuris the Stoic saying that, God gave people two ears, but only one mouth, that they may hear twice as much as they speak; around 53 B. C. , we find Cicero, the Roman statesman/orator, commenting that there is an eloquence of silence to be found in conversations; and, around 42 B. C. , we find Publius Syrus noting that, a person who does not know when to speak does not know when to be silent. ①

Here Bruneau states how silence is perceived in the western tradition, though the western world has a long history of valuing speech and rhetoric from the ancient Greek period, the virtues of silence are also greatly accentuated.

It is generally acknowledged that it is in the Eastern tradition that silence isinterpreted as a positive issue. For instance, the Japanese view of silence can be observed from the following proverbs: "It is the duck the squawks that gets shot", "A flower does not speak" and "The mouth is to eat not to speak with". Thus in Japanese culture, silence is highly preferred while talking is regarded as a negative issue. The Buddhism also holds a negative attitude towards speech by stressing "What is real is, and when it is spoken it becomes unreal". It is the same case with Hinduism, it holds the view that "self-realization, salvation, wisdom, peace, and bliss are all achieved in a state of meditation and introspection when the individual is communicating with himself or herself in silence" ②. Therefore, Hinduism stresses self-realization rather than outward expression and regards that the inner peace and wisdom can only be obtained

---

① T. J Bruneau, "Silence, Silences, and Silencing", In Littlejohn, S. & K. Foss (Eds.), *Encyclopedia of Communication*, CF: Sage Publications, Inc, 2009.

② N. Jain and. Ai Matukumall, *The Functions of Silence in India: Implications for Intercultural Communication*(paper presented at the Second International East Meets West Conference in Cross-Cultural Communication, Comparative Philosophy, and Comparative Religion, Long Beach, CA) , 1993.

through silence. As the famous Indian leader Chief Joseph states: "it does not require many words to speak the truth. "

Nevertheless, in some other cultures, talk instead of silence is greatly valued. A famous Greek idiom says "Nothing done with silence is done without speech", obviously it emphasizes the importance of talk as a means of communication. A similar Arabic saying is "A man's tongue is his sword. "With this saying, a man's tongue is compared to his sword, and the Arabs are taught to value word, to use them as a powerful tool. Mexican culture also enjoys the value of conversation, there is a famous Mexican idiom: "Conversation is the food for the soul. " From the Mexican proverb we see their preference to talking, in Mexican people's daily lives they value talking with their friends and the family, and it has been one part of their tradition.

Many scholars think that silence is not interpreted as a meaningful part of life in dominant American culture, "numerous studies have pointed out that most Americans believe that talking is an important activity and actually enjoy talking"[1]. Most people in the United States spend their spare time talking, watching TV, listening to the radio and take part in other sound-producing activities in order to keep them from silence, thus, American people prefer talking to silence in most cases, as Bruneau notes: "Many people especially in some Asian societies, feel that Americans talk too much, clarifying and explaining and trying to make their meanings more and more certain. But, such talk often happens because these Americans feel that it is only through talk that meanings are conveyed and silences do not imply communication for them. " [2] Althen offers a similar remark of American people's preference with language in the statement: "American depend more on spoken words than on nonverbal behavior to convey messages. They think it is important to ' speak up' and ' say what is on their

---

① J. Wiemann and V. Chen, and H Giles, *Beliefs about Talk and Silence in a Cultural Context* (paper presented at the Annual Convention of the Speech Communication Association, Chicago) , 1986.

② E Fred. Jandt, *An Introduction to Intercultural Communication*, Sage Publications, Inc, 2004.

mind. ' They admire a person who has a moderately large vocabulary and who can express herself clearly and shrewdly. " Therefore, in the dominant American culture, talk is often regarded as a positive attitude and manner. While silence is interpreted as a negative issue, to most American people, silence means lack of attention and lack of initiate. Jandt even thinks that "To most people in the United States silence can mean one is fearful of communicating" and he further uses the term "communication apprehension" to refer to "an individual's fear or anxiety associated with either real or anticipated communication with another person or persons". ①

From the general survey of the different perceptions of silence and talk in various cultures mentioned above, here we notice there are two different views towards the virtues and negativities of silence. One view holds the belief that silence is a positive issue which possesses the rich connotations of credibility, thoughtfulness, meditation and truth. While another view regards talk as a powerful part of life and perceive silence as a negative element. Then, what is the case in traditional Chinese culture?

Perception of Silence in Chinese Traditional Culture

Generally speaking, in traditional Chinese culture, silence is often perceived as a positive issue while talk is deprecated. In Lao Tzu's interpretation of the beginning of the universe, "There was something formed from Chaos, before the creation of heaven and earth. It is silent and formless. It stands alone always and never ceases coursing. You could consider it as the source of all things. I don't know what it is called, but if forced to name it, I would say ' Dao' ". "Dao" is a crucial concept in Dao De Jing, it provides the basic principle for the universe, and Lao Tzu believed that the real "Dao" could not be expressed in words by

---

① E Fred. Jandt, *An Introduction to Intercultural Communication*, Sage Publications, Inc, 2004.

stating "The Dao that can be told is not the eternal Dao; the name that can be named is not the eternal name". He further illustrated the intrinsic connotation of "Dao" from the following famous metaphors: "The Loudest sound can't be heard, the largest form can't not be seen, and The Dao is invisible and nameless, only the Dao excels at creating the myriad things and bringing them to maturity. " In a word, in Lao Tzu's interpretation, "Dao" represents the fundamental force in the universe, yet it operates silently and namelessly in the universe which denies any verbal explanation. Based on the interpretation of the universe, both Lao Tzu and Chuang Tzu deprecated outward expression and speech. As Jensen(1987) points out "Eloquence, and even speaking in general, is deprecated and is associated with highly negative connotations. Eloquence is spoken of as glibness, quickness of speech, noise making and clap-trap, and is identified with shallowness, superficiality, untrustworthy cleverness, pretentiousness, pride, hypocrisy, and flattery"[①]. Confucius shared the same view by expressing his dislikes of the people "speaking flattering words". Confucius also gave some advice on how to behave properly in our life by stressing the prudent use of words in suitable occasions and avoid talking too much.

The traditional Chinese philosophy mentioned above has exerted a far-reaching influence on Chinese traditional arts, such as Chinese painting and ancient poems. For instance, the Chinese "landscape painting"lays great emphasis on the empty space which provides the readers with much room for contemplation, and the Chinese poems contains rich and profound connotations beyond the words. The Chinese traditional culture also affects the Chinese people's thoughts and behaviors. The saying "Silence is gold" is still very popular in Chinese people's minds and offers a guidance in their daily life. In short, in traditional Chinese culture, silence has been endowed with positive connotations of thoughtfulness, productivity and profoundness.

---

① J. V, Jensen, *Rhetorical emphasis of Taoism*, rhetorrical, 1987, pp. 219—229.

However, with the passage of time, Chinese people's interpretation of silence has changed dramatically. Verbal communication has been attached greater importance in Chinese contemporary culture, while silence is not necessarily perceived as a positive issue among Chinese people, especially among Chinese young people. The following is a recent survey based on a questionnaire focusing on the silence perception among the university students in the Ocean University of China.

Research Method

The research method is a kind of questionnaire analysis. The questionnaire is designed to examine the university students' attitude towards silence, and ten questions have been designed to evaluate university students' perceptions of silence and talking. During the author's "Intercultural Communication class" on the afternoon of Oct. 9, 2009, one hundred papers have been handed out to the students in Ocean University of China coming from different departments, and eighty two papers have been collected in class.

Data Analyses and Results

The results show there has been a striking change in Chinese university students' view toward silence.

Question one is about the role of silence in our everyday interaction, and the results show 65% students think silence is very important, and 22% three students regard it is important, only 12% students say it is not so important and 1% students say it is not important at all. To sum up, about 88% students believe silence plays a very important role in their daily life interaction.

Questions from two to four focus on examining whether the Chinese students have preferences for the Chinese proverb "Silence is gold" or for the American saying "The squeaky wheel gets the grease". About 56% students still think that the Chinese proverb "silence is gold" is reasonable, and 37% students believe it is still workable today, only 5% students think it is unreasonable now, and 2% students regard it is out of date now.

In terms of American saying "The squeaky wheel gets the grease", results show 68% students think the American saying is reasonable as well, and 24% students express their views that the American saying is workable, only 6% students think it is not workable in their daily life and 2% students regards it as unreasonable.

It is quite interesting if we make a comparison. It indicates that student show liking for both of proverbs. 93% students think that the Chinese proverb "silence is gold" is reasonable and still workable today, while 92% students think that the American saying "The squeaky wheel gets the grease" is also as a reasonable and workable one. Basically, the Chinese proverb "Silence is gold" and the American saying "The squeaky wheel gets the grease" focus on opposing orientations, yet now the students accept both of them.

Nevertheless, students' responses to the questions number seven and eight show that they have preferences for talking over silence. In answering question number seven, 70% students think they should talk to others on their own initiatives in social doing, 22% students think they should be active speakers, only 3% students think they'd better talk less or remain silent.

In question number eight, when being asked about "What do you think of a person who is good at speech to be". 43% students think of such a person to be a talented person, 37% students regard such a person as a smart person, while 11% students conceive such a person to be. an unreliable person, and the remaining 6% students think of him or her to be a flimsy person. Considering what has been discussed above about Taoism and Confucianism's negative attitudes towards eloquence, here obviously, the students' views towards eloquence have changed dramatically.

Correspondingly, students express a negative view towards silence in the following two questions. Responding to question number five about "Sometimes when you talk with your friend, he or she remains silent, what do you think of his or her silence". 36% students think it is a sign of disagreement, 32% students think it is a sign of lack of attention, and 10% students say it is a sign of contempt, while only 20% students say it is a sign of agreement.

Consequently, in question nine, 63% students regard silence as a negative signal and 37% students consider silence as a positive signal. The students' preference of talking over silence can be further supported by their responses to question number ten, 75% students express their favor of talking while only 25% students show their liking for silence.

However, there remain some complexities in students' perceptions of silence and their actual behaviors in classroom. For instance, in answering question number six about their responses to teachers' questions in the class room, 41% students say they often keep silent, 37% students say they usually wait until teachers call their names, 9% students say they hope not to be asked to answer the questions, and only 13% students say they volunteer to answer the questions.

Discussion

From the findings illustrated above, we can see a kind of complex status in students' perceptions of silence. On the one hand, the traditional Chinese culture's view of silence still exerts far-reaching influences on the students' minds, most students still value the Chinese proverb "Silence is gold" and regard it as a reasonable saying. Moreover, at the present time, in university classes, most students accept the fact they often keep silent and are not eager to answer the teachers' questions, let alone raise some challenging questions to argue with the teachers.

However, on the other hand, most students think of the American saying "The squeaky wheel gets the grease" also as a reasonable and workable one, and most of them think they should be active speakers in social doings. What's more, most students now regard silence as a negative issue and show their preference for talking, thus the findings reflect a tendency that the perception of silence at the contemporary Chinese culture has undergone a striking change.

Many factors may contribute to the changes, among which one leading factor turns out to be the influence of globalization. In the process of globalization, China has learned a lot from the outside world, particularly western culture and values, thus the Chinese people now pay more and more attention to the value of talk and regard it as a good opportunity of showing their talents and a good way of communicating with one another, and silence is sometimes even interpreted as a negative issue which signifies inability.

Conclusion

Silence as the muting form of expressions has its rich connotations in traditional Chinese culture, silence has once been highly valued in Chinese traditional culture while eloquence is depreciated. However, the findings of the questionnaire reveal that at the present time, with the passage of time, university students' perceptions of silence have changed dramatically, comparing with what has been conceived in the traditional Chinese culture. Verbal communication has been attached greater importance in today's Chinese culture.

(The paper is based on the presentation at the Kumamoto International conference on Intercultural Communication in 2009 and made some alterations.)

The Exploration of Regionalism and Universalism in
Shen Congwen and William Faulkners' Novels

Shen Congwen is one of the most representative modern writers in the twentieth century from China. He was once nominated as the candidate for Nobel Prize for Literature and gained his fame both at home and abroad. Since Shen Congwen's novels focus on the regional life of his home town, most of his works are imbued with the folklore and customs of his native western Hunan, and he has often been compared to William Faulkner, one of the most influential American writers of the twentieth century, who was awarded the Nobel Prize for literature in 1950. Faulkner is considered as one of the most important "Southern writers" as well as the one of the greatest American writers of all time. Many researchers have mentioned some similarities between the two writers' novels. For instance, Jeffrey C. Kinkley, a professor of Asian studies at St. John's University in New York as well as the leading American scholar devoted to Shen Congwen research, regards that "West Hunan" in Shen Congwen's novels is an imaginary kingdom, which is like "the Yoknapatawpha world" in Faulkner's works. Another famous scholar Xia Zhiqing points out both Shen Congwen and Faulkner show interest in the naive and innocent nature of human beings. However, there have been no research papers or books focusing on the comparative study of the two writers' novels from an intercultural communication perspective. Thus, this paper aims for this perspective; to be more specific, it concentrates on an analysis of cultural region, value, and time in the two writers' novels and argues that the three elements have played a vital role in helping us understand the writers' novels as well as intercultural communication issues. The research method adopted in the paper is a kind of parallel comparison, illustrating the similarities as well as differences of the two writers' novels from the aspects mentioned above.

1. 1 Cultural Region

Region as a kind of cultural space is a specific area occupied by people sharing recognizable and distinctive cultural characteristics as well as cultural heritage. Consequently, the cultural region consists of a large cultural space which can represent an entire culture system and reflect cultural traits, beliefs, values and complexes. As Dr. St. Clair explained, "Cultures have a geographical dwelling, or a space. They have ontological structures. Furthermore, they are united to a geographical environment, and respond to it. The human environment and the natural environment can never be separated. Human beings leave their ontological markers on their environment. Their reciprocal relation creates geographical milieu and cultural milieu" [1].

Cultural Region has played a significant role in the two modern writers of the twentieth century, the Chinese writer Shen Congwen and American writer William Faulkner. The commonness of Shen Congwen and Faulkner lies in their strong attachment to the particular regions they were born and nurtured, which are respectively "West Hunan world" and "Yoknapatawpha world". The regional life and people portrayed by Shen Congwen and Faulkner possessed the unique cultural characteristics as well as universal ontological significance.

Shen Congwen was one of the most representative modern writers in the twentieth century of China, and he had once been nominated as the Nobel Prize candidate. He gained his fame both at home and abroad. As Jeffrey C. Kinkley, a professor of Asian studies at St. John's University in New York and the leading American authority on Shen Congwen's works remarked: "Shen's masterpieces

---

① R. N. St Clair and W. Song, *Cultural Space and Cultural Materialism: A Theoretical Investigation of the Concept of Cultural Space*, Lewiston, NY: Edwin Mellen Press, 2008, p. 2.

rank with Chekhov's. ''

Most of Shen Congwen's works concentrate on the depiction of the people in western Hunan, where he was born and bred. Region has played a very important role in the writing of Shen Congwen and he became obsessed with his regions' "habits, speech, manners, history, folklore, or beliefs". West Hunan (also known as Xiangxi) is a mountainous region close to the border of Guizhou, in which the upper areas are occupied by Miao minority people and the lower by Han (or a mixture). This region was part of the ancient state of Chu, known for its Chu Wu culture. The area is regarded by the more northern cultures of the time as barbaric and uncivilized. However, Shen Congwen has rediscovered the unique value of Chu Wu culture as well as the life modes of native western Hunan and its moral strength. Though he portrayed his region for its particularity, his works has made it typical of the Chinese rural life and of universal qualities of life in general. Kinkley once commented, "He conveyed a sense of his country folk as a moral community sitting in judgment of modern China".

Since Shen Congwen focused more on the regional life of his home town, much of his works were imbued with the folklore and customs of his native western Hunan, he has often been compared to that of William Faulkner, who as one of the most influential American writers of the twentieth century was awarded the 1949 Nobel Prize in literature. Faulkner was considered as one of the most important "South writers" as well as the greatest American writers of all time.

Most of Faulkner's works are set in Yoknapatawpha County, termed as "postage stamp" by the writer. Yoknapatawpha County is a literary imaginary area in most of Faulkner's works which are based on the Lafayette County in Mississippi State, of which his hometown Oxford is the county seat. Faulkner was raised in Oxford and spent most of his life time in Oxford, thus he was greatly influenced by the history of his family and the region in which he lived as well as the history and culture of the South as a whole. Malcolm Cowley in *The Portable Faulkner* illustrated the deep influence Oxford had exerted in Faulkner's works:

The Pattern was based on what he saw in Oxford or remembered from his Childhood; in scraps of family tradition (the Falkners, as they spelled the name, and had played their part in the history of the state); on Kitchen dialogues between the black cook and her amiable husband; on Saturday-afternoon gossip in Courthouse Square; on stories told by men in overalls squatting on their heels while they passed around a fruit jar full of white corn liquor; on all the sources familiar to a small-town Mississippi boy but the whole of it was elaborated, transformed, given convulsive life by his emotions; until by simple intensity of feeling the figures in it became a little more than human, became heroic or diabolical, became symbols of the Old South, of war and reconstruction, of commerce and machinery destroying the standards of the past. There in Oxford, Faulkner performed a labor of imagination that has not been equaled in our time, and a double labor: first, to invent a Mississippi country that was like a mythical kingdom, but was complete and living in all its details; second, to make his story of Yoknapatawpha County stand as a parable or legend of all the Deep South. [①]

Malcolm Cowley discovered Yoknapatawpha actually served as a mythical kingdom as well as a "parable or legend of all the Deep South", using the oxford as a background, Faulkner not only depicted its geographical milieu and cultural milieu, but also the common situation which the human beings has confronted with. Again, Frederick commented : "He wrote from and about a part of country that has always fascinated the readers the world over; the south has its own sources of profound interests, and Faulkner soon became known as pre-eminently a ' novelist of the South' ". [②]

As what has been revealed above, both Shen Congwen and Faulkner focused

---

① M. Cowley, *The Portable Faulkner Revised and Expanded Edition*. New York: Penguin Books, 1967, p. Viii.

② F. J. Hoffman, *William Faulkner*, New Haven, CT: College and University Press, 1961, p. 17.

on the writing of two particular regions " West Hunan world " and "Yoknapatawpha", and the two areas were the starting points and footstones of their literary world, which reflected the typical cultural legacy embedded in particular cultural space, and the cultural legacy could be observed particularly in their depictions of cultural values in their novels.

1. 2 Cultural Value

Shen Congwen was strongly influenced by the Chinese traditional cultural concept of harmony and he tent to look at humanity and nature in total harmony and in eternal inseparability, while Faulkner held a firm belief in individualism, which was the typical reflection of American culture value.

The literary ideal of Shen Congwen's novels was the pursuit and portrayal of the harmonious relationship in terms of human and nature as well as human beings themselves in society. In Shen Congwen's "West Hunan" works, the relation between human beings and nature was intimate and harmonious instead of being opposite and separated. Human nature was a key word in Shen Congwen's works, and Shen Congwen had his unique interpretation of it. What he appealed for was a kind of human nature which embodied the affinity between human being and nature. In his representative works such as novels *Border City* and *The Long River*, short story collection *Lamp of Spring and Black Phoenix*, he had portrayed a large number of characters who were natural beings, full of natural temperament, vigor and robustness, Shen Congwen addressed them in such a poetic way : "They are like light, heat, spring water and fruit, and in fact they are everything in universe. " [1]Some critics praised Shen Congwen for portraying characters with beautiful souls, who had the personalities of being natural, nave and sincere. In his famous novel *Border City*, Shen Congwen explained his motivation in writing

---

① Shen Congwen, *The Completed Works of Shen Conwen*, Shanxi: Beiyue Wenyi Press, 2002, p. 168.

novels, and said what he attempted to depict was a kind of human being's life style, a kind of elegant, healthy, natural life style which suited the human nature. The life style that reflected the affinity between nature and human being was the highest life style Shen Congwen had pursued. Actually, What permeated his "west Hunan" novels was this kind of healthy and natural life style of the rural folks in his native region, In their daily lives, they just followed the rhythms of nature, and had a harmonious relationship in family and sex by learning from the law of nature.

While Faulkner's novels concentrated on the core belief of individualism. In Faulkner's view, individualism was the true representation of human nature, and he regarded that human beings could only be saved by maintaining their individualistic personalities. Faulkner even asserted that he would be a preacher of individualism and he held a firm belief that the uniqueness of each individual was of paramount value, and thus in Faulkner's view, an individual or "I" identity should be regarded as the most important unit in society, and the value of each individual should be placed in the first position.

This individualistic view could be traced back to the early history of American culture. At the beginning of the nation, most people were immigrants from Europe. When facing with a desolate and uninhabited wilderness they developed their habits of survival based on individualism and great importance was attached to the self-dependence. Later on, America won its independence from England, and founded a federal country based on the principle that "all men are created equal". The individualism was reinforced by Emerson's transcendentalism which laid great emphasis on unique value of the individual life.

Christianity has exerted a profound influence on American culture, which helps shape its basic values, one of which is individualism. Some scholars maintain that "Christianity discovered the individual". In a sense, the western concept of the importance of individual can be linked partially to the Christianity. According to the Christianity; human beings are significant because God created them in his image. God has a special relationship with each person, and each person is important to him. Therefore, individualism in American culture has its rich resources both in history and religion.

In Faulkner's novels, Yoknapatawpha is a fable of the tradition and history of "Old South" which underscores the value of individualism. In his major works, he had depicted a series of characters, who could be regarded as individualistic heroes. These characters were mainly based on his great-grandfather and his grandfather. Faulkner's great-grandfather, William C. Faulkner, was a legendary figure, who was a colonel in the civil war, an owner of a railroad and a member of the state legislature and finally was killed by a business rival. The great-grandfather was the original of the characters in many of Faulkner's novels, *Sartoris, The Unvanquished, Sound and Fury, Absalom, Absalom, Go down Moses* and many other stories, and according to William Van O's Connor(1959), they have become "part of the legend of the Old South, and they has played an important part in Faulkner's Yoknapatawpha saga"[1]. The characters, such as the Compsons, the Satories, the McCaslines were Faulkner's "Mississippi aristocrats", who possessed the personalities of being enterprising, independent, ambitious. Among them, the general Compson was not only a person who had the personalities mentioned above, but also a benevolent character, who had a spirit "capable of compassion, and sacrifice and endurance" by surpassing the gaps of class and race and treat people, including the black people equally.

Under the influence of beliefs of Christianity, Faulkner advocated the dignity and equality of every individual in his works, and in the novels such as *The Hamlet, Go down Moses, the Light in August*, John Pilkington argued "Especially Faulkner insisted upon the dignity of every man whatever his color or condition in life; he continually affirmed that the poor, the sick, the elderly, the young, the

---

① O' Connor W. V. , *William Faulkner*, Minneapolis, MN: University of Minnesota University, 1959, p. 5.

mentally retarded, even the criminal, have yet their claim to the rights of man"①.

1.3 Cultural time

In a sense, space is closely related to time, since time is embedded in cultural space. As Dr St. Clair has pointed out "Time exists within space. The present is embedded in the past and the future is embedded in the present. This model of the stratification of cultural space is also predicated on dialectic between the past and the present in the practical consciousness of the co-present"②.

In the cultural space of "West Hunan world" and "Yokanatawpha County", Shen Congwen and Faulkner have identity themselves with the traditional cultural values of harmony and individualism in Chinese and American cultures. As what has been discussed above, "West Hunan world" is a harmonious mythology of the past, in Shen Congwen's famous novel Fengzi, he spoke highly of the world that was full of love, harmony and regarded it as the age that the God still existed. Faulkner also cherished the past of Old South, and appealed for the precious value of individualism, courage, honor, hope, and sympathy in the Old South culture and further rediscovered a world which symbolized the "Edenic past", As Fredrick J. Hoffman had argued: "a past removed from historical time, an Eden coexisting with society yet never mistaken for society by those who come to it for refreshment and purification. " ③ The "Edenic past" had been described in a large number of images in "The Bear", Absalom, Light in August, Requiem for Nun, among them, Lena Grove was one of the ideal characters, "whose existence in ' pure' Edenic past is marked by her absolute immunity from the

---

① John Pilkington, *The Heart of Yoknapatawpha, Jackson*, University of Mississippi Press, 1983, p. Xii.

② St Clair R. N. and Song W. , *Cultural Space and Cultural Materialism: A Theoretical Investigation of the Concept of Cultural Space*, Lewiston, NY: Edwin Mellen Press, 2008, p. 2.

③ Hoffman F. J. , *William Faulkner*, New Haven, CT: College and University Press, 1961, p. 27.

stresses and strains of human involvement"①.

The reason why Shen Congwen and Faulkner's identified themselves strongly with the past in "West Hunan world" and "Yokanatawpha county" lies in the fact that past served as a kind of cultural legacy that could provide the present with rich resources and helped reshape present. Dr. St. Clair has again pointed out : "As the layers of cultural space are laminated, the present enfolds into the co-present before being redefining or modifying the old-past. " ②

However, with the passage of time, the old ways of living, the traditional values of the old world Shen Congwen and Faulkner cherished had been eroded by the commercialization and mechanization of the present time they lived in. Shen Congwen criticized the materialism erosion sharply in "West Hunan World" by writing: "the beautiful song and beautiful bodies have disappeared, and women paid more and more attention to money now. " ③While Faulkner's novels also portrayed the tragic decay and corruption of the Old South and the rise and invasion of the insidious northern industrialized force such as Snopes, as John Pilkington remarked: "He deplore the materialism that he felt had eroded human values, he saw with the dismay the breakdown of the parental responsibility in the home, the growth of religious bigotry in the churches, the failure of the courts to dispense justice evenhandedly, the ever-widening racial division in the community. He chronicled with regret the decay of the leadership exercised by aristocratic men like his ancestors and their defeat by the rising class of amoral businessmen. " ④

Nevertheless, Shen Congwen and Faulkner had adopted different attitudes towards the past. Shen Congwen identified himself strongly with the pure and

---

① F. J. Hoffman, *William Faulkner*, New Haven, CT: College and University Press, 1961, p. 27.

② R. N. St Clair and W. Song, *Cultural Space and Cultural Materialism: A Theoretical Investigation of the Concept of Cultural Space, Lewiston*, NY: Edwin Mellen Press, 2008, p. 62.

③ Congwen Shen, *The Completed Works of Shen Conwen*, Shanxi: Beiyue Wenyi Press, 2002, p. 202.

④ John Pilkington, *The Heart of Yoknapatawpha*, Jackson, MS: University of Mississippi Press, 1983, p. 296.

harmonious state of the past in "West Hunan world", and believed it to the representation of the perfect status of human civilization, while Faulkner held a dialectical attitude towards the past in the Old South. On the one hand, he cherished the traditional values in the Old South such as "individualism", "courage", "pride", "sympathy", "perseverance" and "sacrifice", on the other hand, he realized the inhuman moral crisis hidden in the slavery-based Old South culture and passed his sharp criticism upon the strict paternal system, the ostensible women moral value and racial discrimination within the culture, and revealed that these elements lead to the disaggregation of the south.

Literary works can serve as good materials for the research of intercultural communication; however, the perspective has often been ignored. The paper focuses on the study of the cultural region, value and time in the novels of Shen Conwen and Faulkner, the two influential writers in the twentieth century, and argues that the cultural regions "West Hunan World" and "Yokanapatawpha" created by the two writers serve as the myths of the past, convey the core values of harmony and individualism in Chinese and American cultures, which can provide the present with the rich cultural legacy and resources.

(The paper was first published in "Intercultural Communication Studies", 2009 XVIII: 2.)

On the Open Value Orientation in John Steinbeck's
Short Stories *The Long Valley*

Being a remarkably candid and prolific writer all his life, in his literary career, John Steinbeck has created twelve volumes of novels, two short story collections, two reportage collections and three travel notes. In his works, he deals with various subjects, tests different forms and raises great varieties of themes. For his outstanding contribution to literature world, Steinbeck was awarded The Nobel Prize in 1962.

In the western academic circle, the study on Steinbeck lays more stresses on the point that he is a naturalist, while in the Chinese research field, Steinbeck is often categorized as a " proletarian " or " social protest writer ", However, Steinbeck's works go beyond the above labels, and in this part, the book will prove into the open value orientation revealed in his short stories. The open value features are mainly reflected from the following three aspects: First, Steinbeck's thinking has a distinctive open characteristics nurtured by the rich American cultural tradition, Steinbeck's mind is in tune with an open, pioneering American spirit and in his works, especially his short stories, he continuingly advocates the American spirit. Next, being aware of his great mission as a writer, he spares no efforts to expose the weakness in human beings, and regards that if only human beings were willing to accept the faults and failures in themselves and did not indulge in the illusion of their self-perfection, they could make improvements. And finally, he underscores the freedom of individual, which should not been hampered by any restrictions.

John Steinbeck is a writer whose writings cover various topics which are presented in different forms. The depictions of his works vary from the humorous, light-hearted life of Monterey bum(*Tortilla Flat*) to the stifling depression hanging around the ranches of the Salinas Valley (*The Long valley*) , from a boy's initiation into adulthood (*The Red Pony*) to two itinerant workers ' cherishing dream of owning a piece of land (*Of Mice and Men*) , from the migratory workers' strike (*In Dubious Battle*) to Oklahoma farmers' westward trek to Callifomla (*The Grapes of Wrath*) , from Steinbeck and his friend Edward F. Ricketts' marine voyage in the Gulf of California (*Sea Of Cortes*) to his personal travel of 40 states with his poodle chaley(*Travels with Charley in Search Of America*) . In dealing with the various subjects, Steinbeck rcpcatedly tests his literary creativity with different forms, which range from the picaresque (*Tortilla Flat*) through the sociological (*The Grapes of Wrath*) and philosophlcal (*East of Eden*) to the warmly personal (*Travels with Charley in Search of America*) .

Though Steinbeck's major attribution is in his novels, his achievement in short stories is equally impressive. Mary Rohrberger has aptly said: "In the end… [Steinbeck's] reputation may rest on the short stories. As a novelist he is competent, as a short story writer he can be superb. " ①Due to his popular success of his short stories, Steinbeck won the O. Henry Memorial Award for prize stories four times, and his work was also frequently honored in Edward J. O' Brien's Best Short stories annuals and in O' Brien's ultimate of select anthologies, 50 Best American Short Stories, 1915—1939.

Steinbeck has altogether published two short story collcctions. One is *The Pastures of Heaven* and the other is *The Long Valley*. Anyway it is *The Long Valley* that can account for Steinbeck's higher achievement in short stories, therefore, this book will focus on the study of the short story collection *The Long Valley*. Fifteen of Steinbeck's finest and best-known short stories are collected in The Long Valley. Most of the stories take place in the Salinas Vallcy, Others on its border,

---

① Rohrberger Mary, *Writing the American Classics*, North Carolina: Duke University, 1984, p. 58.

such as Santa Lucia Mountains, Big Sur and Corral de Tierra, with the exception of a few stories ranging further from the Salinas Valley. The book will mainly concentrate on the detailed analyses of the following short stories: The Red Pony, "The Harness", "The White Quail" and "The Chrysanthemums".

The Red Pony consists of four episodes: "The Gift", "The Great Mountains", "The Promise" and "The leader of People". The structure is panoramic with a strong thematic unity that binds the four episodes together. Their shared reference is one important experience, the process of growing up, and their shared focus is one character, the boy Jody. "The Gift" and "The Promise" are two short stories, which deal with Jody's communion with horses. In "The Gift", Jody witnesses the tragic death of his beloved pony Gabilan, and in "The Promise", he observes the violent end of the mare Nellie as she gives birth of a shiny colt. "The Great Mountains" relates a story of an old Indian named Gitano who returns to his birthplace to die,. While "The Leader of the Peoplc" is about an old man's reminiscence of his "westering" experience.

Apart from *The Red Pony*, "The Chrysanthemums", "The White Quail", and "The Harness" are generally regarded as the best stories in *The Long Valley*. Each of the stories takes place in the Salinas Valley and probes the psychological consequences of unhappy or unhealthy marriages. "The Chrysanthemums" tells of a story of a vigorous, but depressed female character Elisa Allen who is deceived by a vulgar tinker. The latter two stories are about two males' frustrations. In "The White Quail", when Mary Teller orders her husband to kill a gray cat that threatens the quail, Harry Teller instinctively shoots the quail instead of the cat, which is the incarnation of his wife. While in "The Harness", Peter Randall, a model husband who always stands in his perfect straightness, is actually trussed in a harness by his wife.

One theme revealed in John Steinbeck's novels is the appealing of the typical American pioneering spirit. This theme has its historical tradition in American History and literature.

If there is one dream that most American share, it is a yearning dream that sets their eyes straining for a look beyond the horizon, their mind wandering what might be beyond their range of vision, and their feet on paths into the unknown. The horizons keep expanding, but for 100 years after the Declaration of Independence, the adventurers, the millions who braved the wilderness are in a ceaseless quest for independence and prosperity. In a sense, the westward movement was a typical expression of the American character, not too strongly longing for a settled life but dream by moving from place to place.

The American West inspires the imagination of many great American writers. To list just a few out of many, for instance, James Cooper, Mark Twain and Willa Cather are some of them. James Cooper, as a famous writer of American Romantic period is remembered today as the author of "The Leather Stocking Tales," a series of American novels about the frontier life of American settlers. In this book, Cooper depicted a new western world where there is freedom not tainted and fettered by any forms of human institutions and portrayed a typical American frontier character Natty Bumppo who represents the ideal American, living a virtuous and free life in God's world.

The west pursuit again became Mark Twain's major theme. His two famous novels *Life on the Mississippi* and *The Adventures of Huckleberry* Finn were both set in a background of Mississippi river, on both sides of which there was unpopulated wildness and a dense forest. Chang Yaoxin in *A Survey of American Literature* makes such a remark on Mark Twain's works of the west: "Here lies an America, with its great national faults, full of violence and ever cruelty yet still retaining the virtues of some simplicity some innocence, some peace. "[1]

Willa Cather was one of the few "uneasy survivors of the nineteenth century"[2], though born in Virginia, Cather moved at the age of nine with her

---

① Yao Xin Chang, *A Survey of American Literature*, Tianjin: Nankai University Press, 1990, p. 186.

② Robert Spiller, *The Cycle of Amreican Literature*, New York: The Free Press, 1967, p. 170.

family to a prairie state of the West — Nebraska. Old West thus became in most of her novels the center of moral reference against which modem existence is measured. Old Captain Forrester in *A lost lady* is a symbol of old west, one of the pioneers, "great-hearted adventurers", However, new men like Ivy Peters who "would drink up the mirage, dispel the morning freshness, root out the great brooding spirit of freedom, the generous easy life of great land-holder" ① are destroying the traditional and establishing a different value system which is infested with small-town spirit and materialistic standard.

The American theme of the west announces itself regularly in Steinbeck's works. His first novel *To a God Unknown* begins with the departure of Joseph Wayne, from the family home in New England near Pittsford, Vermont, to the green hills of Californla: "I've been reading about the west and the good cheap land there", "It's not just rcstlessness", his father replies: "You may go to the west, You are finished here with me. " ②The process is repeated in East of Eden, when Adam Trask leaves his Connecticut home and heads for California. "It's nice there, sun all the time and beautiful. " ③On seeing his native Salinas Valley in California as a new Eden, the scene of new chance for man, and in transporting his heroes from the exhausted cast to west, Steinbeck is not only continuing in an American tradition, enacting again an old American dream, he is also suggesting that the dream itself has moved west and has settled there. As Tetsumaro?Hayashi remarks, "Steinbeck's instinct at these initial moments was altogether sound, he was knowingly possessing himself of a native theme and a native resource, a resource both of history and literature" ④.

In "The Leader of the People", the fourth story of *The Red Pony*, an old

---

① Robert Spiller, *The Cycle of Amreican Literature*, New York: The Free Press, 1967, p. 333.

② John Steibeck, *To A God Unknown*, New York: Viking Press, 1929, p. 132.

③ John Steibeck, *East of Eden*, New York: Viking Press, 1952, p. 245.

④ Tetsumaro, Hayashi ed. , *Steinbeck's Short Stories in The Long Valley: Essays in Criticism*, Muncie: Ball State University Press, 1991, p. 634.

man's memories of "Westering" become the central focus. The old pioneer (Jody's grandfather) describes a westward migration which he himself once led as "a whole bunch of people made into one big crawling beast—Every man wanted something for himself but the big beast that was all of them wanted only westering"①. Trying once more to explain himself, the old man said, "We carried life out here and set it down the way those ants carry eggs. And I was the leader. The westering was as big as God and the slow steps that made the movement piled up and piled up until the continent was crossed"②.

The tension between the two generations roaches its maximum when Jody's grandfather who reminisces proudly again about "the long phalanxes of humanity crossing the prairie" overhears the scornful remark which his son-in-law has made one morning during his visit to their house, "why does he have to tell them over and Over? He came across the plains. All right! Now it's finished Nobody wants to hear about it over and over". ③

To his grandson who is eager to do the similar deeds, the old man said sadly, "No place to go, Jody, Every place is taken. But that's not the worst—, no, not the worst. Westering has died out of the people. Westering isn' t a hunger anymore. It is all done. Your father is right. It is finished"④.

Jody's father Carl Tiflin represents the tame and settled life mode of the present generation. Being confined to the limitation of an isolated ranch—a narrow world in which he lived, he is arrogant, self-content and narrow-minded and to him, "the westering has really died out". Intrestingly, Steinbeck links grandfather's hunting stories of soldiers, buffalo and Indians with Jody's mice hunt. The story opens with Jody's joyous anticipation of slaughtering the "plump,

---

① Covic Pascal Jr. , ed, *The Portable Steinbeck*, New York: Penguin Books, 1976, p. 414.
② Ibid. , p. 412.
③ Ibid. .
④ Ibid. , p. 414.

sleek, arrogant mice", who have been living comfortably for many months in a haystack. ①To Jody the mice are big game, and he images himself in pursuit of them as a heroic hunter like his grandfather, yet his grandfather says Jody's hunt is typical of "the people of this generation who have stooped to hunting vermin"②. In addition, since the mice are "smug in their security, overbearing and fat in their hay stack" ③, they further suggest degeneration. However, Jody stands for a new generation; he is by no means the same as his father, whose eyes are not always fixed on the narrow limited reality. In "The Great Mountains", Jody's great desire to tap the screws of unknown world is revealed as he watches the mysterious "Great Mountains" he knows little about:

> *"What's on the other side? " he asked his father once.*
>
> *"More mountains, I guess. Why?"*
>
> *"More mountains on and on? "*
>
> *"Well, no. At last you come to the ocean. "*
>
> *"But what's in the mountains? "*
>
> *"Just cliffs end brush and rocks and dryness. "*
>
> *"No. "*
>
> *"Has anybody ever been there?"*
>
> *"A few people, I guess. It's dangerous, with cliffs and things. "*
>
> *"Why, I've read there's more unexplored country in the mountains of Monterey Country than any place in the United States. "*
>
> *His father seemed proud that this should be so.*
>
> *"And at last the ocean? "*
>
> *"At last the ocean. "*
>
> *"But, " the boy insisted, "but in between? No one knows?"*

---

① Covic Jr. Pascal , ed, *The Portable Steinbeck*, New York: Penguin Books, 1976, p. 398.

② Ibid. , p. 404.

③ Ibid. , p. 398.

"Oh, a few people do, I guess. But there's nothing there to get. And not much water. Just rocks and cliffs and greasewood. Why?"

"It would be good to go. "

"What's for? There is nothing there. " ①

But Jody knows that there is actually something wonderful, mysterious and unknown there. Here the "Great Mountains" is a symbol which represents the unknown, unexplored world. Jody's curiosity about the mysterious mountains shows his great desire of going beyond his narrow world and reach for some new and unknown sphere. Moreover, Jody's final decision of giving up the mice hunt and his sympathy towards his grandfather's past experience further betoken the fact that the westering spirit has not died out but has been carried on by the next generation.

In short, the recurring native theme of the American West in Steinbeck's works suggests that Steinbeck calls for and embraces an open, American pioneering spirit the essence of which is the continuous transcendence of the narrow confines of the reality for the purpose of reaching for some new and unknown world.

Steinbeck believes that perfection and imperfection, good and evil are closely related with each other, and there are no absolute rules. In many short stories of *The Long Valley*, by revealing the tragic fates of a group of characters who are destroyed by their futile seek for absolute perfection and goodness, Steinbeck intends to express such a theme: Absolute perfection is not available to man. If one indulges in his illusion of narcissism and refuses making any changes like those characters, his psychology might be enclosed and he will see no hopes for progress and improvement.

Michael J. Meyer, in his disagreement with some critics who consider that

①　Covic Pascal Jr. , ed, *The Portable Steinbeck*, New York: Penguin Books, 1976, pp. 361 – 362.

Steinbeck's The Long Valley offers a mass of confusion, argues that "The whole collection is well crafted, containing apparently discrete tales that are really interrelated by a symbolic valley"①. in his opinion, this valley is a constant part of life, signifying human being's constant struggle to cope with polar opposites of good and evil, perfection and imperfection, and to create a balanced understanding of human existence. Ray Crifflin offers a similar reading of Steinbeck's valley in an unpublished dissertation from Loyola University of Chicago in 1972, he notes:

> *Mixtures of gray tones are more frequent than stark block und stark white. An additional complication is superimposed with Steinbeck's varying attitudes towards good and evil, resulting in an outlook that is tantamount to dual duality.*
>
> *In fact, the two most comprehensive of Steinbeck's themes relate to the nature of man and the universe, this clash between validity of perfection and the impossibility of perfection.* ②

Steinbeck's basic attitudes toward the human race, and his view of human being's attempts of understanding and accepting the continuing existence of both good and evil are told and retold in his short stories and novels.

One message conveyed by Steinbeck in *The Red Pony* is his preoccupation with man's struggle for perfection and his acceptance of imperfection. In "The Gift", Jody's initiation into adulthood begins by his learning lessons from life. The first lesson he has learned is that imperfection is everywhere. Carl Tiflin, Billy Buck and Jody are all imperfect in different ways: Jody's father is a stern disciplinarian, implicitly afraid to express his affection for Jody. His materialistic gift and his claim that the pony will be useful mark his effort to express a love for

---

① Tetsumaro Hayashi, ed. , *Steinbeck's Short Stories in The Long Valley: Essays in Criticism*, Muncie: Ball State University Press, 1991, p. 126.

② Ibid. .

Jody that he cannot express in words.

The irony lies in this: Once seeing the red pony, Jody is filled with wonder and affection for it, not for his father Mr. Tiflin, but for the pony, yet the pony bite Jody's hand, a hint of the latter's forthcoming imperfection. In the final division of the episode, when Jody finds the dying pony's body surrounded by the buzzards, he fights fiecefully with them. Carl Tiflin cannot understand Jody's act: "Jody", he explained: "The buzzard didn't kill the pony, don't you know that?" It was Billy buck who knew Jody's inner feeling. He turned back on Carl Tiflin: "course he knows it. "Billy said furiously: "Jesus Christ! Can't you see how he'd feel about it?" ① Lifting Jody in his arm, Billy Buck can understand Jody better than the well-being but detached Carl Tiflin.

The illness and death of pony occur in this context of imperfect that even happiness does not negate. The central fact is that Jody tends to transfer an implicit belief in his father's perfection to the less awesome Billy Buck, who is aware that he can't bear to seem fallible to Jody. Partly because of this self-knowledge, Billy claims too much good sense, but he is badly mistaken on three occasions: The pony gets wet because Billy misjudges the weather; the pony gets sick in spite of Billy's assurance that he will not; and the pony fails to get better in spite of Billy's careful looking after. To complete the round, Jody's need to place the whole blame for human's imperfection of Billy dissolves when he goes to slecp in the stable, without being aware of pony's wandering outdoors into the chilly night to its death. Furthermore, even the red pony is not quite perfect. He is untrained, acquired at an auction after the bankruptcy of a show. The red saddle he comes with is too frail for ordinary use and he has been paid for by money from butchered cows and the imperfection culminates in the death of the pony.

The ironies increase when the idols of perfection embodied by Peter Randoll in "The Harness" and Mary Teller in "The White Quail", collapse one by

---

① Jr. Pascal Covic, ed, *The Portable Steinbeck*, New York: Penguin Books, 1976, p. 359.

one. Peter Randall is a good model in the valley, a grave man to whom others look for advice and pattern. Unlike the farmers whose bodies are bent from long leaning to earth, Peter stands with the straightness like a solider, a posture which gains an added respect for him. However, Gradually the dual personality of Peter is exposed to the readers. The straightness of his posture is acfually artiflcial, imposed on him by his wife Emma, who insists that he be trussed in a harness. He is noted for his reputation of a good husband, yet once a year he must go away for a week on his "business"trip, actually a trip to the fancy houses of San Francisco. The truly good but fully human Peter is denied in favor of an illusion of unfallen perfection, even after Emma's death, Peter is still harnessed by the illusion and cannot accept the possibility that man can be both good and flawed. He remains in the end and divides against himself.

Mary Teller in "The white Quail" is another character who walls the dangerous chaos of the fallen world out of her perfect unchanging garden. She perceives her garden as all-important and immutable and says, "If one bush dies, we'll put another one like it in the same place" ①, and Mary develops a fear that if the garden should change, it would be like a part of herself being torn out. In her seek for perfection, Mary seems to have become automation, she even condemns the excitement her husband Harry finds in the normal events of lifc, in expressing and sharing emotions. She realizes that such feeling is in conflict with the gentle, almost stagnant picture of her garden, therefore, they must be cvil. A dog "would do things on the plants of her garden, or even dig in her flowerbeds, and worst of all, a dog would keep the birds away from the pool"②. A simllar "civil" reaction is seen when Mary suspects a cat might be lingering in her garden and causing the absence of birds. Her absolution is violent—to put out poisoned fish, to kill to maintain perfection. Again the ironic paradox of man's dual nature

---

① John Steinbeck, *The Long Valley*, New York: P. F. Collier and Sons, 1938, p. 30.
② Ibid. , p. 36.

is emphasized. Is one species to be protected and maintained at the expense of another? In the end, the resulting perfection brings about evil outcomes and the destruction of the character's dreams when Harry shoots the White quail [1] dead. Therefore, in the story, John Steinbeck again reinforces the theme of moral ambiguity—of the necessity to accept perfection and imperfection, good and evil as part of an integral whole.

Perhaps David Bakan's *The Duality of Human Existence* is helpful for readers who wish to understand Steinbeck's perception of the nature of the universe and man:

> The most critical paradox that man must live with, of the possibility that all that is characteristically associated with evil is in some way, intimately intertwined with good, the notion that the sins of mankind—sex, aggression, and avarice are related to the survival of mankind. [2]

Steinbeck also realizes in *Sea of Cortes* that man is a "two-legged paradox, torn between alternatives" [3]. In the book, he describes his voyage in the following words that indicate the difficulty of making absolute decisions: "The sky sucks up the land and disgorges it. A dream hangs over the whole region, a brooding kind of hallucination. The mirage was working, and right and wrong fought before [4] very eyes and how could we tell which was error?" [5]

Here Steinbeck does not waffle on the subject or is ambivalent in a negative sense by presenting his readers a confused picture of ambivalent men. Rather, he uses these to illustrate the difficulty of making absolute choices.

In his "Nobel Prize Acceptance Speech", Steinbeck accepts that "humanity

---

[1] An incarnation of the ideal Mary.
[2] David Bakan, *The Duality of Human Existence*, Chicago: Rand Mc Nally, 1966, p. 37.
[3] John Steinbeck, *The Log from the Sea of Cortes*, New York: Viking Press, 1951, p. 98.
[4] Ibid. .
[5] Ibid. , p. 84.

has been passing through a gray and desolate time of confusion"①, yet he persists in believing in a constantly evolving process of life and progress for mankind. In his short stories, Steinbeck is endeavoring to help break through one's illusion of perfection and encourages people to fight courageously with the faults in themselves. Though the fates of Emma in "The Harness" and Mary in "The White Quail" remind the readers of the human plight, Peter and Harry's rebellions bring the hope that one day the absolutes will be replaced by the mutual understanding.

As far as John Steinbeck's short fiction is concerned, he is often regarded as a modernist, since most of his short stories deal with the modern motif of isolation, loneliness and repression. Whereas he championed proletarian values in his novels of the 1930s, Steinbeck focused in his short stories of that era on the problems of individual beings. As Peter Lisa has concluded, "A common theme in his short fiction, as we have seen, is frustration, blocked communication or sexual repression, and these frustrations occasionally lead to violence"②. However, by censuring against the passive, suffocating forces of humanity, Steinbeck advocates an open personality with broad psychology in which man must both find physical and spiritual fulfillment.

"The Long Valley" is a symbol that can sustain rich interpretations. On the one hand, it offers the positives of the valley with verdant, green pastures, abundant life and potential happiness. On the other hand, the stifling closed-in valley denotes the negatives of repression. The opening paragraph of "The Chrysanthemums" thoroughly depicts the stifling, closed-in valley as such:

> *The high gray-flannel fog of winter closed off the Salinas valley from the sky and from all the rest of the world. On every side it sat like a lid on the mountains and made of the great valley as a closed pot.* ③

---

① Jr. Pascal Covic, ed, *The Portable Steinbeck*, New York: Penguin Books, 1976, p. 690.
② Lisa Peter, *The Wide World of John Steibeck*, New Jersey: Rutgers University Press, 1958, p. 120.
③ Jr. Pascal Covic, ed, *The Portable Steinbeck*, New York: Penguin Books, 1976, p. 56.

It is quite obvious that the Salinas Valley here symbolizes the depressed circumstance in which Steinbeck's characters live in. Dwelling in such a geographically isolated valley, Jody Tiflin, Peter Randall and Elisa Allen, one character after another in the short stories are controlled by the blocked force and suffer the same problems of depression, loneliness and frustration.

Jody is an adolescent who has been reared in the valley. That Jody is geographically isolated on a ranch in the Salinas Valley lies in that he has no contact with the cosmopolitan world of cities and large number of people. His only contact with the world off the ranch is at his school, and Steinbeck only briefly mentions this part of Jody's life, thus suggesting that it is relatively insignificant in the formation of Jody's responses to the world. The distance of other families or neighbors is indicated when Jody takes Nellie to be bred and has to walk steadily for an hour before reaching the road that leads to Tess Taylor's ranch. Having no brothers or sisters, and having only brief contact with his schoolmates, Jody's world is surrounded by a couple of adults.

The adults like Peter, Harry, and Elisa all suffer the same geographically isolation as Jody does. Living on the lonely ranches in the valleg, not only are they closed off from the rest of large cities, but also they are separated among the ranches. However, the problems that the adults confront are more complex and their frustratlons mainly derive from the sexual repression and spiritual unfulfllment.

Steinbeck attributes the causes of the unhappy marriages partly to sexual repression. The short stories like "The Chrysanthemum", "The White Quail" and "The Harness" are typical ones which all probe the psychological consequences of unhappy and unhealthy marriages.

The female character Elisa Allen in the "Chrysanthemum" and the two male characters Peter Randall and Harry Teller in "The Harness" and "The White Quail" respectively all share a deep sexual starvation. In the case of Elisa, her deep excessive energy finds no outlet except for her garden of chrysanthemums and well-tended house. Though the arrival of the manly tinker arouses her deep dormant sexual desire, she returns to her nomal status of stiffness after his leaving and cries helplessly over her frustrated situation. In the case of Harry Teller, the husband views his own sexuality as "unintentionally vile and shameful" since his wife is regarded as a model of woman who is "sexless and inviolable"[1]. However, the long-seated sexual repression in him finally breaks into violence when he shoots a white quail dead, which is the true incarnation of his ideal wife.

While in terms of Peter Randall, the deep sexual starvation causes him to live schizophrenically— a model mason, a farmer and husband-fifty-one weeks of the year, and an irresponsible sensualist the one remaining week.

Elisa Allen in "The Chrysanthemum" is a good example who suffers from sexual and spiritual repression. Elisa Allen, whom Joseph Warren calls, "one of the most delicious character ever transferred from life to the pages of a book" [2]is Steinbeck's "strong woman". Evidence in the story shows Elisa, like the chrysanthemum she plants in her garden is in her prime—strong, talented, and energetic. She cuts her chrysanthemum stalks with excessive energy: "Her work with the scissors was over-eager, over-powerful", and the stems seem, "too small and too easy for her energy". [3]She has "strong, terrier fingers", which destroy pests, "before they get started", even her gardening clothes suggest power: "heavy leather gloves", "clod-hopper shoes", "a man's black hat" and "a big corduroy apron with four big pockets to hold gardening tools". [4]

However, such an energetic woman lives on an isolated ranch, and is married to a well-being but unexcited cattleman. In the beginning of the story Steinbeck's Elisa is a kept woman. The opening paragraphs that describe the valley mentioned

---

[1] John Steinbeck, *The Long Valley*, New York: P. F. Collier and Sons, 1938, p. 62.

[2] Lisa Peter, *The Wide World of John Steibeck*, New Jersey: Rutgers University Press, 1958, p. 167.

[3] Covic Pascal Jr. , ed, *The Portable Steinbeck*, New York: Penguin Books, 1976, p. 57.

[4] Ibid. .

above suggest her isolation and her suspended life. The figurative language, which conveys a sense of mechanized, transformed nature, also helps characterize Elisa. Fog sits like a lid; the Salinas Valley is a closed pot; earth gleams like metal; willow shrubs, "flame with a sharp and positive leaves, as if etched"[①]. Nature, now held in check, has undergone a metamorphosis into something static and vaguely forbidding, and Elisa, the woman closest to nature is similarly checked.

Steinbeck states Elisa's age clearly thirty-five, and also implies the message that the couple have no children. The two elements placed together further suggest the sterility of their marriage and the sexual depression Elisa is suffering from. Thus, being a human being, a woman bored with her husband and her childless stifling ranch-wife's life, the major outlet for her passion is her well-scrubbed house and well-tended flowers, but frustrated passion remains in her scornful attitude toward her husband and her cruel treatment of him: "Henry came banging out of the door, shoving his tie inside his vest as he came. Elisa stiffened and her face grew tight. "[②]And later, before they go to town for dinner, she deliberately delays her appearance to inconvenience him, to punish him for being so boring: Elisa went into the house. She heard him drive to the gate and idle down his motor, and then she took a long time to put on her hat. She pulled it here and pressed it there. When Henry turned the motor off, she slipped into her coat and went out. [③]

However, the repression that Elisa has endured is not merely limited to the sexual one, though the sexual depression is one of the important causes of their unhappy marriage. Elisa's frustration also derives from a spiritual unfulfllment. Critics have suggested various reasons for Elisa's attraction to the tinker. Apart from the sexual attraction, William V. Miller notes that she responds

---

① Covic Pascal Jr. , ed, *The Portable Steinbeck*, New York: Penguin Books, 1976, p. 56.

② Ibid. , p. 67.

③ Ibid. , p. 68.

to the romanticism of his "vagabond life"①. In one of the best analyses of the story, Marilyn Mitchell argues that "both Elisa and Mary Teller of ' The White Quail' are trapped between society's definition of the masculine and the feminine and are struggling against the limitations of the feminine".

Elisa has been repressed by the very things which, while gardening, she achieves physical distance from——the tidy house behind her and the men conversing "down " to her, but no psychological escape follows/ The syntax of the first sentence describing Elisa conveys her awareness of the male prerogatives: "Elisa Allen, working in her flower garden, looked down across the yard and saw Henry, her husband, talking to two business suits. "②The main clause addresses her awareness of the empowered male, but the phrase suggests her avocation. In the second page of the story that describes her gardening activities, there are four references to Elisa's glances toward this authoritative group, each of whom stands "with one foot on the side of the little Fordson tractor"③.

Steinbeck repeatedly shows that the bourgeois world restricts Elisa's self-deflnition and creativity. When first being described, she wears male clothing like a shield: "Her figure lookcd blocked and heavy in her gardening costume, a man's black hat pulled low down over her eyes, clod-hopper shoes, a figured spring dress almost completely covered by a big corduroy apron with four big pockets… She wore heavy leathering gloves to protects her hands while she worked. " ④The male attire compromises Elisa's sexual identity and this blurred identity causes much of her frustration. The softness that she later so poignantly reveals, is initially concealed beneath the unwieldy clothing. Unconsciously, she "pulls on the gardening glove again" ⑤, when Henry approaches, not only steeling

---

① William V. Miller, "Sexual and Spiritual Ambiguity in ' The Chrysanthemum' ", *Southwest Review*, 61 Summer, 1972.

② Ibid. , p. 56.

③ Ibid. .

④ ˝Covic Pascal Jr. , ed, *The Portable Steinbeck*, New York: Penguin Books, 1976, p. 57.

⑤ Ibid. , p. 58.

herself against him, but revealing the impossibility at this point of identifying herself outside a male sphere.

In a sharp contrast with her stiff and cautious attitude towards her husband, with the tinker Elisa expands gradually, since she finds a breakthrough of her limited female role. Unlike her terse comments to Henry about her "planter's hands, Elisa's responses to the tinker's flattering arc expensive:

> *Well, I can only tell you what it feels like. It's when you're picking off the buds you don't want. Everything goes right down into your fingertips. You watch your fingers work. They do it themselves. You can feel how it is. They pick and pick the buds. They never make a mistake. They are with the plant. Do you see? Your fingers and plant. You can feel that, right up your arm; They know. They never make a mistake. You can feel it. When you're like that you can't do anything wrong. Do you see that? Can you understand that?* [①]

In Elisa's longest, most impassioned speech, she finds words to express what Edward F. Ricketts called the experience of "breaking through". To complcte from somebody's woman to her own, she must both flnd physical and spiritual fulflllment. Nevertheless, this fulflllment can never last long, as what has been mentioned above, in the last few paragraphs; Steinbeck emphasizes the finality of her retreat from fulflllment when she spots the sprouts of the chrysanthemum being thrown away by the sordid tinker. Elisa cries weakly like an old woman—she has to accept her fate. The open road is really a dead road for her.

In *East of Eden*, Steinbeck defines his philosophy as a writer, what he believes is "the free, exploring mind of the individual"and what he would fight for is"the freedom of the mind to take any direction it wishes, undirected" ; and what

---

① Covic Pascal Jr. , ed, *The Portable Steinbeck*, New York: Penguin Books, 1976, pp. 63—64.

he will flght against is "any idea, religion, or government which limits or destroys the individual"[①]. By revealing the tragic fate of the characters, who fall victims to the various limitations and depressions, Steinbeck hopes that both men and women may find their physical and spirtual fulfillment.

(The paper is based on the master's thesis "On the Open, Local Cultural Values in John Steinbeck's *Long Valley*" in 1999.)

---

① John Steibeck, *East of Eden*, New York: Viking Press, 1952, p. 132.

The Racial and Cultural Identity Analysis in American African Novel *See How They Run*

In the foreword of a collection of Short Stories by American Woman Writers in Chinese Translation published in 1983, Zhu hong, a famous Chinese female scholar major in the American and British women writers study as well as the editor of the book spoke highly of a short story See "How They Run" written by Mary Elizabeth Vroman, she regarded the short story as a piece of work of being the most vigorous and hopeful among all the collected short stories in the book, since most of stories focused on the writings of women's suffering, puzzlement, holiness and desperation. It was the first time the name of Mary Elizabeth Vroman and her short story "How They Run" being mentioned, from then on, however, Elizabeth Vroman has remained unnoticed in the Chinese academic circle, and no researchers have commented on her short story "How They Run". For this reason, my paper aims at analyses of the short story "How They Run", hopefully the Chinese readers could know more about the story through my introduction and review.

As an African American writer, Mary Elizabeth Vroman showed her great sympathy for the life of the black people, but unlike other African American writers who focus on the the themes of racial prejudice, puzzlement, desperation and even hatred of the American African people, Mary Elizabeth Vroman's short story "See How They Run " is a carol of love and hope.

Being an African American writer, Mary Elizabeth Vroman showed her great sympathy for the life of the black people, in this short story, Vroman reveals in depth the plights of poverty, illiteracy and loss of identity American African people are experiencing, and Vroman's exploration of the fate and suffering of the black people are profound, it rested not only on the material sphere, but also on the cultural and educational aspects.

Firstly, in terms of the material sphere, the story depicted in detail about the poverty and miserable life the black people had suffered from. When Miss Richards, a new primary school teacher first met her pupil C. T. Yong, she found him to be a small, thin boy who looked like a boy of only eight years old, with hunger seemed to be written on his face, actually C. T was already twelve years old. There are eleven children in his family, and he was the seventh of them. We can imagine what kind of life it is in a family with so many children. In the story, there is an interesting dialogue between Miss Richard and C. T. Yong. When being asked about what he had eaten for breakfast, C. T told a lie that he had eaten fried chicken, rice and orange, and drank coffee. , when further being curious about the reason why he didn't turn up in the lunch room, C. T lied again by saying he did not feel hungry at all since he had eaten too much at breakfast. When talking about his father, he boasted that his father earned a lot of money in the biggest factory of the town; the real fact was that his father was unemployed.

However, Vroman thought that the problem of poverty to the black people were not so severe than that of education. In the story, the more serious problem in C. T. Yong was his illiteracy. When Miss Richard picked up the new class of grade three, C. T. Yong failed to go up to grade four, it seemed that it was quite difficult for him to go up to the next grade since he had no desire for learning and refused to learn anything. Miss Richard had made great effort in helping him, for instance, in order to help him to set up a new image, she bought him new clothes, taught him to have a bath before wearing new clothes and sent him to the barbershop. As a result, C. T. 's new appearance had stirred up a shake in the class. However, C. T. 's vanity caused him to puff, he even boasted that he could wear new clothes whenever he liked, but he distained to follow the fashion like other students. Hence, to Miss Richard's great disappointment, he made no progress in study. What's more, he became a trouble-maker in class by keeping on interrupting the class with teasing words. He even run out of the class room during Miss Richard's leaving for a while and declared to the other children he would not stay in the classroom any longer. Therefore, Miss Richards' great challenge is to fight with C. T. 's illiteracy.

Another serious situation the African American people are facing with is their loss of identity in some extent. When Miss Richard took charge of the new class and called the roll, she was surprised to find the last name on the rolls was C. T Young, and then she asked the boy what his full name was, the boy told her C. T was his full name. Puzzled by the name, Miss Richard insisted on inquiring about what C. T stood for, "Charles or Clarence". The boy replied it didn' t mean anything, it was just C. T. his father simply called him C. T after his name. Later on when Miss Richard talked about the puzzlement about the name of C. T with another teacher Miss Nelson, the latter took it for granted by saying there were a lot of students in their school whose full names were just initial letters, and there was nothing strange about it. Here the author had revealed a thought-provoking issue. These black children are living in a status of nameless. They do not know who they are, and their personal identities were unconsciously aware of. In a sense, personal identity is closely related to ethnic and cultural identity. C. T. and other black children' loss of personal identities manifested the fate of the African American people. They are in a state of losing their own identities, they are so careless about who they are that they casually use meaningless letters as their children's names.

However, to illustrate the plights of poverty, illiteracy and loss of identity American African people are facing with is only part of the story, the short story centered more on the themes of love and hope. It speaks highly of Miss Richards' effort in helping the black children fighting against all the barriers. It was due to her devotion, love and perseverance; we see new hope of the life of the American African people.

Basically, the short story "How They Run" is a very simple one, it is about how Miss Richards, a new teacher in a primary school helped her black pupils whole-heartedly and selfishness. In particular, the short story focused on the depiction of Miss Richards' offering sincere helps to two black pupils. One is a black girl named Tanniya, another is C. T. Yong.

In the former part of the story, it gave account of how Miss Richards spared no effort in helping Tanniya, a black girl who fell illness. In Miss Richards' eyes, Tanniy was a pretty girl like a lovely angel, she really liked her. but one day Tanniya told her she felt sick. By gently letting Tanniya sit beside her, Miss Richards showed great concern for her illness, she asked Tanniya whether she felt uncomfortable in the morning at home, Tania said yes but her mother thought her daughter played truant, and insisted her going to school. Tanniy sighed over the pitiful, good-will and enthusiastic parents who placed great expectations on education and thought that was the only way to change their fates, But Miss Richards believed what children really needed was love and care. So she helped wash Tanniy's forehead with cool water and arranged a tall boy to give Tania a ride in his bicycle to take her home, and told the boy to take good care of Tania. The next day, Miss Richards went to see Tania and knew Tania had a serious disease, but her family could not afford to see a doctor. Without any hesitation, Miss Richards volunteered to go to the town to call a doctor by herself, though she herself had not enough money to pay for the doctor. Then she tried to ask help from her colleagues. But those selfish colleagues were very stingy and only donated eight dollars altogether while the doctor's medical charge were fifteen dollars and Miss Nelson even warned Miss Richards that a teacher should not care too much for a single student, since there were almost fifty students in a class. Here we see, in contrast with her selfish and hardhearted colleague Miss Nelson, Miss Richards was a teacher whose heart was full of love for her pupils. The love was based on her respect for every individual's life. Though she knew life for those black children was particularly rough, but she tried her best to help them to gain the opportunity of survival. After hearing from the doctor that Tania were getting better, she was so delighted that she made a plan to celebrate a special Christmas for Tania by delineating such a wonderful picture: Tania had grown stronger and healthy, she would act as a lovely angel, and she would get a lot of delicious food such as milk, oranges and eggs as well as many interesting cards. But Tania died before Christmas.

Nevertheless, Tania's death didn't mean the failure of love. On the contrary, we see the flame of love still shined, not only Miss Richards' heart, but even in C. T. , the naughty boy's heart. The next day after Tania's funeral, C. T brought a pot of rose to Miss Richards and asked whether it would look nice if it was put in front of Tania's grave. C. T admitted having stolen the pot of rose, since he had no money to buy it, but he just wanted to express his love for Tania with it. Miss Richards was deeply touched, she started looking at him with new eyes, before that, C. T appeared to a demon and a trouble-maker, who always told lies, played truant, did poorly in study, but now Miss Richards was rejoiced to find that C. T had a caring heart for others, and she thought there was a valuable thing that could not be bought by money in the world, that was love.

What happened later made Miss Richards appreciate C T. and see hope on him. After the winter vacation, Miss Richards asked students about how they spent their Christmas, all the other students talked about the presents they have got, for instance toy, bicycle and the food they have eaten, such as ice cream and cake, when it was C. T's turn, he said frankly he had got nothing except for a small gift from Miss Richards. Because his mother was ill, he had to do some chores in a store, and earned three dollars. With the three dollars, he bought his mother a nice handkerchief and a comb, his father a tie brooch and his sisters and brothers some candies. Hearing what C T had said, Miss Richard 's heart was filled with. ardent passion, and in the story, there is a vivid monolog paragraph depicting her appreciation of C. T, it says her heart is singing a song, she even regards C T. as her son in her deep mind, and thinks that C. T has brought a new and bright hope to the distrustful world. , since C T is almost penniless, yet he tries to offer something to others by his own effort, As the Novel says in the end "Therefore, Miss Richards, Therefore, Miss Richards saw new hope".

(The paper was delivered as a speech in "The International Symposium on African American Literature in 2009".)

On the Modernity Pursuit in *The Kite's Ribbon*

As one of the most influential writers in the contemporary Chinese literary circles, Wang Meng is well known for his " grand narration " of Chinese Contemporary history. Wang Meng has the rich experiences in depicting such a splendid picture of China, of its past and the present, However, behind the "grand narration", Wang Meng's works pay more great attention to the ordinary people's lives, and his short story The Kites' Ribbon offers us a good example. In the story, he not only depicts the lives of the ordinary people in the early 1980's by showing his great concern for their fates, expressing the sweetness and bitterness of their life, but also reflects their modernity pursuit of personal rights and happiness. In a sense, he has become a spokesman of the ordinary people at that age.

After sixteen year's life of staying in the countryside in the remote China's northwest —Xinjiang, in 1979, Wang Meng returned to Beijing and reverted to his writing again. This particular experience of living with the common people causes a great change in his view of life as well as that of literature. Instead of being fascinated with the " romanticism " and " heroism " as he were in his novels of 1950's, his works of 1980's concentrate more on the depiction of the life of the ordinary people, their desires and rights as individuals, and his short story *The Kite's Ribbon* is one of them.

The Kite's Ribbon was written in 1980, a period when China had just ended its "Cultural Revolution" and it was also termed as the "transitional period" in which China's reconstruction was under the way. *The Kite's Ribbon* presents a vivid and realistic depiction of that particular period.

The protagonists in the story are no longer intellectuals, communist party's leaders or young students, instead, they are common people from the lower social class. The leading characters in *The Kite's Ribbon* are a young girl Su Su and her boyfriend Jia Yuan. Although Su Su has ever had the ambitious dreams of becoming a medical doctor, or a sword-fighting champion or something like that, she finally gets a job as a small restaurant waitress. The boyfriend she has pictured in her mind should be a handsome prince, actually he is just a young man whose job is mending umbrella. Therefore, there are two worlds in Su Su's life, one world is made up of dream, fantasy and ambition, another world is the reality she has to face with as a humble waitress every day. In the story, Su Su's former world is occasionally mentioned, yet it merely serves as a contrast. Obviously, what Wang Meng attempts to stress is the latter's world—the reality world. The significance of putting the two worlds in comparison lies in the fact that Wang Meng tries to remind the readers of the illusion of the fantasy world and the solidity of the reality world. For more than 30 years, the Chinese people have addicted to the unrealistic fantasies and crazy dreams, now it is the high time they faced the reality.

In the short story, the reality world is manifested to us in the eyes of Su Su. As what has been mentioned above, the story was written in 1980, and it was a period in which China had just recovered from ten year's upheaval. Though China's economy was in its development, the shadow of the old world was still there. The living status of the common people in city was extremely poor during that period. In the story, Wang Meng particularly depicts the poor condition of some public places such as parks, restaurants and hospitals to illustrate the terrible living standard of the ordinary people in city. For instance, whenever Su Su and Jia Yuan go out for a walk in the park, they cannot find any empty chairs except for the one, under which there is a heap of vomit, and there are various kinds of bulletins of prohibition and forfeit everywhere in the park. In the crowded restaurant, they have to wait for hours until the other customers slowly finish their meals, sometimes unexpectedly, the customers waiting behind them occupy the seat swiftly. There is also a detail about the wretched condition of the hospital in the story. Su Su's grandma once suffers from a severe heart attack and her parents have no idea as to whether to send her to hospital or just leave her at home. However, Su Su strongly opposed to sending her grandma to the hospital, since she thought the condition in the hospital was extremely bad, it was better to stay at home than to go to the hospital.

In addition to the description of the barren material life the common people, Wang Meng places more emphasis on the revelation of their poor spiritual life. To most of them, they live in a state of ignorance and trust crisis. For instance, when Su Su's parents know their daughter is in love with a young man, they are shocked and get very angry. They cannot understand why their daughter chooses a lover without even knowing his social class status, they still regard class status as the main criterion in choosing a son-in-law. Furthermore, the issue of mistrust among the people is also revealed in the story. Jia Yuan's good will to help an old lady who is knocked down by a young man's bicycle does not earn him any gratitude but mistrust and mock from other passers-by, who believe him to be the troublemakers. Cultural Revolution has caused a severe problem of trust crisis, and in some of Chinese people's common sense, only foolish people help others without asking for reward, hence, people tend to be on the guard of others and shrug off other people's sincere help in suspicious eyes, and it is really a big issue.

Ten year's upheaval in China leads to the decline of people's life, either in material or in spiritual aspects. *The Kite's Ribbon* depicts such a realistic picture of the populace's life in the early 1980's in China. However, as a great writer, Wang Meng reveals some deeper thoughts in the story, and he pays more attention to the common people's rights as individuals, particularly the rights of pursuing happiness and enjoying privacy.

The story is about the love story between Su Su and Jia Yuan, but unlike the common love stories which focus on the depiction of young people's love affairs, the love story in *The Kite's Ribbon* partly serves as a plot to illustrate the conflict between the individual's normal right to pursue happiness and the reality which makes the pursuit seem difficult. In the story, Su Su and Jia yuan even find it hard to find a place to stay together. As the story describes, "For three years, their weekends have been spent in search of a place, they look for a place to sit on. They keep on looking for and looking for. It is often the case the whole night has been spent in search of a place to stay together. Our country's vast sky and land, our splendid three-dimensional space, in which corner do you provide the two young men with a place to enjoy hugs and kisses to their hearts' content? They only need a small place"[①]. Actually, Su Su and Jia Yuan's longing for a small place to stay together was the strong desire of pursuing personal happiness. Nevertheless, they found it very difficult to satisfy their desires in reality.

In connection with the right of pursuing happiness, the right of enjoying privacy is also put forth by Wang Meng. In Chinese traditional culture, the value of collectivism is held in the first place, it is especially stressed in Chairman Mao's period. People often entrust themselves to the collective organization, and they have no secrets to themselves, hence, the individual's right of privacy is always totally deprived of. It is the true case in the story. Su Su and Jia Yuan's love affair suffers strong opposition from Su Su's parents, and their privacy is kept on being interfered by the outside world. As the short story humorously depicts, there are still some people who might be caught up with the disease of epilepsy on seeing them walking hand in hand because of rage. Wherever they go, in the park, along the city river, or in the street, their privacy is constantly disturbed, even naughty children laugh and yell at them. The story reaches its climax when it describes the following scene: on one windy and rainy night, the lovers are lucky

---

① Meng Wang, *The Collection of Wang Meng's Works* (Volume 11), Beijing: People's Literature Publishing House, 2003, p. 271.

enough to find a newly-built, 14-story apartment building, where they regard as a safe place to stay together and enjoy the sweet kisses when they are interrupted and investigated by a group of safety inspectors, who scold them for the conduct of a rogue.

Why can most of the Chinese people in that period not be ensured the right of enjoying personal happiness? Wang Meng raises such a thought-provoking question. There are perhaps many reasons. As Wang Meng revealed profoundly in the story, one factor is the problem of privilege and corruption. Privilege means a particular group of people can enjoy special rights while others cannot. The reason why one of Su Su's primary classmates owns an apartment even though he is just a single lies in the fact that his father has some privileges. It is a great irony if we compare it with the case of Su Su and Jia Yuan who are in urgent need of small house, but find it rather hard to obtain one by the means of their own efforts. Social injustice and privilege are the damages to the individual's equal rights. Wang Meng shows his deep solicitude for the Chinese common people's equal rights.

Nevertheless, Wang Meng is by no means a pessimistic writer. Despite of the fact he exposes a series of problems in China in "the transitional period", Wang Meng feels very hopeful about China's future. His confidence is built on his belief in modern knowledge. "*The Kite's Ribbon*", which is mentioned several times in the story, serves as a symbol, it symbolizes the surpassing of the reality and the pursuit of the ideal world. From the story, we know Su Su and Jia Yuan are not willing to yield to their fate, instead, they feel quite confident of themselves, and the weapon in their hand is modern knowledge. Su Su starts to learn Arabic while Jia Yuan tries to grasp every chance to study for the purpose of becoming a college student and even becoming a postgraduate. Actually, it is Wang Meng who believes that knowledge is the premise of social progress and ensurance of the individuals' rights of gaining happiness.

Above all, *The Kite's Ribbon* leads us enter a world of the common people, a world which is filled with the populace's weal and woe, sorrow and happiness. In the short story, Wang Meng not only provides us with a lively picture of the common Chinese people's life, their feelings and desires, but also expresses his great concern for their modernity pursuits of personal rights and happiness, which still has its significance today.

(The paper was first delivered as a speech in "the First International Symposium on Wang Meng's Works" and later collected in Wang *Meng in the Multidimensional Perspectives.*)

An Interview with Professor Michael H. Prosser:
On Intercultural Communication

Li Mengyu(Li for short hereafter) : As we know you are one of the founders in intercultural communication in Northern America, and you are actively involved in the field; for instance, you started the early teaching of intercultural communication courses in the US, helped organize many international conferences on intercultural communication, and edited and wrote a large number of books related to the field, could you please introduce in more details about your major contributions to the field?

Michael H· Prosser(Prosser for short hereafter) : In 1967 when the Speech Communication Association Committee for Cooperation with Foreign Universities met, we began to discuss informally the need to create an academic field of intercultural or cross-cultural communication. We weren' t quite sure of the precise name. In the mid to late 1960s, courses began to develop in various American universities. I taught my first intercultural/cross-cultural communication class at Indiana University in 1970, using Everett C. Rogers' book on innovation in Latin America. In fact, this made this course more of a class on communication and social change than just intercultural/international communication. In 1970, K. S. Sitaram and others initiated the Intercultural and Development Division for the International Communication Association. In 1995, he and I cochaired the first of six Rochester Intercultural Conferences (1995—2001), celebrating the founding of the academic field of study, 25 years earlier.

In 1971, the Speech Communication Association sponsored a consultation at Indiana University (Brown County State Park) to begin to establish intercultural communication as a distinct subject of academic study. Speech Communication Association President William Howell, Canadian Speech Communication Association President Grace Layman,

Edward C. Stewart, Edmund Glenn, Fred Casmir, I and others plus about a dozen of my postgraduates, most notably, William J. Starosta (my first Ph. D. in intercultural communication) . Barbara Monfils, Sherry Ferguson, and Iris Gonzalez, met to discuss two key topics: the content of the future academic study field and the process of developing it.

In 1973, at the University of Virginia (Masanettan Conference) , about 55 of us met to develop academic syllabi in intercultural communication and communication and social change. In practical terms, the US Navy sent a small delegation too. My book, *Intercommunication among Nations and Peoples* was published that year. In 1974, 200 of us met in Chicago, under the sponsorship of the Speech Communication Association, International Communication Association, and the International Society for Intercultural Education, Training, and Research, using Edward Stewart's "Outline of Intercultural Communication" as a foundational document for building the field's content. A Proceedings was published by the Speech Communication Association. Also, in 1974, a bicultural Japanese/ American research conference was held in Nihonmatsu, Japan to discover the similarities and differences in the two cultures' communication patterns. I have described the dialogue which took place there in my book, The Cultural Dialogue (1978, 1985 and 1989) and translated into Japanese in 1982.

In 1974, Fred L. Casmir became the first editor of the *International and Intercultural Communication Annual*, published annually for twenty-five years under the sponsorship of the Speech Communication Association/National Communication Association, when it became a regular journal. In 1978, under the sponsorship of L. Robert Kohls at the United States Information Agency, I had the opportunity to teach a course in intercultural communication for midlevel executives, and served as a consultant to the vice director of the Agency. Later, in

1979 and 1980, I was the coordinator for 23 half hour programs on intercultural communication for world-wide broadcast in English.

These were the formative years of the development of intercultural communication as an academic field of study. As I described in my essay for Steve J. Kulich's and my coedited book *Intercultural Perspectives on Chinese Communication*, the 1980s and 1990s saw the maturation of this field of study, both in North America and abroad, including its rapid development in China. Professor Sitaram and I returned to work together by hosting the six Rochester Intercultural Communication Conferences (1995—2001) on specific themes, and by coediting two volumes on intercultural and international communication and media. In 1998—2004, I served as the series editor for the publication of 18 books related to intercultural and international communication and media under the sponsorship of Ablex, Praeger, and Greenwood Publishing Group. From 2001 to 2009, I taught intercultural communication or global media at several Chinese universities, including most recently in 2011 at Ocean University of China. During the 2010/2011 period, you, Professor Li Mengyu, and I coauthored an intercultural communication text book, Communicating Interculturally, which is now in press with Higher Education Press. We hope that this book will become a model for understanding the importance of intercultural communication for Chinese students. In 2009 and 2011, I was pleased to receive a special contribution award for contributions to the development and study of intercultural communication in China by the China Association for Intercultural Communication.

Li: You like to quote Socrates famous saying "I am a citizen, neither of Athens, nor of Greece, but of the world. " What is the significance of the quotation to intercultural communication?

Prosser: In 1986, the International Society for Intercultural Education, Training, and Research gave me an award entitled Global Citizen Award, based on the statement of Socrates. This has encouraged me to make this my most favorite secular quotation in all of my teaching, whether in North America, Swaziland, or China. I firmly believe that it is an obligation for those of us who teach intercultural communication to assist our students both to become critical thinkers, and also to become more and more multicultural in their outlook, ending as true global citizens of the world. I have moved several steps in that direction, as explained in my keynote address at the Shanghai International Studies University June 2010 symposium on intercultural communication: "Being There: Steps along the Way in the Development of Intercultural Communication as an Academic Study. "

Li: You often call yourself "Chinamerican", after many years of living in China, what do you think of your cultural identity now?

Prosser: Actually, in 2009, some of our Shanghai International Studies University MA students started calling me "Chinamerican" neither fully Chinese (as a foreign teacher), not entirely American (retaining my American identity, but becoming broader in my outlook. Having spent nearly 10 years in China, I have assimilated some of the very positive aspects of Chinese culture, while also being fully American. There is a saying: "You can take Michael out of America, but you can' t take America out of Michael. " I like the term, Chinamerican, and am pleased that some of my students began calling me that name.

Li: You have taught in China for nearly ten years, and got to know Chinese culture and people quite well, what do you learn from Chinese culture and people?

Prosser: Socrates not only made the famous quote above, but he said that his goal was to become truly wise, just, honest, and a good person, and if one were to accept the name of a philosopher, he would aspire to be such a person. In Plato's Socratic dialogues, he has Socrates give the impression that he seeks to know more, and in fact to be a"gadfly on the horse that" is the establishment. Reading the dialogues, however, we become convinced that Socrates is indeed one of the wisest early thinkers and philosophers, seeks through dialogue (dialectic) to seek the truth by discussing ideas with wise others. In China, my fondness for western philosophy, and Decartes' famous quote, "I doubt, therefore I think; I think therefore I am" has blended with an increasing interest in the wisdom of Confucius and Mencius and their applications to modern Chinese life. Although, I have in fact learned almost no Chinese, I have been a serious student of contemporary China since its founding in 1949 and read as many books as possible to give me a clearer understanding of Chinese culture. Having taught 2, 300 Chinese students, and giving lectures to another 8, 500 Chinese secondary and university students, as well as giving volunteer classes for Chinese kindergarteners, primary school pupils, secondary students, and university students, I have developed a special interest in Chinese youth, as has been demonstrated in our joint book, Communicating Interculturally to be published soon by Higher Education Press.

Li: What do you think of the western and eastern civilizations' contributions to the world respectively? Particularly, what do you think of the far-reaching influences the great thinkers such as Socrates and Confucius?

Prosser: I have briefly discussed these points above. It appears to me that western and Asian thinking, philosophy, and customs have often merged, although recognizing that there are still many major differences between the cultures. . As Deng Xiaoping claimed, the Chinese have learned a lot from the west, and it is wise to take the best of each culture as complimentary, while acknowledging that there are major differences between the cultures. Now, there are 100, 000 young Chinese studying in the United States alone on an annual basis, and perhaps 100, 000 young Americans studying Chinese language and culture in China (including, for example, nearly 7, 500 studying Chinese at the Beijing Language and Culture University, and also as exhibited by the many Confucius Centers and Chinese language classes which have developed in Western countries. The fact that US, Australia, Canada, New Zealand, and Belgium) is itself a major contribution to intercultural understanding. Personally, without the ability to teach my courses in China in English, many foreign experts and I would never have had the opportunity to learn so much about contemporary China and Chinese youth. For this I am quite grateful.

Li: As we can see, there is a growing tendency of globalization in today's world, on the one hand, the American culture appear to be the most powerful, for instance, Hollywood movies, fast foods like McDonald and KFC seem to sweep over the world; on the other hand, with the rapid economic development, China seem to exert more and more influences on the world, what is your remark on the phenomena? How can globalization and localization be balanced for the world?

Prosser: Martin Jacques, in his 2010 book, *When China Rules the World*, argues that although much modernization in China and more broadly in Asia is western-oriented, which can be tested by such comparisons as clothing and cosmetics, food, language, power and policy, there are indeed many western influences, depending on which Asian country we are considering. Nonetheless, he proposes that in the end, Asian, and Chinese society will determine its own modernization by what works in each of these societies. Although we think that McDonald and KFC have large market shares in several of these countries, in fact, Yum owns many more franchises than the western restaurants—both with western and Chinese franchises, in fact, at the end of the day, each Asian society adopts what is practical for it, and rejects what is not practical.

Li: Ever since intercultural communication has been introduced to China, it has developed quite rapidly; in your view, what are the strengths and weaknesses of intercultural communication.

Prosser: With China just beginning to develop intercultural communication as a field of study in the mid 1980's as it was becoming mature in North America, it has indeed moved forward very rapidly, and is now entering its own mature stage. Progress is increasingly rapid today, both in technology and in idea development, but in the latter case, still within the context of traditional and modernizing societies. I like to think of two events in recent Chinese history, the

2008 Olympics, and the Shanghai World Expo, as major indicators of the possibility of positive intercultural interaction and exposure. Although the Han culture plus 55 minorities are in frequent interaction, more and more westerners, Africans, Middle Easterners, Latin Americans, and other Asians need to come to China to work or study, and more and more Chinese should go abroad to work and study. Being a short-term tourist is a good start, but only when we spend a long time in another country, do we begin to understand our own culture better, and then see how it interacts with the new culture in which we are a part.

Li: Until now, you say you have traveled to 64 countries and numerous cities in the world, you seem to be a global citizen; what do you think of the international traveling experience helping to widen your horizon as well as your understanding of various people from different parts of the world?

Prosser: Fourth century Augustine of Hippo claimed that unless we have traveled, we have not yet opened the book of life. Personally, I traveled briefly in North America with my parents as a teenager; then when I graduated from university, I began to travel for a two month period in Europe. Then many more trips developed with my family and personally. Since I came to China in 2001, I have also traveled to Japan, India, Cambodia, Vietnam, Thailand, the Philippines, Singapore, Malaysia, Indonesia, South Korea, Australia, New Zealand, Latin America, and Europe. I always encourage young Chinese to get a passport, as they never know when an opportunity might develop to go out of China, and have their world broadened. I have taken 7 young Chinese out of China, and almost all of them have a much broader world outlook because of this travel. Three of my young grandchildren have come to China, and one has gone to Spain, setting the stage for more broadening international travel in the future.

Li: You prefer to say "Thinking Globally; Acting Locally", what does this suggest to be a global citizen?

Prosser: This is an international slogan. Toward becoming world citizens, we need to know as much as possible, not only about our own society, but also other societies near and far from our borders. When an earthquake, or tsunami, or typhoon strikes one country or region, we all have an obligation to help in such situations to the extent possible. For Chinese, it may mean becoming friends with foreigners, or letting go of past national injuries or insults. If I had never gone to teach in China, I would have had contacts with American born Chinese, or Chinese overseas students, who are already westernized, but I probably would never have learned to have deep friendships with Chinese colleagues and students.

Li: You have written one paper entitled " One World, One Dream: Harmonizing Society Through Intercultural Communication: A Prelude to China Intercultural Communication Studies" ; then according to your opinion, how can we harmonize the world through intercultural communication when political, cultural and religious differences still prove to be hidden barriers to mutual understanding in today's world?

Prosser: The late D. Ray Heisey gave me three pieces of advice when I was first going to China to teach in 2001: 1. Patience; 2. Patience; 3. Patience. The same holds true for Chinese going to work or study abroad. It is not so easy to promote intercultural and international harmony, but it is a requirement for a more cooperative and positive relationship to develop. The Confucian concept of "ren" (benevolence, kindness) helps to lead us all toward a deeper understanding, wisdom, and happiness as a means of moving toward "the good life" means that we all must seek this harmony together. Or, as the ancient Chinese saying goes, "if you want to travel 1, 000 kilometers, you must begin with a single step". As the anthropologist Margaret Mead said, it takes a community to begin to build a better world, or as Hilary Clinton proposed, "it takes a village to grow a child". While building a better and harmonious domestic, regional, and international society, we need to acknowledge and practice these words of United Nations Secretary General Ban-ki Moon. " The biggest crisis is a lack of global leadership. There are too few citizens with an entirely new vision for the world, a vision that is informed by a sense of global responsibility. " So, truly, we need to think globally, and act positively on a local level.

(The paper was first published in: Shan dong Foreign Languages Teaching Journal, 2011/6.)

Culture, Language and Communication:
An Interview with Robert St. Clair

Li: Dr. St. Clair, as a distinguished professor in the Department of Communication, University of Louisville, you have a wide range of interests in research, could you please introduce yourmajor research fields as well as your major achievements in these fields?

St. Clair: I approach scholarship as a search for insight into solving problems that I am working on. This commitment means that if I need to learn another language in order read documents in their original language, I will study another language. When I received my BA degree, I was comfortable in 11 languages. I have now studied 28 and my 29th will be Chinese. In terms of content areas, I will sit in classes in other fields and read voraciously in other fields when I am trying to solve interdisciplinary problems. My home field is linguistics but I am comfortable with such fields as philosophy, communication theory, sociology, political science, and bilingual education. It has taken me years to become competent in these fields but the journey has been worth the travel. I am now looking at sign theory from the perspectives of structural epistemology and structural ontology. I want to expand on the work of Hjelmslev and redo the model of Charles Sanders Pierce. I want to revise the model of symbolic interactionism to include a philosophical statement about human cognition and information processing. This is the current problem that I am working on.

Li: You have your own academic website, until now more than 65, 000 people have paid a visit to your website; it shows that your research has exerted a great influence in the internet as well. You also have your intercultural Forum website, what role do you think the internet has played in making your academic research widely known to the scholars as well as the ordinary readers?

St. Clair: One of my areas of commitment has been to language renewal. I did my doctorate on Eskimo and I have studied seven of the indigenous languages of North America. As a consequence, I belong to an organization of Teachers of Indigenous languages. In that organization, we hold a conference with about 200—300 teaches of the indigenous languages of the Americas and shortly after that we publish the proceedings for each member. Two weeks later, those same proceedings are place on the internet. The result has been phenomenal. The number of people at the conference amounted to a few hundred. The number that accessed that information over the internet amounted to millions of scholars around the world. This speeds up the process of problem-solving. We all learn from each other and information sharing plays an important role in contemporary research programs. I have created website with the intent of sharing information. I created an institute (The Intercultural Forum) in which we have online journals, online monographs, and online textbooks. All of these are peer reviewed and refereed. We are in the process of obtaining ISSN and ISBN numbers for these publications. Scholarship is not jeopardized by this process.

When I was in Harbin for an international conference, one of the professors from Iran came up to me and said that he uses many of my publications in his classes in Teheran. I believe more scholars should share their knowledge through the internet. In Western thinking, people own ideas. They copyright their works and claim ownership to them. This is not a problem because scholars should be recognized for their creativity. What is a problem, however, is the commercialization of ideas where they are financially controlled and placed in journals that demand expensive access to the materials. This leaves out scholars from countries that are beneath a certain economic scale. It is a capitalistic model of access to knowledge. It is a model of the few, by the few and for the few. It is not a model that is open to all scholars. Hence, I favor more online journals.

There is another reason why online journals should increase among intellectuals. It has to do with the fact that many countries are moving rapidly from Print Cultures to Media and Visual Cultures. Online journals are about the new communication paradigm. In my classes, I used course management software through which my students post their papers on an intranet system. They are allowed to use audio files, film clips, graphics, charts, hyperlinks, and a rich array of hyper-texts. This is the future of communication. The internet is driving this new paradigm.

Li: It seems that you have been greatly influenced by the Chicago School of Sociology. For instance, I notice you focus more on the study of culture, language, communication from sociology perspective, why do you think the sociology perspective is so important in these areas?

St. Clair: Westerners love to think of themselves as individuals. They love to think that what they have achieved is due to their own hard work. They think that they are self-made. This is a form of mental blindness in Western thinking. The fact is that for every successful person there are six or seven layers of people who played an important role in making that person successful. In Asia, this view of life is obvious. People life in a society in which there is a strong social self and one must take others into consideration while doing things. One does not act alone. One acts as a member of a social group. One has a social self and the individual self is involved in a matrix of relationships with others. Harmony has to do with the role that the individual self plays in a larger social context. One needs to respect those who also participate in this social matrix. The Chicago school of sociology is something unique to American scholarship. It provided a model of the social self in American culture. Irving Goffman provided wonderful models of the dramaturgical self (the egocentrical self) while his colleagues went on to further articulate the role that the social self plays in modern society. Related to this research was the model taken by the New School for Social Research in Frankfurt, Germany, in which it was argued that the self is socially constructed. These sociological traditions fascinate me. It provides great insight into how human beings see themselves. What I find missing in this model, however, is a lack of detailed social structures. It is not enough to know how reality is socially constructed and distributed I want to know how these structures relate to other kinds of social and linguistic patterns. As a consequence, I have been working on social script theory because such a model does provide detailed information on how human beings pattern their lives. It articulates the various roles that human beings play in society. Most sociological models just admit that roles exist. This is just the beginning of a far more interesting journey of discovering those roles, articulating them, and relating them to a coherent model of social and cultural life.

Li: One of your research fields is linguistics; could you tell me what the main approaches in contemporary linguistics study are? Again, it seems that you focus more on the sociology of language, what do you think of language as a social system? Particularly what do you think of the significance of phenomenological sociology language theory raised by Foucault?

St. Clair: This is not an either or situation. There have been wonderful ideas that came out of formal linguistics. The various model of generative grammar have been intellectually exciting. My own research paradigm goes beyond the confines of formal linguistics. I am not against it. I just want to expand it so that it includes more sociological information. I make a distinction between sociolinguistics (society as seen through language patterns) and the sociology of language (language as a function in society). The latter begins with social theory. It places language within a social system and not as an isolated entity (sociolinguistics).

My focus on Foucault is not about the sociology of language. It is about his brilliant insights into society. He belonged to the Annals School of History, an interdisciplinary model of historiography. He was able to articulate how the middle ages transformed human cognition (les mots et chose). He was able to develop a model of social change that sees culture in the form of layers of cultural space (l' archeologie du savoir). He was able to document has social forces that began in the past continue to influence power in the present. Foucault has made great contributions of historiography. I use these insights in my own writing. Many use Foucault as a device to push their postmodern philosophies. I consider these acts of justification as a distortion of the contributions made by Foucault. He is much more than postmodernism. The label does not do him justice.

Li: In one of your books, you illustrate how cultural metaphors can be combined to create a cultural profile for a cultural system. Could you please explain it in more detail?

St. Clair: There are many social metaphors but they are not all used in the same way. The metaphor of the journey, for example, exists in modern American culture, but it is not a major metaphor. It is not a cardinal metaphor. It is not ingrained in American culture. The metaphor of growth, however, is a cardinal metaphor. It is part of Western thinking. The metaphor of progress is about 300 years old and it is a related metaphor of growth. It forms an intrinsic part of how Americans see the world. The metaphor of the journey may function as a cultural metaphor (a cardinal metaphor) in Asia, but it does not do so in the US. For this reason, I found it insightful to look at those cardinal metaphors that constitute a culture. In the US, they are the metaphors of growth, the machine, the world as a stage, linear time, and Euclidian space. China has its own cultural metaphors and one of my doctoral students is working on that area of research right now. He is documenting the cardinal metaphors of China and demonstrating how they combine to create a cultural profile of Chinese thought.

Li: Could you make a comment on the present research status ofintercultural communicationin the United States?

St. Clair: Linguists love to deal with theory and systems of thought. Most communication scientists fail in this regard. They create research projects and provide them ontological status by layers of quantitative research. They do not really address the far more important questions of the philosophy of communication. I just created a new website where I am beginning to address those issues. I begin with sign theory and the role that structure plays in human communication. I am in the process of developing my model of intercultural communication theory and it should be completed in about a year. I have the global outline worked out and I am now documenting the details. For example, intercultural communication is not recent. It began in the trade routes of ancient empires. I am researching this process and documenting how the model began and how cultural knowledge and interaction styles were created in these contexts and shared through cultural diffusion with others.

Li: It seems that the Chinese scholars as well as the Japanese scholars are very active in the field of intercultural communication at the present time, what do you think of their researches as well as contributions to the field?

St. Clair: There are certain individuals who led the way in their own countries in the area of intercultural communication. In Japan, Masanori Higa (University of the Air) was an outstanding scholar. He lived in several countries and was fluent in Spanish, Portuguese, and English. He did much to create awareness of intercultural communication in Japan. Also, Nobuyuki Honna (Aoyama Gakuin Daigaku) led the way in developing this way of thinking in Japan. Both Higa and Honna were active members of the International Association for Intercultural Communication Studies that I led as Executive Director for over a decade. These are the people who started the research model in Japan. Honna has gone on to do research in the various forms of English emerging in Asia. He has done excellent work but his model is not fully recognized outside of Japan. If his journal was made into an online journal, his contributions would be better recognized.

In China, Prof. Jia Yuxin of Harbin Institute of Technology has been an active leader in the area of Intercultural Communication Theory. He has hosted two very successful conferences in China as a member of the International Association for Intercultural Communication Studies. The conference in Harbin had over 700 participants. Prof. Jia has also directed many doctoral dissertations in this area. He played a large role in creating intercultural communication as a research paradigm in China. Jia is now the President of the Chinese Association for Intercultural Communication (CAFIC) . That organization will be holding an international conference in Beijing in June of 2009. Professor Hu Wenzhong, the Honorary President of CAFIC is another very important figure in the study of intercultural communications in China. His research has drawn the national media in China and he is well respected for his many publications in this area. The role that Professor Hu has played in the development of intercultural communication studies in China needs further articulation as his contributions have been many.

Professor Guo Mingchen, the current Executive Director of IAICS and a faculty member in the Communication Department at the University of Rhode Island is another active person involved in the development of intercultural communication studies in China. He works with the faculty in intercultural communications in Guanzhou and has done much to bring this area of research to the forefront in China.

Finally, one should mention the program in Shanghai headed by Kulich and Professor. Both have worked with the aforementioned scholars to develop intercultural communication studies in China.

The research models in intercultural communication studies are excellent. What is needed is for these scholars in China to make their organizations more international and to command important international journals that emanate from China. The problem is not one of quality, but of recognition.

Li: There is a growing tendency toward globalization in the modern era, what do you think of the influences globalization has exerted towardsculture and communication in the world? What do you think of various globalization theories?

St. Clair: Globalization is not new. There have always been patterns of cultural diffusion. There are two things about the current models of globalization that merit comment. One is that the scale of diffusion is extraordinary. The rate of cultural exchange and influence has been amazing. This is due, in part, to the cultures of modernity in which information exchange and product exchange is massive. The second thing that merit comment is that the model of globalization that being promoted by scholars is too narrow in its focus. It is essentially an economic model. It provides an unbalanced picture of what is going on. One of the things that it overlooks is the fact that a new culture of modernity is being developed internationally. This new models is driven by several forces: the business models (the seven cultures of capitalism), global business exchange, modernization of building, highways, traffic, air travel, etc. I am currently working on articulating his model of cultural modernity.

Li: Visual communication has been paid more and more attention; could you please tell me why it is important? What role does it play in communication?

St. Clair: In Western thought, logic plays a huge role in the philosophy of language. Logic is based on hypo-deductive thinking. This is where one has a major premise, minor premise, and a conclusion. It was assumed that this rational model of thinking was adequate in explaining how people think. There have been several reasons to challenge this model. One comes from the study of metaphor. This is a form of analogical reasoning. One takes some concept, idea, form, or pattern as a source and creates a new object in the process through analogy. One begins, with the solar system, for example, in which planet circle around the sun and then one uses this model to create the new model of the atom in which electrons circle the nucleus. What is important about analogical thinking is that it is a dominant model of how people negotiate themselves through life. They go from the known to the unknown by creating analogies. Visual communication is important because it also uses analogical thinking. However, visual thinking differs in many ways from verbal analogies. In visual thinking, one creates a cognitive space and organizes objects within that space. It is the organization of objects in a cognitive visual space that provides the source of visual analogies. In Western thinking (Cf. Rudolph von Arnheim), one look at the center of a square visual space and balances objects around that space. Visual artists are aware of this process and use it in their visual productions. The problem, however, becomes challenging when one realizes that not all cultures use the Von Arnheim model of the visual center. There are many cultures in which visual space is vertical and organized from right to left, etc. Visual communication in the context of intercultural communication is in need of a new research paradigm and that is why I am fascinated by this area of research.

Li: Could you introduce or make a remark about the "Cultural Network theory"

St. Clair: If one looks at systems theory, one finds that things do not operate alone and in isolation. Everything is connected into a larger network of connections. The components within a system interact. Currently, most researchers in culture theory are unaware of system theory. They are unaware of the fact that a human system differs substantially from non-human systems. In the areas of business and advertising and mass media, these two kinds of systems are conflated. They provide a challenge as theoretical constructs. Cultural network theory is the beginning of this research paradigm. It attempts to see culture as a system and it attempts to describe the components within that system and how they interact. In addition to these concerns, there are systems that are creative and they proliferate into new systems. This is true of both human and non-human systems (the second generation of systems theory). More scholars should engage in systems thinking in order to develop better models of human communication and intercultural communication.

Li: You have also another research focus, it is called "Media and Cognition, The Embodied Mind", could you illustrate in more detail about it? What do you think of the American media industry and its impact toward the contemporary American culture?

St. Clair: These are two different things. The Embodied mind has to do with the fact that the brain is not limited to the cranium. It is connected to the whole of the human body. My interest in this are of research has to do with the fact that most linguist infer biological information from their linguistic models. What is needed is for one to study language from the inside out. One needs to look at how phonation or audition works physiologically and then develop a model of linguistics based on that information. Current linguistic work on the biology of language is mostly inferential. t lacks physiological and biological depth. The model of the embodied mind that I am working on with my colleagues in the medical school begins with biology, physiology, and chemistry and works outwards towards linguistic theory.

The question about the media and its impact on American culture has to do with socialization. Mass media plays a major role in the socialization of people within a society. It provides social scripts and tells people how to perform them. Most people are unaware of these influences and how it is changing American culture. Once I have articulated social script theory in sufficient detail, I will be able to articulate just what these influences are and how they operate. One needs structure and patterns in order to articulate this paradigm. We are not yet there.

Li: More and more visiting scholar from different countries have come to your institute working under the supervision of you, what do you think of their visits?

St. Clair: We all learn from each other. We are all experts in our own areas of study. When we come together, we share our search for insight and understanding. We create our own think tanks and explore wonderful ideas. It is not a matter of supervision as much as a matter of learning together. We are all experts in something but we are also children in other areas of life. One may be a brilliant linguist, for example, and know little or nothing of systems theory or sociological theory. By coming together, we learn from each other. These are the values that visiting scholars bring with them when they come and join us.

（The paper was first published in the *Journal of Ocean University of China*, 2010/4. ）

On William Faulkner: An Interview with Robert W. Hamblin

Li Mengyu: (Li for short hereafter): Ever since 1934 when William Faulkner was first introduced to China, the Chinese scholars and readers have shown an interest in Faulkner's works. Especially since the 1980s, there has been a heightened interest in the study of Faulkner's novels among the Chinese scholars. In fact, Faulkner has become one of the most important western writers the Chinese scholars pay great attention to, and a large number of papers and some books on Faulkner's works have been published so far. However, there are also some limitations on Faulkner study in China. Most Chinese scholars read Faulkner's novels in the Chinese translations of his novels, and only his major novels have been translated into Chinese. Additionally, most Chinese scholars cannot get access to the related papers and books on Faulkner written by western scholars. All these factors have prevented the Chinese readers and scholars from better understanding Faulkner's works. Therefore, there is a great necessity of building a bridge of research between Chinese scholars and western scholars; especially it is of vital importance to introduce Faulkner study in the United States to China. This afternoon, I' d like to have an interview with you on Faulkner's life and works; hopefully you can share some information as well as your insight with Chinese scholars and readers.

Hamblin (Hamblin for short hereafter) : Thank you very much; I look forward to talking with you.

Li: Thank you. My first question is: could you please describe the general status of Faulkner study in America?

Hamblin: Sustained scholarly study of Faulkner in the United States began in the 1950s, shortly after he won the Nobel Prize for Literature, and Faulkner study still remains very strong in this country. I think one reason for that is that Faulkner's novels are so open-ended, lending themselves to a wide variety of critical approaches. The early study of Faulkner, influenced largely by New Critical theory, focused on a close reading of the text, analyzing the form and structure of the work and the use of language. There were also numerous studies early on that examined Faulkner as a "Southern" writer, specifically one who explores the tragic legacy of the Civil War and Reconstruction. More recent study of Faulkner focuses on race, class, gender, post-colonial, and even environmental issues. One might have thought that there would be a decline in Faulkner study after so many years, but that is not the case. Even today, six decades after Faulkner won the Nobel Prize, there are on average more than one hundred books and articles per year on Faulkner, so he continues to be considered one of the great American writers, and contemporary American scholars continue to study his works diligently.

Li: To be more specific, could you introduce some famous American scholars who have done quite well in Faulkner study and their representative books?

Hamblin: An early highly influential treatment of Faulkner was Malcolm Cowley's introduction to *The Portable Faulkner*, published in 1946. The first full-length book on Faulkner, *William Faulkner: A Critical Appraisal* by Harry Campbell and Ruel Foster, appeared in 1951. Perhaps the best of the early overviews of Faulkner's work is *William Faulkner: The Yoknapatawpha Country by Cleanth Brooks*(1963). Other good early books on Faulkner are those written by Richard P. Adams, Michael Millgate, Melvin Backman, Olga Vickery, Walter Slatoff, Hyatt H. Waggoner, and Irving Howe. The most prolific of the current group of Faulkner scholars is Noel Polk, who has done textual, psychoanalytic, and thematic treatments of almost all of Faulkner's books. Another outstanding contemporary critic is Philip Weinstein, who deals with Faulkner's treatment of race. Thadious Davis has also written extensively on Faulkner and race. John

T. Irwin's *Doubling and Incest / Repetition and Revenge* is the best-known psychoanalytic treatment of Faulkner, but Doreen Fowler has also published Freudian and Lacanian interpretations of Faulkner. Two historians, Joel Williamson and Don Doyle, have produced detailed analyses of the historical contexts of Faulkner's fiction. Minrose Gwin, Deborah Clarke, Sally Page, and David Williams have studied Faulkner's treatment of women. Lewis Dabney has written about Faulkner's treatment of Native Americans. James Carothers and Theresa Towner have defended the quality of Faulkner's post-1942 work, which was frequently disparaged by the earlier critics. Post-colonial critics such as Deborah Cohn and Mark Frisch have examined Faulkner's influence upon Caribbean and Latin American authors. My colleague at the Faulkner Center, Christopher Rieger, has related Faulkner's works to ecological and environmental concerns. Judith Sensibar, the foremost critic of Faulkner's poetry, in *The Origins of Faulkner's Art*, examines the influence of that poetry upon the fiction. Bruce Kawin, Gene Phillips, Louis Daniel Brodsky, and I have written about Faulkner's movie work. The first detailed biography of Faulkner, written by Joseph Blotner, was published in 1974. Later biographies have been written by Frederick Karl, David Minter, Stephen Oates, Richard Gray (who is British), and Jay Parini. I recommend Blotner's biography for the facts of Faulkner's life and Parini's for the commentaries on the works.

Li: The second question is quite related to the first one. Could you please introduce the major approaches which the American scholars employ to interpret Faulkner's works? There are different approaches of studying Faulkner's novels, for instance, the historical approach, psychological approach, new criticism approach, religious approach.

Hamblin: In the early years particularly after he won the "Nobel Prize for Literature" in 1950, scholars focused primarily on Faulkner's texts. Faulkner is a very difficult writer, and we all need a lot of help with his texts. Take *The Sound and the Fury* as an example: given the shifting viewpoints and the multiple time shifts, we need assistance in putting the book together, in understanding the structure and the narrative technique. Other early studies examined the ways that Faulkner is a "Southern" writer. These early studies helped us to have a better understanding of his texts and their historical contexts; they assisted us in discovering his themes, such as the degeneration of the South, the relationship of the past and the present, and the universals of the human condition, what he called "the conflict of the human heart". Faulkner was very fortunate to have good critics working on his books; I think his reputation has been well served by the quality of the scholars who have studied his works. Over the last twenty or thirty years, there has been more focus on race, gender, and class issues – specialized studies dealing with the contexts of Faulkner's work. The early study was more general, more humanistic; more recent study deals with specific aspects of Faulkner's works.

Li: I think, at the present time, the Chinese scholars have paid little attention to gender and class study in Faulkner's novels, and American scholars' research might provide them with new insights.

Dr. Hamblin, I know your center has played a very important role in Faulkner study. As the director of the Center for Faulkner Studies at Southeast Missouri State University, could you please make a brief introduction of your center and its contribution to Faulkner study?

Hamblin: We have a Center for Faulkner Studies here because of the Brodsky Collection. Beginning in 1978, Louis Daniel Brodsky and I worked for ten years or so, throughout the 1980s, in publishing books and articles, mounting exhibits, and giving lectures based on his private collection of William Faulkner materials. Then in 1988, he made his decision to place his Faulkner collection at this institution, and now our center has become one of four major Faulkner collections in the world, the others being at the University of the Virginia, University of Mississippi, and University of Texas. When Mr. Brodsky placed his Faulkner collection here, we opened it up for any scholar doing research on

Faulkner. We have been very pleased to host scholars coming not only from the United States but also from China, Taiwan, Japan, Korea, Canada, England, France, Germany, and Romania to use the materials in their research for their articles and books. So you cannot really separate our Faulkner Center from the Brodsky Collection. It has been my privilege to work with Mr. Brodsky, and with his collection, now for some thirty years. And because of him and his collection, I now have the opportunity to work with scholars like you. And that is a great honor and privilege.

Li: Yes, I think your center has provided the scholars, especially the international scholars, with good opportunities to get access to Faulkner's research materials. On my visit to your center, I'm finding here plenty of helpful collections of criticism devoted to Faulkner's works, including *A William Faulkner Encyclopedia* and *A Companion to Faulkner Studies* which you have co-edited with Charles A. Peek. Yesterday, I also used the Brodsky Collection and went through the manuscripts of Faulkner's poems, letters, and speeches.

Hamblin: We also have a website to assist the scholars who cannot come personally. We are happy to provide them materials through the internet: photographs, copies of letters and scanned documents, answers to their questions. We are always pleased when we host people for personal visits, but we also use the modern technology of the internet to offer help to people all over the world. Since many people cannot afford to travel here, or it is not convenient for them to do so, it is very fortunate that we can supply materials through scanned documents. The internet is a very important part of our operation at the Faulkner Center.

Li: Actually I also got to know your center through the internet.

Hamblin: I think most scholars will continue to learn about the Faulkner Center the internet. More and more people are coming here for personal visits, but, yes, I think most scholars learn about the Center through our website. I hope that through this published interview, even more people will get to know about our Center and website. Whether we have contact through the internet or host visitors here, we enjoy assisting scholars with their research, and we are grateful for their interest.

Li: I think in the meanwhile the visitors like me who have come here also enjoy our visits and benefit a lot from your center.

Dr. Hamblin, When did you start doing research on Faulkner? Could you please tell me your major achievement in Faulkner study?

Hamblin: I became interested in Faulkner as an undergraduate student at the Delta State University in Mississippi, Faulkner's native state. I had a wonderful, very influential professor there, Dr. T. D. Young. It was in his Southern literature class that I first read Faulkner. The first novel I studied and wrote a paper about was As I Lay Dying; it remains one of my favorites. Then, later, during graduate school at the University of Mississippi, I had an opportunity to study with another very fine scholar, Dr. John Pilkington, the author of a very important Faulkner study titled *The Heart of Yoknapatawpha*. Dr. Pilkington is my mentor; he directed both my master's thesis and doctoral dissertation, both on Faulkner. As a native Mississippian, I was curious about Faulkner, since he came from my home state, and I had two wonderful professors along the way, both of whom had a special interest in Faulkner, and they encouraged and inspired me to study Faulkner. Later I met Mr. Brodsky and was given the opportunity of working with him and his collection, so I have now devoted over forty years to reading Faulkner, studying Faulkner, writing about Faulkner. Most people who are familiar with my work probably know me as a partner and collaborator with Mr. Brodsky. We have done eight books together based on the materials in this collection, so I suppose my main achievement in Faulkner study would be the work I have done with Mr. Brodsky, bringing his collection to public awareness.

I also have many years' experience of participating in the Faulkner conferences at the University of Mississippi. I have spoken at the conferences on a number of occasions, and I initiated the "Teaching Faulkner" sessions which have become a regular feature of the conference. I think, all told, I have attended twenty-three of the annual Faulkner conferences. So some people would also know me through my work with the conferences over the years, particularly in the area of "Teaching Faulkner". We've created a network of Faulkner teachers, and I edit a newsletter devoted to the teaching of Faulkner's works in university, college, and high school classes.

I would say that the work with Mr. Brodsky, the work with the Faulkner conference, and my work in the area of teaching Faulkner are my primary contributions. But, as you noted above, I have also co-edited, with Charles A. Peek, *A William Faulkner Encyclopedia and A Companion to Faulkner Studies*, and I have also co-edited three additional Faulkner volumes with other scholars. All of these activities have led me to realize that the more we study Faulkner, the more we realize we don't yet know him. As we re-read Faulkner's works and re-discover them, we recognize that we can never exhaust Faulkner's texts. James Joyce once said that it would take a lifetime to understand him. It will take a lifetime to understand Faulkner. Writers like Joyce and Faulkner are so difficult and complex, so profound, you could spend your lifetime studying them and find you still have only scratched the surface of their works.

Li: In addition to Faulkner study, I remember the other day you mentioned that you also write poems and short stories.

Hamblin: Yes, I have published three volumes of poems, as well as a few short stories and personal essays, in magazines and journals. I don't write much fiction, I write poems. And I have another book of poems almost finished. I write about family, grandchildren, friends, memories of Mississippi, vacations and travel, my own thoughts and reflections. Initially I had no intention of publishing the poems. I wrote them as some people make photographs, just to capture precious moments for remembering and cherishing them later. I love writing poetry, but I don't think I will ever be primarily remembered for my poetry. I will be remembered, if at all, for my Faulkner study.

Li: Yes, I think you are a Faulkner expert.

Hamblin: Thank you.

Li: By the way, is there a conference on Faulkner held annually?

Hamblin: The University of Mississippi has held an annual Faulkner and Yoknapatawpha Conference every summer since 1974. It is the longest running conference devoted to a single writer in the United States. Here at Southeast Missouri State University we now have biannual conferences hosted by the Center for Faulkner Studies. The last one we did was on Faulkner and Kate Chopin; previously we did Faulkner and Twain; and in 2010 we will do Faulkner and Toni Morrison. There are also Faulkner sessions at the annual conferences held by the Modern Language Association, the American Literature Association, and the Society for the Study of Southern Literature. Many of those sessions are organized by American William Faulkner Society.

Li: How about the participants? Are there any international scholars?

Hamblin: The Faulkner and Yoknapatawpha Conference at Ole Miss is attended by scholars from all over the world. Over the years Japanese scholars, Chinese scholars, and Russian scholars have been regular participants. Faulkner's novels inspire Latin and South American writers who are interested in post-colonialism, so people from the Caribbean also attend the conference. Our Southeast Missouri conference also attracts international scholars. For the Faulkner and Chopin conference, we had scholars from six different countries, so even for a small conference like ours, in a relatively unknown place like Cape Girardeau, Faulkner still attracts people from all over the world to participate.

Li: Hopefully more and more Chinese scholars will come here to attend your conferences.

Hamblin: Yes, I hope so.

Li: Now, let's focus on Faulkner's works. As we know, Yoknapatawpha created by Faulkner is often regarded as the myth of the Old South as well as the myth of the modern world. What do you think of Faulkner's mythology of

Yoknapatawpha?

Hamblin: Faulkner's Yoknapatawpha fiction is grounded in the South, in Oxford, so it is modeled on the real world. Faulkner grew up and lived in that experience, so it is understandable that his fiction reflects that place. But Yoknapatawpha is about more than Oxford, or Mississippi, or the South, or America. It is a mythic rendering of the human condition. It is an expression of Faulkner's view of human nature, human social structures, religion, race, all these things. It is a tremendous achievement, a great creation of the imagination. There is really nothing like it in American literature.

Li: Yes, it is quite unique. Then what do you think of the themes revealed in the mythology of Yoknapatawpha?

Hamblin: There are hundreds of scholars who study Faulkner's themes, and they find many themes. One of the most prominent ones is the influence of the past upon the present. As one of his characters, Gavin Stevens, says, "The past is never dead, it is not even past". In the American South, in addition to the legacy of slavery, the Civil War and Reconstruction, and the struggle of poor people for justice and equality, there are a lot of past influences upon the present, and one of Faulkner's grand themes is how his characters negotiate the past and present. As with any cultural history, there are a lot of things from the past that you cherish, you admire, you preserve. But there are also parts of the past we need to get rid of, things we have to change or transcend in order to move on, just as in our personal lives there are unhappy and tragic events that we have to put aside and move on; and I think it is this need to escape to the past and move on to the present and future that engages many of Faulkner's characters. Sometimes the past can be treated as a positive heritage, because there are a lot of traditions we do need to preserve and cherish. But much of the past has been a burden, a curse, like slavery, so the tension between past and present is one of Faulkner's major themes.

In his fiction Faulkner also expresses his views toward the federal government, the North, gender issues, the roles of women, race, social classes, religion, war, and the conflicts between rich and poor. Marxists find his books quite interesting, because he often shows the plight of the poor, both white and black, and their struggles against an economic system that has left them behind and shut off opportunity. So there is a conflict between the social classes, you often find that in Faulkner's novels. But I would say the struggle between the past and present is the dominant theme.

Li: The relationship of the individual to society is a major theme in American literature and politics. Does Faulkner treat this subject as well?

Hamblin: Faulkner holds traditional views concerning a sense of human responsibility to other people, to community. Extreme individualists in Faulkner, living isolated and alone—Joe Christmas would be a good example—are typically tragic figures. When it comes to personal responsibility, we need to remember that Faulkner is part of a Southern literary tradition that is not bound to a deterministic view of human behavior. Southern writers generally think we need to make responsible choices; we cannot excuse our failures by blaming them on hereditary or environmental influences. Naturalistic and deterministic philosophies became very dominate in American literature at the end of the nineteenth century and early in the twentieth century, with writers like Stephen Crane, Frank Norris, Jack London, and Theodore Dreiser. Faulkner was influenced by such writers, especially early in his career, but he, like most writers of the Southern Renaissance, was never willing to give over the notion that human destiny is the matter of one's choice and free will. We make choices. If we make good choices, we can be happy and productive, we can live happily and successfully in a community; if we made bad choices, we suffer and we pay the consequences. Faulkner's characters are Shakespearean, not Greek, governed by choice, not fate. They are responsible for their own destinies through the choices they have made. That belief made Southern writers, especially Faulkner, much different from many other writers in the twentieth century, who place more emphasis on a deterministic philosophy. In Faulkner's works, choice, free will, personal responsibility play dominant roles. Faulkner's characters can be satanic, like Flem Snopes or Popeye Vitelli, or saintly and good, like Dilsey and, one of my favorites, Byron Bunch in *Light in August*. In Faulkner there is always a struggle between good and evil, since the human heart is conflicted and divided. There is the pull of the old, ugly past and also the pull into the bad side of human nature. You have to resist, you have to choose what is good and acceptable, and it is always difficult. Faulkner's theme in this regard is very consistent with Christian philosophy. Faulkner was raised in a Christian background; thus he was heavily influenced by *The Bible's* view of the world. You know that in the Christian philosophy, if you make good choices, you go to heaven; if you make bad choices, you go to hell; it is the choices you have made that determine your destiny. Faulkner believed that in the world we make our choices; we either make good choices which lead to happiness and productivity in relationships, or bad choices leading to tragedy and grief. His native South had made some bad choices: slavery was a choice, civil war was a choice, destroying the big woods was a choice; but you have to remedy the bad choices you have made previously and you have to make better choices in the present. But you don't make these choices in isolation, you are a part of the human community.

Li: I know there is a theory called existentialism, is it related to Faulkner's view?

Hamblin: Existentialism emphasizes free will and choice ("You are condemned to freedom"the existentialists say), and may be understood in part as a resistance to determinism. But Faulkner's view is existential only to a degree. Faulkner holds some views in common with existentialism, but he does not share the nihilistic and pessimistic view of the world that existentialism embraces. He would not call the cosmos and our existence "absurd" : he is more positive. But yes, there are a lot of common points between existentialism and Faulkner's views of human behavior and history, particularly in relation to human freedom and responsibility.

Li: As Faulkner reveals in his works, the American South has undergone a process of change under the invasion of Northern commercialization. What is Faulkner's interpretation of change and commercialism?

Hamblin: He loves nature, he loves the land; thus he is very suspicious of industrialization and commercialization. At the same time he realizes, it is not an either/or situation; these are things that have to be negotiated. Benjy lives in the world of nature as an eternal innocent: he is three years old, mentally, and will always be three years old. But Faulkner does not represent Benjy's world as a perfect state; rather, it is sad, pathetic, to be trapped at any one point of history, to be unable to grow and advance. That is a tragedy. The challenge is taking what is best out of the old world and taking it with you as you go into the contemporary world. The past is not always better than the present, and vice versa. Some things in the past may be better than the present, some things in the present may be better than the past; you have to choose wisely, you have to judge between them. And so it is with nature versus industrialization. Faulkner was always in favor of preserving the land, respecting the wilderness and old landmarks and buildings. For example, he made quite an effort to preserve the old court house in Oxford, when many of his fellow citizens wanted to tear it down and build a new one in the name of progress. And when you go to visit Oxford and see the magnificent old court house, you know Faulkner was right. Faulkner has a great respect for the good things in tradition; he believes you should honor what is good in the past, bring it forward, but there are many things in the past we need to throw away and leave behind, since they are not good for us.

Noel Polk, an outstanding Faulkner scholar, calls Faulkner a "man in the middle". His characters, too, are often caught in the middle; they have to negotiate the opposites of past and present. And Faulkner wants his readers to do the same. That's why Faulkner's novels are open-ended. He does not tell the reader what to think; rather, he dramatizes the problems, the situations, and then he leaves readers to make up their own minds about what the stories mean and what is the theme and meaning of the story. He does not try to force the meanings upon readers because he knows we always have to negotiate meaning for ourselves, and we each do that in a different way. Faulkner does not favor a return to the past. Benjy shows the tragedy of being trapped in the past, as Quentin and Gail Hightower and Thomas Sutpen also do. Faulkner's characters who cannot move forward into the present are tragic characters. At the same time, his characters who live in the present without any ethical grounding or tradition, like the Snopes clan, are tragic too. The Snopeses survive into the present and future, but they have no humanistic foundation—no value system, no ethnics. They are amoral; they have power, money, greed, but they are animalistic, lacking in the human qualities they need to negotiate change positively. The secret is not to go back to the past or leave all the past behind, it is to find a proper balance between the two, and the best of Faulkner's characters, like Dilsey, or Byron Bunch, or V. K. Ratliff, are successful in negotiating these oppositions.

Li: Race is a very important factor in Faulkner's novels. What is Faulkner's attitude towards it?

Hamblin: Almost all Southern writers deal with race, so it is no surprise that Faulkner's novels also deal with race. Faulkner's great-grandfather owned slaves, and he may have fathered children by one of them. Thus, in the story of L. Q. C. McCaslin in Go Down, Moses, Faulkner may be writing about his own family history. Faulkner had great sympathy for the little people of the world, whatever their color. In the American South, historically, black people have been discriminated against as second-class citizens; they' ve had to ride in the back of the bus. Faulkner appeals for justice, fairness, and *Go Down, Moses* is his best testament that regardless of the color of a person's skin, they are equal, they should be fairly treated under the law, they should have equal opportunities in economics, business, and politics. That said, I don' t think Faulkner is a liberal on race; I would call him a moderate. He is a white Southerner who did not live to see the Civil Rights Movement and the changes it brought to the American society. He lived in a different time, in a more conservative era. He believed that blacks should have equal schools and equal opportunity, but I don't believe he would approve of social integration: I think he would have been very upset if his daughter Jill had brought a black boyfriend home with her. Once again, we see Faulkner as a man caught in the middle. Concerning race, Faulkner is very much a product of his time and place. I'm sure he would be amazed (and I think pleased) to see that we have an African-American president now, only fifty years after the Civil Rights Movement. Faulkner thought it would take at least a hundred years for American racial attitudes to change significantly. So I am convinced that Faulkner would be amazed at the enormous change in race relations in the American South.

Some of his best books such as *Go Down, Moses* and Light in August center on race, particularly on biracial characters. Faulkner understood that most blacks in the United States are not black, that is, only black; they also have white ancestors. Dr. Martin Luther King, for example, was called a Negro, but he actually was part black, part white, and part Native American. Faulkner's Joe Christmas is biracial; in truth, he does not know what he is. Maybe his father was Mexican; maybe he was a black; Joe doesn't actually know. But our history, our culture even today still clings to that outdated, outworn notion that if you have the smallest trace of black ancestry (the "one drop rule"), we are going to call you black. As the post-colonial critics remind us, it's interesting that farther south, in the Caribbean and throughout Latin America, this is not an issue. There you are allowed to take pride in your mixed ancestry; but in the American South, historically, blackness, even partial blackness, has been treated as a curse. And while that attitude is changing, it is still present to a degree. No matter how many times Barack Obama reminds us that he is not only black, that he has a white mother, white grandparents, there are still people (both white and black) who will insist that he is black and only black. This is why scholars today point out that race is in part a "social construct", that is, black is whatever society decides to call black. Obama honors both sides of his heritage. He is proud of his black ancestors; he is also proud of his white ancestors. We should not force him to choose between the two. Most Americans, in fact, are a mixture of racial and ethnic identities; that is the result of our egalitarian history. Thus it is not accurate to call a biracial person black, because that is only part of his identity. Faulkner understood all of this long before the rest of our society, so he depicts his biracial characters as being caught in a culture that will not allow them to be biracial, that forces them into the box of being black. That is the situation with Joe Christmas and Charles Bon. If they lived somewhere other than Mississippi—maybe California or New York, or Europe, certainly in the Carribean, maybe even in today's Mississippi—their color would not matter. But in the South that Faulkner knew, because race was still such a crucial issue, they were regarded as black, no matter how light their skin.

Li: Then what is the situation today? Do the people still hold the attitude?

Hamblin: As in any culture, many of the old folks still hold to the old ways of looking at things. But in contrast to that, the situation has changed a lot. When we conduct our national census every ten years, you have to fill in the box to identify your ethnic identity. You can check Caucasian, Hispanic, Asian, African American, Native American, or a box labeled "Other". This last box is the fastest growing category because more and more young people who are bi-racial or tri-racial are uncomfortable privileging only one line of their ancestry. Many people, especially young people, no longer view themselves as Asian-American, African-American, or Hispanic-American, they see themselves as "other", that is, biracial. In a country where immigrants come from all over the world, we go to school together, we go to church together, we marry and intermarry, thus we can no longer say we belong to only one group. The old folks may still put you in a box, but more and more Americans are beginning to accept and celebrate their diverse heritage, and this is a positive thing, since it leaves behind the old racial stereotypes and prejudices and treats people as individuals, regardless of their background, ethnicity, or race. We like to say that justice is color blind, so ideally in any society we should get to a place where color does not matter. And that's why Barack Obama's election is so important and, I hope, prophetic.

Back to Faulkner's stance on all of this: we must remember that he died in 1962; he did not live to see these radical changes coming to American society in terms of race, and his characters and even he himself are still locked into their old ways of looking at the world. But Faulkner was fortunate, he was not a provincial: he worked in Hollywood and traveled in Europe and went to New York. And when he left Mississippi, and went to New York, California, and Paris, he was exposed to a cosmopolitan view of race. But when he went back to Mississippi, he was back in the provincial view. When you grow up as I did in the rural South, and you are poor, you don't travel, so you think the whole world is like your little province. But if you are lucky enough to travel, to go to college, to get an education, then you read some books, you travel to Europe, Japan, and China, or Hollywood and New York and Paris as Faulkner did. And then you begin to see that the reality of the world is quite different from your little reality of home, and that can be liberating. So that is why we try to ensure that everybody receives a good education and has the chance of travelling, because then you grow, you enlarge your vision, and you move away from that provincial view which is often associated with that prejudice and narrow-mindedness.

I believe that Faulkner personally was bigger than his characters. His characters are locked into a provincial way of looking at the world, and Faulkner can show the shortcomings of that, because he has seen a larger world. And one of the best places you see that paradox in his works is in his treatment of race. Faulkner's characters view race in the old way, but Faulkner himself is moving to a larger view of that subject. That is the history of America. We have painfully, slowly, but progressively moved away from the old ways of looking at race and are trying a new way of looking at it. Race should not be used to define characteristics of any person's identity or value, but some people still hold the old-fashioned view, and it is hard for them to let go of that view.

Li: Could you make a brief comment of Faulkner's male characters and female characters? How does Faulkner interpret femininity and masculinity in his works?

Hamblin: Again, as with race, Faulkner's characters reflect the time in which they live. There are some male characters who abuse women (Popeye, for example); there are some who don't (Byron Bunch); there are some female characters who are fixed in the traditional role of female characters; there are others like Caddy Compson who challenge the traditional role of female characters. Faulkner's novels have different types of female and male characters. Sometimes they mirror the gender roles of the time in which they live; at other times (as with Caddy Compson) they are in opposition to those roles. Faulkner presents a large variety of types.

More and more Faulkner studies are appearing that deal with gender issues, not only the female and male issue but also the question of heterosexuality versus homosexuality. Just as we have learned in the field of race, there are emerging new perspectives on gender. These studies reflect the influence of Sigmund Freud and Carl Jung, especially Jung. Jung taught that every individual possesses both female and male attributes. Even if we are males, we have female tendencies, and females have some male characteristics. In the development of the psyche typically either the male or female side will come to dominate, but you still need to have a harmonious balance between the two. Males need to keep in touch with their feminine side; females need to maintain touch with their masculine side. Jung argued that suppression of either side of one's personality will lead to neurosis, or worse. Faulkner's successful characters (for example, Dilsey, Lena Grove, Byron Bunch, V. K. Ratliff, Gavin Stevens, Ike McCaslin, Lucas Beauchamp) are not aggressive, violent, or destructive; they create a harmonious psychology which enables them to live peacefully and productively with themselves, their neighbors, and their community. They seem to be characters who mirror the Jungian ideal: female characters in touch with their male side and male characters in touch with their female side. As with other Faulkner subjects, such as time and individualism and race, there is a negotiation, in this case between the female and male principles. And the solution, I would argue, is not to be found in the conflicts of genders and gender wars, with one side winning and the other losing; it is to be found in the peace and harmony and balance of male and female principles. You can study Faulkner's characters in terms of Jung's theory and see which ones are able to negotiate these opposites in a healthy and productive way. Jason Compson, for example, who hates women, completely denies his female side, he is all masculinity. Ike McCaslin, on the other hand, is a male who seems to be very much in touch with his feminine side.

Some critics find the basis for Faulkner's examination of gender roles within his own biography. If you look at Faulkner's picture as a boy, he is delicate, pretty, almost like a girl. Perhaps the reason why Faulkner grew a mustache is so he would appear to be more masculine. It seems to have bothered him that he did not present more of a masculine image, so he lied about going to the war; he went hunting, even though he did not like killing animals; and of course he drank excessively. In all of these actions Faulkner seems to be trying to create the image that he is more masculine than he appears. In this connection, there may be a good deal of Faulkner's own feelings in his portrayal of Quentin Compson. Quentin is not masculine in the traditional sense, and he worries about his gender and sexuality. He is wrestling with his inner urges and drives, and ultimately he is unable to find a happy and harmonious reconciliation of those conflicts. But Quentin is only one character. Faulkner gives us a large variety of character types.

Li: What do you think of Faulkner as a short story writer?

Hamblin: A large number of critics think Faulkner is a better short story writer than he is a novelist; I think Malcolm Cowley may have been the first one to offer that theory. Cowley, a very influential critic who edited *The Portable Faulkner*, points out that several of Faulkner's novels were basically made out of his previous short stories. Moreover, Faulkner's short stories are relatively easy to understood, while his novels are so difficult and offsetting to read. Among recent critics, James Carothers has done a book on Faulkner's short stories, and he agrees with Cowley that Faulkner is a masterful short story writer and argues that critics should be spending more time studying his short stories. In ranking the degree of difficulty of producing the various genres, Faulkner put poetry at the top, short stories second, and novels third. So he apparently thought of himself as a pretty competent short story writer. I think most scholars agree with him.

Li: Then, how about Faulkner's poems? It seems that they are paid less attention.

Hamblin: Yes, that is certainly the case. Maybe it is unfortunate, but Faulkner did not stay with poetry long enough to develop his full talent in that area. When he wrote poetry, he was imitating Eliot and Swinburne and Housman. Most beginning writers are imitators; they start imitating the masters and eventually move toward independence. But Faulkner never stayed with poetry; all of his poems were written in his early years (even those that were published later). So Faulkner quit writing poetry when he was still in the imitation stage. I think Faulkner's poems are quite interesting, I like quite a few of them; but he did not stay with it long enough to really discover how good he could be in poetry. Judith Sensibar has made the most extensive study of Faulkner's poems; her study shows how the themes, use of language, and character types in Faulkner's poems find their way into his fiction. Even though she admires his poetry and studies it closely, she considers Faulkner's poems to be apprentice works, interesting primarily in relation to his later, greater fiction. But there remains a lot to be done on Faulkner's poetry.

Incidentally, another area of Faulkner study that has been neglected is his movie work; very few critics—no more than a half-dozen—have studied Faulkner's

Hollywood career. In general, these are the two areas are most neglected by scholars: the poetry and the movie scripts. There is a lot of work yet needed in both of those areas.

Li: Could you make a general comment on Faulkner? What do you think of Faulkner's literary achievement? What is his influence towards the American writers as well as the other writers in the world?

Hamblin: Faulkner is without question one of the truly great American writers. He has been called "the American Shakespeare", and I agree with that assessment. Among American novelists he ranks with Melville, Hawthorne, Poe, Twain, Henry James. I would not go so far as to claim that Faulkner is the greatest American writer, though he is often called the greatest of the twentieth century American writers, and he surely deserves to be included in the top rank of the best writers America has ever produced. I think the tremendous amount of scholarship devoted to his work demonstrates this point. There are hundreds of books and thousands of articles that testify to how significant he is.

Ironically, as great as he is, he is not a popular writer, and he will never be a popular writer, because his works are very difficult to read. His books are not bestsellers. Faulkner's success is largely with academic and intellectual readers, the elite readers, not the masses. Faulkner's case is similar to that of Eliot, whose *The Waste Land* is not easy to read. People sitting on an airplane or in a bus station reading books for leisure might not pick up Faulkner's novels. Faulkner is definitely an acquired taste, but he is unquestionably a great writer. One proof of this claim is how other writers feel about his work. The American writer William Kennedy, the Columbian writer Gabriel Garcia Marquez, the Japanese writer Kenzaburo Oe, and the Chinese writer Mo Yan all admire Faulkner and have been influenced by him.

Li: Yes, a lot of Chinese contemporary writers are greatly influenced by Faulkner. Mo Yan once mentioned that when he started writing novels, he went through one of Faulkner's novels and was inspired by it to take his home town

Gaomi as the place to start with in his novel.

Finally, could you please tell me what do you think of the Faulkner study in China?

Hamblin: I have only come to know about the Chinese study of Faulkner during the past few years, only since Chinese scholars have been visiting our Faulkner Center, so I am just recently aware of the popularity of Faulkner in China. But I would stress that we learn from you too. As I noted earlier, a big tendency in Faulkner study in the United States has been to identify Faulkner as a Southern writer, but when the Chinese scholars come here, they tell me how they read Faulkner, and I learn from them to view Faulkner in a different context. In the United States, we keep putting Faulkner into the box labeled "Southern writer", but the Chinese scholars, who may not know much about the history of the American South or might not have a detailed knowledge of the Civil War, do not read Faulkner from a Southern historical perspective; they approach his work from a broader humanistic view, looking at the characters, the language, the themes such as the mixture of tragedy and comedy and the struggle between good and evil. The Chinese scholars are not as grounded in the Southern context as we American scholars are, and, as a result, they are free to give us a new perspective on Faulkner. We help the Chinese scholars see how Faulkner is a Southern writer, for example, when we show you Oxford, the geography and landscape of his work, the old court house, the house where he lived. But you read Faulkner with Chinese eyes instead of American or Southern eyes, so you are in a position to remind us that Faulkner is bigger than his Southern context because he is more universal.

All great writers, of course, deal in universals. Shakespeare does not belong only to Stratford, he is universal. Likewise, Faulkner is much bigger than Oxford and the American South. I think that the right way to read any great writer is from the humanistic perspective, whatever region or locale he might represent. Of course, as Faulkner says, you cannot sit down to write a universal novel, you have to write what you know; but if you are any good, or lucky, what you know will be translated into some universal themes. And somebody from another part of the world reads what you have written and says, I feel the same way, I am not a part of the writer's world, but I feel the same way about my children, my government, my dreams, whatever. So with the Chinese scholars and me, it is a mutual exchange. We benefit each other: I learn something about reading Faulkner from them, and hopefully they learn something from me.

Li: Yes, we need to learn from one another. I really appreciate the interview, and I hope the Chinese scholars and readers will have a better understanding of Faulkner through the interview. Thank you very much.

Hamblin: Thank you very much.

(The paper was first published in *Foreign Literature Studies*, 2010/1.)

The New Approaches in William Faulkner Study:
An Interview with Dr. Christopher Rieger

Li Mengyu (Li for short hereinafter) : Dr. Rieger, It's my great pleasure and honor to have an interview with you on William Faulkner, since you are an expert in this field. My first question is, as the director of the Center for Faulkner Studies in your university, could you please introduce your center briefly? What role does it play in Faulkner studies in the US as well as outside of the US?

Christopher Rieger(Rieger for short hereinafter) : The Center for Faulkner Studies here at Southeast Missouri State University was established in 1989 at the same time that we acquired the Louis Daniel Brodsky collection of William Faulkner materials. So it was because we acquired the Brodsky collection that we started the Faulkner Center at the same time. Mr. Brodsky was a famous collector of Faulkner, and he collected the largest personal collection of Faulkner materials, at that time, over 10, 000 items. After working with Dr. Hamblin, who was the founding director of the Faulkner center, he eventually donated the collection to our university. So he wanted to make sure that the collection was used by scholars and that it didn' t just sit in a room somewhere and one could never see it. So the Faulkner Center was established to try to promote the collection and bring people from around the world to use it, and promote the study of Faulkner's work. We host visiting scholars, we have people working on books and articles on Faulkner who come to use our collection, the Blotner papers in particular, and we host a conference every two years that brings scholars together from around the world to present their work on Faulkner.

Li: So I also know you have an online course on Faulkner?

Rieger: Yes, that was another thing we did to promote the collection of our university; a massive open online course or MOOC was created to help people read Faulkner on their own. A lot of times, people don't have a chance to read Faulkner with a professor or in class, and sometimes it can be difficult to read by yourself, so we created the MOOC to help people read Faulkner's novels and understand them.

Li: OK, actually, in China last year, I received an e-mail about your MOOC from professor Hamblin. I was very pleased to get the news, and also visited the MOOC course website and registered, and I found many very interesting topics and also introduced it to my students. Next question: You are a Faulkner expert, could you please introduce your study on Faulkner ?

Rieger: Yes, a lot of my work on Faulkner is ecocriticism, that's the main approach I take, which is a study of the natural world, the environment and how they are related to Faulkner's work. So, for instance, I have a book with a chapter on Go Down Moses, which is Faulkner's important novel that most tackles the questions about the environment and the relationship between humans and the nature, and I recently published an essay on *The Sound and the Fury* using an ecocritical approach to that book also, to see how nature and the environment are significant in the novel as well.

Li: And I found this approach in China is also very popular. Many scholars use this ecological approach to study Faulkner's novels. Previously, I published a book *On the Study of Shen Congwen and Faulkner's Novels in Multidimensional Perspectives*, I have also made a comparative study of two authors from the ecological approach.

Rieger: That's great! We have a scholar from Japan who has come here to our conference who also does ecocritical approach to Faulkner too.

Li: So, It is a very insightful approach to get close to Faulkner's novels and works. Next question, Could you please introduce the contemporary criticism on Faulkner in the US? What are the major approaches in Faulkner studies in

American contemporary academic circles?

Rieger: There is still a lot of work being done on Faulkner. People use a lot of different approaches, and one of the newer ones that people are using more would be disability studies, a fairly new field. There is recently a book, published by Taylor Haygood using disability studies applied to Faulkner, and we have published some essays in our books using that approach as well as the approach of trauma theory. Also popular recently have been cultural approaches to Faulkner, especially looking at popular culture, and how that has a lot of intersections with Faulkner's work. We usually don't think of Faulkner as a popular author, but some new work has been done about how his work has connections to popular culture, music, movies, popular literature, magazines, things like that. This year "The Faulkner & Yoknapatawpha Conference" at the University of Mississippi was about Faulkner and print culture, and many of the presentations looked at how Faulkner's work engaged with the popular culture from that time period.

Li: So, I'd like to know more about the "The Faulkner & Yoknapatawpha Conference 2015" conference held at the University of Mississippi this year. I know you have just returned from the conference. Could you please tell me about the conference?

Rieger: Yes, again, the theme was Faulkner and print culture, so there are a lot of different presentations, but like I said, a lot of people looked at Faulkner's connection to the publishing industry, and popular culture, so there were presentations on magazines, and how he was portrayed in the popular media. The cover art of his books, and how his novels fit into the paperback revolution of the time period, connections between Faulkner and other important figures in publishing and literary industry at that time, some of those were included also too. So, there was a wide variety of presentations.

Li: What was the topic of your presentation?

Rieger: My topic was Faulkner's revision process during his novel A Fable, some last minute revisions that he did to this novel. I used some materials from our Brodsky collection to illustrate how Faulkner worked and how he make changes. Especially in this novel, he made some important changes very very late in the publishing process, when it was almost ready to go to press.

Li: A very interesting approach, and as we know, Faulkner is often labeled as a writer of the south in US. What do you think the significance of the south is to the understanding of Faulkner's works?

Rieger: Well, I think if you want to do a historical or cultural approach to Faulkner, then you need to understand southern history and southern culture; otherwise, you have an incomplete view of his connections to his history and to his culture, because Faulkner himself was very much interested in southern history, and the way that southern history has been presented to southerners and non-southerners over the years. And he also engaged with some of the issues of his day, things that are history to us now, that were very much contemporary issues to him. Faulkner would often engage with those issues as well too. You don't have to understand the south or think Faulkner is only a southern writer. And I think meeting with some international scholars has helped us to see that Faulkner can be thought of in other ways too, not just as a southern author.

Li: Just now, we talked about cultural contexts; if we examine Faulkner's works in cultural contexts, what other cultural contexts have exerted influences on Faulkner besides southern culture?

Rieger: One example in southern studies these days is to look at is what called the global south. So, not just the American south, but South America, the Caribbean, even Africa or other parts of the southern hemisphere around the world, and to see connections between the American south and other souths. Faulkner sometimes can be placed in that context as well too. He has novels that touch on Caribbean settings, for instance, like *Absalom, Absalom!*, and he engaged in other issues that go far beyond the south to other places.

Well, and also we can study Faulkner in an American context, not just southern, but as an American writer, because many of the issues he is talking about are really American issues and are not southern issues. He happens to use the south as his location, because that's what he knows, that's where he's from, so he can write about that more authentically. But he uses that to talk about American culture as a whole. So when he is talking about race, for instance, he is not simply talking about race relations of the south, or not only about race relations of the south, but American race relations in general.

Then, you can also see him in international contexts too. I think that helps explain why his works are popular in places like China and Japan, because he writes about issues that affect all humans, universal issues, so you can see that clearly in a novel like *A Fable*, which was set in Europe, not set in Mississippi or the south at all. The south in other works too could be extended to that larger context, for instance, the problems of rural people and farmers and those issues I think can be understood by people in a lot of countries. That might be one reason some Chinese respond him, because he is talking about the clash between urban and rural and something like that is still happening in China, small towns versus big cities, and past versus the present, and so a lot of cultures can identify with that.

Li: Ok, just now you talked about cultural contexts and the global south, and it is a very interesting topic. In China, some scholars have made some comparative study of Faulkner and Su Tong, who is also a very famous writer whose writings focus more on southern settings of China, and this global source reminds me of this situation in China. Among various approaches in Faulkner studies, and also I notice there are the modernity approach and post-modernity approach, and what have scholars found out by using them?

Rieger: I think the modernity approach you are referring to is a historic one namely, looking at the whole artistic movement of modernism in the past. The first three or four decades of the 20th century, would be the chief time period for modernism. So scholars have looked at other modernist authors, like James Joyce and Virginia Woolf, and how Faulkner's style and literary, writing are similar to theirs. They have looked at modernism in other forms too, like painting, in particular. So we know, for instance, that Faulkner when he traveled to Paris in 1925, viewed many modernist painters, and this was influential on him. So some critics have looked at connections between modernist painting and Faulkner's modernist writing. Those would be the main ways to look at modernism. There are several books that study Faulkner in connection to modernism as a whole.

Li: How about post-modernism approaches?

Rieger: Post-modernism I think again would be a method of connecting Faulkner to areas of the culture that seemingly don' t have much connection. So again you could go back to the popular culture approach that I mentioned earlier, that would be popular in post-modernism approach, or also the ways that Faulkner often reuses his own material. After he wrote a story he would often come back to it later and take some material from it and use it in a different way in a future story. Those are techniques of post-modernism in particular too. That would be a couple of examples.

Li: I am also very interested in Faulkner and psychological approaches; could you please introduce this research approach in the US?

Rieger: Yes, the psychological approach was very popular with Faulkner, particularly in the 1980s and 1990s, and it is still used today, but it's not quite as popular as it was in those days. Freudian approaches were some of the early ones. John T. Irwin has one of the most famous and influential books on Faulkner using a Freud psychological approach, called *Doubling and Incest/Repetition and Revenge*. Lots of other approaches have been used since then, not just Freudian, but Lacanian approaches and using more contemporary psychological theories to understand Faulkner as well. Faulkner certainly writes about the unconscious a lot, people who do things without knowing why they do things. The return of the repressed is a big feature in Irwin's book, and because Faulkner's characters are psychologically complex, I think there is a lot to study. He depicts characters who are very complicated, he often gives us their inner thoughts, and a lot of their family history and memories and stories. So compared to some other authors, he provides us with a lot of information about primary characters who lend themselves very well to psychological study.

Li: In China, there are also scholars who show some interest in Faulkner psychological approaches. For instance, some scholars have made some particular studies using Freudian theory. I know you have published a book *Clear-Cutting Eden: Ecology and the Pastoral in Southern Literature*, could you please you explain a little bit about the title, "Clearing-Cutting Eden" and the book as well ?

Rieger: The title refers to a couple of different things. One is a historical tendency of authors and another people to refer to the south as a paradise or Eden. In the early part of the 20th century, in particular, the natural world has been destroyed at a very fast rate in the south, in America as a whole, but particularly in the south. Because it was a more rural place, you could see the destruction of the natural environment more clearly there. So that is one aspect of the title reference and also Eden refers to an imagined place of perfection that may not have ever existed in reality. There is a tendency by some people to romanticize the past and to think of the past in the south as better or more perfect, and to want to reclaim that somehow, even though it may not have really existed. So the book uses an ecocritical approach to study four southern authors, all of them writing during the Great Depression: Faulkner, Erskine Caldwell, Zora Neale Hurston, and Marjorie Kinnan Rawlings. So I use ecocritical and also historical approaches to look at how the Great Depression affected those authors' portrayals of nature and the environment in their fiction.

Li: You have just mentioned that in the final part of this book, you have made a study on the post-pastoral perspective of William Faulkner's *Go Down, Moses*. Could you please introduce your main view and how it is reflected in Faulkner's *Go Down, Moses*?

Rieger: In the book as a whole, I talk about how the pastoral originally in southern literature is seen as a balanced middle ground, between the city and wilderness. So in older southern literature, traditional pastoral versions had a farm or the plantation as a pastoral space where these competing forces were balanced. It was a kind of paradise in that sense. But as we get into the Great Depression era, there is so much environmental devastation and destruction that the plantation and farm now come to be seen as very problematic places, and authors are not willing to look at those places in the same ways as previous authors were. So even though these new authors still use versions of the pastoral, the pastoral middle ground moves from the farm and plantation closer to the actual wilderness, in order to achieve or hope to achieve that sense of balance, such as the balance between the human and the nature, or between technology and wilderness, or the urban and rural. The writers are still trying to use the pastoral mode to find that balance with the middle ground, but the location of it has shifted.

Li: How do these changes in the pastoral relate to ecology?

Rieger: I think that you see in this time period of the 1930s and 1940s that these southern authors put more emphasis, for instance, on cooperation, collective action, and interdependence among people and between people and their natural environment, so that a more interdependent and cooperative ecological model replaces a more individualistic and competitive model from the past. As I argue in the book, I think this is largely because of the effects of the Great Depression. For example, environmental disasters of the era, like floods, droughts, soil erosion, widespread logging, and a boll weevil infestation, illustrated to many people the ways that the human and natural worlds were interconnected.

Li: I have another question: I'm very interested in Faulkner's cultural setting. For instance, Faulkner's novels are set in the Bible belt. We know Christianity has also exerted very strong influence on Faulkner.

Rieger: That's true. Faulkner certainly was raised Christian. Later in life he was not necessarily a very devout churchgoer or devout Christian. But he knew the

Bible very well. He often used story patterns or themes or motifs or character types from the Bible. In his fiction, there are a lot of references to the Bible, so I think it is helpful to understand Christianity and the Bible in order to understand Faulkner. However, Faulkner at times could be very critical of religion too. I don't think he was critical of religion itself, as much as he was critical of the ways that people sometimes use or misuse religion for their own purposes, so he could show the problems with doing that, just like with everything else. Faulkner was very willing to show problems with Christianity and religion.

Li: How about the issue of race? Even nowadays, for the black American, there are still some problems, so what do you think of the significance of Faulkner's writings in terms of this racial problem?

Rieger: Faulkner in some ways is very ahead of time when he writes about race. He shows us in *Light in August*, for instance, that race really has nothing to do with skin color, and so he is writing that book in early 1930s, and this is a topic that still gives people trouble today. But we still have many of those same racial issues in our society today, although they may take different forms now. So he still has something to teach us or something to say about contemporary American society.

Li: Ok, it still has a significant meaning today.

Rieger: There is a recent journal article that talked about connections between *Light in August* and Barack Obama, and his own personal story and the way that he has been treated by some groups in the country or media figures. So I think that is an interesting connection to the present.

Li: How about women's issue or gender issues? What is Faulkner's attitude towards women?

Rieger: Well, that is a good question, and there is still a quite bit of debate about Faulkner's women characters and how he presents women. So, some people see a lot of problems what the way the presents his women characters, that he uses stereotypes, that he shows a very limited picture of women, but other people would argue that he has a lot of strong women characters, and he is showing us these very limited women characters. but he is doing so in order to point out the problems of male dominated culture or patriarchal culture, so that he showing us the realities but he is not necessarily agreeing with those realities that may be oppressive to women. Rather, he is showing us how difficult life is for women, that it is men who make it so difficult for women. So that is still a topic of debate: how we should view Faulkner's female character and Faulkner's own view about women.

Li: You delivered a speech on the comparative study of Faulkner and Mo Yan at the Faulkner & Yoknapatawpha Conference last year. I am glad to know you have showed an interest in Chinese contemporary writers. Now I' m doing a National Social Science Fund project on Faulkner's influence on contemporary Chinese writers, and also you have written one paper on that topic.

Rieger: Only one, so far, I will be very interested to see your work as well too.

Li: Hopefully later on we can cooperate in this field and do some more study in this field.

Rieger: Sounds good, I look forward to it.

Li: I have read your paper, which is very insightful. What do you find are the similarities and differences between the two writers? And what has caused you to do this kind of research?

Rieger: I think there are a lot of similarities between Mo Yan and Faulkner, their experimental narrative technique for one thing. They both use stream of consciousness techniques or they shift viewpoints a lot in the same story, and they move around in time a lot in their stories, so the past and the present are mixed up together in the ways they tell their stories. My presentation last year at the conference was specifically about two novels, Faulkner's *The Unvanquished* and Mo Yan's *Red Sorghum*.

Both those novels dealt with war and civil war, particularly, so I am interested in how they both portray war in their home territories, civil war, particularly. And there are a lot of similarities. In particular, I think they have very similar relationships with the past. Both authors seem to be very critical of the past and to look at the past with a critical eye, and they want to tell the truth about the past, where others have covered up the truth. But yet, both of them also retain a dialectical view of the past in some ways, and there is something very positive and appealing about the past to them as well. So in my presentation I talked about how figures from the past in both novels take on legendary status almost. And people in the present can never hope to measure up to these legendary figures of the past. Even though they are very critical of the past, both authors see the present as smaller and less significant than the past. The past is full of giant and mythical figures, deeds, and stories, and the present is very small and uninteresting by comparison, at least in their characters'minds. So, I think both of the authors have that ambivalent relationship with the past: they don't like it and they want criticize it in some ways, but they are still attracted to it.

Li: As you have mentioned in your paper, that is a complex attitude which reflects the two enchantments and disenchantment with the past.

Rieger: Yes, exactly. Both opposite feelings at same time are present.

Li: And I found your views about strong women also very interesting.

Rieger: Yes, that is another interesting comparison. Because both stories are set far in the past from when the writers are writing them, both of them project very strong female characters backward into the past who are more brave and better equipped to deal with the war in some way than the male characters. Some male characters are very dishonorable in the war setting. But each of these authors uses a strong female character who is a real leader of the people in both novels, and these women are very dedicated to their families, showing loyalty, courage, strength, and bravery.

Li: At the beginning of your talk, you mentioned that your center, hosts visiting scholars every year, including Chinese visiting scholars and Japanese visiting scholars?

Rieger: We have quite a few Chinese visiting scholars who have come in the last 10 years. Usually there are an average of two or three Chinese scholars every year, who come and stay with us, sometimes just for few weeks, sometimes for an entire year, and they are very interested in Faulkner and interested in the way we teach literature and writing. They have other interests besides Faulkner, too, sometimes that bring them here. We also have quite a few Japanese scholars. We have annual program with a local company here in town, called Biokyowa, Biokyowa has an office in Japan and a factory in Cape Girardeau, and this Japanese-American company helps us to pay for a Japanese scholar to come over once a year for about two weeks and do research in our collection. At our conferences, we have scholars from Japan and China, Canada, Nigeria, Australia, and France come to present their work. Just in the last year, we have had a visiting scholar from the University of Dubai, who came for several weeks and do some research while, and we got scholars visiting from all around country. We also have graduate students and scholars who come to use our collection for particular projects. They are working on books, dissertations, or articles, and that has been great for us to have different people to come to visit us here and use our resources.

Li: Just now you mentioned so many scholars from all over the world visiting your center. Could you please share your comments on Faulkner from an international perspective?

Rieger: It's interesting that Faulkner appeals to so many people from different parts of the world. Because sometimes in the United States, people do still think of Faulkner as a southern writer, but I think that is a limited way to view him. I think Faulkner's popularity in so many other countries proves that he has appeal that is not just a regional appeal or even just a national appeal. He writes about topics that people anywhere can identify with, the gender issue, for instance, or the community and the individual, past and present, how they clash. People everywhere can identify with a lot of those themes.

Li: Thank you very much for sharing you insights of Faulkner. You are warmly welcome to visit China to give lectures on Faulkner and on the comparative study on Faulkner and Chinese writers.

Rieger: Alright, I' ll see you in China.

Li: I look forward to that day. Thank you very much.

Annotation: Special thanks to my postgraduate student Yangyan who helped edit the recording interview.

后　记

　　此自选集是我这些年来从事学术研究的一个结集，分为三编。第一编"跨文化认同与中外文学综合研究"，此部分一方面对"跨文化认同"、"全球化"、"深生态学"、"后殖民主义"等重要理论范畴进行了学术探究和考辨，另一方面则运用上述理论视角对一些中外重要的文学作品进行了分析和阐释。第二编"中西文学关系研究"，主要以沈从文与福克纳比较作为中西文学平行研究的一个聚焦，所选的论文从宗教学、生态学、神话原型批评、后现代性、文化空间、时间、价值观以及文化特质和价值评判等多维角度，较为系统、全面、深层次地比较了两位作家创作的类同性与差异性，以期丰富沈从文和福克纳的比较研究。此部分还收入了我目前所主持的国家社科基金项目"威廉·福克纳对中国新时期小说影响研究"阶段性成果——福克纳与新时期文学三种思潮即"寻根小说思潮"、"新历史主义小说思潮"及"先锋小说思潮"关系研究。该书第三编"跨文化沟通与对话"收入的文章大多为我在国外刊物或国际学术研讨会上所发表的跨文化传播研究成果的中文译稿。附录部分还收录了 10 篇英文文章，包括对西方福克纳研究专家和跨文化传播知名学者所做的几个重要访谈。此外，有几篇论文与温奉桥教授、庄冬文副教授、魏李梅副教授全作完成。

　　本书所收的文章，从最早的 2001 年根据硕士论文研究内容发表的"《长谷》压抑主题阐释"，迄今写作时间跨越了 15 年。研究生阶段的求学是我学术研究的一个起点，我的主攻方向为美国文学，硕士论文做的是美国作家斯坦贝克的短篇小说集《长谷》研究，颇感自豪和欣慰的是，当时作为一名研究生，在国内较早对这部作品进行了较为系统的研究，并且为完成此论文的英文写作，专程赴中国社会科学院外国文学研究所及其他高校查阅了很多关于斯坦贝克的外文研究资料，所以今天读这篇文章，感觉内容似不陈旧，在借鉴外文资料的基础上形成了一些自己的观点。回想往昔的写作岁月，颇为感慨，那时连电脑都没有，只好在系资料室的电脑房"蹭"电脑用。博士阶段，我主要的研究课题是"沈从文与福克纳比较研究"，博士论文"全球化视野中的沈从文和福克纳小说"运用本土化、后现代性、生态学、宗教学、原型批评等多维理论视角，结合作品细读，对两位作家的作品进行了较为深入、多层面的分析和阐释，本书第二编所收录的一些文章，即是基于博士阶段的研究所发表的系列论文，因在国内较为系统、全面地对沈从文与福克纳进行了比较研究，国内著名福克纳研究专家——北京大学陶洁教授在其主持的国家社会科学基金重大项目阶段性成果"新中国六十年福克纳研究之考察与分析"中论及了此研究的影响，谈到了该比较研究的成果已经进入美国一些大学图书馆，这对我的学术研究是一个很好的激励。

在中国海洋大学任教以来，因教学所需，我又开辟了一个新的研究领域"跨文化传播"。十多年来，从自学英文原版著作，其后到美国路易斯维尔大学跨文化传播学研究所研修，积极参加跨文化传播国际学术研讨会，在国际学术期刊上发表英文论文，我在此领域也逐渐积累了一些成果。在本书稿下编收入的论文中，如《试论中国传统文化和谐理念对跨文化交际学科的贡献》《论中国传统文化时间观的独特价值——兼与西方文化时间观比较》《中国文化沉默观的再考量》等论文，在借鉴西方跨文化传播学研究成果的基础上，我试图立足于中国传统文化之根基，挖掘其对跨文化传播研究独特的资源借鉴价值。因为从事上述研究的机缘，我还有幸结识了一些国外福克纳研究专家和跨文化传播知名学者，这促成了系列学术访谈，他们的研究阅历、智慧和独特的研究视角和观点，对拓展我们的学术视野大有裨益。

回顾我的学术研究成长的道路，诚挚地感谢给我诸多指教、启迪和帮助的良师益友。感谢我硕士学习阶段的导师清华大学刘世生教授，博士学习阶段的导师山东师范大学的杨守森教授，感谢路易斯维尔大学访学时的导师罗伯特·圣·克莱尔教授，感谢美国跨文化交际学科的创始人麦克·H. 普罗斯教授，与他在此领域的合作令我受益良多，感谢中国跨文化交际学会前会长、哈尔滨工业大学的贾玉新教授，感谢他为我和普罗斯教授合著的《跨文化交际教程》所撰写的热情洋溢、高屋建瓴的序言，此书得以在高等教育出版社出版，后又得到美国 Dignity Press 的 Dr. Spalthoff 的支持在美国出版。感谢美国东南密苏里州大学福克纳研究中心的两任主任罗伯特·罕布林教授和克里斯托弗·瑞格博士，他们在福克纳研究领域的学术洞见对拓展国内福克纳研究视野具有很好的启发性。同时感谢《外国文学研究》的聂珍钊先生、《中国比较文学》的宋炳辉先生、《齐鲁学刊》的赵歌东先生、《东方论坛》的冯济平女士、《名作欣赏》的吕晓东女士、《中国海洋大学学报》的高雪女士等，他们的支持和厚爱使得上述论文得以问世。感谢本书责编安芳女士，感谢她所付出了的巨大心血。最后还要感谢中国海洋大学文学与新闻传播学院的大力支持，感谢学院比较文学与世界文学团队，一路走来多谢他们的扶持和帮助！感谢我的研究生王梦瑶、杨燕、罗紫晨、吕越等同学，在我工作繁忙之际，协助翻译了此书的几篇英文论文和访谈，并对书稿部分注释的编辑工作提供了诸多帮助。

由于水平所限，浅陋之处敬请读者朋友批评指正、不吝赐教！

当我完成书稿的三校时，正是初春的一个上午，阳光洒在眼前的稿纸上，有一种莫名的感动，这令我想起前年的初春写的一首小诗"春天等待开放的花蕾"：

> 院落的那片草地，
> 依旧沉睡在枯黄中，
> 草间青青的芽儿，
> 却在悄然生长。
> 早春的风，
> 依旧凛冽，来势汹汹，
> 无力摧毁，却催生了，
> 枝头那繁星般，

等待开放的，
倔强的花蕾。

又一个春天悄然而来，静静等待花儿的绽放。

李萌羽
2017 初春